W9-CLP-757

Family Trouble

Other Books by

WILLIAM McFEE

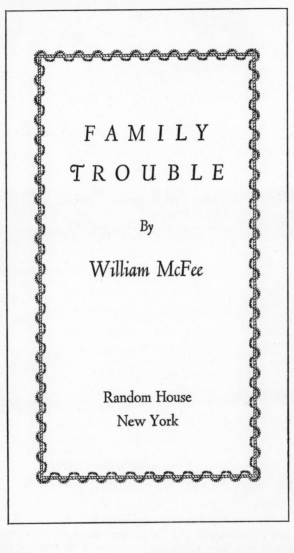

FAMILY TROUBLE

By

William McFee

Random House
New York

First Printing

Copyright, 1949, by William McFee
Copyright, 1949, in Canada, by William McFee

ALL RIGHTS RESERVED
UNDER INTERNATIONAL AND PAN-AMERICAN COPYRIGHT CONVENTIONS
PUBLISHED IN NEW YORK BY RANDOM HOUSE, INC., AND SIMULTANEOUSLY IN
TORONTO, CANADA, BY RANDOM HOUSE OF CANADA, LTD. 1949

MANUFACTURED IN THE UNITED STATES OF AMERICA
BY KINGSPORT PRESS, INC., KINGSPORT, TENN.

TO

Captain Sir David William Bone K.B.E.

A GOOD SHIPMASTER

A GOOD SHIPMATE

Let me not injure the felicity of others, if I say I am as happy as any. . . . In brief I am content, and what should providence add more: Surely this is it we call Happiness, and this I enjoy; with this I am happy in a dream, and as content to enjoy a happiness in a fancy, as others in a more apparent truth and reality.

SIR THOMAS BROWNE

Happy families are all alike; every unhappy family is unhappy in its own way.

Anna Karenina.

Family Trouble

CHAPTER

1

LOOKING back to that summer day, when they had landed in England—like Pilgrims in reverse, he had pointed out to Perdita and Sonia, but they had been too excited to reply—he made no bones about admitting that at first he had felt no sensation of coming home. England had been marvelous in many ways, but it had always been marvelous to him when he had returned from one of his long absences. This time the most marvelous feature of England had been the way it had changed. He realized that, in spite of his shrewd surmises and suspicions about it during the past ten years, while he was at sea, he had retained a lot of sentimental illusions about his native land. It had changed tremendously. So had he, he decided, with a grimace, when he heard an argument at a hotel bar, as to what part of America he came from. One of the arguers said, 'Texas, probably. Down there, you know, they're . . .'

The changes, however, turned out to be in both cases largely superficial. As the months passed, he found less and less to criticize in the country, and he himself no longer attracted attention as an alien. He even began to grant to the English the right to run their own country in their own way, which is the expatriate's rarest and handsomest concession.

He was too wise to confuse his sensations with an alien's. He had lived long enough in America to discover that 'naturalization,' as they called it, was a myth. You could not divest yourself of your own manifold nature. The odd thing was, native Americans, who believed in it for foreigners, were the most resistant of all human beings when it was applied to them. There was nothing in the world to compare with the shocked expression on an American's face when you suggested to him that he change his nationality. And it was, he reflected, as the train approached Marks Tey Junction, where Perdita would meet him with the Virago, one of the wonders of the world, to observe Americans abroad when they had an attack of homesickness and patriotism. He remembered one or two occasions when he and Perdita, in London, had heard the eagle scream, by Jove! Talk about hearing the chimes at midnight, Master Shallow!

That was all in the past, of course. The first impressions, which are always grotesque, always unfair, always inaccurate, soon faded. The illusion, that England was populated by unintelligible idiots with bad teeth, that Americans were always rude (when they were merely nervous of being misunderstood) faded too. One wondered how it had ever been entertained in the first place! It was true, to be sure, that the hotels seemed a little unenterprising, a little reluctant to admit guests to their mysteriously dark dungeons. He had enjoyed Perdita's caustic comments on returning from a bathroom contrived in some distant turret of the building. He reminded her that she had had no previous experience of English hotels outside of London. Like many English girls, she had seen almost nothing of England before

4

she had left it, a young married woman, to go to live in California. If she had known those hotels in her childhood, she might have found no bathrooms at all, he said.

But the compensations had been marvelous. After America, everything was marvelous! Now and then he himself had a sudden dizzy glimpse of how this clean, cosy, quiet, nook-shotten England must appear to a native of the roaring Middle West when he came over to visit it in summer.

The night they had left New York in the *Queen Mary* he had made a list of the things they would infallibly do, the places they would visit before the great day when they would have a house. They had done everything on the list. They had seen all the places before Sonia had gone to her school in Switzerland, and Louis, Perdita's old house-man, had gone for a vacation in his native Belgium.

He had been astonished to find how little Perdita knew of England, how limited had been her actual contact with the country. She was an intelligent member of the upper-middle classes. She had been to a school near Brighton, to an aunt in a 'crescent,' near Paddington Station, for several visits, which had given her a slight acquaintance with the region west of Cambridge Circus, south of Oxford Street and east of the Cromwell Road. She knew some of the theatres, and her mother would sometimes take her to Frascati's for lunch and to the Trocadero (in the downstairs grill) for a rare dinner. She knew Harrod's and Peter Robinson's and Marshall and Snelgrove's, and they would stay at Brown's Hotel, which was in Bond Street.

That was really all Perdita knew of England before she went to Hollywood on that long-ago honeymoon with her first husband. It was grotesque. When he told her of it, she agreed amiably that it was grotesque.

'You can't say you left England,' he told her, smiling,

5

as they watched the shores of Ireland rushing past them at thirty knots. 'You've never really seen it. You don't know much about it. You haven't actually been there.'

'True, oh King,' she said. 'A woman without a country.'

'Who stood and smiled amid the alien corn,' he went on.

'You mean, in Hollywood? Are you referring to the whine of the country? The stuff in the studios?'

He had not pursued that theme. He knew that when she talked nonsense Perdita was secretly happy. There were occasions when she betrayed the secret to him. As the weeks passed into months and their relations remained perfect, she relaxed.

'I hadn't any intention of doing anything else, darling,' she told him. 'I wanted to be with you so much, but I didn't know if it would work. I'd been so disillusioned, I didn't really believe in happiness any more. Well, it seems there is such a thing, after all. And Sonia, too. She's pleased. She said she felt she could safely leave and go to school now.'

'Sonia feels her responsibility,' he said, nodding.

That was in September, just before they finally came to anchor in Essex, where they were now living, in a house called, to Mr. Spenlove's delight, Layer-de-la-Pole. It was, he remarked, even more traditional than Brandiston Knights.

'And a jolly sight healthier,' Perdita declared, when they saw it together. 'Gravel soil with chalk underneath. You know, Brandiston, for some mysterious reason, has clay. The only clay in Suffolk, I fancy.'

There had been a period of confusion at first, for Louis had not returned from his native land. Much to their astonishment, Louis suddenly got married to a girl in Antwerp. The laconic news came on a post card through the bank in London, which was the only address Louis knew. They were

6

going to New York to a job he had heard of. On Long Island. Best regards, Louis said.

There were many trips in the Virago to London before the house was ready and life began to settle into some sort of pattern. Mr. Spenlove had turned a small, gloomy chamber, which had been a sort of buttery, near the kitchen, into a study. It was in this room that he kept his own books, the worn, sea-stained volumes he had carried with him for so many years. He had a table and a chair and a cot-bed. There was also a box of cigars and writing materials. He smoked, but the pen was not often in his hand. His idea was to make a sort of small, private corner for himself where he could think. Perdita did not ask him what he might be up to in there, which only intensified his love; she warned the maids to keep out of that room. It was understood that so long as he stayed behind that door he was not to be disturbed.

He told her once that he had an idea for a book, but he had been forced to the conclusion that it would never be written because he was 'no hand with a pen.' Moreover, he had a lot of thinking to do before he would have it arranged. She had asked the usual question, what was it about? He said he would tell her the moment he made a beginning. With a diffident air she had asked him if he couldn't dictate it. To whom? he asked, in alarm. She had told him how her first husband, Elliot Ducroy, the phenomenally successful writer, had used a rented machine. 'A dictaphone, or dictograph, I forget which it was,' she said. 'When he had a secretary she would put the record on another machine and type from that. Couldn't you do that? You can talk for the record.'

One day she had said suddenly, in a sort of mild panic, 'You aren't going literary on me in there, are you, ducky?'

He had reassured her smilingly. He had no intention of

7

competing with Mrs. Price, who did her four thousand words a day, at three guineas a thousand, as regularly as though she had been wound up like a clockwork mechanism. He said he had 'other fish to fry.'

'Of course. I was only getting the wind up for a minute,' she had said. 'But you try that machine thing, if you have anything you want to get off your chest, old dear. Elliot said it was only a matter of practice. He said he got so he forgot it was a machine, and yelled at it.'

'Thought it was a human being,' he said lightly.

His attitude toward his predecessor had remained somewhat shadowy, and he had refrained from defining it in words. Elliot Ducroy had been a master of words, in a sense, unless, as Mr. Spenlove suspected, words had mastered him, so that he had become uncertain about realities. Mr. Spenlove knew very little about writers as a class; he did not assume that they were all like Ducroy; but he divined that their communings with eternal truth were less important than their skill as magicians or medicine men. They had a collection of lay figures and masks painted to resemble terrifying, consoling or thrilling characters. He detected, behind the immense façade of the financial and social grandeur of authors, the basic design of the old penny gaff of his youth, the cheapjack performances at fairs, with the hero and the heroine, the villain and the fool, doing their stuff. The raucous and irreverent apprentices had called them the hero, the shero, the hardroe and the softroe, in derision, for apprentices had always been derisive since the Norman conquest. It was the truth, however; the stories he read in magazines were all built on that ancient plan. The catch lay in merchandising the particular, individual grimace of the author. They claimed to 'exploit their own personality'; but what personality had a man like Ducroy, who had turned

8

himself into a sort of fiction machine, grinding out patterns as alike as the newspapers which flowed from a printing press?

No, he had said later to Perdita, when they were discussing the matter again, it was not that Ducroy thought the machine had become human; it was the other way around. He experienced a mystical sympathy with the machine, having become one himself to a certain extent. She had nodded, and then laughed, a little wrily.

Layer-de-la-Pole was a seventeenth-century structure, a red-brick, rambling, oft-added-to house at the end of a winding narrow lane turning off what they called a second-class road. Mr. Spenlove had smiled at the definition. It was a very good road indeed, with a surface as clean as polished granite, with ditches and hedges on either side. He wondered what class they would give to some of the roads, the unimproved kind, around Norbury, Connecticut, U. S. A.

It was the only large house in a tiny village of a dozen cottages. Part of the roof was red tile, part heavy thatch. A brook, a tributary of the River Wiven, dribbled along past the meadows. The eighteenth-century owners of Layer-de-la-Pole had dammed it and dug irrigation ditches, and a fish-pond designed for carp. There were no carp now.

Remembering his garden at Norbury, he was awed by the lush fertility of the English earth. There was a piggery and some cows, and in a cottage with a thatch nearly three feet thick there lived an ancient couple, who went with the house. They had spent something like half a century in that cottage. Mr. Spenlove supposed they were what used to be called chattels. Their lack of ease over Americans coming into the place occasioned him real pleasure.

'You might as well save your breath,' Perdita told him.

'They've decided that we're Americans. We'd better act the part. God help them if . . . Some of those Beverly Hills people, you know . . . Ah, well! They wouldn't stay long.'

Mr. and Mrs. Bobey reminded Mr. Spenlove of old Mr. and Mrs. Mudge, who had owned the Norbury place before he left the sea. He had owned the mortgage in those days. Old Mr. and Mrs. Bobey did not own their cottage, but they seemed to belong to the land much more inalienably than the Mudges. Perhaps that was one of the real differences between Old and New England, he supposed.

Those differences impressed and moved him deeply. He did not want to sink into an old country house and perish of inanition. He found Perdita an extraordinarily easy woman to live with in England. She seemed completely cured of the troubling neuroses of the days in California and New York. There was a jolly look in her eye as she moved around Layer-de-la-Pole, as though she were the heir of all those Englishwomen who had struggled with its primitive conveniences since 1611.

'The year the Bible was translated. The King James Version,' he told her.

'How much you know!' she sighed. 'Do you happen to know that the Grid will come across the ten-acre meadow next month?'

'The Grid? Oh, the high-tension lines? They want to pay us five shillings a year for each pair of poles.'

'And if you'll pay fifty pounds deposit they'll sell us electricity.'

'And scrap our nice little private power plant!' He pretended to be shocked.

'You'll spend more than fifty pounds on your nice little

power plant if you hang onto it,' she assured him. 'It would pay us to give it to the South Kensington Museum.'

Perdita got on very well with the Bobeys, too. They thought her an unusually nice kind of American, but it was difficult to imagine what stood in their minds for Americans in general. Mrs. Bobey had once remarked, in answer to an inquiry from Perdita, that 'Some Americans came.' To look at the place, with a view to leasing it. They had not been satisfied with the plumbing, or with what Mrs. Bobey called 'the garridge.'

Old Bobey seemed only to putter around the garden, but Mr. Spenlove, who had had a long experience of men working, noted that things got done in Mr. Bobey's department. His chin whiskers were worth what he cost, in Mr. Spenlove's view. The former tenants had been journalists, who rushed down in a fast car on Friday nights, bringing many guests. They left on Mondays for London in the fast car, leaving all the beds in disorder, many ash trays full and many bottles empty.

Those tenants had been noisy and untidy, but they had worked. They made a lot of money, somehow, and never inquired what Mr. Bobey did or did not do. The Bobeys had been accustomed all their lives to gentry, who did not make money, but who had it. The Bobeys had scant respect for employers who earned their living. They had decided that Mr. and Mrs. Spenlove were rather nice and eccentric American millionaires, which was the next best thing to gentry.

Perdita could laugh at them and make them like it. Mr. Spenlove did not interfere. That old chin-whiskered Bobey could stand among the flowers in his own microscopic private garden at twilight, behind his cottage, like a dead tree, he was so still. Perdita told her husband that Mr. Bobey was enjoying himself. He was a wonderful gardener, she said, and knew every inch of the estate, man and boy.

Mr. Spenlove had a fancy for a more dynamic type. He told Perdita that old Bobey was probably a pre-Faustian man, a species belonging to the Middle Ages, but occasionally seen nowadays in secluded corners of the world. They occupied a position between the trogloditic types and the more recent slot-machine organisms. Perdita did not argue about that. She said young Bobey was in South Africa, growing oranges, and their daughter was married in Canada.

'We can't all be like you, darling,' she said.

Perdita took a practical line with her husband. He had a number of ridiculous illusions. He imagined, for instance, that he was not adapted to the social life of a country place, and would only be in the way at tea time. What frightened him, he said, was always meeting the same people month after month. He had been used to life on the ships, when they got a new lot every voyage! So stimulating and refreshing, didn't she think? Wouldn't it be a good suggestion for shore life, to have a new lot of friends every month? Perdita was not so sure about that.

Their first visitor, the rector of the next parish, who looked after Layer-de-la-Pole as priest in charge, was a vigorous man of sixty, to whom Mr. Spenlove at once took a liking. Father Soames had started life in the Navy, but had not gone on with it. He had made a voyage to Australia in a sailing ship in 1893 before deciding to enter the church. Mr. Spenlove had his own views of men who go to sea and give up after one voyage, but he found Father Soames too good a listener to criticize him. The parson enjoyed paying a call after dinner, with a cigar and a tot of rum. Perdita said he was a lot more pleased than he admitted to have them in the village, in what really was the manor house. It was that sister of his, Miss Soames. She was very churchy, and belonged to the White Ribbon Brigade or whatever it was they called themselves. Miss Soames kept house for her brother and did practically everything around the church except preach and ring the bell. Perdita wouldn't put even those activities past Miss Soames.

'He likes getting off the chain,' Perdita said.

He had another theory about his present life, that he had a duty toward Perdita's mother. Mrs. Price had a flat in town; she was a busy writer of serials for girls' papers; but she still had the old house at Brandiston Knights, some ten miles toward Ipswich. Mrs. Price was Mr. Spenlove's idea of a duchess. He used to call her the dowager. She was neither haughty nor high-toned. Mr. Spenlove's conception of a duchess was not based on conventional fictions but on historical examples, like the first Duchesses of Albemarle and Marlborough. Women with capacity and good looks. Mrs. Price was that sort of duchess. She liked large picture hats, feather boas, high-heeled shoes, fur coats and elbow-length kid gloves. She wore several large, valuable diamond rings and elaborate earrings.

She was very bustling and good-humored. In that, she reminded him at times of his old friend on Long Island, Mrs. Colwell, but Mrs. Price lacked that lady's grasp of ideas. Indeed, for a woman who wrote fiction very rapidly and sold it as rapidly as she wrote it, she had literally no ideas at all. The World War had conveyed nothing to her mind except that 'If you ask me, it was six of one and half a dozen of the other.' Her admiration of the new régime in Italy was extravagant because the Rome Express was now 'so punctual.' Mr. Spenlove had no idea, she told him, how bad it was in the old days, before the Duce, when she was in

Italy on her honeymoon. It was, in her opinion, 'the coming thing,' meaning the new régime of *Fascismo*.

She had a number of such phrases, which she used as conversational counters. Her ideas of America were a constant delight to her son-in-law. She had been often 'on the Continent,' but had never even thought of going to America. 'What on earth for?' was her inquiry. Wasn't it a 'scientific fact,' she asked, that American women were descended from Negresses? Mr. Spenlove assured her that it was an understatement. Many of them *were* Negresses, he told her, adding, American men all had Indian blood in them, hadn't they? Hadn't she noticed their keen, aquiline profiles, so like Fenimore Cooper's Indians? American boys were carefully bred to resemble Indian braves, he told her. And as for the scalping that went on in New York, right on Broadway . . .

Perdita warned him on one occasion, after Mrs. Price had gone rustling back to Bayswater from Marks Tey, 'Don't you worry about Mother. She's really happy, now she's on her own. All that about America . . . She doesn't care a rap about America, except she'd like American money.'

'You mean, she wasn't happy before?'

'Oh, yes! But now she's on her own, free of us kids, she really *is* living. She gets a new religion every year now.'

'A new religion?' Mr. Spenlove said faintly. He had imagined Americans had a monopoly of that sort of thing. Perdita laughed.

'I don't mean the Aimee Semple MacPherson business, or the Hollywood yogi-bogi boys. Mother's religions are more like sacred hobbies. She doesn't ram them down your throat. She's very High Church just now. She and Miss Soames are in perfect harmony. She does a little curtsey to the altar and crosses herself, if she remembers. You wait till she hears about the Rosicrucians. She'll be on it like a bird!'

'But she surely isn't serious about America.'

'Of course not! She thinks they wear paint and feathers and tomahawk their enemies. She believes you get shot at if you go into the street in Chicago. But she doesn't really give the matter much thought. She's thinking of more important matters, like her soul, and her serials. You can't sniff at anybody who makes five hundred a year with a postoffice pen and some penny exercise books.'

Mr. Spenlove, as a matter of fact, learned to like Mrs. Price and enjoyed having her for week-ends. Perdita was amused to see them get on together so well. She herself was not really any more interested in world affairs than her mother. She was afraid of the world outside of the circle in which she now resided, a circle whose center was Layer-de-la-Pole, whose circumference included her mother's flat in Bayswater, Brandiston Knights, the Royal Hotel at Felixtowe and one or two country places in Essex and Suffolk. To have her mother and husband so very matey was great luck, she told herself.

The train had left Witham and Kelvedon and would be at Marks Tey in a few minutes. He took down his bag and umbrella from the rack and filled a pipe. One of Perdita's few idiosyncracies was a pretense that to see him smoking a pipe gave her a feeling of security!

He smiled as he looked out of the window at the summer afternoon. England was being kinder than he had expected. The little house on Long Island Sound, between Norbury and the shore, would seem strange now. Stranger than his own house would be hers, the arrogant, empty shell of the fantastic personality known as Elliot Ducroy, the famous writer of swift action stories for magazines. Perdita had said she could never live in it again. As if she ever had lived in it,

15

really! It was rented on a long lease by a successful writer of advertising copy, a man who made even more than the successful Elliot Ducroy. But his own little place was closed, with temporary shutters over the windows. Sometimes they had discussed going over and opening it up for a season, just to feel again the emotions of their early meetings. They had discussed it, but they had not carried out the scheme. There had been so many other places to visit. And they were satisfied, very well indeed, with their emotions.

One of his fancies had been to take Perdita to some of the ports he had adventured in in his old days. She had never been anywhere, he discovered. The Mediterranean, for instance, had been unknown to her. He suspected her of being geographically indolent. He said, if no one *took* her anywhere she would remain where she was, like a limpet on a rock.

'Well, you're the rock,' she had said, quietly, and he had nodded.

'A clashing rock,' he amended, and spoke to her of the floating rocks of Sicily.

'Go on,' she said, but he said it was a long story. In Homer. 'But you wait,' he said, 'and I'll show you.'

So he did. In the Mediterranean she had had something to say of the sort of life he must have led in the old freight steamers, tramps he called them, of his youth.

'Were you tramps really?' she asked. He said many men were just that, but they would have been tramps in any walk of life.

'Sailors!' she had said, fascinated, watching some of them in Genoa as they drove along the Principe late at night. The idea was evidently novel to her. It had amazed him to discover her vast ignorance of life outside her own limited experience. Of course she didn't read very much. She really knew less than Sonia at her Montreux academy for young ladies. When he mentioned this ignorance, calling it in-nocence, she remained incurious.

'It doesn't matter,' she said. And 'Never mind, ducky. You know enough for us both!'

She was waiting at the barrier when he appeared, very much part of the scenery, a mature, splendid creature. Some-one had told him she had 'poise,' but he disliked the word. It implied artificiality. It also implied a precarious balance, as though, if she were not both lucky and clever, she would fall over. He preferred to think of her as safely, buoyantly afloat on the centuries of English life. She was at ease in the English Zion in which she had been born. It gave her a kind, calm, good nature. What she had been through gave her strength to enjoy, but it had not made her voluble about it. It was impossible, for example, to associate her with philosophy, but even if she did not know it, she had it.

'On the dot,' she said, very pleased, looking at her wrist-watch. 'Have a good time? Was it all you expected?'

'I didn't expect so very much.' He put his bag in the car and got in beside her. 'Oh, yes, it was amusing. I found Romaine in a pokey little hotel opposite Victoria Station. I got him out of it. He's at the Royal Colonial, near Sloane Square. It's neither royal nor colonial, but Romaine doesn't know that. It's comfortable, and clean, and it has several bathrooms. And decent grub. Romaine's a bit scared of his native land still, after being away so long.'

'Is he coming down to see us?'

'I insisted. He has a trip of some kind to Glasgow. Rela-tions, I imagine. You phone him. He's a bit shy. And of course he has that occupational hazard of all good stewards: he knows his place.'

17

'What a thing to say! He's one of your old friends.'

'Old shipmate, rather. Yes, I like him. You phone him.'

'Tad wants to come down again. He says he needs a change.'

Tad was Perdita's energetic young brother. He was an advertising executive. Mr. Spenlove was able to restrain his enthusiasm for Tad because of his inordinate admiration for Sir Oswald Mosely. He made a faint sound to indicate he had heard.

''I'll tell him to wait a week or so,' Perdita said. 'Don't be uncharitable, ducky. He's young.'

'Well, he can do what we all do, get older and be his age. Why doesn't he get married, and have a place of his own to have a change in?'

Perdita smiled. 'He says he hasn't found anybody rich enough or intelligent enough. He says all the pretty girls are radicals nowadays and he detests radicals. He'll grow out of it.'

'I'm glad to know it. I don't really mind at all. He's your brother. Only, the young people are not always easy to figure out. Their standards are different. There's a gap we can't bridge. It would be no use my trying to treat young Tad in a fatherly way. Being filial is not his strong point. And there's always an uneasy suspicion in my mind that the new generation are much smarter than we were at the same age. They are much more sure of themselves. Look at Sonia. I remember my sister at Sonia's age. See what I mean?'

'Don't I? I remember myself at Sonia's age!' Perdita said, frowning over the steering wheel and then smiling. 'I'm not sure I would go back to those days.'

'Nor I. We have to be charitable. So we'll hear what Tad has to say about the state of the nation. First, we'll give old Romaine a few days of country life. I don't know why I

call him old. He's not much older than I am. It's because he's
such a steady old wheel-horse. You know, he's well off. It
was ridiculous going to that little hotel! He sold his business
in New York, a restaurant, for forty thousand dollars, two-
thirds cash. He still has his stock in the Line which he
bought, as I did, for eighty-nine. It's nearly a hundred and
sixty now. He could have a suite at the Carlton or the Ritz.'

'Why doesn't he settle down? He may not be old but he
isn't young.'

'He can't. He knows how to make money, but that's all
he does know. He hasn't the faintest notion of what to do
with it, apart from investing it, of course. And he's a New
Yorker by instinct, if not by birth. He was born in England,
but he couldn't live here any more. He never has lived here,
for that matter, since he grew up. He went to sea in a tramp's
galley when he was sixteen.'

'A miser?'

'A capitalist. It's not the same thing. He didn't use to be.
When he was at sea and had a few hundreds to invest, he
was in a dither. He really trembled about it. I had bought
some aeronautical shares at the suggestion of my old friend,
Mr. Merry, that banker you met. He told me frankly they
might blow up instead of go up and I wouldn't get even the
principal back, but he thought it a chance. In those days
buying such things was exactly like backing a horse you have
never seen. I took the chance, and when old Romaine asked
me what I thought was good I said I'd bought this stuff, and
why didn't he take a chance too? He nearly had a nervous
breakdown for the first few voyages after he had sunk his
five hundred dollars in that stock. Then, after the Lindbergh
business, it began to go up, and up, and up. Remember?
It became ridiculous. We gave fifteen for it and there it was,
hovering around a hundred and thirty. Romaine came to me

19

in Havana one time and looked haggard. Not even his tropical fish could hold his interest. What did I suggest? I said I thought it would be a good thing to sell out. Romaine was in an agony when we got home, for it had rocketed again, and he wanted to hold on. I said I was getting nervous and would sell. I found out later that he did too. He was like a man who had been near death's dark portals. It was his baptism of fire. He found that it was his element! He became accustomed to living in it. He found he had a talent for business and investing money. When he finally had the capital he bought that Third Avenue restaurant and turned it into a mint. It was his hobby as well as his business. Now, instead of owning his capital, it owns him! He's going to invest in a road house on a New Jersey turnpike, and turn that into a mint! His mind works in the American tempo, so he couldn't possibly stay away from it very long. Men like him are always desperately unhappy in England. I have a suspicion they are unhappy if they go to the colonies. They have to go to America to find the air they can breathe.'

'I wonder why. I used to feel I was dying for lack of air in America.'

'D. H. Lawrence said he felt like a drawn chicken there,' Mr. Spenlove said. 'I don't feel that way myself. I can breathe anywhere.'

'You're lucky. I suppose it's due to sailing all over the place for so many years.'

'Well, so did old Romaine sail the seas for a good many years—longer than I did. The fact is, since he sold his business he is only half alive. His occupation's gone. He has no idea of what to do with his time. He thought it would be grand to come back to the Old Country and do nothing, but he is finding it a washout.'

Perdita swung the Virago into the winding driveway

which led to the front door of Layer-de-la-Pole. She sounded the horn to warn her cocker spaniel, who liked to sleep in the exact center of the gravel drive.

'No occupation?' she said as the car stopped. 'You haven't any occupation either in that sense. Well, I suppose you have me. I'm an occupation. But I know what you mean about Mr. Romaine. He's a bachelor, didn't you say?'

'Widower. It isn't only that. It's because he has the business disease. His business was his whole life. It absorbed him. He had a talent for that sort of thing. But he didn't realize it until he sold it. He thought it was a financial transaction. It turned out to be a spiritual amputation. He had become so indentified with that successful restaurant that he is no longer really alive without it. He was a happy man when he was at sea, with his tropical fish for a hobby, his job, and the staff he managed so well. A happy man! Now he is owned by the investments he has made or is going to make. When he comes, we must take him out of himself. If he comes. He may take fright at the last moment and bolt back to New York.'

'Hasn't he any tropical fish now?' Perdita said.

'You can't make a career out of tropical fish,' Mr. Spenlove said bleakly. He got out and reached for his bag. He set it down in the open brick porch and they went in together.

The hall had been originally much larger. It was low-ceilinged and paneled, and the rafters were of oak. A side door opened into a small parlor; at the far end a green baize door led down three steps into a billiard room. Mr. Spenlove noted a lady's visiting card on the big brass tray on a table where candlesticks stood with matches.

The sight of the card reminded Perdita. She followed Mr. Spenlove into the billiard room. Holding the card she said, 'Do you know a Mrs. Bannister?'

21

He was standing at an oak dresser pouring himself a whiskey and soda. In the mirror she saw him pause and thrust his bushy eyebrows forward. He finished with the siphon and set the bottle back in the tantalus. Without turning around at once, he said, 'I knew a Mr. Bannister. One of my old shipmates—one of our chief engineers. He was with me in the war. I should say, I was with him, I suppose. I was his second. He was the youngest chief engineer in the service, I believe. He was twenty-three or -four when I knew him. Then we met again in the old Maracaibo Line, and stayed with them when it was merged in the Afro-Iberian. You say, Mrs. Bannister?'

'Yes, Mrs. John Bannister. Very nice, too. She drove over from Tollemache St. Marys. That's just over into Suffolk, seven miles from Brandiston Knights. Said she saw your name on a box at Marks Tey station. Damn nice kid. They have Moat Farm.'

'They live there?'

Perdita nodded and held up a card.

It was an authentic card. Holding his glass to one side, Mr. Spenlove leaned over and examined it, sharpening those eyebrows which seemed to grow no whiter with the years. *Mrs. John Bannister.* A bold schoolgirl hand had scribbled on the lower portion, *Tollemache St. Marys, 6 mi. from Marks Tey.* Then, in the corner, she had added more clearly, *Thursdays.*

'She said her husband knew me?'

'You knew her, too. On a ship, as a passenger. Her husband was on a ship called the *Sandringham*, she said.'

'Yes, he was. I was, too. But that was a very long time ago. How old is she?'

'In the twenties, I would say. Not more. Her name's Candace.'

'The *Sandringham* was before she was born, then! Oh, I

22

know! She was the kid we used to carry across the Atlantic, a kid at school in Switzerland.' He nodded as the memory came back. 'But the *Sandringham!* He must have told her about it. That was a transport in the war. He and I were ship-mates. A very young chief. And he was also a hero! He had covered himself with glory by rescuing a lot of people when his ship was torpedoed. I remember.'

'You don't seem to remember him with much pleasure, darling,' Perdita said. 'What about Mrs. Bannister? She . . .'

'Oh, pleasure! The fact is, I had forgotten about Jack. So he's married again, after all! Our hero! We used to harp on our peculiar luck, working under a hero. Well, he's married three times.'

Perdita passed him on her way to the door at the far end of the billiard room, a door which led to the kitchen. This door gave her a feeling of satisfaction. Mr. Spenlove had designed it and had it installed. It was covered with red leather and studded with bright brass nailheads. Like the divan, the stools and the top of the brass fender around the stone fireplace, it had inspired Perdita to say the room looked like a club. He had agreed amiably.

'And you're a member in good standing, my dear,' he said.

Now she realized the door was like him. There was no pretense about it. It was oak, but the oak was concealed within a handsome, substantial exterior. It led to important regions. And it swung either way without noise.

She gave him a glance of calm interest as she passed him and went on into a passage leading to the stone-flagged kitchen. He continued to take sips of his drink and think of his friend, Jack Bannister, whose young wife had come to tea in a good old convertible two-seater. Perdita had described it and had said Mrs. Bannister was nice. She seemed to have a sound, sensible strength about her. There seemed to have been an understanding between them. They had recognized at once the identity of their backgrounds. Mrs. Bannister had said her name was Candace, which would remind Mr. Spenlove, she said. It had. She said they had been in America, although she herself was born in Paris. And she had a little boy. She had looked at Sonia's photograph with critical approval. And she had surprised Perdita very much with a statement about her childhood.

While she was talking to the apple-cheeked maid, who had become a good plain cook, Perdita wondered what her husband would say when she told him what Mrs. Bannister had said.

'I don't know why she mentioned the *Sandringham*,' Mr. Spenlove remarked. 'It was such a long time ago. Jack was married to another woman. He was on the *Camotan* when he met this one. He has been what you can call a marrying man. Several—and there was one he would have married if she had lived. I never thought anything would come of his meeting this girl. Dear me!'

'All I know is,' Perdita said, 'she came over here on her own. She asked for you. She remembered you on a ship. In America.'

'How did she know we were living here?' he asked. 'We aren't exactly celebrities.'

'She saw your name on a trunk at Marks Tey. She asked the stationmaster, and I suppose he described us.'

'And yet Jack didn't go to the telephone and get in touch with his old shipmate. I suppose he would have a certain delicacy. I was once his second engineer, and I had seen him in a very embarrassing situation. In fact, I knew his first wife before he married her. And I met him afterwards.

Now he's got another wife, he might have a delicacy. Yes.'

'Was he divorced?'

'So he said. She went to Paris and got a divorce because she was going to marry a middle-aged man with money. Jack said he would never love any other woman, but she had a right to get a divorce if she wanted one. The strange thing was, that when he said he would never love any woman as he loved her he was living with a girl and they were in love. Jack has had a number of what I would call exhausting relationships. When I first knew him he was unmarried. Then he became a hero.'

'Where was this new Mrs. Bannister when you met her? She's the competent young matron type, quite good family, I would say.'

'I remember her. She crossed with Bannister on several occasions. Crossed with me. I had some talk with her. We had lots of them, girls going to school in Europe, convents mostly, and returning to their parents, or to the parent who had the custody. This kid was at school in Switzerland.'

'I was going to tell you,' Perdita said. 'She was at Montreux, where Sonia is.'

'That's right. I remember the Switzerland part of it because that was where her parents met, before they were married. Not Montreux, Davos Platz. They ran away to Paris. She, the kid, was born in Paris.'

'She said her father was American, her mother English.'

'That's right. He died rather suddenly. In fact he threw himself out of a hotel window in New York, during the great depression. It all comes back now, when you mention the name, Bannister. But it isn't easy for me to believe Jack has retired to, well, this sort of life. Jack was emotionally a rolling stone. His first marriage started him rolling, you might say.'

'Was her father a writer?' Perdita said. 'I had some sort of impression . . .'

'No, an illustrator. One of the biggest illustrators they had, when he was the vogue. His name was Deming. Don't you remember Deming's Damsels? And Deming's Demons? He drew silly, fat-headed college boys. And big, square-shouldered executives in the business stories, fellows with massive muscles and jutting jaws.'

Perdita smiled. She always did when he got onto the subject of conventional art and fiction.

'She told me her father was a genius,' she said.

'She made the same remark to me on the ship. Perhaps he was.' He rubbed his beard reflectively. 'Perhaps he was. He was more famous than the writers he illustrated. The women loved his men, and men were crazy about his girls, very much as they were crazy about Gibson Girls a generation earlier. They were luscious creatures, scornful, brave, tender, voluptuous, long-legged and deeply reverent. They always got their men. They, and the men, were all seven feet tall, if you scaled them against the scenery. Yes, he was certainly the vogue in the great national weeklies. And then, suddenly, almost without warning, he wasn't the vogue any longer. The American public, or the American editor, or the American advertising men, suddenly dropped him. Like that!' Mr. Spenlove opened his hand and made a gesture of dropping something. He looked suddenly stern.

'Did you know her mother?'

'For a while. I hadn't much opportunity, and after that awful Christmas party, I hadn't the heart to keep in touch. And she wasn't the one to keep in touch either. She went over with me once or twice, which was how I got the invitation to go with Jack Bannister to the party. As her kid was going to and fro she had the habit of watching the ship arrival columns in the shipping news. She was at my table the time she went over to visit her child in Switzerland. A bright, little woman, with a sort of high-bred, nervous force about her. She had a very attractive, disarming and confusing smile when she was talking about herself and her child as though she was a bit astonished herself at what she had gone through. She had crossed with Jack Bannister, and she confided in both of us. When the kid, this Mrs. Bannister, if she's the same one, crossed alone, she had notes of introduction to me and Jack, in case either of us was on board. She would be sure of meeting someone who had met her mother. Mrs. Deming thought we were the sort of chaps she could trust her child to.'

'Don't keep me in suspense. Is he like you?'

Mr. Spenlove laughed. 'A difficult question to answer without guile,' he said. 'In some ways he was. In others we were poles apart. He's much younger than I, and he had that early sorrow.' He laughed again. Perdita looked at him with sympathy tinged with impatience. 'Then,' her husband continued, 'he did something I never could have done. He had a love affair with a cantina girl, or rather a girl who had been brought up in a cantina owned by her mother. It was in Puerto Balboa, in Costaragua. You've heard me speak of it. She was the nursemaid who pushed the harbor-master's baby's perambulator.'

'Really a love affair? Not just one of those sailor's Jack-ashore things?'

'Really a love affair. It always is, with Jack. He lived with her up the line. He went to the hospital and so had to leave his ship. When he was convalescent he saw her in the plaza, pushing the perambulator. So he took a job ashore, running a steam shovel, and he lived with her up the line. I saw him. I visited him, in fact, up the line. It ended in a tragedy. He came back to the ships later and took the Sansovino when I was transferred. It was while he had the Sansovino that he had another romantic adventure, which led him to get married again. But that didn't last long. A stewardess. She got a separation almost at once. That's what makes me incredulous of him settling down in England. He is so romantic. An undisciplined romantic.'

'That's why I asked you if he was like you. You're a romantic. Very much so.'

He finished his drink and took Perdita in his arms. The newspaper slipped from her hand. 'We've been over that before,' he said quietly.

Behind her he saw the sunlit garden, the warm red brick of the outbuildings, the cooing pigeons, the golden weathercock on the stable roof. He did not think of himself as a romantic; but as he would have been the first to mention, nobody does. There had been nothing romantic about his hard, lower-middle-class upbringing, his lonely years in London, the lonelier years of his apprenticeship to the sea. He had often asked Perdita why he seemed romantic to her. What was there different in him from the ordinary humdrum man of middle age?

'It's you yourself,' she had told him. She said it again now, as though reading his thoughts. 'It's an emanation. You give it off!'

'Well, I am romantic in a way different from Jack Bannister!' he said, smiling. 'I get your point, of course. I've been lucky, that's all. I'm like the buccaneers who came home to settle in England and reformed, bringing their treasure with them. But I never went in for the adventures Jack went in for. I rather admired him for his flouting conventions in Puerto Balboa, but I couldn't have done it myself. As for marrying that beautiful stewardess on the Sansovino, that was quite out of my range.'

'What did he rescue her from? You said he was always rescuing girls.'

'Always. He rescued her from a passenger's unwelcome attentions. An old, rather fuddled tycoon. My friend, Romaine, was chief steward. Romaine is the sort of man who can sail with a dozen beautiful stewardesses and never turn a hair. Her certainly wouldn't marry any of them. As usual Jack did the right thing. He hated injustice, when the victim was a girl, or misfortune. You see, he would always be busy!'

'You were enjoying the whole thing, too,' Perdita said. 'You'll enjoy seeing him again and bringing it up to date.'

He took her arm and they went out into the garden. It was a very old garden, and like so many old gardens in the lush East Anglian land, rather congested. The English passion, very strong in old Mr. Bobey, for crowding innumerable species into a small acreage, had been given full scope. He was also partial to glass bottles and jars for borders. They were set into the earth on the slant and the green grass grew brightly within them. He had arranged them around the flower beds, and they encircled a sun dial on the lawn. Mr. Spenlove's theory was that old Bobey had been a Druid in a previous incarnation. His fancy for jam pots and pickle jars for the garden was an atrophied vestige of an ancient British passion for stone circles and glass forts. The Druids began it, Mr. Spenlove argued, and we had been going around in circles ever since.

Mr. Bobey was smoking a black clay pipe in a shady corner of the garden. He watched his employers walk across the lawn to the line of aspens which screened the garden from the slow-moving Wiven. They were more of a mystery to him than he was to them. There was always a mystery about anyone who came from America. His daughter had gone to Canada, but Mr. Bobey had never been farther than

London. He could form only a vague conception of distances in excess of a hundred miles. But the mystery about Mr. and Mrs. Spenlove was not the place they had come from, but their place in the world they had come to. They weren't tradesmen who had got a bit of money. They didn't do anything to earn a living, yet they weren't in the hunting set, and they didn't entertain to any extent. The master (him with the beard) was a great one for walking, he was! Walk to Colchester, he would! Missus 'ud drive her big motor over and bring him back. Cigars he smoked. He warn't gentry, nor yit trade . . .

Old Bobey, wearing chin-whiskers, was slightly huffed because Mr. Spenlove apparently paid no attention to what was done in the garden, never entered the greenhouses or the potting shed. Had he done so, Mr. Bobey would have been huffed again, fiercely resenting intrusion into his department. Mr. Spenlove was perfectly aware of this.

Old Bobey credited his employer with a youth of sensational adventure among redskins, train-robbers, and stage-coach bandits who wore handkerchiefs over their faces and wielded six-shooters. In his own youth Mr. Bobey had acquired these ideas of America from paper-bound volumes with richly colored covers. They were known in those days, to those who disapproved of them, as penny dreadfuls. The country boy, gaping around Colchester, received simple but indelible impressions from the pictures and the stories. By an obscure association of the pictures of Buffalo Bill and Mr. Spenlove he identified the latter gentleman's idiosyncrasies and general behavior with that of a retired and reformed frontier desperado. There had been a picture in one of Mr. Bobey's penny books, of a frontiersman with a beard like Mr. Spenlove's. It was reasonable to believe that such a person would seek asylum with his loot in England.

CHAPTER

2

'IT WILL indeed seem fantastic to meet Jack Bannister as a genial host,' Mr. Spenlove said as they crossed the lawn. 'Any kind of host, in fact. I don't remember him ever being hospitable, or genial.'

'Ducky, has he any money?'

Mr. Spenlove followed her into a sort of sentry box, a fairly roomy sentry box, with a thatched roof, which stood at the corner of the estate, overlooking the road that led down to the village and the calm waters of the Wiven. It was technically a gazebo. Mr. Spenlove took pleasure in the word. They sat down.

'He doesn't *need* any money, my dear! That was the joke on Jack Bannister! He thought of himself as a knight errant rescuing a penniless damsel from a fate worse than death!'

'Are her people wealthy, then?'

'The Enderby-Bretons have had money for generations. I mentioned an Enderby-Breton who played county cricket for Hampshire. When I was a boy, I mean. Don't misunderstand me. They have been county-folk since George the

Second's time. And all the money will come to this kid, as you call her, or her kids. The rest of the family seem to have died out, burned out, perhaps, by luxurious living on the Riviera, and that sort of thing. You see before you the beginnings of a new ancient family. There are no other children. That fellow Deming, the illustrator, may have been a genius or he may not. But he did something the others couldn't do. He begat an heir. So, when the uncles and aunts at Torquay and Mentone die off, the money comes to the Bannisters. And she inherited an income from a great-aunt when she was born. Trust fund.'

'Do you like her? You seem to have made an impression on her.'

'I can't answer that. I didn't when she was a schoolgirl. She was very brusque when people merely tried to be nice to her. She put on airs. I don't know, I'm sure.'

'You wouldn't have liked me when I was a schoolgirl,' Perdita said. 'I was an unpleasant creature. I'm curious about her husband. You haven't told me about him before, have you?'

'I don't think so. I had forgotten about him. You see, he dropped out. What I heard was, he had got a job in England, something on shore it was, and had gone home. I had no idea he would marry that kid! He wasn't so scandalously old; but Candace, the kid, was about fifteen then. Jack may have been forty. I must admit, if she hadn't given you that card and said she was Candace, I would think it was some other woman who had got hold of him later on. The fact that he did marry her still astonishes me. Of course I know what the girl went through with that family of hers, but still . . . Hm! I suppose that Jack, who had taken a beating the first and second times, would feel safer if he

32

married a very young English girl, of that class. Just for a change!'

'Tell me about that first time,' Perdita said.

'Ancient history now. It was during the war, the Great War for Civilization, as our medals say. I wonder if it was! Jack and I were in it. We were fighting for Civilization, no doubt, but we were not aware of it at the time. Jack was a married man when he came aboard the *Sandringham* in London River. He was also a hero. He was more than that. He was the youngest chief engineer any of us had ever heard of. Most of us had started going to sea at the age he reached the top. It made him a sort of prodigy, and prodigies are not popular in my profession, I may tell you. There was nothing we could do about it, however. There he was, chief of the *Sandringham*, six thousand tons register, twelve and a half knots, and brand new. We went to Alexandria in Egypt, and stuck around there for months, when Jack suddenly left us and went home.'

'We had a skipper named Bowen, an old cock who had come out of retirement to go to sea again. He had sons and daughters married and with families, and he had no earthly use for his new young chief engineer. He disliked having what he called "a conceited jackanapes" for chief engineer. Old Bowen had come back from his retirement like a lion refreshed. He had left the sea in 1913, he told me. His children all married, he was comfortably off, with two houses in Penarth; he had settled down to "keep chickens," as he put it. It was a phrase for taking it easy. I don't think he actually kept chickens. But he discovered that retirement wasn't at all what he had imagined. He was like old Romaine. He had no occupation. He had been skipper for thirty years, and he missed his position as a tin god on the bridge.

He missed the deference paid to the senior commander in the office, the excitement and novelty of sailing to new places, of being received by agents in old places.'

Perdita smiled in reminiscence. He was off on one of his favorite themes, the astonishment of most men of his own calling at the real character of shore life when they come to sample it. What they had thought to be Elysium turns out to be boredom.

'Old Bowen was bored stiff by retirement, and the war, in 1914, saved his sanity. You see, he had never lived with Mrs. Bowen for more than a week or two at long intervals. When the chance came to live at home permanently, he found he didn't like what she had grown into at all!'

'Tut-tut!' said Perdita. She bent over and took the cocker spaniel in her arms. 'How do you know he didn't?'

'Never mind that now. I did know! I'll tell you. I merely mention old Bowen because he was as full of chest as a turkey cock, on account of serving his country, "coming out of his well-earned retirement," as the Cardiff paper said. He had a clipping which was pretty worn with being shown around to other captains. The paper said he was "sacrificing his ease and leisure, etc." I doubt if old Bowen ever sacrificed anything to anybody else in his life! If the *Sandringham* needed a hero, however, old Bowen was going to have the job. And he didn't like the office shunting this precocious young whippersnapper, as he called him, on to the *Sandringham*. As a matter of fact, he got my job. I'll tell you.

'Bannister had been chief of the *Lavenham*, the smallest ship in the company, a coaster, really. Her run was from the Thames to Antwerp. She was in Antwerp when the Germans came roaring over the Belgian frontier, overwhelming the gallant little Belgian army. The *Lavenham* was one of the last ships to leave, full of refugees, before the place fell.

34

'The *Lavenham* was so small Jack could easily stand on the low-pressure cylinder and look out on deck. He was watching the deck crowded with refugees when a torpedo hit and he was blown out of his engine room into the sea. He went down into a sea full of refugees, and he came up with a girl in his arms!

'He was making for a lifebuoy, intending to save his life if he could, when he saw a boat turn over. For the usual reason: the refugees had all crowded to one side. The whole boatload were decanted into the water. Jack saved them all.

'He did it in a cool, professional style too. He swam to the boat, got the people ranged on the lifelines, and, as a destroyer came storming along, just too late as usual, Jack took command. One of the passengers had slipped from the lifelines and he dived after her. She was floating face down. Jack got hold of her and hauled her head out of the water. He told me her hair was hanging over her face when he found her, and she might have been fourteen or forty, for all he knew. He said to me, when he was unusually loquacious, that he thought she was dead anyway.

'Whatever he thought at the time it was a reflex action to get her head above water and tow her alongside. He was hardly aware of what he was doing. The excitement kept him up. The explosion, you know; the feeling, "By Jove, I'm in it at last!" and the peculiar effect of being levitated literally out of his warm engine room into a cold sea by a tremendous puff of hot wind. It was stimulating.'

'And he married her?'

Mr. Spenlove had been looking at Perdita's profile as she bent over the recumbent Rover. He had given the dog this name 'Because he has never been anywhere, but has dreams.' He smiled now at the question.

'Yes, he married her. The newspapers insisted on it. He was a bachelor; she was married, but her husband, a chap named Heller, was drowned. The hullabaloo in the papers over the heroic seaman who saved the passengers, including the young widow just turned twenty-one, practically forced Jack Bannister, "the youngest chief engineer in the Merchant Service," to do the romantic thing. You could call it a shot-gun marriage.'

'Was he in love with her?'

'Of course! Inevitably! She was very pretty; she was a foreigner; she had lost her husband; Jack had rescued her from a watery grave, and he was a single man. A single man with a remarkably high position for his age. I doubt if the history of the world affords us any instance where such a situation was not followed by love and engagement and marriage!'

Perdita smiled as she rose to go to the kitchen. 'Where were you all this time?' she said.

'Oh, I was less than the dust beneath Jack Bannister's chariot wheels,' he said. 'In plain words, I had been promised the *Sandringham*, but when the fuss over our hero arose, I was asked, as a patriotic gesture, to step down and make way for Jack. I was shown the newspapers about him. Captain Bowen knew about my stepping down, so when Jack rushed home from Alexandria, Bowen gave me his job. I was glad, for being second in command to a hero needed a lot of tact.'

'What did he rush home for?' Perdita halted and looked over her shoulder.

'His wife had run away. Like Nora in the play about a doll's house. Only Roxane didn't slam the door. She didn't even close it. Left it open!'

Perdita walked away, nodding but not turning around. He watched her lithe easy grace. Then he saw her shrug, and understood. He wondered how he could explain Bannister's situation to her, if the chap was living at Moat Farm, Tollemache St. Marys, unless he went into Jack's background.

It was only a dozen miles away. They would come into Perdita's social orbit. Candace was now a capable, attractive woman, it seemed. That was natural. She had been a disdainful, rather aloof kid, with a chip on her shoulder. Of course she had had a difficult childhood on both sides of the family. Yet she had remembered him and asked about him, and regretted he had not been at home when she called. He tried to recapture their conversation on the ship. He had not realized he had made any impression—a favorable impression, he added to himself.

Jack had always had a sort of desperate facility in his relations with society. As when he made old Bowen send him home on a compassionate pass because he had, as he said, 'family trouble.' Mr. Spenlove had not been too happy as second-in-command under a man so much younger than himself. Bannister had had irritating idiosyncrasies, and he had been a hero in the days when men were still starry-eyed about the war. Until he had run off home in such a hurry . . . Because of 'family trouble.'

As he heard the mellow rumble of the dinner gong, Mr. Spenlove decided that meeting old Romaine in London had done him good. He must keep up these contacts. Meeting Jack Bannister, however, after all these years, would be an adventure. He had an infinite curiosity about people, especially people who were unaware of the impression they created in the world. Jack was one of the oblivious souls. He was, or had been, completely egocentric. It would be interesting to see what living with a nice girl, a lady, had done to the shining surface of his self-esteem. Before he met Candace, he had always been entangled with a woman

(Mr. Spenlove made a queer face as he thought this) of his own class. This new Jack did not seem in character.

'What was her name?' Perdita said, when they were at dinner. 'The one he saved from drowning?'

'Roxane. A Belgian. That is, I assume she was a Belgian. I am not sure Jack himself knew just what she was before she married a fellow named Heller, who was drowned. Those ships crowded with refugees had quite a few German secret agents. As I remember it, the British Consul-general at Antwerp told Naval Intelligence that Franz Heller was a German from Stuttgart. I happened on that item in one of the confidential reports we had when I was on the *Sycorax*, a naval sloop in the Mediterranean. Roxane was a girl this Heller had married when he was living in Belgium as a lodger in her parents' house. He was going to London to open a branch office for his optical-instrument firm in Stuttgart. There was strong presumption that this branch office was just the usual pretext for a spy headquarters. There were dozens of them in London. I could tell you! But Roxane had nothing to do with that. I'm sure she knew nothing of it. She was not interested in espionage. She was not interested in anyone in the world but Roxane.'

'She wasn't in love with him, then?'

'How should I know? She ran away with a man when she left Jack Bannister. I heard about him in a roundabout way while I was in the Hamlet Line. The office had told me to stand by for the *Sandringham*. So I was staying at home in my Liverpool lodgings, feeling very pleased with myself. The *Sandringham* was new and she was comfortable. I was staying with Mrs. Collins, the wife of Harry Collins, chief of the *Letheringham*, another nice ship of the line. He was in the Pacific somewhere. Or perhaps he was already sunk. The *Letheringham* was one of the ships sunk by Von Spee's squadron before Sturdee caught him in the Falklands and battered him to pieces. Anyway, Harry Collins was at sea, and I was in the spare bedroom.

'Annie Collins was an old-fashioned engineer's wife. She'd been a barmaid at the Blackpool Metropole before Harry asked her to come out from behind the saloon bar and get spliced. She was an ideal chief's wife, just as Roxane Heller was about the last girl on earth to fit the job. Annie Collins was a good-looking woman of the buxom type, with a very fresh complexion and pretty hair. She was also an ideal Penelope for a sea-going Ulysses. He could come home at any hour of the day or night, and find the house dusted, scrubbed and polished, and Penelope ready to take off her apron and fold him in her arms. No suitors need apply! She was the sort of girl, when she married, married for keeps. Ideal landlady, too. I was extremely comfortable in Sefton Park.

'The day we saw the news of the *Lavenham* being sunk and Jack Bannister's heroism, Annie Collins gave me my first information about him. I had heard in a dim sort of way that the chief of the *Lavenham* was a young chap who was supposed to be a friend of the management, but it was nothing to me. I had no interest in coasters. You can never save any money in a ship with a short overnight run and a place like Antwerp at the other end. But Annie knew all about him. He had been an apprentice in the same yard as Harry. We were looking at Jack's picture in the paper, with the account of his heroic rescue of a girl, and I said, if he knew his duty he'd marry her.

' "Not Jack Bannister," Annie said. "It's one of his fancy ideas that a seafaring man is a fool to marry. And what would he want to marry one of these foreigners for? Why not a nice, honest English girl?"

'I didn't argue about that. We read the papers, and when the Royal Humane Society gave Jack a medal, we had a visit from a reporter from the *Echo*. He told us the girl, Roxane Heller, was a widow. Her husband had gone down with the *Lavenham*. When he heard that Chief Engineer John Bannister was a bachelor, he was delighted. Jack's address on the Company's books was "Care of Mrs. Harry Collins." Jack had been a lodger often, and had now no other home. So the Sunday paper had Jack's and Roxane's photographs side by side. I said it looked like fate.

'Not Annie. She was sure Jack wouldn't marry. I had, and still have an idea she didn't *want* him to marry. Nothing improper, you understand. She hadn't any children, and Jack may have been a substitute. I don't know. But it had usually been Jack who occupied that back bedroom, and she liked him. They had known him a long time. I wasn't as involved as they were. But what I didn't bargain for was Jack's heroism doing me out of my job as chief. On the *Sandringham*.'

'I have an idea,' Perdita said, 'as a matter of fact, you had been torpedoed too. Wasn't that why you were at home without a job? I seem to remember something you said . . .'

'Never mind,' Mr. Spenlove said, without looking up from his dinner. 'It can happen to anybody. But I wasn't a hero! The Royal Humane Society never wasted any time over me. They should have, I admit! I have been marvelously humane at times! But I never had my picture in the paper. I was merely eager to get to sea again. I had put in an application for the Naval Reserve, but nothing had come of it, and I couldn't stick around wearing out shoe leather forever.'

'But why should you have had to?'

'The publicity Jack Bannister was getting. His heroic

exploit had involved the Company. They too had had to make a patriotic gesture. Newspapers and the public never have any sense, you know. The Company announced, after reporters had made a lot of inquiries as to what was being done for the heroic Jack, that in recognition of his gallantry Mr. Bannister had been appointed chief of the *Sandringham.* I pocketed my dignity and took the second's job.'

Perdita, her elbow on the table, pointed a finger at her husband.

'There was no humiliation in that for you, darling. You only pretend there was! Men are of different sizes. You're trying to make Mr. Bannister seem bigger than he really was. Or is, for all I know.'

'I don't know how big he is now, my dear. I'm curious to find out. I can't imagine Jack a country gentleman! You're right, as usual. I didn't care very much. The Company was decent about it. I went to London to wait for the *Sandringham.* And I met Jack there by accident. We always stayed at Hartigan's Hotel in those days, and Jack was there when I arrived.'

'Did you go to Hartigan's this time?'

Mr. Spenlove made a gesture. 'They're pulling it down!' he said, somberly. 'The Cosmopole has built practically all round that old place. They've wanted Hartigan's corner for years. I suppose Hartigan's great-grandson has capitulated. It had to go eventually. It only suited old fogies. I liked it when I was on shore. It was a favorite hangout of skippers who were attending Admiralty Court cases and officers working with a coach for the extra-master's examination. People from the Clyde and Mersey used Hartigan's. We had old-fashioned ideas; but lots of tip-top people had the same, or how would Brown's Hotel have lasted so long?'

'What's the matter with Brown's?' Perdita said. She

had often stayed there when she was a girl. 'I liked it. It's a bit stuffy, I suppose, but . . .'

'So was Hartigan's, but it was luxurious after most British steamers. And only men of courage, strong will and real standing in their profession could make their way into that dark interior! It was forbidding to a stranger. It had, to a very high degree, that marvelous quality of the English hotel. They gave you the impression that they didn't give a damn whether you patronized them or not. They made me feel, when I first went there, that they would like it just as well if I went away and never came back.'

Perdita smiled and nodded. 'What a press agent you'd make for your native country!'

'Hartigan's wouldn't have known what you were talking about if you mentioned a press agent. They lasted a hundred and twenty years. I doubt if a press agent could improve on that. Well, Jack was there, while he attended the inquiry into the loss of the *Lavenham*. I asked about him in the dark little office, and they directed me to the smoking room, which was three steps down after you passed a green baize door with a round window like a porthole in it. I looked through the porthole to make sure he was in there. He was—in a brand-new suit of tweeds that made him look like a book-maker, and he was talking to an extremely pretty girl.'

'She was all in black, with a trig little widow's bonnet. They were widow's weeds, but extremely smart weeds, I can tell you. They had a distinctly frivolous appearance on Roxane Heller. And what was more, she was smoking a cigarette.'

'And you went in?' Perdita said. The maid was removing the soup plates. Mr. Spenlove shook his head.

'Not immediately. I had had my orders to join the *Sandringham* when she arrived. I was merely being sociable when I called on Jack Bannister. I went to the dark little bar and ordered a drink. While I drank I had a few thoughts about Jack. I was shocked. You probably can't imagine it, but the sight of a woman smoking shocked me. It was nineteen fourteen, remember. I had never seen such a thing outside of houses of—you know what I mean. Loose women were known to smoke, but not in public. And in Hartigan's, where a woman would be ordered out of the bar as if she were a leper, it was incredible.'

'Didn't they have barmaids?' Perdita asked, trying to remember.

'Certainly they had barmaids. That was respectable. But not on the other side of the bar. And the barmaids wouldn't have dreamed of smoking.'

'No, she wouldn't. I remember now. A man would stop smoking if he met a woman in the street. Father used to say a gentleman shouldn't smoke except in a smoking room and he should wear a smoking jacket even there.' She went on remembering, biting her lip.

'That's right. Ladies left the gentlemen to their cigars,' she went on. 'I was about Sonia's age. Father took the men guests to his den after dinner.'

'Yes, it was the age of dens. Men accepted the convention that they were wild beasts as soon as the ladies left.'

'How did we stand it?' Perdita wondered, staring at the tablecloth.

'I didn't stand it, my dear. I went to sea! I don't say sea life then was a bed of roses or without any conventions, but we had some release from Victorian stuffiness. We would all have been shocked if we had seen any of our own female relatives smoking, or sitting in public houses, unless they were charladies, of course. So I was shocked. I wasn't used to seeing a woman smoke. I had the same feeling when I first saw a woman in the streets of Norbury naked clear to her crotch, with a naked midriff and not much above that. But she was modest; she wore sun-glasses! It took time, but I got used even to that. And I can't quite recapture the emotion I had when I saw Roxane, in her sweet widow's rig, smoking.

'She wasn't doing it for bravado either. It was, I heard from Annie Collins later, for her a necessity. Jack told me she smoked fifty cigarettes a day. She was a forerunner of our modern women. Egyptian cigarettes, Samsuns, she smoked. She had a downy upper lip and it was faintly discolored with nicotine. Strange to say, it was attractive.

'Well, I had my drink and hung around a while, reading the newspapers in the library, and looking at the leather-bound works in a locked bookcase. Then I wandered down to the smoking room again.

'They were still there. They were in the same pose as when I first peeped in at them. There was Jack in his snappy tweeds, leaning forward in his chair, and Roxane, very erect, smoking like a chimney. She was wearing black gloves. She was dark, with a black bob, such as girls in their teens wore in those days, and she had a very white skin. She was looking at Jack with those brilliant dark eyes of hers.'

'French?' said Perdita.

'Her maiden name was Vermandois. She came from Ghent. The word to describe her was brilliance. The dense black costume, black hair, black gloves, shoes, stockings, against the dead-white skin, reminded me of those portraits of Alexandrian Greeks on the late Egyptian mummy cases. Her eyes were very large, and they could open wide, like those portraits.

'I walked in, and Jack looked round. He didn't know

me then from Adam, and he gave me a blank stare. He had the Englishman's look of sulky resentment when someone else comes into a public room, as though his own privacy was being invaded. I made a wide circuit of them and sat down. Roxane took no notice of me at all. She had her brilliant gaze fixed on Jack and had no intention of letting him go merely to look at a passing stranger!'

'You exaggerate!' Perdita protested. 'Wasn't she in love with him?'

'She was very interested in him! Imagine her situation! She was married to this Heller, representative of a Stuttgart camera film. Nobody knew anything about Heller except that our consul-general in Antwerp believed him to be a secret agent. No matter. He was dead, drowned in the *Lavenham*. Roxane was living with a family of Flemings in Hatton Garden. They were diamond cutters, Jack told me, as if it conferred some sort of luster on Roxane, and on him, at second hand. They knew the Vermandois family in Ghent. No, she wasn't necessarily in love with him. Not then. Why should she be? If a woman saves a man's life, would she be expected to fall in love with him?'

Perdita nodded in agreement. 'No,' she said. 'No, but she might.'

'She was looking at Jack with a sort of alert brilliance, and Jack seemed hypnotized. Her personality was like a jewel with facets all over it. I went over, introduced myself, and he became the famous young chief engineer at once, the character we got used to on the ship. He looked down at my feet in a way he had, and said, in a lofty tone, "All right, Mister, I'll see you later." He didn't rise to shake hands or ask anything about me, and he made no move to introduce me to the girl.'

'Shy,' Perdita said at once.

'I dare say. Roxane looked at me and I saw what an extraordinarily attractive girl she was. She was alluring. She gave one the impression she was appraising one as a possible source of assistance.'

'A gold-digger?'

'I may be prejudiced. She treated Jack in a very scurvy way and I never heard any good of her.' Mr. Spenlove took up the carving knife and cut Perdita some more mutton. 'We were not sympathetic,' he added.

'She was probably afraid of you. How could she help it, when you were taking it all in, watching her as if she were a specimen in a museum?'

'No!' he protested. 'I got it from Jack, and from Annie Collins in Liverpool.'

'She wouldn't like you coming in just then,' Perdita said. 'Go on. What happened?'

'Yes, about the hotel. The *Sandringham* didn't arrive for some days and we were together in the hotel. Jack began to thaw and even took me into his confidence. He probably thought it would not be such a bad idea if he had a second engineer of my experience, but he found it hard to get rid of the notion that anyone who hadn't been in the Hamlet Line all his life wasn't of much account. I could tell you of absolutely incredible lengths that idea is carried by some men. If you have been in the Hamlet Line, or whatever line they belong to, and get out, they think of you as a lost soul! If you come into their marvelous line, you are a brand plucked from the burning! So he thawed and became con-descending, which was as far as he could manage in those days. He would suggest we go to the theater together. We had dinner in restaurants and we sat in bars. Jack was a Lancashire man and really knew London only as a tripper knows it. I was a Londoner in the sense that I had served my

46

time there and worked there and lived there. It was natural that Jack gradually accepted me as almost an equal. And the time came when he mentioned Roxane. I was curious to learn how he came to meet her after the boats brought the passengers ashore.'

'It seems she saw his picture in the paper. She had been sent by the Belgian consul to the family of diamond cutters in Hatton Garden. The reporters had been to Hatton Garden, but Roxane wouldn't see them. She spoke a pretty broken English. In fact, I imagine that her English was one of the reasons the man Heller had wanted to marry her before he went to his assignment in England. And she knew enough about her late husband to make her think the British might lock her up. But when she saw Jack's picture in the paper, the *officier*, the hero who had saved her life, she got into action. Roxane was one of those individuals who have a short range emotionally but tremendous energy at that range. While they have the emotion they are great! And Roxane had the drive of another emotion, fear. She didn't know what was going to happen to her.

'The Flemish family in Hatton Garden had made it clear, and the Belgian consul had made it clearer, that she was in a jam. She was legally, by marriage, a German subject. She would have to look out for herself or be interned. The Germans by that time had occupied Belgium, so she couldn't be sent home. And any way she could expect no help from her family.

'So she got into action when she saw Jack's picture in the paper. She came out of her seclusion in her bedroom in Hatton Garden and went to see the Belgian consul. He located Jack for her. Jack was attending the inquiry, as the consul was, too, for a lot of genuine Belgians had been drowned in the *Lavenham*. Next day she was at Hartigan's

Hotel inquiring for Monsieur Bannister. She had run him down.'

'You needn't gloat,' Perdita protested. 'I can understand. . . . He was very young, you say?'

'Come come, I wasn't so old! He had done me out of a job I had been practically promised. He seemed to think this affair of his with Roxane lifted him far above us common seagoing mortals. He looked down on us. Perhaps I do gloat a little. Why, when he got that medal for life-saving, up he went another notch, into a region we couldn't reach. We were given a copy of the citation, you know. A bitter pill!

'I admit I was startled when I heard from Captain Bowen that our young chief was married. It was all done from Hatten Garden and nobody we knew was present. He got a week's leave to take her to Liverpool, where he left her with Annie Collins. This was just before we sailed from London River. Annie told me about it when I got home. If it hadn't been for Annie's information I wouldn't have been able to get Jack's adventures straight. Because Jack was not a good informant, even if he had not been, well, a victim of circumstances.'

'I know your Annies!' Perdita said, smiling. The red-cheeked maid clumped around the table, removing the plates and setting the jam roll in front of her mistress. Mr. Spenlove glanced at the glass of Burgundy, 'good old Beaune,' at his elbow. He liked it as a rule, but tonight he was not so sure. He had had a lot to drink with old Romaine in the Trocodero bar and in a pub near Victoria. Romaine had been quite expansive. He had forgotten for a while that he was a business man. It had been curious to see him disentangling himself, with many grimaces, from the hard, jagged-edged shell of business, the almost impenetrable carapace which he had evolved during the past ten years. For a while he

48

had been just a veteran chief steward trying to be convivial ashore. Well, they had been good shipmates for a long time, and it might not be too late for Romaine to live any other way.

Mr. Spenlove had asked him why he did not get married and have a home. Old Romaine had mumbled that 'Nobody 'ud have me.' But had he tried? Another mumble. Mr. Spenlove had not pressed him. It was his own affair, of course.

He took a small piece of jam roll. No cheese; black coffee, and a brandy later.

'My Annies, as you call them, are the salt of the earth,' he said, smiling. 'This Annie was one of the best of the boiling, as we used to say. Seamen have a very limited choice of wives. Even old Bowen had married his landlady's daughter. He told me so. He was a first mate at the time. Quite an ordinary occurrence in our lives. Mrs. Bowen was another Annie, to judge from what the Old Man said. Her mother ran apartments for officers. This particular Annie I am talking about, who had been a barmaid at the Metropole at New Brighton, was the daughter of a Cunard steward with seven children. We didn't really go out of our own class if we married our landlady's daughter. Or a barmaid either, come to that.'

'We didn't?' Perdita said, gently.

'I get carried away,' he admitted, smiling, 'but you understand I am speaking generally, not of particular cases. We—and I mean the run of seamen—knew where we were with such girls. If you married out of your class, or a foreigner, as some occasionally did, you had no charts, no pilot, no sailing directions. You sailed out into an unknown sea.

'And being a barmaid was an education in itself. If a girl was intelligent, she became tolerant and civilized. She

49

met a variety of men and women, with a good solid bar between her and them. Met them when they were off guard, at times. I suppose it's different now.

'So Annie, my Annie, was well equipped to handle Roxane, if anyone was. Roxane has probably forgotten Annie long ago, wherever she is—forgotten me, and even Jack Bannister. Girls like that advance from tree to tree, like their prehistoric ancestors, springing lightly from man to man across perilous places.'

'She sounds as if she'd get on well in Hollywood,' Perdita said. The red-cheeked maid came in with the coffee-tray. 'In the billiard room, please, Polly,' Perdita rose as her husband withdrew her chair.

'Oh, yes, she could get on anywhere, I would say,' he said. They settled in the deep chairs by the fireplace. 'She had chic. She didn't look like a penniless alien, an enemy alien by marriage. She sat looking at Jack Bannister, a cigarette in her black-gloved hand. I had the idea she was exerting hypnotic power over him, he was so still.

'Whatever power she had, it worked. We were no sooner over the shock of reading about our young chief engineer getting a medal for his heroism than we were bowled over by seeing his picture in the paper again, with his bride, the lovely Mme. Roxane Heller, nee Vermandois. Here was romance brought right into our engine room with a vengeance.

'And we didn't care much about it. The sudden rise of Jack Bannister, not only above me but above several other men, was not popular. It never is. They say you can't keep a good man down. Nothing easier, sometimes. Jack wasn't popular either, because he was on a high horse. He was unapproachable. His sudden, secret marriage, about which we had been told nothing at all in advance, made it worse. The steward, who was also our purser on that ship, a bit of a toady, started a subscription with a guinea to buy our hero a wedding present. He gave me the job of pinning up the list in the mess room and collecting the contributions from my juniors.'

Perdita passed him a cup of black coffee. 'You mean he didn't tell you, in the hotel? That he was going to get married?'

'He told me about Roxane. Later I had the pleasure of her company. He didn't say he was going to marry her. He used me as a sounding board for his sentiments. My impression is, that until the last few days on shore he didn't know himself whether he was going to marry her before he sailed. Roxane did that. Jack's background, once he had got rid of his personal prejudice against a seaman being married at all, would call for a long engagement. Engagements in the lower-middle, or upper working-class circles, used to be long. I knew men who were engaged for years! Unless you had a mate's job, or a chief's, you simply hadn't the means to support a wife. Roxane knew nothing about that. She had to make sure of him. When I think back to that first scene in Hartigan's Hotel, I have a feeling that even then she had made up her mind to make sure of him. Think of her situation. Think of what had happened to her the only time she had ever been on board of a ship! His ship, too! It might happen again; and if she weren't married to him, where would she be? It would be a case of Mr. Heller all over again. She'd be right back where she started! And in a foreign country!'

'You surely don't believe she thought it all out like that!' Perdita said. He shook his head. 'No,' he said. 'Roxane's mind didn't work that way. She didn't think anything out. She arrived at her conclusion in one lightning flash of intuition. Call it instinct, if you like. Girls like her have an instinct when they are hunting their prey. Heller was very flush with money when he was staying in Ghent. I learned that from my invaluable Confidential Report (for officers only) in H.M.S. *Sycorax's* wardroom. The reason he became interested in Roxane, as I told you, was her pretty English. They were going to live in England, where he was to start a branch agency for his firm. They made complicated cameras and optical lenses. Roxane's English was pretty, but it was limited, and she neither read it nor wrote it. An ideal combination, from Herr Heller's point of view. Especially when combined with Roxane's glamorous aspect and attractiveness, if he ever had any young British officers to deal with.

'Jack, in short, was hooked, and it was because he was hooked that he was so off-hand with me when I introduced myself that day in Hartigan's Hotel. I thought at the time he was merely heading for one of those tremendous wartime love affairs, in which everything is speeded up as when a motion-picture machine is driven too fast; affairs which everybody knows are not intended to be permanent. I had no reason to suppose he would have a wedding in a Soho church, attended by only a few friends of the bride, who were all foreigners. They were headed by the consul and the diamond-cutting family, who gave the bride a diamond brooch.'

'I should have thought he would have left her with her diamond-cutting friends instead of taking her to Liverpool. A girl like that,' Perdita said.

'Naturally,' Mr. Spenlove said. 'But Jack went all out when he decided to get married. He revealed all the usual characteristics of a seaman getting spliced. He had about four hundred pounds invested, and his new *Sandringham* job, being a bigger ship, raised his pay. When he got back from this voyage, or after the war, he was going to have a house near the Collins' place in Sefton Park, and set up house-keeping. He told me this after we had been at sea a week or so,' Mr. Spenlove laughed reminiscently. 'He had it all planned! I would stand just within his cabin door and listen to the plans. Roxane was giving me a brilliant smile from the bulkhead. It was a large photograph, and she was what they call nowadays very photogenic.'

'You keep on about Roxane,' Perdita said. 'What is *he* like?'

'Tall, high-shouldered. He used to wear a dark tooth-brush mustache. He had good features, rather dark, with brown eyes. He had a sort of haughtiness in his manner. He had something of the look of Cecil Rhodes. The minute you spoke to him he seemed to withdraw into himself. He would look down at his feet, as though he were trying to suppress indignation at your cheek in addressing him. His voice was harsh and flat. He had an exasperating trick of saying, in a superior manner, "It's lucky I have a sense of humor." As a matter of fact he had no sense of humor whatever, or he would never have bragged about Roxane.

'Perhaps bragging is too emphatic a word. It implies expansiveness and there was nothing expansive about Jack. His method was to tell us, in curt tones, that "my wife this" and "my wife that." Very curt and definite, and with a touch of condescension.

'Doesn't it tell you anything about him to know he never looked at the person he was talking to? The moment you came into his field of vision you saw he wasn't looking at you. When I went to him for orders, or to tell him some-thing, he would stand looking out of his after window, and talk to me as if he were addressing someone outside on deck. He seemed to be holding himself in all the time.

'He had his chair at an angle to Roxane's, when I saw them, with the light on his face. She had the light on her profile. I glanced through the little round window, like a porthole in the door. Jack was speaking. He was looking down at his clenched fist, in a way he had. I became familiar with that pose of his. Very intense, he was! Then Roxane, leaning forward, raised her black-gloved hands, clasped them to her breast, and spoke with what seemed to me, peeping in on them, with intense emotion also. Her smile was brilliant. It seemed to illuminate them at that table. I say seemed. The rest of the room was rather dusky. Hartigan's were thrifty with electricity.

'That was all I had to go on. Later, when we were out together, when we had become acquainted while waiting for our ship, I could see Roxane was trying to impress herself on me as Jack's girl. Jack had a way of striding along, his hands in his pockets, head down, looking severely pleased with himself, so to speak, yet rather as if he were trying to lose Roxane. That's just my impression!' Mr. Spenlove smiled. 'Roxane was not the sort of girl to be shaken off. When we were out walking she snuggled close to Jack, holding his arm, her face close to his shoulder, every now and then giving me a ravishing glance from her brilliant eyes. I had to walk fast to keep up with this procession, and Roxane had to run. You would have thought Jack had a train to catch, and a last train at that! We must have seemed slightly strange to anyone watching, as we raced along.'

Perdita laughed, not only at the picture he had drawn, but at something she was thinking of. She was wondering whether anyone else in the world got so much amusement out of his fellow men as her husband seemed to do. Possibly that was the reason he was so easy to live with. He had a profoundly enjoying nature. Elliot Ducroy, with whom she had tried to live in Hollywood and Connecticut, made an immense amount of money and lived on a lavish scale. He had made that money by exploiting the craving for vicarious adventure and mystery in the American public. They had clutched eagerly at his pictures of luxurious living and desperate villainy, yet the man himself had never seemed to enjoy his own life. Even when he plunged into an affair with another extravagantly talented purveyor of imaginary happiness he seemed to be doing it out of some feeling that fate demanded it, rather than something to be enjoyed.

CHAPTER

3

T HERE was another strange thing about Jack at that time,' Mr. Spenlove went on presently. 'He gave me a distinct impression that he wanted me to think it is only an affair. As though he wanted to put me off the track.

'One day, walking along the Strand to Hartigan's, after we had been out with Roxane, Jack said to me, "What do you think of my little piece of skirt?"

'It sounds pretty crude. Even then, when "bit of skirt" was the regular slang for the girl a man went out with, it sounded crude.

'I said nothing, and he went on, "She wants me to be her steady. I don't know! Can't say I want to keep another man's daughter! Not until the war's over, anyway; and that's a long time yet." He meant it would be more than six months. That was how we thought in 1915. We thought it would be over in six months. We were the pessimists!

'I asked him why didn't he get married before we sailed? It was taking them a long time to convert the *Sandringham* into a transport. We knew we'd have another month at least in dock.

'He fixed his eyes on the distance and stared indignantly. He asked me what I was talking about. He said he didn't believe in seagoing men getting married. Anybody who did was just a plain idiot. "You take me for an idiot?" he said.

'And you want me to believe he was in love with her?' Perdita exclaimed. 'What a thing to say!'

'Yes, it sounds odd, I know, yet that is what he said. That's the kind of thing men like him, in that level of society, in that time, used to say. It wasn't their real thought. Their real thought was not to be expressed. Why, you would be horrified if I told you some of the things men of that grade will say about women. They have strange ways of expressing themselves, or rather expressing what they want you to think is themselves. It is hard, when you have made an image of yourself as a sharp, cunning, wise man of the world, to confess tender emotions. The thing to do is to assume that the real thought is the exact opposite of what they say. Men like Jack have no tradition of lovemaking and lack the originality to make one. Jack's class, our class, had no articulate conventions. We were something new in the world. Poets, dramatists, novelists and painters didn't even know we existed!

'Jack knew his job, and as he started his apprenticeship at fourteen, the usual age, his education at a common school stopped then. He knew his job, but he knew precious little else. His sudden elevation to the role of hero had done something to his balance. His rise to chief engineer at a preposterously early age—quite deserved, mind you—oh yes, quite justified!—had altered his traditional humility toward the world outside our professional horizon. It had made him slightly eccentric and disdainful of us plodding mortals. You could call him conceited if you didn't understand him.'

'I'm relieved,' Perdita said. 'I thought you were working up to one of your climaxes, when some man you used to know and thought was marvelous turned out to be just a papier-mâché imitation. You have a weakness for them, you know.'

'I do. I know I do. No, Jack wasn't papier-mâché. He was a really good chief engineer, but rather difficult for us common mortals to get along with. And he suffered from the fact that his commanders, especially Captain Bowen of the *Sandringham*, couldn't stand him. And commanders didn't have to conceal their feelings about him as we did.

'So when he told me, in so many words, that he was thinking of Roxane as his fancy piece, I didn't like it at all. I had an idea that Roxane wasn't the type to be anybody's fancy piece unless there was something substantial in it for her. I needn't have worried. Roxane happened to be in urgent need of a husband at the moment. When Jack made off-hand remarks about her and his disbelief in marriage, it was his way of telling me that Roxane was the divinest creature he had ever seen, that he was madly in love with her and could not live until he had made her his dear darling little wife. That was what he meant. But he could no more have told me that than he could have taken a guitar and serenaded her window in Hatton Garden. I would have known this if I had been more experienced. But we live and learn.'

'You mean other people live and you learn,' Perdita teased gently. 'Go on, darling.'

'There's something in that!' he admitted. 'What I was going to say, the *Sandringham* got away at last. Jack came back from Liverpool the day we sailed, a married man. He had a new and difficult attitude toward us. He had been rather aloof before. Now he was unapproachable. There we were, with a young chief engineer, the youngest chief engineer in the world, I dare say, and he would hardly speak to us. To make it worse, our steward-purser, as I mentioned, the sort of chap who never misses a chance to ingratiate himself in the most irreproachable way, started a collection for a wedding present for Jack. It came to twenty-seven pounds and nobody knew what to do with it. We had sailed suddenly and without any information where we were going. Old Bowen had his orders in a sealed envelope which he was to open off Ushant. You can imagine the conjectures! And the ribald remarks to our steward-purser.'

'To do him justice, Jack probably never even imagined a present from us. He was new to the ship and his aloofness prevented him from getting any hint, even from the steward-purser. He came back from Liverpool full of the pride of possession, which was the reverse side of his former antagonism against marriage. Anything that happened to him personally was important, and his marriage must have taken on something unusual in his view because he was the youngest chief engineer in the service.

'The fellows on the *Sandringham* put the blame on the hero business. If he hadn't happened to be a public hero, they argued, he might have been easier to get along with. He came up from below one day while I was in my cabin and stood there looking furious. "They're all dead!" he said to me. I found he was referring to the two juniors on watch. He had found the evaporator shut off. I told him it was shut off by my orders and they were obeying orders. He walked off without another word.

'When Captain Bowen opened his sealed orders he wouldn't tell Jack where we were going. That increased the tension. It was only natural that I should ask my chief if he knew our destination. Jack wanted me to think he knew, but wouldn't tell me for reasons of national security. He said it was confidential. He was fond of phrases like that. When the rumors circulated in the mess, I told the boys they were wrong to make such guesses. Our destination was confidential. Our fifth engineer, who was the electrician, and naturally chummy with the wireless operators, suddenly let the cat out of the bag. He said we were going to Alexandria. He had seen a naval signal on the desk in the wireless room. I might have had fun with Jack if I had told him what I knew, but even then I had learned that it is a good thing to know more than one's superior thinks one knows.'

Mr. Spenlove stopped to listen to the sound of a car on the driveway.

'It's Father Soames,' Perdita said. 'He said he'd drop in this evening.' She went to meet the visitor.

'For a tot,' Mr. Spenlove smiled and rose. 'It's a pleasure.'

He was sincere. Sky-pilots were not much in his line, never had been, but Father Soames was no pious proselytizer. He had nothing sacerdotal about him. His clean-shaven, ruddy features and resonant, baritone, pulpit voice might have belonged to a character actor. Mr. Spenlove thought him more like a stage parson than the real thing. Perdita, who attended the morning service every other Sunday in the little old church of Layer-de-la-Pole, said his sermons took exactly fifteen minutes and were always cheerful.

Father Soames came in with evident shy pleasure. He shook hands with his host with the sincerity which means, in an Englishman, that he accepts you not merely as a human being but as a member of his own class. Or very nearly. Father Soames was not deeply introspective. He imagined it was his own carefully guarded secret that he looked forward to these evening visits. Mr. Spenlove chaffed him about the heathen atmosphere of the house; Father Soames said he came in a missionary spirit. He said he didn't hope to convert Mr. Spenlove. He believed in miracles, but not that kind.

He had sufficient intelligence to find his usual cronies occasionally boring. They were social crustaceans. They were county-minded, as he said at times to Mr. Spenlove, who was not at all county-minded, and chaffed Perdita's mother, Mrs. Price, when she told Father Soames that he, Mr. Spenlove, came of an old Hampshire family.

He sat down with a gleam in his eye as Mr. Spenlove set the brandy bottle at his elbow and opened the cigar box. Mr. Spenlove remembered the parson's embarrassment when he had been offered a cigar with the fingers, American fashion. He was never embarrassed again. The host held a match to the cigar and told him what had taken him to London. He added a short account of Mr. Romaine's career and said he might be coming down. Father Soames had been to sea as a boy after giving up the navy. He had made a long voyage in a four-master Australian ship, an experience which had turned his thoughts to spiritual things. He and Mr. Spenlove had discussed certain men who had written sea books, and Father Soames spoke up for Frank T. Bullen as a much under-rated author. There was, he mentioned a book of Bullen's, *With Christ at Sea*. He admired that book. He admitted, with a smile, that if he himself had been going to write one it would have had to be called *Without Christ at Sea*. 'They were a very irreligious crowd in that ship,' he said, shaking his head. 'Very irreligious. But you can't make silk purses out of sow's ears.'

He was interested in Mr. Romaine's reaction to a life of leisure. He nodded and blew out a cloud of smoke with enjoyment.

'I've known that to happen. We had a man here some

61

years ago. Made a fortune out of a patent washing-machine. Or an ironing-machine; I forget which it was now. He hadn't done anything since he was fourteen except work in a factory. Sold his business to a big combine and bought that house on the way to Sutton Marney. Didn't ride, didn't shoot, didn't play golf. Garden didn't seem to mean much to him. Left it to the gardener. Didn't read except the *Times*. He died in a nursing home. You're wise, Spenlove. You haven't let Mammon take charge.'

'Luck, not judgment,' Mr. Spenlove warned him. 'I always lacked the nerve to go into business for myself. Of course, I lacked the capital; but if I'd had it, I would still have lacked the nerve. Passengers used to frighten me. They would say, "It takes so much capital to start and run a business nowadays." I would ask them what they meant by "so much" and they would frighten me with "Oh, fifty thousand dollars—sixty thousand—eighty thousand, perhaps." The way they said it showed they thought such sums extremely conservative and reasonable.'

Father Soames smiled. 'Americans! Money's different over there.'

'Well, I would tell them, if I had had any such sum, I would not put it into a business. I would live on the interest and enjoy myself. They would look at me as if I had gone insane! To them I *was* insane, because I worked for someone else and did nothing with my money but spend it or put it in the bank. My old friend Romaine is one of them. They usually die in the fifties, of a heart ailment. I have warned Romaine to take life easily now. He has about fifty thousand dollars, and at present his idea is to go back to America and start in some business and make another fifty thousand. Then he would do what he calls "retire." I advise him to get married, but he thinks the fifty thousand would vanish like smoke if a woman got hold of him. He no longer thinks of money as a means of exchange. It is capital. He can't break into capital, he says.'

'That's what I mean by Mammon,' Father Soames said.

'Well, it's his money, darling,' Perdita said. 'If he likes to do it that way. It isn't very interesting to hear about.'

'Capital? No, it isn't,' said Mr. Spenlove, looking at his visitor. 'We were discussing another old shipmate of mine when you came in. Not a capitalist, by any means, but his wife called to see us while I was in London. They live at Tollemache St. Marys. His wife is young. It so happens she went to the school where our Sonia is now, at Montreux.'

'My husband's been telling me about Mr. Bannister's past,' Perdita said. Father Soames was interested.

'Bannister? I've heard of them. She's an Enderby-Breton on her mother's side. Her uncle used to be deputy-lieutenant of the county. What about Mr. Bannister's past?'

'Nothing scandalous,' Mr. Spenlove explained briefly what he had been talking about. 'I simply don't see him as the master of Moat Farm, Tollemache St. Marys.'

'The Enderby-Bretons are an old family, as families go nowadays,' Father Soames said comfortably. 'Made their money in India, you know. East India Company.'

'And it all comes eventually to this young Mrs. Bannister, as I understand it,' Mr. Spenlove said. 'Through her mother. That's what makes it interesting to me, for I knew Bannister at one time, rather well. And it means an immense change in Jack. I remember his first wife, when I first knew him.'

'Sounds like one of your yarns,' the parson said.

'There were certain unusual features about him,' Mr. Spenlove went on, rubbing his beard. 'Jack was precocious. He was an orphan and lived with an aunt while he was an apprentice. Then he went to sea in the Hamlet Line and by a stroke of luck he served under the son of the old superintendent, who was grooming this son for a successor. Jack must have been smart, of course, but he had the luck. When young Dalgleish took over on his father's resignation, he shoved young Jack ahead. The rise to the top with most of us is slow and, occasionally, very slow. With Jack it was meteoric. It made him conceited and hard to get along with. The result was, that when the war began in 1914, Jack at twenty-three or -four was chief of the *Lavenham*, a small ship trading to the Continent.

'Annie told me Jack got the idea he was reserved for some great destiny. I believe it was a fact that Dalgleish tipped him off to take a course of study in Diesels at a time when most of us had no use for anything but steam. As soon as Dalgleish had a clear field and the Company were ready to build, he got them to see that Diesels were coming. He was going to shove Jack onto one of them. They were building a new fleet when the war started. And it would only be a matter of a few years before Jack would step ashore as assistant superintendent. Jack got this bee in his bonnet, and he became very reserved. He never had a girl in those days, Annie said. In fact, he had no friends of either sex, apart from Annie and her Harry, who was at sea as often as not when Jack was at home. He became very severe when he got this chief's job. Juniors used to quit because they couldn't stand his lack of appreciation. Young Dalgleish backed him. He too thought the young fellows were lazy, ignorant and independent. He wanted what he called "dead wood" cut away.'

Mr. Spenlove struck a match against the stone fireplace and relighted his cigar. He blew a cloud of smoke and pointed the cigar at his listeners.

'So here was our Jack suddenly bowled over by a foreign girl, whom he had saved from the water, married to her too, and off to a foreign station for years, so far as any of us knew.

'What held him up during the time he was with us? I, as second, was the cushion between him and the others. There was no cushion between him and old Bowen, the skipper. Old Bowen couldn't stand him, wouldn't speak to him, or have anything to do with him directly. If Jack wanted anything he had to write a chit and send it to the captain, who would send an answer by the third mate. Old Bowen used to remind me of that naval captain we heard about, who never would see any of his officers. If one of them came to his cabin, and the marine at the door brought in the news, the skipper would say, "Ask him what he wants, and tell him no." We lay in Alexandria harbor, with an occasional run to Salonika or Malta, while the war dragged on. It was the most boring war you can imagine for us, but we made the best of it, and stuck it out.

'Well, Sefton Park, Liverpool, was a change all right for Roxane! She had some definite ideas about honeymoons, ideas which included marvelous clothes, jewelry, shoes, silk stockings and underwear. Silk was an obsession with her, Annie said. She shocked Annie by telling her that if she could get them she would have silk sheets on the beds! That was her idea of starting housekeeping for a seagoing man who might be at home three weeks in a year.'

'What I really wanted to know was, how they got on together. Annie said it was "sunshine and storms all day," and even part of the night. Annie thought Jack did not quite realize what his obligations were as a bridegroom. Roxane had a temper. Jack seemed to think all he had to do was to exist. He didn't exert himself; he didn't, as we say nowadays, splurge at all. Annie said he ought to have taken a suite at the Metropole and ordered a champagne dinner once or twice. She said it wasn't that he was stingy. He just didn't *think* of anything dramatic or spontaneous to do. Yet he was absolutely infatuated with his Roxane, Annie assured me. When Roxane got mad, he was in despair. When they made it up, he was in the seventh heaven!

'Naturally, a young woman, even if she has been suddenly and violently widowed, wants to be taken out. Jack seemed to feel that, having saved her life, it wasn't up to him particularly to make her life worth living. I don't say he actually put it that way to himself, but Annie said it really seemed to her as if he figured Roxane must henceforth be so wild with gratitude to him for his services in saving her, that he didn't need to do anything more!

'When he left, Jack gave his wife fifty pounds for expenses, and of course she would receive his half-pay. Roxane slumped when she was left alone. She lay in bed smoking, worrying the life out of Annie on account of fire, and often going twice in a day to the movies. If a letter came from Jack, Roxane would leave it around for days without opening it.

'What worried a woman with Annie's instincts, was Roxane's dreadfully egocentric character. She was apparently uninterested in anything or anybody but her own personal comfort. Annie wanted to teach her how to cook, how to market economically, how to serve a nice high tea to guests. It was a fact, Annie admitted, that Roxane knew a lot more about it than she did, but she wouldn't *do* anything at all. She was preoccupied with the problem of how to get out of the fearful hole she had got herself into by marrying Jack. For it *was* a hole. Annie told me she found Roxane one day lying on her bed, looking at the ceiling. When she looked at Annie, who wanted to know if she was not feeling well, she gave Annie a funny look, and said, "How can I feel well when I am living like this? In hell! Much better in a prison than here! My God! Feel well!" And she turned over and tore at the pillow and almost went into hysterics.

'Don't forget, she'd had a miraculous honeymoon the first time. It took place in Ostend with Heller, she told Annie. Germans were real men, she said, not like Englishmen, stingy. She'd had champagne suppers, diamonds, silks and furs. Paris clothes and huge boxes of chocolates and cigarettes. All gone down in that horrible English ship.

'She had imagined that Jack, being a hero, would live the life of a hero, in a big London house, with servants and motor cars and aristocratic friends. And here she was, stuck away in a miserable little suburb of a town she had hardly heard of. And she was straining every nerve of her brain, trying to seek a way out.

'She would dress herself—Annie said she was a fair dazzler when she was dressed—and go into Liverpool. Annie was shocked at the way Roxane went to the movies. Dreaming, Annie supposed. Then she'd take the electric tram home. When summer came Annie took her to New Brighton, and that was a revelation for Roxane. That was what she wanted, the glittering beach, the bright lights, the big hotels, the bands of music, and the shows. She soon got in the way of going there by herself.

'Annie knew it would be difficult for Jack when he came home. He wrote to her, asking how things were. Roxane wouldn't or couldn't write to him. I expect that was the real reason. She couldn't sit down before a sheet of paper to *write* to Jack, she couldn't tell him anything. She said she couldn't write English, so Annie offered to write it for her. Roxane said, "Yes, yes! You write. Anything you please. No matter." Annie was scandalized!

'You have to say this for Roxane, she was all of a piece. She had a hard, tight, compact character. Every particle of energy she possessed was directed to one object, the personal welfare of Roxane.

'Annie was getting a little tired of Roxane's indolent habits when something happened which precipitated what you might call a crisis. Roxane got picked up in New Brighton. An officer on a Belgian steamer loading in Liverpool. One afternoon Annie, who had been visiting relations in Bootle, came home and found her house full of foreigners.

'It was not only full of foreigners, it was *open!* In a place like Sefton Park, no matter how warm the weather may be, privacy is observed. People sit in their back gardens, safe from observation.

'Annie, to her horror, found her front door open. She could see clear through the house into the back garden. The front-room windows were open, and all the lights were on. Harry Collins had had electricity put in on a lavish scale, and the sitting room had plenty of lamps, floor-lamps, table-lamps and sconces. Every blessed one of those lights was on, and the French window at the back leading onto a little brick terrace, was open too. The visitors, whoever they were, had carried a table out there, and it was loaded with bottles of wine and beer.

'Annie nearly had a fit. The piano was being played loudly and the first person she actually caught sight of was a stout man wearing a huge black beard and a naval sort of uniform. He was holding up a glass and singing. Annie remembered his red lips and tongue in the black beard, and his white teeth. She had read somewhere about a character named Blackbeard and she had a sudden, fleeting panic that there were pirates in her house!

'Her first impulse was to call a policeman, but she didn't. She has plenty of courage, and she walked straight through the house into her nice little back garden. She admitted to me that it was the "openness" of the place which outraged her feelings. Nobody had ever been able to stare straight through her house before that day. An Englishman's house is supposed to be his castle, and an Englishwoman's house, in Annie's social stratum, is a castle with the drawbridge up and the curtains drawn.

'Straight through she went and found Roxane with a young man, also in some foreign naval uniform. Annie said she could see, the minute she saw them, that there was something between those two. Roxane turned on Annie a brilliant smile—and how she could smile!—and introduced her to Lieutenant——, some foreign name, Annie did not catch it.'

'He had had his arm around Roxane's shoulders. He had glossy blond hair which Annie thought had been marcelled. Roxane introduced him in what I call her bravura manner, "My cousin." He may have been her cousin, of course. I doubt whether any of us ever knew that. He was very polite and bowed to Annie.

'Annie couldn't do anything at all. Roxane, just a shade defiant as well as bravura, led the way into the front room and introduced Annie to the blackbearded person. *Capitaine* Somebody, from the *bateau* in the river. There were other lieutenants and two foreign women, refugees living in Wallasey.

'To Annie's Sefton Park mind it was an invasion! It was shocking, outrageous. She closed the doors and windows, turned off the lights, and cleared away the cigarette ashes on the tables and carpets. She gave Roxane what she called "A good talking to," but Roxane retired to her room and lay on the bed smoking cigarettes and lost in thought. What did she think she was doing, allowing that young man to put his arm around her? Roxane shouted, "He's my cousin! Go away!"

'Annie calmed down after a while and decided that the only thing to do was to ask Roxane to leave. But she was worried as to what Jack Bannister would think. She was very fond of Jack. He had been a sort of kid brother. She hesitated about throwing Roxane into the street. If she had known anyone who could have taken her—but what can one do with a foreign girl?

'While she thought the matter over Roxane disappeared.

'Girls like Roxane are not so difficult to understand, after all. The springs of their conduct run near the surface. They run bright and clear when they emerge from their characters. I doubt if Roxane, for instance, had the slightest conception of what we mean by love of country. She was at home wherever she could find ease and security and gaiety. There is an austerity about a place like Sefton Park, a dullness, a drabness even, which simply suffocated her. And a good many other Gallic refugees. Like many girls clever enough at domestic tasks, Roxane was lazy. She hated housework. Her interest was in beautifying herself, wearing extremely high heels, and silk wherever she could wear it. If Annie didn't actually think Roxane was immoral, she thought her reprehensible, because she didn't earn her living.

'Annie was writing a letter to Jack telling him, as well as she could, what had happened and why she had to ask him to put his wife somewhere else. She didn't mention the Belgian lieutenant. She said Roxane was "running around too much." She said she was afraid Roxane might get into some sort of trouble. She hinted at the number of refugees idling about in the Liverpool district, foreigners whom it was difficult to be sure about.

'It was this letter I was going to tell you about, because when Jack received it, he was brought up all standing. His dream world came crashing down around him.

'The first thing we knew about it was a rumor that our young chief engineer had had a row with the skipper. This was the story I heard when I came up from below one day and took my place at the head of the mess table. Yes, the chief was having a row with the skipper. I asked, what about? They didn't know that. It was something I had accidentally discovered myself that very morning. I had had two embarrassing experiences.

'I had gone to Jack's cabin to see him about some professional matter. The door was closed and I knocked. There was no answer, so I tried the door gently. If it was locked I could come back again when he was on board. But in spite of my gentle movement the door opened in my hand and I saw him.

'He was sitting on his settee, his face in his hands and there were tears falling through his fingers. His shoulders were heaving. I was appalled, for I know nothing worse for a man than to find another man crying. He was like a small child! *Blubbering!*'

Mr. Spenlove got up suddenly and took the decanter. He stood for a moment, the stopper in his other hand, as though even the memory of that scene had embarrassed him. Then he refilled the glasses.

'Horrible!' he said, sitting down again. 'It wasn't just a matter of, as we say, having tears in his eyes. He had lost all control of his facial muscles. His mouth, under his tooth-

71

brush mustache, was a gaping hole, out of which came gasp after gasp as he looked up and saw me. It was as if I had found a stranger stark naked. As he was, in a sense. I mean his soul was at that moment stripped of everything.

'I started to close the door at once, of course, but he put up one hand to stop me and went on blubbering. I don't know any other word for it. Then he got hold of himself and said, very quietly, with only one gasp, "What do you want, Mister?"

'I must have closed the door between us involuntarily, for he said it again, louder. When I got the door open again he was standing by his wash basin bathing his face. His back was toward me. He took a towel and leaned forward to examine a spot on his chin. He glanced at me in the mirror for an instant and said, "What's the matter? Can't you speak?" And he gave a sudden hiccup.

'I told him what I wanted. He put the towel down, turned to his bunk and said, "All right, Mister." I closed the door again and stole away, very much shaken.

'That was the first thing. I was in a state. I had no way of knowing what the trouble was. Jack had spoken to me from time to time about "my wife," as he called Roxane, in a rather smug tone, as though he naturally had a specially excellent and remarkable wife, but the impression he had given me was that he was very much cock of the walk at home. He said he gave her "an allowance" and she was expected to keep within it. He thought men were very foolish to let their wives be extravagant. "A tight rein," he assured me, was his idea of the right thing. He made these sage remarks from time to time when we happened to be alone, walking to and fro on deck. He didn't go ashore much, and I often stayed on board to read and meditate. If I had any thoughts at all about Jack at that time and his inamorata, they were chiefly that he was making a grand success of marriage, as in every other department of his life. A precociously successful human being!'

Mr. Spenlove shook his finger at Perdita, who was smiling skeptically, but he spoke to Father Soames, who was also smiling in his attempt to capture the mood of the moment.

'She,' Mr. Spenlove said, meaning Perdita, 'cannot believe that I was not always what I now am, a combination of sage and philosopher! But it's obvious, isn't it, that to reach such perfection I had to have experiences? That I had to indulge in weakness and folly? That to understand a fellow like Jack Bannister, for instance, I had to see him from below, as it were, when he was elevated on his pedestal? Well, I assure you that in those days I had the most fantastic ideas of the perfection of other men. I even dabbled, on occasion, in humility! It never did any harm. Old Bowen, for example, would never have unburdened himself to me about Jack if I had not been one of the quiet, efficient young men who knew their place in the world. That was my caper in those days! Impenetrable neutrality combined with impeccable efficiency! I tried to give the impression that I had no private life whatever, because when you have no private affairs, your superiors, for some reason, think you are less likely to neglect *their* interests. I really believe I fooled them, too. But I didn't fool myself. I had an intuition that if I took what you may call a psychological back-seat, I would do better than if I threw my weight about and tried to impress them that way.

'Yes, Jack was a precociously successful man! I knew he was good professionally. He couldn't fool me there. I had a vision of him reaching the position of superintendent in the Line, or even a bigger line than ours, a powerful and prosperous citizen.

'So I was in a great state when I saw him in *déshabille*, so to speak. I had no idea at the time what the trouble was. The first thing that occurred to me was that he was likely to do away with himself. There was a lot of it going on during the war: a fellow would get a letter telling him his wife had gone away with another man.

'A shot from behind a closed cabin door doesn't reach very far, and after I had been down below and seen everybody at work, I came up again by the fire-room ladder, which led clear up to the top deck. I think I had the idea of taking the skipper into my confidence. I don't remember just what was in my mind. I was just uneasy. I went along and down to Jack's room again. I had thought of a pretext, and I knocked. There was no answer. I turned the knob. The door was locked.

'I was in a state again. It seemed to me that what I had imagined was taking place right there behind that closed door. I shook the door and said, "Are you there, Mister?" No answer. I came out on deck and went straight up to see the old man. When I got topside again I crossed the boat deck, dodged around a pile of life rafts and made for Captain Bowen's quarters.

'I stopped behind a ventilator. Jack was up there standing beside the old man at the rail. Old Bowen was smoking a cigar very fast and staring across the harbor, taking no notice at all of the man talking to him. Jack had his fists clenched on the rail and he was looking down at his feet. I could see his shoulders heaving.

'Suddenly old Bowen turned to Jack and stared at him with his mouth open, his cigar cocked, as though he could not believe his ears. Then he led the way to his cabin, Jack followed and the door closed. So I went down to my work again.'

74

Mr. Spenlove looked at Father Soames, who was looking at his own cigar, and smiled.

'Here was a case, Father, when ghostly counsel was needed. When Jack Bannister got that letter from Annie Collins, he felt that Roxane had merely used him, had never really cared a snap of her fingers for him. It must have been a blow. He had been nothing but what he was in the first place to her, a life-saving apparatus, which she had discarded as soon as she was in safety. The moment something else a little more buoyant, in this case a Belgian lieutenant, had floated past her, Jack was forgotten.

'Captain Bowen told me later that when Jack went to pieces in the old man's cabin, it was an embarrassing moment. It became even more embarrassing when Jack went down on his knees to him and begged him to have mercy and let him go home by the next ship.

'I don't suppose Jack had any clear ideas as to how far old Bowen could help him. He had to apply for a pass, for what they called "compassionate leave." After that letter he was ready to jump overboard and swim ashore, or to another homeward-bound ship. The only clear idea he had was that he must go after Roxane.'

'He was in love,' Perdita said.

'Yes, he was in love, the sort of love that is a blend of pride, sex, fear, and a dash of hate! It affects romantics and egoists. It's a sort of soul-sickness. Jack had built up in his imagination a Roxane not at all like the real one. He had imagination, you see, but it was not warm. He had become, on account of his easy success in life, an egoist, a romantic egoist who was conceited. Thinking of himself as Roxane's savior, and he thought that she would be eternally grateful to him.'

'He surely didn't go on his knees,' Father Soames suggested.

'No, I don't suppose he actually did genuflect so as to touch the floor. He certainly must have made some gesture which stuck in old Bowen's mind as amounting to the same thing. Old Bowen turned out to be a talkative old cock when I took over Jack's vacant job, and he used vigorous expressions. I suppose he had had it all bottled up inside him for so long that he was glad to uncork himself to me.

'You see, he had had almost no direct communication with Jack. He would never let him into his cabin, but talked to him with the door opened a crack. So when Jack rushed up to him while he was taking his morning constitutional on his sacred private deck, and began to pour out an incoherent yarn about how he had to go home at once to look after his wife, old Bowen hardly knew what to do. He naturally asked him what he wanted to go home for. Jack said, "Family trouble." But it wouldn't be possible for old Bowen to get a pass from the naval commander without something a little more explicit than that. It was when they were in the old man's cabin that Jack elaborated the family trouble into what old Bowen called, "The usual thing—his wife's left him. And he wants to run after her! The damfool!"

'Old Bowen thought Jack had gone off his chump and would have to be put away. Go home? He asked Jack, how he thought anybody could go home with the country at war. Wasn't he doing his bit? So on and so on. There's no patriot like an old one. And anyway he, Captain Bowen, couldn't give anybody permission to desert, yes, sir, desert, and run off home. It would be necessary to put in a request to the Resident Naval Officer. This was a naval captain fished out of retirement, who hated everybody in the Merchant Service. We fellows were a low lot, to his way of thinking. He was a crusted martinet who wanted us all put under naval discipline. He hated what he called our damned civilian cheek.

It never occurred to him that if he had had his way, he would have to give us all pensions and treble our personnel. I can remember when that priceless relic ordered half a ship's crew into the brig for sixty days for refusing to take orders from a naval man, and then expressed amazement because the ship did not sail on time. Oh, the Navy! In my time they were fearfully and wonderfully made!

'Old Bowen said, "I thought he'd gone batty, so I humored him. If he had gone mad I'd have to get him sent home anyhow. So I jollied him along." Old Bowen honestly thought anybody who would want to go home was out of his mind. We had a fine climate; nothing much to do, good grub without the rationing they were getting at home, shore leave, interesting places to visit. We were getting what only the rich had in peace time, and we were getting paid for it! He couldn't understand a man wanting to go home to England. He was old, and he had a good bank. All he had to do was to sit tight and watch his shipping shares go up and up and up. He dreaded most of all returning to his nice, mortgage-free house, and his nice dull wife, and his nice, dull retirement. He had had some! Nobody has ever put into song or story the frightful boredom of a sailor home from the sea for good!'

'But you gave it up,' Father Soames said suddenly. 'You're home from the sea for good, aren't you? You . . .'

'Ah, yes, but you miss the point,' Mr. Spenlove said. 'I should have been more explicit. I said "a sailor." I meant, of course, a deck officer, or even more explicitly, a shipmaster. Ancient mariners of our day! For years they have been doing nothing save accept the burden of command. We put it that way delicately, to avoid hurting their feelings. There is precious little they can do nowadays. Their owners send them orders by wireless, and their propulsion, to put it

77

delicately again, is not a matter they meddle with. Even the seamen's unions poke their obscene noses into his authority nowadays. Well, after years of that sort of thing, with nothing to do, they retire and enter into their reward, which is an infinity of vacuity for most of them. For old Bowen it was a miracle of luck to get on a ship again, with higher pay than ever, very little sea-voyaging, and most agreeable conditions.

'I had the same reluctance to go home, but for fundamentally different reasons. I was recovering from an unfortunate love affair at the time.' He nodded toward his wife. 'She can tell you all about it. It has nothing to do with Jack Bannister. He was having his unfortunate love affair right in front of all of us.'

Mr. Spenlove paused for a moment, as though to think of a phrase. He frowned and nodded again toward Perdita.

'She often tells me that my stories of the war have no patriotism. We lived in a moderately strong solution of patriotism. We were saturated with it. It colored our entire existence. We were not aware of it because we all had it. On ships, we simply went about our usual business.'

'You may wonder why I am so steamed up about all this dead past. You may even feel surprise that we would be talking of an old shipmate. But Jack's new wife was here this afternoon and that in itself is to me an extraordinary thing. My friendship with him, if you can call it that, dates from a later time, in the Afro-Iberian Line. It was the Maracaibo Line then. I saw a lot of Jack at different times, and the fact that he is a neighbor of ours now is difficult to fit to the image of the Jack I used to know. There was Roxane, his first wife, who ran out on him and vanished. Nobody on the ship ever heard of her again. And it really looked, when Jack boarded the British India steamer, that nobody would ever hear of him again either.

'Imagine demanding a home leave from Egypt for what he called "family trouble!" Old Bowen posed that one to me, when we were discussing the business calmly. He had asked Jack whether he couldn't be a shade more definite. Did he see him, Captain Bowen, going ashore and asking for a new chief engineer, and compassionate leave for a fellow who merely talked about "family trouble?" I've told you what sort of crustacean we had for a Resident Naval Officer.

'When they got inside old Bowen's cabin, Jack jabbered like a monkey, the captain said. "Yes, but what's the matter?" the old man shouted. "What is it? Wife run off with somebody else?"

'It was like a blow in the face to Jack to hear the truth spoken right out like that. "Know who she's gone with?" Jack absolutely shrank back from the captain. Collapsed on the settee and buried his face in his hands. "And then," the captain told me, "before I knew what he was doing he was half on his knees, begging me to get him a pass, so he could go home. At once! Half on his knees!"

'Nice kettle of fish for a skipper. In more than one way it was an embarrassing situation for him. Nobody in our trade cared to show up his shipmates as crazy and unpatriotic to the Navy. They had a poor enough opinion of us anyhow. But on looking back I am not sure about the motives of anybody. Old Bowen said, "All right. Get ready and come with me to the R.N.O. Let him hear your story. But we have to get the approval of the N.T.O. first."

'Now the N.T.O., the Naval Transport Officer, was as difficult in his way as the R.N.O. was in his. The N.T.O. was a retired commodore of one of the very biggest lines in the world, a line that regarded the Hamlet Line and all cargo carriers as scows and riff-raff, flotsam and jetsam of the sea. Old Bowen never would say anything about that chap, but I knew he wished they didn't have to take orders from the old fellow. The N.T.O. would at once conclude that Captain Bowen couldn't keep discipline on his ship, that the Hamlet Line was a pain in the neck.

'Still, he probably would say yes. Captain Bowen wanted him to say yes. Captain Bowen, I suspect, wanted to get rid of Jack without doing himself any harm. So they went off together an hour later and I suppose they succeeded in getting the compassionate leave of absence for Mr. John Bannister, Chief Engineer of S. S. *Sandringham*, to go to England, on account of family trouble.'

'What good could he do when he got home?' Father Soames said. He had had experience of married soldiers who went off their heads when they received letters from home from loving friends.

'I asked that question in the messroom when the boys began to chatter about how the refugees were sleeping with the soldiers' wives at home. What I said was, if a woman goes off with another man, what can her husband do about it? Our electrician said at once, "Shoot the bastard!" All right, I said, agreeing to that, consider him shot. And what then? Does the injured man, after shooting the other man, resume his connubial bliss? One of the juniors said he ought to shoot her, too. I agreed to that. Consider *her* shot. They were both dead. Does he then shoot himself?

'I wanted to find out what their ideas really added up to. I found they hadn't any ideas. They were merely reacting unconsciously to a pattern of behavior that had no bearing on our social class. No bearing on our century; the twentieth, I reminded them. The joke was, those young men made no bones about going with girls ashore. I don't mean with girls in the licensed quarter, but girls they might meet in stores or on the street. And I don't mean the single men either. I mean the young married men among them. They were the fiercest defenders of the sanctity of the British hearth and home against defilement by alien refugees!

'The business went much more smoothly than anybody expected. Why? Because the transport officer and the naval resident officer cherished the same traditional illusions as my juniors. They honestly believed they were helping Jack in some way by taking him from his job in the war and sending him back to his deserted home. They imagined they were complying with the ancient chivalric code. I suppose a Crusader, out in Palestine, when he got word that his wife was off the chain, would be given leave to gallop to the nearest port, jump on a ship and sail home. He would then put his sword through the local boy who had lured his wife from virtue, lock the lady in his dungeon, and hurry back to help capture the Holy City. He had avenged his honor, and though he might dally awhile with a Saracen wench at times, his wife was secure until such time as he could return and make her life a misery again.'

Perdita pulled Rover's ears slowly. She made a face at her husband and said to Father Soames, 'Wouldn't you like to read a history of the Crusaders if he wrote it?'

'I could write a history of our 1914–18 Crusade which would be a lot truer than some I have read,' Mr. Spenlove said with warmth. 'A history of its boredom and its silly stupidity. The histories I have read don't mention the strutting of little bounders, the sadism of middle-class clowns invested with a little brief authority, the corruption of decent men who were thrown without lifebelts into an ocean of evil waste!

'When old Bowen sent for me to his cabin, Jack was already being carried over to the British India liner, just in from Port Said. It was calling at Brindisi, and Jack was to go overland from there to Paris and London. We were awed by this in our messroom. I had not rushed to occupy Jack's quarters. I felt quite competent to run my chaps without interposing the whatever-it-is that doth hedge a king. I listened to the awed comments on Jack's traveling overland. I was a bit awed myself. He was rushing home as fast as possible, with the idea, I suppose, that he would be able to catch up with Roxane and her ravisher.

'They say travel broadens the mind, but Jack's mind was never broadened. He had the sort of mind which takes in nothing from its surroundings. In all the time I knew him in the Caribbean, when he was working with us and when he wasn't, he never mentioned his trip through Europe. I know because I asked him about it. I had not had that experience myself at the time and I envied him. Not a word to show he had even looked out of a window. He must have been in or close to an air-raid while passing through Paris, but he never mentioned it. When he was having an extraordinary adventure in Central America, the sort of thing one reads about in adventure books, he never seemed to notice anything which would make you feel he was thrilled by what he was doing. Indeed, he gave me the impression at times that he was an unquiet spirit hurrying through our world, in search of a better one.'

'Perhaps he has found it,' Perdita said. Mr. Spenlove smiled apologetically.

'Ah!' he said, 'it's *possible*. I'd have to see it to believe it. But he was like a man in a desperate hurry to reach his destination, never noticing the scenery, the climate, or the local inhabitants. Yes, he may have found what he wanted subconsciously, at Tollemache St. Marys. He may have been aware of that, when he met Candace Deming. In those days he was often like a knight who had mislaid his armor and who was not a very good judge of the damsels he suc-cored. He was defenseless against women like Roxane. Then there was Chiquita. But Candace was different. Even when she was a school kid, when I first met her, and didn't much care for her, she gave me the impression that she was more adult than her parents, to say nothing of Jack Bannister. Candace didn't exactly resemble a clinging vine.'

'Funny sort of knight,' Perdita said.

'Well, it was a knightly gesture to marry Roxane, wasn't it? I dare say medieval knights often rescued girls who were doing very well in the wicked count's castle. I can imagine those ladies hoping the war would last another year or two . . .

'That was the last of Jack, so far as we, on that ship, were concerned. I once asked old Bowen if he had heard anything from the office. He hadn't; but then he didn't want to hear anything about "that damned, conceited, cocksure . . ." He used to think up all kinds of adjectives to describe Jack. He was a pretty conceited old cock himself. Let us say, he never had any news of Jack. My source of information was Annie, a year later, when I was home getting a com-mission in the Reserve.

'I think that was in 1919. Harry Collins had sailed in a new ship and I was at home waiting for one. I was living in Princess Park, nearer the city; but I liked to go over and talk to Annie. We discussed what had happened to Roxane. It seemed natural to discuss her. She was the type that ex-cited one's imagination.

'It seemed to me an extraordinarily foolish thing for her to run off with another man, even if she did not love Jack. If she had been a bad girl she would have remained, as so many other wives did, getting the half-pay and keeping her standing as a married woman, and having an affair on the quiet. The young man she was supposed to have gone off with was a Belgian pay-master. He had been in an Antwerp office.

'Annie thought Roxane was in love with the man. It seemed to me a much too easy explanation. I have always had a suspicion that she used him to get away. The secret of my friend Annie's success in her married life was that she had a simple philosophy. She would tell Roxane that when Jack came home "Everything would be all right." Why not? When her Harry came home she was in heaven. She never even thought about the possibility of him not coming home. She had no conception of Roxane's experience in being nearly drowned.

'Roxane had no such simple ideas. To her, Jack coming home, after their short and stormy honeymoon, offered no solution to the problem of how was she to live a comprehensible life? When later I heard she was in London, I suspected she had wanted that all along. She had constructed a world in which she would be able to expand her personality. This is merely a hypothesis, of course. In this case we are groping into the working of an alien intelligence, a sharp, possibly limited intelligence, but not a bad one, as Annie insisted. "She's a wrong 'un, if you ask me," Annie would say. I wasn't so sure. I thought Annie misjudged Roxane. I thought it showed a certain honesty, to abandon the security of Sefton Park, to bring things to a head.

'Another thing struck me at the time. I have said Roxane was intelligent. She had probably learned about the social standing of men who go to sea. It's a delicate point, but a young man who was, in civil life, in an office, would appear to Roxane to have superior attractions over a seaman. This doesn't mean she would be mercenary or no longer had any regard for Jack. What she was seeking, almost unconsciously, was a world she could live in. The Sefton Park world was, as she said, impossible. She would rather be dead than stay in it.

'And of course she wanted to rejoin the kind of people she knew. All the domestic details Annie made so much of, Roxane would have enjoyed, perhaps revelled in, if she had had the environment she understood. Annie never understood, either, that to Roxane, personal chastity, what is known as virtue, was irrelevant. She had the larger virtue of honesty. She might have inquired, where was Jack's virtue? And if Annie had insisted that she was sure Jack was remaining faithful to Roxane, Roxane would have waved this away as irrelevant.

'It was a cruel thing to marry a girl like Roxane and go off to sea, leaving her in such loneliness. She had no resources at all. She wanted life and gaiety. In Sefton Park, a suburb of a provincial city, neither town nor country, she was suffocating. She began to take the trolley car into Liverpool, and she would sit all afternoon in a movie house. Other trolleys carried her out to the seaside places. She spent a lot of time on her clothes, and when she walked to the end of the road to wait for the car, the neighbors would peep through their curtains at the foreign girl, with her high-heeled shoes, her provocative hat, her expensive gloves and stockings, as she went quickly along the street.

'I suggested that perhaps she had the same feeling for this Belgian young man, who was rescuing her from Sefton Park, as she had had for Jack when he rescued her from drowning. Annie said it wasn't so simple. Roxane could not understand how she was expected to love a man who wasn't there any more. Sometimes she would talk wildly to Annie. She would say, "Jack, he is good man. Very good to Roxane. But he is not here! I cannot live in this place!" Annie would say, every woman who married a seaman had the same problem. Roxane would say it was *impossible* to support such a life.

'Annie told me she knew Roxane would never stand Sefton Park. Moreover, she didn't think Roxane was the kind of girl to make a man happy. She was not quite prepared for what happened, but she became convinced that Jack had made a terrible mistake in marrying Roxane. Roxane, when Annie made the suggestion, said she had no house, and no husband, so she wasn't really married. Why did not Jack give her a house and live with her? It was plain enough to Annie that Jack and Roxane had got married in a very peculiar state of mind. Roxane, at any rate, had had no idea at all of what was in store for her. Before she could realize it, she was carried away to a place she had never heard of, among people she could not understand, and Jack had vanished. Probably having a good time!'

'Think of what must have gone on in her mind! Her first husband had been drowned while she was with him on that ship. The explosion, and the sudden plunge into the sea; the return to consciousness among strangers; the realization that she was a widow in a foreign land. The new world of London, and the awakening to the fact that she had been saved by a young man who was a hero. And now that young man had vanished to a distant part of the world, of which she had only the faintest conception. As far as her sharp, concrete little mind could fathom it she was a widow again.'

Mr. Spenlove laid down his cigar and finished his brandy. He thought Father Soames was about to make a remark. The clergyman did seem to have such an idea, but he was not a thinking man, and outside of his special line, had no great facility in expression. He knew, as the rector of two parishes, with a house and a comfortable income, that he enjoyed a sheltered existence. But he was aware that things were changing. The young people were all going to the cities, and the farms were gradually getting into the hands of large limited companies, so that his parishioners were the employes of absentee directors in London. Then he had the novel experience of government inspectors supervising the subsidized beet farms. His neighbors said it was Socialism.

All these things had an effect on Father Soames, and he had a feeling that his class, the hunting people, the retired colonels, the gentry, were being left high and dry, and were on the way out. What he liked about the Spenloves was that they came from beyond the frontiers of his English world. Mr. Spenlove was not at all the usual type of retired professional man. In a deep sense he was not retired at all. He gave Father Soames the impression that he was at work, contemplating the comedy of his own existence. He always had a story to tell and his stories were about unfamiliar people in America. America was certainly a very strange place, if you listened to Mr. Spenlove.

He was, Father Soames thought, a man of the Homeric age, born out of his age. He was a modern Ulysses, who had passed safely among the clashing rocks. From his stories he had known the song the sirens sang, and he had reached the far Atlantic shore, and had settled in Arcady. But he had preserved a detached view even of Arcady.

Father Soames cleared his throat. 'There was a lot of that during the war,' he said gloomily.

'You mean desertion? Polygamy? Yes, there was,' Mr. Spenlove agreed. He smiled. 'There was also a lot of fidelity, but it never got into the newspapers.'

'I mean writing letters to service men to tell them,' Father Soames said. Mr. Spenlove agreed again.

'People exaggerated,' Father Soames nodded and went

on. 'In this village there were people who exaggerated. Motives of jealousy. I was told that there were suicides at the Front, in France, on account of letters they received. We had Canadians here, you know. Very bad situation. They weren't given leave to go to Canada and their wives could not come to England. We had a lot of trouble with the—the children born here.'

'Annie didn't mean to exaggerate,' Mr. Spenlove said. 'And it was not, in her case, jealousy. She had a maternal jealousy, or the embryo of one. She had also a highly developed sense of justice. Roxane was getting Jack's half-pay. That was the king-pin of the peculiar institution of marriage as practised in our Merchant Service. You probably don't realize what that means. Annie saw the letter come from the office every month. She had been going to the office with Roxane at first, to show her how to cash the note. She had a note of her own to cash every month, and she knew the men in the office. And a wife who cashed the half-pay note and went with another man had to be stopped. The streets of Aigburth, Seacombe, Bootle, Birkenhead and Wallasey were full of women who would stop her dead if they caught her. There is a solidarity among those sea-wives, and perhaps a little jealousy too, in the case of a pretty girl like Roxane. She never was and never could be one of them.

'Annie was one of the best, but she had to tell Jack the plain unvarnished facts about the half-pay note. I asked her, when I came home, if she regarded it as a painful duty. She said it was a pleasure! Annie was honest. If Roxane had been a silly chit carrying on a casual flirtation with some boy, Annie would have been wise and diplomatic, knowing it would pass off. But Roxane wasn't the one to have silly flirtations.

88

'She came flying home one day, began to pack a couple of suitcases, making a great rumpus upstairs, dropping things on the floor, flinging what she didn't want in a corner. She left all the house-dresses, the aprons and dust-caps Annie had bought for her. She even left Jack's photograph on the dressing table. There was a taxi waiting at the door, and she came down dragging her baggage. Annie stood watching this performance, thinking, well, she's going, all right. Roxane opened the front door, turned to Annie and pointing to herself, said, "I go!" And she went, leaving the door open, much to Annie's indignation, and drove off in the taxi.'

'Didn't he ever speak of her?' Perdita said.

'You can believe I asked him, when I met him out on the ships in New Orleans. I remember the first time, in Royal Street. He was staying in a boarding house down there until he got a ship. I said, "What became of Roxane, Jack? Ever see her again?" Just like that. I had a natural desire to know if his frantic trip home from Alexandria had any result. He knew I had been on deck when he had that family trouble, as he called it. I used that expression to him, to recall my part in the business.

'He began to walk a bit faster toward the Cosmopolitan Café, where we all went in those days in New Orleans. It was known as the Monkey Wrench, on our account. It looked as if I was going to be brushed off, but I suppose it dawned on him that we were both exiles in America now, and I occupied a special position. He halted in front of an antique shop and stared into the window. He was one of those who can spend years in America, or any other country, for that matter, and remain absolutely incurious about everything native to it. Even when it took a fortnight for a Liverpool paper to reach us, he never read a local paper, never made a comment about native customs. As for what he saw in that window, the old furniture from the plantations, the Audubon prints of strange birds, the fans and the bits of lace, they made no impression on him at all. Suddenly he said, without looking at me, "It's a long story." He started along again, very fast.

'And that was all I ever heard him say about it. For a long time after he came to us, he kept very much to himself. He had been in the Birkenhall Line after the war for a while, and when they sold one of their ships to the old Maracaibo Line, Jack came out in her as second engineer. That was how he turned up. He didn't take much to the lively young fellows who lived far up Canal Street, in a boarding house that was more like a boarding school when one of the ships was in port. He had a room in a house down near the French Market. It was only when he was promoted to chief and started on a regular run to Puerto Balboa that he had a word to say to anybody. Then he got sick, and was taken to the hospital down there, and met the girl I was telling you of. But I had no news of Roxane. I have often wished I knew what had become of her. In a way she captured my imagination. I have thought of her going over to America with her Belgian boy, and starting on a career of matrimony over there!

'You may say, she was a little bitch, and Jack was well rid of her. But I can see her side! I can even admire her final words, "I go!" She had that incisive quality. She had got herself into an impossible situation, cooped up in a provincial English town without a single congenial companion. She had no compensation for what she was going through. Jack had proved a slow learner at the art of living with a woman. The years stretched ahead of her—in Liverpool—and she was nerved to desperation. When the chance came for her to extricate herself, she did it with one quick, clean, incisive stroke. No sentimental returns for her. Annie said she used to walk around the house, savaging herself for being in such a terrible town, and muttering, "Finish! Finish!" When the chance came, that was what she did. She finished.'

CHAPTER

4

SO, to get back to the war days, we lost our young chief. This big new liner, *Lord of the Indus*, sailed away with our Mr. Bannister to deal with his family trouble. I had my reward for standing down so nobly and got his job. Captain Bowen would never have admitted it made any difference to him who was running his engine room. He was one of the old-fashioned skippers who always spoke of "my chief engineer," as though he had got the fellow cheap somewhere at a sale. But he took a fancy to me. I was so completely the exact opposite of Jack in temperament, he could not help enjoying the change. He would even invite me into his sacred cabin occasionally, and he would break down and ring for drinks. We didn't actually become bosom friends, but we got along very well. No fights at all!

'In fact I got along with all of them. I wasn't brilliant, like Jack. I wasn't a hero. I hadn't saved a beautiful girl and had my picture in the paper. I had had no medal for life-saving.

'However, I had been chief in the Mediterranean, long

before the war, and I knew all the moves. I had a totally different background from Jack's, and it was a background my shipmates could understand. Jack had spent his entire sea time in the Hamlet Line. He had spent most of his apprenticeship in the yard that made Hamlet Line engines. He had brilliance and precocity, but it had been in a narrow, professional groove.

'You would be surprised how many young fellows used to get stuck in a trade like that. It not only limited their professional experience, it made them remarkably silly in their ideas. They would get into a way of thinking that they were a chosen race, a sort of élite of the sea because they spent their lives in their precious Line. Jack was like that. The Hamlet Line ships were all built in the same yard, and naturally they resembled each other a good deal. They were all dry-cargo ships and they were amazingly well-kept up. Another thing, being a Liverpool line, all the Hamlet personnel came from around Liverpool; Mersey men, we called them. They are all right, but they are a special crowd. I had had everything, from West African niggers to Bengalis and Chinks. After riding some pretty wild horses I found it easy to amble along with the Sandringham crowd.

'I got along with them all, but there were no flies on me! There are times in a man's life when he reveals his fundamental qualities to his superiors without exerting himself, or, as we say, sweating to get his name up. So far as I can perceive, it corresponds to the period when an artist emerges from the status of improver to that of competent craftsman, one who puts a trade finish on his work.'

Mr. Spenlove saw Father Soames move as though to ask a question. He took the decanter and filled the clergyman's glass.

'What, precisely, did you do?' Father Soames said.

93

Mr. Spenlove smiled. He had often had that question leveled at him while he was at sea. What did he do, apart from entertaining passengers with his yarns?

'Nothing!' he said emphatically. 'It was my doctrine, and I hold to it still, that a chief engineer, or a chief officer, or a chief of state, if he has to work, is not a good chief. Call it a trick. The quickness of the brain deceives the sly! The cunning subordinate, the lad who is as good as his master, is the victim of a psychological illusion. He thinks he is doing it all, while the chief has a good time. He does not understand the holy mystery of management, of dispensing a benign, Olympian supervision.'

'Didn't Mr. Bannister have it, the Olympian . . . ?' Perdita smiled at Father Soames. She had listened to sermons on this text before. It was the bee in his bonnet, that management was an art. 'You said he was a good chief,' she pointed out.

'Yes, he was a good chief in a certain way, but he didn't have it,' Mr. Spenlove said. He got hold of some of it later on, when he came into the Afro-Iberian Line. He had had more experience then. He was good in the sense that he knew his job, and all the jobs under him. He ran the ship all right, and he got her along fast, too; but his men weren't happy. You aren't going to tell me that is not important in our civilization? He gave you the impression that he, the chief, was doing it all. The art of being a good chief is to give the junior the idea that he is doing it, while you, the chief, emulate the lilies of the field because you toil not, neither do you spin anything, except of course a yarn with the passengers. You are arrayed in fine linen and in a clean uniform. I've seen Jack Bannister plunge down into the engine room and get as dirty as any of his juniors and leave them all in a thundering rage for being interfered with. And

94

he hadn't done any good, either! If he had kept out of the road they would have done the job better and quicker. And he would have kept his white uniform clean. But it pleased him to come up and stand by the rail, fuming, his clothes all dirtied, his opinion of everybody on the staff going down.

'I didn't do that. You can't expect me to divulge all the secrets of the trade, I hope. Jack Bannister, whatever he might have been, burned his boats in those far-off war days when he boarded the *Lord of the Indus* and went home. My captain expressed to me the irritated opinion that a fellow like that would always have "family trouble." Well, to jump a few years, Candace Deming, the girl you had here,' he said to Perdita, 'had family trouble too, in an acute form, so perhaps that was why they, she and Jack, have made a go of it.

'Jack's defect, in spite of his real ability, was a lack of warmth. He never seemed to be able to sweeten a junior, make him feel important and valuable. He could inject neither praise nor friendliness into a remark. Something held him back from admitting anybody else was worth much. When a job was done to his satisfaction he would walk away without a word. If something came out well, or was done faster than he had anticipated, he would say it was "more by luck than judgment." He had a number of disparaging comments like that. They made us want to kill him. Lack of warmth in human relations is a bad thing.'

'Perhaps he's changed,' Perdita said, doubtfully.

'In one sense he had. He realized by degrees that it paid to get along with the crowd. Out where we were, it wasn't so easy to pick up replacements from the dock-side. The Company didn't care for a rapid turnover of the staffs. But he did inspire loyalty in some of the boys. I had a chap who told me, although it meant promotion, he was sorry to leave

Jack, who, he said, was "One of the finest men who ever stood on two feet."

'That was after he was down in Puerto Balboa, on the beach. I'll tell you about that in a minute. What I was thinking of was Mrs. Bannister, and how she came into Jack's life.'

'Did she have family trouble too?' said Father Soames.

'Very much so,' Mr. Spenlove said. 'International complications. She had an American father and an English mother.'

'A misalliance?' Father Soames said. Mr. Spenlove shook his head. 'Deming's family, on his mother's side, was old New York. You know what that means? Knickerbocker, I believe. Mrs. Deming, Candace's grandmother, was born on Washington Square. So far as birth went, one was as good as the other, if not better. Candace herself was born in Paris, so she is an international person, if such a person exists. And if there is such a thing as blue blood, she has it.

'The Germans were heading for Paris and the French had turned them back. You remember the sudden swerve of von Kluck's advance when the unexpected French Sixth Army arrived in taxi-cabs? Jack Bannister had arrived from Egypt and was passing through Paris from the P.L.M. to the Nord station,' Mr. Spenlove said. 'I have often wondered whether he had difficulty in getting a taxi. I would have walked. From all he could tell you about Paris, he might have crawled through a sewer or have been led, blindfolded, like a prisoner of war. You have to know these things to understand how Candace has come to be what she is.'

'But how do you know what she is, dear?' Perdita said. 'You haven't seen her.'

'I deduce,' Mr. Spenlove said, gravely. 'You have told me something, and that card tells me more. Oh, yes! I doubt if she has changed in essentials. In essentials!' he repeated.

Father Soames finished his glass and rose. 'You have a lot of gaps to fill,' he said. 'The man rushing home when his wife ran away. He didn't spend years doing that, did he? Or don't you know about that?'

'Oh, yes, I know,' Mr. Spenlove said comfortably. 'He was having adventures. I was, you may say, on the spot. He had that marvelous adventure in Central America. A love-affair with a girl in a small village on the shore, a few miles from where we used to dock and discharge cargo for the railway and the factories in the capital in the mountains. Don't misunderstand me. It was a grand passion, while it lasted, and it lasted a long time. You remember the twenties, the years after the war?'

'Darling, what do you mean by a grand passion?' Perdita said. 'My parents were always using the expression,' she added to Father Soames, who looked at her with benevolence. He liked Perdita's mother, Mrs. Price. 'In their fiction, I mean. Mother still does. What's so grand about it?'

Father Soames laughed as he turned to shake hands with Mr. Spenlove. 'I'll leave you to answer that,' he said, and laughed again as he walked to the door. The back of his neck was pressed against his Roman collar. Mr. Spenlove followed him out to the two-cylindered, two-seater Jowett runabout, which carried the clergyman around his parishes.

'Do you think I can't answer it?' he inquired. Father Soames settled in the car, shrugged his shoulders and switched on the lights. Then he laughed again.

'I hope she doesn't ask *me* that sort of thing!'

'It's very simple,' Mr. Spenlove said, leaning into the car. 'I almost said it was elementary theology. It takes place in the imagination, of course.'

Father Soames started his two-cylinder engine and sat looking straight ahead, as though he contemplated a sudden escape from Mr. Spenlove's badgering. He had once had a grand passion. He had an idea that Mr. Spenlove had heard something from Perdita, who had had it from Miss Soames. The lady had married another, and had died, far away, the wife of a colonial governor.

'Stendhal,' Mr. Spenlove went on slowly, 'used the metaphor of crystalization. The lover covers the loved one with a shining crystal deposit, precipitated out of his own imagination. I prefer to think grand passions derive from religion.'

Father Soames was a little startled, but he did not show it. This was his idea too. He had enshrined the memory of the lady, but he could not accept such a theory publicly. He said shortly, 'Heathen? Pagan?'

'Christian, I regret to say, if you'll excuse a quotation in reverse. It's medieval. Have you read the *Vita Nuova*? The lover identifies the loved one with celestial beings. He sees her in an unearthly radiance. *La Belle Dame Sans Merci!* The religion has been eroded away in our time, the age of mechanism, but the grand passion still survives here and there. Men do sometimes worship women. They are generally worthless women; or we would call them worthless. Or else they go over to Rome. But it is Dante's Rome they are seeking, not priests bawling over the wireless. Well, good night. I run on, I'm afraid. The garrulity of age! Come soon. Come soon.'

The old car gave a jerk and crackled away down the drive. The red tail light seemed to give a profane leer as it vanished around the curve.

Mr. Spenlove lingered in the soft summer night before going in. He saw a light in the bowed lattice window of his wife's room. It was "the knight's chamber" in the old days,

98

and Mr. Spenlove took pleasure in the name. Now it was the chamber of the knight's lady. It was very large, with low, black beams across one part, while the western and more modern end was sharply, loftily gabled. It had a small adjoining chamber, reached by two steep steps. It was a bathroom now. Originally the knight had hung up his armor and other hardware in it. There were large hooks for corselets and shields. That room had been used for escape in emergencies too, possibly, for there had been a small postern door, later bricked up, which led to the attic over the kitchen, and thence to the stables, by a low tunnel.

It was their favorite room. Mr. Spenlove, coming in early in the morning, would take his breakfast by the wide, bowed, mullioned window which looked out upon the lawn. Perdita, sitting up in the four-poster, would pour the coffee and munch her dry toast.

He walked under the apple trees bordering the turf, enjoying his thoughts. Now that he was in what the world called retirement, nothing interested him more than the behavior of his contemporaries. He supposed this curiosity of his was no nobler than the sharp scrutiny, by some elderly shellback, of his fellow boarders in an almshouse. Perdita had refused to believe in his pretended senescence. 'You'll never be an old man in that sense, darling,' she had said comfortably. 'There's something about you that makes it seem unsuitable. Anyhow, let's not discuss it.'

After being with old Romaine for a couple of days in London he thought there might be something in Perdita's ideas. 'Old Romaine,' he called him, yet in age they were only a year or two apart. Romaine seemed old, though! Mr. Spenlove had a puckish notion that Romaine needed one of those glandular transpositions which were supposed to restore a man's youth. He had read about the marvelous things done by the rejuvenation experts. He wondered about them sometimes, thinking of certain people he knew! But the trouble with old Romaine was not decay, but rather atrophy owing to lack of use. Partial atrophy, anyway! There must be some method of restoring a man's interest in the world, even when far gone in commercial cancer. Romaine was only emotionally rusty. He needed limbering up. The job was, to get him into a suitable, congenial environment. What was one to do with a man whose idea of seeing the sights in London was to fiddle with the electric map in the Central Tube Station? He would press the button to show him the way to Walham Green or Wormwood Scrubs, and see the route flash on with satisfaction. Mr. Spenlove had told him sarcastically that there was another way to get to Wormwood Scrubs, in a private, closed conveyance, if he was that keen about it.

He wondered now, about Jack Bannister. Jack wasn't old. He wasn't fifty yet. Say about forty-five. He had packed a lot of experiences into his life, however. What a man he had been for foreign entanglements! There was Roxane, and then that girl in Costaragua, and later there was a Swedish stewardess. By Jove, Mr. Splenlove told himself, he had completely forgotten that affair! One old shipmate had remarked that 'Jack Bannister was one of those beggars who always wanted to marry every girl they slept with.' Something in that, Mr. Spenlove, thought, smiling.

Now Jack was retired, it seemed. That would be a problem. He had no interior resources to sustain him when he had no job. No hobbies; not even Romaine's tropical fish, which, God knew, was a pretty feeble pastime at best.

The last time he had been in Jack Bannister's cabin on the *Camotan* he had noticed that the bookcase contained no books and the only reading matter had been a month-old newspaper or so, and some magazines with torn covers.

Mr. Spenlove began to think of that time the two of them were together at the Demings' place in the country. Somewhere in Connecticut. Mrs. Deming had invited them for a Christmas party because she had been so appreciative of their attention on the trips over from France. They had taken care of the kid when she finally left school and came to America. It had been a remarkable experience, and possibly Jack's reluctance to make any American contacts was due to the way Deming had acted.

It was not, Mr. Spenlove reflected, a novelty for him or Jack to see passengers letting their hair down at sea or in a foreign port. Deming was in his own house and he was presumably the host. But it took no time to realize that the atmosphere in that house was very tense. The guests avoided each other's eyes and pretended not to notice Deming's condition. They ignored the raised voice of the successful illustrator when Mrs. Deming tried to persuade him from opening another bottle. He had been drinking for several hours, from his appearance.

The girl, Candace, had been the problem. Everybody had brought her presents and there was a general movement to keep near the Christmas tree with her in their center. It was almost as if Deming had been aware of this. He came staggering into the room, plunging into the group and falling over the tree. He had kicked the gifts around and flung a bottle into the fireplace. There was artificial snow all over the floor, and Deming had some tinsel hanging over one eye and he looked around uncertainly. A vivid, nightmarish memory!

Mr. Spenlove remembered the terrible sound of the

girl's strangled screams as she rushed up the stairway to her room, while her father suddenly sprawled on the hearth rug.

Seen in perspective, after years of forgetting all about it, that incident would be a turning point. Jack was a born savior of women, and here was the chance of a lifetime, Mr. Spenlove thought, wryly. Always rescuing women! Jack couldn't break himself of the habit when he saw a distressed damsel like Candace at home in an ogre's castle. Mr. Spenlove himself had been so stunned he could think of nothing, save that he wanted to get his hat and coat and walk quickly to the station. He had been almost pitiably sympathetic toward that brightly smiling, plucky little Englishwoman, Mrs. Deming, when she said, "Will you excuse me? I must go to my child." She had gone quickly up the stairs and vanished. Deming had sunk into a dead stupor on the hearth rug.

It had not seemed safe to go on living in a world in which a man who made a lot of money, who was famous and successful, could do a thing like that. Why he did it was something Mr. Spenlove had to discover later. At the time the thing to do was to be taken in somebody's station wagon to the station. They had an hour to wait in a cold wind for the late train to town.

Jack had been silent all the way to New York, but in the taxi, when it stopped to let him get out at his pier, he had said, under his breath, 'Must get her out of that!' Mr. Spenlove sunk in thought, had said, 'Who?' Jack had said, his hand on the door handle, one foot on the pavement, 'The kid, of course!'

Mr. Spenlove had gone on to his own pier in a state of exasperation. He had not been thinking of Candace, but of her mother. He had been scandalized to see an Englishwoman of Mrs. Deming's quality facing such fearful odds. He was thinking of her spending Christmas night (*Heilige Nacht!*) with a hysterical child-woman upstairs and the unconscious genius on the hearth rug, in front of the burned-out fire. He saw her hurriedly and incompetently thrusting rags into the broken panes through which the genius had tried to hurl the Christmas tree, tripping over the electric cords and gashing his hand on broken bulbs. He saw her dousing the fire, turning out all lights save one, in case the genius awoke in the night and began resentfully to smash things in the dark.

Mr. Spenlove always thought of him as "the genius" because Candace, when she came over on his ship that time, had used the expression. They had been discussing a magazine she was reading in the music room, a magazine with a story illustrated by Deming. Mr. Spenlove had said that they were clever, but were they art? gently paraphrasing Kipling. She had turned on him a cold, strange gaze, and said haughtily, 'My father's a genius!'

So in Mr. Spenlove's thought he remained, though heaven only knew what that firm young creature's conception of genius might be. Deming had all the eccentricities of the breed, anyway.

That Christmas had been a bit too much for Mr. Spenlove. He resented Mrs. Deming having to experience such an ordeal. What was the matter with those people? he inquired of himself, angrily. Of course he could not do anything. It was not his affair. He had merely been invited because that little woman was extremely sensitive to casual kindness. He had been 'so very kind' to her on her voyage across the Atlantic, 'the herring pond' she called it, 'to see to my child.'

Finishing his cigar before going in, Mr. Spenlove heard

the telephone buzzing in the entrance hall. He saw a quick shadow on the ceiling of his wife's room. She was going down. He knew what she was expecting. He smiled and returned to his own thoughts.

Of course a third party, like Father Soames, would find it easy to assume that one should have realized at the time the significance of Jack's remark, that he would have 'to get the kid out of that.' The fact remained that Mr. Spenlove had been fully occupied with his own affairs as senior engineer of a fast liner, occupied with his own future. He had let the matter slip from his mind.

It was a sound rule with passengers, once they were safely down the gangway, to forget them. With few exceptions he had followed that rule. There was Mrs. Colwell, of course, and Mr. Merry, the banker. In offering Mr. Spenlove that first mortgage on the property at Norbury, Mr. Merry had had a great influence on Mr. Spenlove's life. He had been responsible for everything that followed. If he had not been sold the mortgage, he would not have gone to live there. He would never have met Perdita and Sonia, and hence might not have been in England at this moment of 1935. He wouldn't be meeting Jack Bannister again. That is, if he were meeting him. Mr. Spenlove was not at all sure about that, even now. He had a strange feeling about Bannister. He knew so much about him.

After the incredible finish of that Christmas party in some lonely spot in the hills of Connecticut, he had felt that no one in his senses would meddle with the Demings. He knew shipmates who had become entangled with passengers, and it always led to trouble. Family trouble, as Jack Bannister phrased it. He knew of skippers who had favored some tycoon's daughters, to the exclusion of some other tycoon's wife or mistress. The skippers had been fired. Mr. Spenlove had met one or two of them, commanding sticky molasses tankers or cheap little banana boats in the coast-wise trade, pretending they were damned glad to be shut of the Line and passengers. The lesson was, you never knew where you were with the rich, especially the very rich. It was a good rule to have nothing to do with them in your private life.

While he was in the Central American trade Jack had kept away from passengers. He had had a painful experience after he returned from the Puerto Balboa adventure. He had rescued that Swedish stewardess from a passenger's importunities, and the results for Jack had been sudden and swift. Fortunately for him he had escaped from the affair almost as quickly as he had got into it. Mr. Spenlove remembered now how surprised everybody had been to discover that Jack had actually married her. He had secured a separation (or she had, nobody knew just what had happened) before anyone heard of the marriage. Jack had gone into his shell with a vengeance after that while on the voyages. Lived all the time in his room. Even had his meals there.

But when the *Camotan* had been switched to the Atlantic run, Romaine, who was steward for a trip, to get the service organized, had sent the headwaiter to Jack's cabin with the news that there was a very nice English lady at his table. Mr. Spenlove recalled that headwaiter's calm, episcopally persuasive manner and husky, port-winey voice.

Romaine said that he and Jack had got along pretty well. No superlatives for Romaine. He had gone to Jack's cabin one evening about something and Mrs. Deming was there, showing Jack some photographs of her child. The cabin door was open, of course, but it was impossible to imagine anything remotely improper connected with Mrs. Deming. She was that sort of woman. She showed Romaine her photographs of the daughter too. Romaine was moved to say he thought her a very nice refined little person. He was never very articulate about passengers. He had given a faint grin when his old friend, Spenlove, had alluded to them as 'perishable freight.'

It was when he began to think distinctly about the present Mrs. Bannister that Mr. Spenlove found himself standing still in his stroll. Perdita had said she liked her. Threading his way among dusty mazes of his memories, which resembled those dim corridors where were stored the old wooden patterns used in the foundry of his apprenticeship, dusty racks and shelves loaded with strange, carefully wrought shapes, he began to clear away the figure of the girl who had told him, her nose in the air, that her father was a genius. He remembered the hysterical cry as she stumbled up the stairs, while her father was tearing the place to pieces, that Christmas night. Now, if she had been one of the timid spirits, a normal school-chit suffering from fright, she wouldn't have uttered that tragic cry.

He had another memory of her which he thought valuable. She had had a French weekly magazine with her on that trip and they had been speaking of the advertisements for *marraines* in it, frankly phrased requests for friends among the opposite sex. He had asked if she would insert anything like that, jocularly, of course, just to make a conversation. She had taken him seriously. She had said she wished it was the custom in America. She would insert an advertisement: 'New parents wanted. Present ones unsatisfactory, Apply Miss Candace Deming, Box XYZ, Montreux Post Office, Switzerland. References exchanged.'

From that they went on to a brief, intimate conversation. Why were they to be replaced? he inquired. She had not been what he would call communicative, in spite of the introduction her mother gave her, saying that Mr. Spenlove had been 'so very kind,' and so on. Watching her among the passengers, he noted that Candace had a chip on each shoulder. It wasn't shyness, but hauteur. Apparently she thought the others were not quite good enough for her highness! She had been, to tell the truth, aloof and chilly. Yet she had suddenly confided to him that she thought her parents very unsatisfactory. And he asked her, why?

The answer had been equally surprising. Simply because, she had said, they didn't get on. They didn't live together in a proper manner, for one thing. Not live together? he had said. Not in the past. Of course, now she was going over, they might 'give it a try.' When Mr. Spenlove inquired why they didn't live together, the girl had given him her strange cold glance, as though she suspected him of a lack of intelligence. Well, they didn't, that was all. And she had never had a home since she was two. So she thought, he said, that an advertisement might produce a better couple? To which she had shrugged and said the advertisement couldn't possibly produce 'anything rottener than what she'd had, so far.'

It hadn't been what she said, he reflected now in his garden at Layer-de-la-Pole, but the character which had suddenly come through in her face. She was nothing to fool with, he had thought, and decided that he was not sure he would care to be her parent. She had been at that moment, like an edged tool, young as she was.

Now, he asked himself, how would she work out in marriage? He knew enough about married life himself by this time, but it wasn't the kind of knowledge to give him a lead about that girl. Perdita was quite another cup of tea, he thought with excitement. She was marvelous! And perhaps he was marvelous too, come to that! It probably took two marvelous people to achieve what they had done. Perhaps three. Sonia . . .

He went into the house. Perdita was at the telephone. She made an agitated beckoning signal with her disengaged hand, and Mr. Spenlove drew up beside her. She regarded him with shining, abstracted, maternal eyes, and went on listening. Then she said, 'Yes, ducky, he's here now,' and offered him the receiver. 'Speaking from Paris,' she said quickly, 'crossing tomorrow morning.'

She stood close to him, smiling at the sudden, luminous benevolence in his satiric dark eyes, her arm in his.

'Oh, is that so?' he said, smiling at Perdita. 'You amaze me! What? Yes, of course, We'll be there. No trouble at all, mademoiselle. A pleasure—yes—yes . . . Good-bye.'

He replaced the receiver, smiling.

'It's an extravagance,' she said, as they went upstairs. 'A person-to-person call from Paris! I suppose to her it's natural. Sure you want to go in to meet her? You've just come back. She can take the train. Big girl now.'

'I wouldn't miss that boat-train for anything!' he said. 'When I was eighteen or nineteen I used to hang around Waterloo Station and watch the first-class passengers from the boat-trains from Southampton. I was living in lodgings in Kennington at the time. I'd see them, with their expensive luggage, getting into hansoms or private broughams, with luggage on top, driving off to smart addresses like Bruton Street or Dover Street or Park Lane, or the Carlton. I would pretend that I hated that kind of life. As a matter of fact, I wanted to live that way, terribly!'

'It doesn't sound like you. I thought you were superior to that kind of thing. Tad would roar if he heard you.' Tad was her young brother. Tad had been to Eton, and thought England needed an élite.

108

'If one is immune to the green-sickness of youth, one goes to pieces in middle life,' Mr. Spenlove said.

Perdita got into bed and watched him as he sat by the window. Above his head was the high-pitched part of the room which had been added in the seventeenth century. He looked medieval, or perhaps Elizabethan, as he sat in the high-backed chair.

'I suppose it's because you're so philosophic now,' she remarked. 'Mellow.' She looked for a cigarette. 'I sometimes think you have too slow a life. After your exciting existence on the ships. You stick around because you think it suits me. We ought to go to town more, and to Felixtowe.'

'I'm all right,' he said, looking at her in a way she knew well, and to which she responded by her own look. 'Many people have that idea. If a man goes to sea he is living an exciting, thrilling, glamorous existence. It's really a rather sedentary existence, especially when one is in charge. I have been lucky. Men who retire from active life, I mean from responsibility, for that's all it is, go to pieces. They have nothing to occupy them. Old Romaine said, when I told him I lived in the country, what business was I in now? He thought I ought to have something to do. He had assumed I had a business; selling something, he meant, of course. He said, "I guess you have a business." '

'Let's have him down,' Perdita said, comfortably.

'Yes, well, I was thinking that, as Romaine knew Mrs. Deming, it might be interesting. He knew the daughter too, when she was a kid. Did she say where Mrs. Deming was?'

'She didn't say in so many words, but I gathered she's with them, at Moat Farm.'

'She used to cross on the *Camotan*,' Mr. Spenlove explained. 'She and Jack met there, on the *Camotan*. You'll like

Mrs. Deming. Did I tell you about that Christmas Jack and I were at their place in Connecticut?'

'Were they in Connecticut?'

Mr. Spenlove told her briefly what had happened on that occasion.

'But why did he act as if he hated them?' Perdita said. 'Was it—you know? Was it? Of course Elliot didn't drink. But Elliot didn't hate Sonia and me . . .'

'Well, Deming had the idea that his wife and daughter had simply ruined his emotional life. He had a model in Greenwich Village who encouraged him to believe he was being frustrated. He wanted to rid himself of his family completely. He wasn't doing any too well at the time professionally, and I fancy he depended to a great extent on Mrs. Deming's family. They used to send her some of her money they had in a trust. And that made Deming hate the English.'

'The kid, this Mrs. Bannister, she isn't English,' Perdita said quickly. 'I must say I thought she was, but she says she's American!'

'Legally. She was born in Paris, so I suppose she had a choice of nationalities. Her mother is very English, but she's legally American too, as she married an American. The kid was like her father in some ways and he knew he would never be able to dominate her as he did her mother. He knew, too, that when she grew up and had her own money, he wouldn't get a cent of it. His wife used to give him money, and he would go off with this model he had to the Cape, or to Long Island.'

'Did you ever meet her? You surely never got that out of his family,' Perdita said.

'Yes, I met her, after Deming had gone the way of all flesh. She was a passenger, and she was on her way to

Havana to the races. She told me she had been a professional model. We were discussing an artist on board, a famous painter, not an illustrator. Then I mentioned Deming, and she began to talk about him. She was rather proud of having known him. She had the same opinion of him that his daughter had, that he was a genius. She said his family never understood him.'

'Of course she would say that. They always do,' Perdita said cheerfully. 'Never mind about her. I'm afraid I take his wife's side, and his daughter's. What were they doing in America? Oh, you said he was an illustrator, didn't you?'

'Did I? Yes, he was, a genius at it, they assured me, whatever that may mean.'

'You didn't like him, I can see that. He got tight at Christmas. Well, lots of people do.'

'It wasn't that in itself. It was the breakdown of a personality in front of strangers. We had a dreadful feeling that the man hated himself more than anything else, and was taking it out on us. If he had been a cipher, a nonentity, we wouldn't have minded so much. But there were his own neighbors present, his wife and child. He was a famous person in a way. He was the creator of the Deming Damsels and the Deming Demons. They had quite a vogue in the magazines at one time.'

'I seem to remember,' Perdita said. 'How did he come to meet his wife?'

'In Paris, just before the war. Well, some time previous to the war. He was an art student. He was broke most of the time, I understand. He and his brother went around together. They were what is called nowadays café society. They had a somewhat uncertain allowance from a stepfather, a rich old chap who had married their mother, and was impressed by her pedigree. We call them remittance men, and don't think much of them. They were great card-players during the tourist season, according to what Mrs. Deming told me when she was in a confidential mood.'

'Did they get married in Paris?'

'Later. Deming had one of those French motorcycles and he nearly ran Mrs. Deming down. She was a girl just out of the schoolroom, going with her parents to Switzerland. She wasn't very clear in the details about this, you know, but I got the notion her people, the Enderby-Bretons, had no use for Americans, and they drove away to Rouen in their big touring car, with chauffeur and maid, with the intention of shaking off the two Demings, who were making advances on the strength of the chance meeting. But Deming rode after them on his motorcycle and met her again in Rouen. They left for Davos Platz and he turned up there.'

'He was in love with her.'

'The Enderby-Bretons thought he was a fortune hunter.'

Perdita smiled.

'I've never been able to understand how you can hunt a fortune,' she said. 'My parents used to have them in their stories. Mother often does it even nowadays.'

'Well, there must have been some of the species around. The Enderby-Bretons believed in their existence, and they forbade their daughter to have anything to do with Deming. But they couldn't control all her movements in a place like Davos. She went in for bob-sledding, just as Sonia does now and her daughter did too, I suppose, when she was at Montreux. And Deming was a great star bob-sledder. He must have been in funds, for the next thing the family knew he had gone back to Paris and taken their daughter with him, and they had a wire from her announcing her marriage and begging forgiveness.'

'Did she tell you this?'

'Not with any continuity, but in snatches as we talked on the ship. She was very sporting about it. She had had, she told me, a wonderful time. Her father cut her off with the traditional shilling; or he would have if he had been able. She had inherited a trust from an aunt or a great-aunt. But he said she was never to darken his door again, and so on.

'Then came the war. They were keeping house in Paris on his allowance and an occasional run of luck with cards, and she was going to have a baby. She had it in the American Hospital, during an air-raid. After the war, of course, they went back to America. Mrs. Deming told me it was her dream, all the time she was keeping house and learning everything the hard way, in Paris, to go to America.'

'Poor kid,' Perdita said. 'I bet she was disillusioned when she got there.'

'No, she wasn't. She had a wonderful time. She always has a wonderful time. She has a highly resilient and plucky character. Not even that awful Christmas night really got her down. Optimism doesn't describe it. She bounces like a rubber ball under misfortune. She never ceased to believe her husband would eventually settle down and be a faithful citizen.' He looked at his watch. I'm keeping you up. We have to make an early start tomorrow to meet that boat-train. I'll just go down . . .'

'Now don't spend half the night in there,' Perdita said. She meant the private study to which he often retired for meditation.

'No, but I'm in the mood,' he said, looking down at her. 'I feel as if you had inspired me. I don't know how you do it, but you do.'

'It's a secret,' she said, smiling, watching him as he went out.

He descended to the billiard room and poured himself a

whiskey and soda and took it with him to his study, where he filled an old briar. For a while he sat with an open book before him, one of his favorite volumes. The green-shaded lamp, the dusky beauty of the book-lined shelves, the faint, distant hum of the little dynamo, filled him with peace. He read the page again before he closed the book.

"Let me not injure the felicity of others, if I say I am as happy as any . . . In brief I am content, and what should providence add more? Surely this is it we call Happiness, and this I do enjoy; with this I am happy in a dream, and as content to enjoy a happiness in a fancy, as others in a more apparent truth and reality."

It seemed to him, as he turned the page and continued to read what he had read so often before, that he could sub-scribe to those words.

CHAPTER

5

M R. ROMAINE was not exactly tired of his stay in England, but he was beginning to feel a trifle home-sick for the United States. He had taken an option on a road-house in New Jersey and was looking forward to reinvesting in the new business.

He had paid a visit to a married sister in Glasgow, and what he had learned there of the stagnation in trade made a deep impression on him. Unemployment (her husband was a shipyard foreman) had led Mr. Romaine to offer a loan, to tide them over. But from what he saw it would be a long time before things were any better around there. He was un-easy concerning what was happening to Britain. But he had not said anything about it to Spenlove.

Now he had received a telephone call from the Spen-love place. He was to go down to Layer-de-la-Pole.

Spenlove was to Mr. Romaine a man of mystery, though they had been shipmates and friends for so many years. He was almost a legendary character in the Line, many of whose officers used the Romaine Bar and Grill on Second Avenue.

They thought of him with awe, as one who had achieved what used to be called the sailor's dream. He had retired, married a rich woman and gone to live in the country. Keeping chickens, as some of them phrased it.

Mrs. Spenlove had a very nice voice over the telephone. He had been rather afraid that Spenlove had gone what he called passenger on him. He imagined Spenlove as he used to be on the crack liners, in a bum-freezer evening uniform, in the saloon. He had no desire to dress for dinner nowadays. Mrs. Spenlove, however, had made it clear that it was to be all informal. She said the three-ten was a convenient train and they would meet him at Mark's Tey.

He looked out of the window of the third-class compartment and contemplated the quiet beauty of the trim Essex scenery. Very different from what he had gone through in the Glasgow suburb, near the silent shipyards and foundries.

His large pale face resembled those of prelates who have become great executives, but who are aware of the secular value of abstinence as well as continence. There was faint sign of a double chin coming, but there was nothing about him to suggest he was a member of the domestic servant class, which in fact he had been, a sort of seagoing butler, for many years.

Now he might have been a retired butler, or in fact an American business man on a holiday in England. Like Perdita Spenlove, the lady who was to meet him at Mark's Tey station, he had been born in this tightly cultivated country, but he had not seen much of it before he left it, to go to sea.

Mr. Romaine had never analyzed his feeling toward the chief engineer with the sharp, pointed beard and black, tufted eyebrows, who seemed to spend his time either meditating in his cabin or conversing with passengers. The significant feature of their relations was that Mr. Romaine's own

116

department never had any trouble with Mr. Spenlove's department. The purser had defined it one day for Mr. Romaine: 'The chief's a good politician.' The chief steward knew what he meant at once. The purser's private conviction was that Mr. Spenlove would in all probability be promoted to a superintending position on the shore-staff. Good politicians usually were sent up higher. Mr. Romaine would have regretted this, but it did not happen. What did happen was that Mr. Spenlove, reaching retirement age, had gone ashore and become a sort of legend. That was after Mr. Romaine had swallowed the anchor himself and started his restaurant on Second Avenue.

The train stopped. Mr. Romaine saw the door of the next compartment fly open. A lady stepped out. He saw Mr. Spenlove looking along the train. He took his bag from the rack and was about to open the door when he saw Mr. Spenlove approach the lady and take her in his arms for a moment. The lady then took a girl of about sixteen in her arms. Mr. Romaine did not expect to be embraced, but he waited a fraction of a moment before he alighted. Mr. Spenlove's sharp eye saw him. That gentleman at once came forward. He took Mr. Romaine's bag and led him to the lady and the girl of sixteen.

'Mr. Romaine,' he said, 'Mrs. Price.' He added, 'One of my old shipmates. And this is Sonia, my stepdaughter.'

If Mrs. Price was Mr. Spenlove's idea of a duchess, she was Mr. Romaine's idea of a grand duchess. He bowed and said it was a pleasure. To Sonia he said he was pleased to meet her. Sonia smiled as though to her it was a pleasure also. She led the way through the wicket, where Mr. Romaine and Mrs. Price were relieved of their tickets, and then Mr. Romaine saw the Virago. The other passengers got into various Austins, Fords and Morris-Cowleys. One, a gentleman with a handlebar mustache and wearing rough tweeds, got into a long low vehicle which resembled a cross between a canoe and a hip-bath, so that he was almost lying down to drive, and roared away without a muffler. Sonia said something about 'that Lagonda!' and got into the driver's seat of the Virago.

'If I'd known you were both coming by this train,' Mr. Spenlove said, 'I'd have told you to look out for each other.'

Mrs. Price smiled at Mr. Romaine. 'We could have worn red roses,' she said comfortably, 'so we'd have known who we were.'

'Or a feather. Well, you know who you are now. Or do you? Mrs. Price is Mrs. Spenlove's mother.' Mr. Spenlove turned to his new guest. Mrs. Price said, looking straight ahead as Sonia turned the car into the road to Layer-de-la-Pole, 'He doesn't like the expression "mother-in-law." I don't either. We never use it. How do you like the country, Mr. Romaine? Is this your first visit to England?'

Mr. Spenlove laughed.

'Mr. Spenlove always finds me amusing,' Mrs. Price said. 'I don't know why. I always ask Americans if they've been here before. It breaks the ice.'

'Well, I was born here,' Mr. Romaine said, but without emphasis, as though he had no desire to enter into an argument about it. It was a fact of no particular importance to him. Mrs. Price, intent on breaking more ice, took no notice of his statement. She merely inquired whether there was any truth in the old adage that a sailor had a wife in every port.

Mr. Spenlove was sitting beside Sonia, and he turned. 'You'll embarrass him,' he said. To Mr. Romaine he continued, 'Mrs. Price is very disappointed with us. When she first met me, after hearing I had been to sea, she expected me to appear with a rolling walk, a parrot on my shoulder and a quid in my cheek. I ought to have warned you to get a parrot, Romaine. Mrs. Price is a writer. She writes stories. She expects you to give her some local color. Think you can? You aren't tattooed anywhere, by any chance? You needn't expect her to believe you ever went to sea if you haven't any nautical evidence to offer.'

Mr. Romaine recognized the old Fred Spenlove getting wound up. That was the way he used to razz the passengers. Now he was doing it to his mother-in-law!

'I'm not a sailor that way,' Mr. Romaine told her courteously. 'I'm a businessman.'

'And instead of being ashamed of such a confession, he is proud of it,' Mr. Spenlove said, without turning around. 'A butterfly on the financial wheel of the world. Or was. He's retired now, you know. Statesman, businessmen and bandits all go into retirement, if they aren't bumped off first.'

'You mustn't take him seriously,' Mr. Romaine said to Mrs. Price. She said, 'I don't! Nobody does except my grand-daughter there. Sonia thinks he knows everything.'

'I mean, about retirement. I'm not retired. I sold a little business I had, and—well . . .'

'And now you've come back to the Old Country,' Mrs. Price exclaimed. 'I think that's always such a fine thing about the English, don't you? They always come back.'

'After the scandal has died down,' Mr. Spenlove said.

'Well, you did yourself, Fred.'

'Ah, that was different,' he reminded her. 'I haven't promised to stay here, you know. And Romaine won't. You won't get him back here. Eh, Romaine?'

Mr. Romaine did not reply at once. He had caught himself just in time talking about his business. He did not suppose Mrs. Price would have any use for the fact that he had an option on the Cloverleaf Casino in New Jersey. But the charm of conversing with this magnificently cordial and friendly lady, in a superb car driven by a very pretty girl, had carried him away. He had forgotten his inflexible rule, never to mention his business affairs to strangers. Moreover, he had a suspicion that to speak of business in his present circumstances was not refined. Not quite refined, anyway.

There was no doubt in Mr. Romaine's mind now that the story of Spenlove marrying a rich woman was true. He didn't see Spenlove, for instance, paying for a car like this. But then the funny thing about Spenlove was you didn't associate him with money at all. He never mentioned it. He had a remote air about that sort of thing, as though he lived in a philosophical vacuum, a region exhausted of the air on which ordinary mortals depended for economic respiration.

Spenlove's habit of yarning with passengers had seemed to Mr. Romaine to have in it something of impudence. It was nerve for a man, who had been a mechanic, who had been at sea for so long, to put himself on an equality with first-class passengers. Certainly he could talk the hind leg off a donkey, and he seemed wonderfully well-posted as to education; but Mr. Romaine had had a feeling in his bosom that as Mr. Spenlove really was one of the proletariat, he couldn't be genuine when he put himself on a level with the passengers. He must be merely showing off.

It seemed that he was genuine—very much so! There he was, on the front seat of this magnificent vehicle, beside his stepdaughter, a pretty girl who thought he knew everything, according to her grandmother. He had none of the air of a man who had promoted himself by marrying above him. He was absolutely at home among these people. Mr. Romaine was aware of a sort of awe when he reflected that Spenlove was the head of this refined and fashionable establishment in the country. He himself and Mrs. Price were guests. It was like the things he had read in novels of English life, novels borrowed from the ship's library. He pondered this as the car flew along, silently, save for the crackle of the tires. They spelt tire with a *y*, he remembered. He listened to Mrs. Price's shrill but exciting voice telling Mr. Spenlove about an American author she had met at the Club, a story which was making Mr. Spenlove shake with amusement; but whether at the American author or at Mrs. Price's method of telling the story he could not determine. But their laughter was infectious, and he smiled.

Suddenly the car swung into a winding drive and drew up in front of an ancient, gabled dwelling whose latticed windows and ivy-covered walls were to Mr. Romaine something out of real life altogether, something he remembered to have read about in Dickens. He enjoyed a good book now and then.

Mr. Romaine got out stiffly, and after offering his hand to Mrs. Price, watched Mr. Spenlove extracting the bags from the rumble. He turned to the porch and found himself facing Perdita Spenlove.

Standing in the Tudor archway of the porch, she seemed to him a marvelous person. She held out her hand and said in a lovely voice, 'How do you do, Mr. Romaine? I'm so glad you could come. Mother dear, how are you?'

In the small powder room, with ivy screening its mullioned window, Mr. Romaine was thoughtful. He hardly knew what to think of Mr. Spenlove now. His own wife, so long parted from him, was only a vague memory. He had spent so little time with her, after all, being at sea so much, that he had never acquired the close intimacy that marriage on shore brings. She had been a girl of his, and Mr. Spenlove's, own class. In spite of himself he had imagined Mrs. Spenlove to be a woman of mature presence, probably stout and, as she was supposed to have been an actress, with the remains of a striking beauty. He recalled a famous actress who had been a passenger with her new young husband on a cruise. She had had a face like a ruin. In some fashion he had thought that Spenlove had formed an attachment of this nature, with a woman who had money, who wanted a man in the house.

Mr. Romaine had no high notions of himself with regard to women. Constant preoccupation with the business, incessant association with men and women, cooks, waitresses and so forth, had kept him from feeling solitary. He had, moreover, a talent for continence. Spenlove had told him he was lacking in ambition, or he would marry and have a family to carry on the business. That was as near as Mr. Spenlove had got to mentioning his own state while they were in London together. Mr. Romaine had said that marriage was 'a gamble.' Mr. Spenlove had agreed. It was a gamble, like buying aeronautical stock, and look what had happened.

When he came out Mr. Spenlove led him up a wide staircase with shallow steps. He wondered why Spenlove lived in such a place instead of a modern house. Mr. Spenlove made no attempt to tell him. He merely led him into a bedroom with a huge fourposter.

'You'll find us in the billiard room,' he said, and made a gesture of drinking.

Mr. Romaine felt he was in a dream world. He looked around. Accustomed to the spaciousness of America, everything seemed on a small scale, as the cars on the roads seemed built for pigmies and the railway coaches resembled portable but comfortable padded cells. Looking out of the window, he saw a sundial amid roses. A tennis court was marked out on the lawn, and beyond, in a field, a donkey grazed. In the distance a faint breeze made ripples across a field of golden-bronze wheat.

He dried his hands and went quietly down the thickly carpeted stairs. He entered a long low chamber. Mr. Spenlove was standing at a sort of bar at the end, a glass in his hand.

Mr. Romaine thought this was all right. It was a man's room, and very well fitted up. He settled into a leather chair with a drink and looked around at the Hogarth pictures, at the big fender and the leather-covered door. He gave a slight nod.

'How d' you like it?' Mr. Spenlove said, meaning just that. It was obvious he wanted to know how it was striking Mr. Romaine. That gentleman hesitated a moment. He took a sip of Scotch and soda. He frowned, in the effort to co-ordinate his thoughts.

'Pretty soft,' he said, and took another sip. 'You thinking of settling down here? Rest of your life?'

'Looks like it,' Mr. Spenlove said, glancing into his own drink. 'You think I'm getting soft after a life at sea? I'm not. Get married, Romaine, and you'll see for yourself.'

'You took your time about it,' Mr. Romaine pointed out mildly. 'Did pretty well for yourself, though.' He looked around again, as if to resolve any lingering doubts as to what the whole place must have cost. That billard table! And that car!

'Get your mind off money,' Mr. Spenlove said gravely. 'I wasn't thinking about that. You have a different view of it, if you . . . As the businessmen say, you get a fresh angle, if you have another person alongside.'

'I ain't having any trouble taking care of myself,' Mr. Romaine said, and took a larger sip. 'I'm a widower, if you've forgotten, Spenlove.'

'I do forget it sometimes,' Mr. Spenlove admitted. 'That's a long time ago, Romaine. I had a loss long ago. Did you ever hear me tell of a girl I knew in Salonika?'

'I never heard you tell of any girls you had,' Mr. Romaine said sincerely. 'It was always the other fellow.'

'Well, naturally. I thought I might have mentioned it. I didn't *have* her, as you put it. I knew her.'

Mr. Romaine was not the man to go into a matter like that. He let it pass. 'Well,' he said, 'you're doing all right. I didn't figure you were as snug as this. Not sure I wouldn't get spliced myself if I . . . This new business I been thinking of buying into needs a woman to run it. You got to have a woman in a hotel business. Same as a stewardesses on a ship. I been thinking about that angle.'

Mr. Spenlove saw his wife coming down the steps into the room. He smiled. 'You always were a sensible, level-headed chump, Romaine.' He said to Perdita, 'Mr. Romaine is thinking of getting married again. He's been a widower for years. I think we ought to be able to fix him up. He demands wealth, high rank, beauty and the abilities of the manager of the Ritz-Carlton. He's going into the hotel business.'

Perdita looked at her guest with amusement and sympathy. Mr. Romaine looked at her gravely, and nodding toward Mr. Spenlove said quietly, 'You know what he is.'

'Don't I?' she said, smiling. She accepted a glass of sherry from her husband. 'Of course we have a waiting list. The only thing is, women like that always want references.'

Mr. Spenlove laughed as he refilled Mr. Romaine's glass. 'Yes,' he said, 'and what's more, she'd need some very special inducements to go to New Jersey. It's tantamount to being sent to Siberia, Romaine.'

Mr. Romaine started on his new drink. He was aware

of the slightly artificial nature of this conversation. He suggested that it might be better to cross bridges when they came to them. He added in a low tone that, for him, mind you, marriage was a serious business. Nothing to make a joke about.

'You'll see it differently, I hope,' Spenlove said, 'when you find something you like. To change the subject . . .' He looked at Perdita. 'We've heard from a chap you knew in the old days. Jack Bannister. Remember him?'

'What's he doing? I heard he came home and got married again.'

'That's right. He did. And he's living a few miles away. I've been telling her about Jack's early adventures. You know, we were together before we came into the Company, in the war.'

'Well, well!' Mr. Romaine wagged his head slowly. 'Two of you, eh? You seen him? I didn't know him very well. We were on the Atlantic run together for a while. Never had much to say, but I wouldn't call that a fault. We heard some queer yarns, though.'

'We haven't seen him. His wife called. She says she happened to see our name on some things at Mark's Tey Station. She came over while I was with you in London. The point is, you and I knew her mother when she was crossing. She crossed with you and Bannister. Which was how he got to know the kid daughter. A schoolgirl.'

Mr. Romaine nodded several times. 'I remember her,' he said. 'I remember her. Nice woman, that. Yes. He married the daughter? Well, she'd grown up by then, eh? I remember Bannister had her at his table. She was all by herself. What was the name again?'

Mr. Spenlove told him. He nodded vaguely. His memory was more for faces than names.

'Mrs. Deming was a nice woman, a very nice woman. There was nothing la-di-da about her, but you could see she was a lady. She told me she was going to live in the States. Showed me a lot of snapshots of her little girl. She was just a kid the first time she went over with me, I remember. Fifteen or sixteen, maybe.'

'My wife seems to think Mrs. Deming is living with her daughter. Place called Tollemache St. Marys, just over in Suffolk. It must be a change for Jack Bannister. You know, he was at a loose end for a long time when we were in the Maracaibo Line. He'd had a lot of family trouble in England. Wife ran away. His first wife, I mean.'

Mr. Romaine's large pale face took on the expression of calm neutrality he had found so useful while at sea. He never took sides in private matters, or expressed any views about behavior outside of his own department. He regarded human life ashore as suitably segmented into departments, as on a ship. It made enormously for easy operation, he had found.

He permitted himself a glance at Mr. Spenlove when he heard that gentleman say that Jack Bannister, in Central America, had been 'at a loose end.'

Mr. Spenlove smiled. He knew Romaine knew what he was talking about. Everybody out there had known. But what they had known was only the externals of the affair, the bare facts. Only he himself knew what was important about Jack Bannister's life with that girl. He had been thinking a lot about it these days, since Mrs. Bannister had made her call.

'First wife?' Mr. Romaine said, hoarsely. 'First? Which one was that?'

'You never knew her,' Mr. Spenlove said. 'That was when he was in the Hamlet Line, during the war. Never mind

that. This wife he has now is another. Young and . . .'
He made a sign of rubbing thumb and finger together. Mr.
Romaine nodded. In his own peculiar way, Mr. Romaine
was extremely interested in this new development. It was
one of the stock jokes of the profession, like finding a tow
and getting rich on salvage, this marrying a rich wife. Yet
here were two of them actually doing it! He nodded. As he
glanced at Perdita he had a sensation of having committed a
social error. He decided that Perdita was different. So, for
that matter, was Spenlove. Men like Spenlove didn't
marry money. That had been just an accident.

'Any family?' he inquired. Mr. Spenlove held up one
finger.

'So I hear. When you come to think of it, it's a marvelous
thing for Jack Bannister. I can hardly see him as a pater-
familias in an English country house, I admit. I wish I'd
been here when she came,' he added to Perdita. 'And I'm
still wondering why he didn't come with her.'

'Is it as important as all that?' Perdita inquired. She
set down her glass and prepared to go to the kitchen. She
said to Mr. Romaine, 'My husband thinks husbands and
wives ought to go everywhere together. I had to insist on
his going in to see you in London.'

'That doesn't explain it,' Mr. Spenlove said, rubbing his
beard roughly. 'Reconstruct the story as you've given it to
me. At Mark's Tey Station she sees luggage with our name
on it. One of those labels, probably, I had printed. All
right. You wouldn't expect her to recognize the name,
would you?' he said to Perdita.

'That's exactly what she did do,' Perdita said. 'I told
you, dear. She remembered your name and told her husband.
She said he was in London; she mentioned it when he came
home. What *he* said was, it couldn't be the Spenlove he

knew. She said she would go and see. So she did, and when I told her you'd been in that line she hoped you remembered her, on the *Sansovino*. I'm perfectly certain she's on her own, as far as coming here is concerned. I mean, she isn't the sort of girl to need anyone to *tell* her what to do.'

'No,' he agreed musingly. 'She's the kid I remember,' he went on. 'Character, eh? Now where do we go from there? She marries Jack, and they settle down in the country. It sounds reasonable enough, unless you know Jack.'

Mr. Romaine watched Perdita pass along to the red door beyond. He didn't see himself talking about that menage in Puerto Balboa to a woman like her, a lady if he ever saw one. He was somewhat surprised at Spenlove bringing it up. He merely shook his head, not venturing on a comment. He saw his host fix him with a frowning scrutiny which changed at once to an ironical smile. Then Mr. Spenlove shook his head slowly.

'We'll see,' he said. 'But don't forget this house has a telephone and so has his Moat Farm at Tollemache St. Marys. Yet we haven't heard from Jack yet. His wife said he was shy with strangers. Would you say you, or I, are a stranger to Jack? A few miles as the crow flies. Jack isn't a crow, but his wife drives a car; and anyway, if he wanted he could hire a taxi for a couple of pound notes. If he wanted.'

Mr. Romaine sat in deep thought. The conversation was bringing back those days in the Caribbean, when Jack Bannister left his ship on sick leave in Puerto Balboa. His second took the ship back to New York and a new chief took her out next trip. Jack, in the hospital on the hill, outside the town. Jack, as a convalescent walking around the bandstand in the little Plaza de Armas, or along the sea wall. And then Jack the beachcomber. That girl wheeling the harbormaster's baby in a perambulator. . . .

The unblended Scotch Mr. Spenlove had brought out to celebrate his old shipmate's visit was taking hold of both of them. Perdita, who had given up spirits since she returned to England, had told him that the stuff he had in the cellar was much too potent for untried victims. Jack Bannister was beginning to assume in Mr. Romaine's imagination a heroic dimension, as though he were some legendary hero. Perhaps he was a hero. He had chucked his job in the Company for a cantina girl, or a girl who had grown up in a cantina. The point was, in Mr. Romaine's view she was not a suitable theme for conversation in such a refined place as he now found himself. He ignored Mr. Spenlove's smile and reassured himself by another glance around at the refinement, which was such a contrast to his host's lack of refinement in bringing up Jack Bannister's past.

'What do you think, Romaine?' Mr. Spenlove said.

'I couldn't say,' Mr. Romaine said hastily. 'Not at this distance of time. Ask him yourself! Twelve miles, you say? Twelve miles for you too, eh? You ask him. You knew him better'n I did.' He rubbed his nose with the back of his hand.

'Well,' Mr. Spenlove said, 'Jack's memory may be as bad as yours. It's a long time ago, anyway. Still, there is always a chance they might come over to see us. His wife did. My wife invited them, you know.'

Mr. Romaine seemed to be thinking it over. He said, heavily, 'She was a very nice young lady. And her mother, what was the name again?—she was a decent lady. Very refined.'

'Mrs. Deming? She's living with them,' Mr. Spenlove said. 'Mrs. Bannister told my wife over the telephone. I liked them too. Yes, I liked them; but the fact is, I'd forgotten about them, the way you forget about people you used to know, but you've heard they died, and that's that. You neither mourn their passing nor feel any emotions one way or another. When my wife told me, when I finally understood, that Jack Bannister's wife had been in this house, I had a feeling for a moment that she had returned from the grave!'

'He's done pretty well for himself,' Mr. Romaine said, and there was awe in his voice. He looked around him again, at the panelling, the red leather, the oak table by the window, the oak sideboard with the bar alongside, the billiard table, the oriental rugs and the heavy dark oak beams of the ceiling. So had Spenlove done pretty well for himself, he thought.

It wasn't, he reflected, a case of these people returning from the grave. They had got into heaven! If Jack Bannister was living out here he wasn't in any business. He would be living like a toff, as they used to say. And where would he get all that money? The answer must be, his young wife. Mr. Romaine thought back to those days and evoked the picture of that school-kid, a blonde, haughty sort of young lady; but the real thing, like her mother.

'You mean financially? Yes. But that isn't the whole story. Jack's done well for himself socially, you know. And morally too, when you think—eh? It's a case of redemption. In the old days it was the thing for a man who had, well, lived the way Jack did out on the coast, to be redeemed by the love of a virgin. I have often doubted whether virgins had this power. It seems they have. Here he is, settled down in the country like an old-fashioned English squire. He's been redeemed from that life out there.'

Mr. Romaine did not reply. He was wondering if Spenlove meant all this. You never knew whether he was pulling your leg or not. He was never serious for long. The funny thing was, he seemed to be so gabby, yet he never said much about himself. More than once, in London, Romaine had been on the point of trying to find out how much money Spenlove had and what it was in. After all, he hadn't been secretive to Spenlove about his own affairs. He had hesitated each time. He had an idea he would not find out. Strangely enough, this augmented his respect for his friend. It took character to have done what Spenlove had accomplished, put himself on easy street, and keep quiet about it. Mr. Romaine knew in his heart that most men he had sailed with would have been pretty cockahoop if they had done anything one-half so remarkable.

This talk of 'redemption' was over his head. Jack Bannister had never been a soak, and Mr. Romaine's ideas of redemption were somehow associated with recovery from alcoholism. Then again, Jack had gotten back his job in the Line, long before he met this kid he was now married to. If there had been any redeeming, the credit was due to Jack's shipmates, who had held their tongues and showed a sporting spirit about who he had been living with in Puerto Balboa. To the New York office Jack had been in the hospital; on coming out, had got himself a job operating a dredger, or steam shovel, scooping out an unusually large irrigation ditch in the jungle behind Puerto Balboa. Very sensible of him.

'You remember?' Mr. Spenlove said. 'It was near the snake farm.' Mr. Romaine nodded. 'I had an idea,' Mr. Spenlove continued, 'that Jack thought he was in the Garden of Eden out there. Remember the serpentarium? Jack always had to have something special, something superior to ordinary mortals. Adam had a serpent. Jack had a serpentarium, and an anti-venin laboratory, in his Eden!'

'Yes,' Mr. Romaine said. 'The snake had the last word too, if you remember?'

Mr. Spenlove gave him a quick glance.

'He usually does, if you live in Paradise. Or in Arcady. You asked me, in London, why I left America. I expect it was too much like the Garden of Eden for perpetual occupancy.'

Mr. Romaine looked down between his knees at the rich oriental rug, as though he were studying the pattern. Perhaps he had better not have any more of that high-test Scotch just now. It was evoking the past. Those days in Costaragua were days which he did not wish to remember particularly. He had nothing of his own to regret, no skeletons in his cupboard; he did not want to peer into the cupboards of his shipmates, as Spenlove seemed to enjoy doing. He had easily forgotten the life on the ships. It had been a way to make a living, but when it was over and he became a New York businessman, the former life had faded like a very old photograph. He could hardly remember the skippers and other officers. Only Spenlove. Spenlove had put him in the way of making his nest egg. And he remembered Mrs. Deming too. He was a bit surprised about that. He had liked her very much, but—hm! A very refined lady.

He had a feeling of discomfort when he recalled Jack Bannister personally. A man shouldn't go off into the bush like that. Garden of Eden, indeed! That was Spenlove, all right! He could talk about the Garden of Eden and bring in serpentariums and anti-venin laboratories!

It was of course the sort of things fellows would always talk about. A man like Jack Bannister, a chief engineer too, whether married or not nobody seemed to know, living in a railroad caboose, with a girl. The crowd had talked of nothing else, the trip they heard of it. There was nothing anyone could take exception to—except the girl. Jack had been offered the job when the other chap was struck by a falling derrick. He was Johnny-on-the-spot, Jack was. Just out of the hospital and without a ship for three weeks, took the job and stuck to it until—hm! Mr. Romaine had a sudden vivid memory of the lonely little funeral procession, wending its slow way along the beach, to the cemetery behind the ice plant. Poor thing!

Spenlove knew all about it. The tracks were laid along the side of the ditch as it was dug, and Jack's caboose, the tool car, the old box car with a kitchen range in it and a crooked chimney at one end and a bunk-car for the crew, followed along day by day into the jungle.

Spenlove knew all about it. He would either get aboard the switching locomotive which ran up each day to push them along and bring the stores, or he would get a ride on the little Ford rail-car the superintendent used for inspections. There was another car, a station-wagon on the rails, which the girls in the office used to make trips on. Spenlove would always get a ride somehow, and go to see Jack at a time when everybody else just let him alone. And he would go to the house where the girl lived before Jack rescued her from what Spenlove called 'a fate that was worse than death!' From the way he said it you knew he was only kidding, yet not kidding. What he was kidding was the customary phrase of saying what happened to a young girl in her position. Spenlove would go to the house and jabber Spanish to the old woman, what was her name?

It was the Casa Something. Yes, Casa Raquel. That was the grandmother's name, and it was down a wide dirty street which became a torrent of muck in the rainy season. Mr. Romaine had no use for such places. He had been taken there once, by a chief mate in search of adventure, but he disliked such places.

This girl had been living in that house when Jack Bannister first met her. She had a day job as nursemaid with the harbormaster. Mr. Romaine remembered that much, but he felt he did not want to remember any of it while in this house in the English country. He did not want to recall that life down in the hot countries. It was all very well for Spenlove to pretend the United States was too much like Paradise, or the Garden of Eden. He had done very well there. Mr. Romaine would be glad to get back to it.

'That's no way to talk,' he said. 'It's good enough for me. I'm a citizen.'

'I understand,' Mr. Spenlove said. 'It's only my way of talking.' He saw Perdita come in and make a gesture. 'I think the guests are coming now,' he said. 'Don't move. I'll bring them in. . . .'

Mr. Romaine heard him greeting the newcomers in the hall. He heard a new voice, yet a vaguely familiar one. He was sure of the owner of it. He had a sudden pleasant memory of Mrs. Deming in his cabin, showing him snapshots of 'my child.'

CHAPTER

6

BECAUSE he had been a widower and a ship's steward for many years, and had followed up that career by running a restaurant in New York, Mr. Romaine had become accustomed to eating his meals alone, day after day and year after year. It made him a little shy in company.

He followed the other guests into a bare-looking dining room, gently propelled by a hand on his shoulder. Mr. Spenlove understood his old friend's state of mind. He too had eaten his meals in solitude for many years.

He eased Mrs. Deming's chair under her, a service Mr. Romaine, due to his monastic way of life, had not thought to render. Very few ladies came to the Bar and Grill on Second Avenue.

The shining mahogany of the table, the austerity of the paneled walls, each panel with its one small picture, the silver candlesticks with tall yellow tapers, the bronze sconces on the wall above a plain oak sideboard, these things impressed Mr. Romaine. So did the circular convex mirror, in which he could see, in a perfect miniature, the scene as in a Dutch painting.

He saw Spenlove at the far end of this reflected interior, not yet seated, talking to Mrs. Price. He saw a far from ascetic-looking clerical gentleman opposite, who sat between a young woman whose face struck him as familiar yet strange, and the girl who had driven the car from the station. That was Spenlove's stepdaughter, a calm young lady of going on fifteen or so. On Mr. Romaine's right was a somewhat dry gentlewoman of mature age who wore a string of beads and a gold cross.

It was Mrs. Deming who enabled him to get his bearings. There was a moment of uncertainty when he looked at her, while he adjusted his mind to the fact that they were both guests, equal in the sight of man and God, and that he was in no way responsible for her safety and comfort, as he had been when he met her on board his ship.

Mrs. Deming said she had never expected to meet him in England. It was a small world. Was he now settled in the Old Country?

The apple-cheeked maid set a plate of soup in front of Mr. Romaine as he explained. He was going back to New York on the first of the month. On the old *Mauretania*.

'Lucky man! I envy you so much!'

Mr. Romaine did not reply for a moment. English people were not so easy to understand as Spenlove made out. Spenlove had told him, in London, 'When you come back, it's like being in a foreign country where you happen to know the language. Remember that and you'll be all right.' Maybe, maybe, Mr. Romaine thought.

'It must be awfully interesting, a sailor's life,' Mrs. Deming said. 'You people on the boats have the best of it.'

There must be some way, Mr. Romaine thought, of correcting Mrs. Deming's ideas. He was not a passionate man. Very few men are at his age, which was just over fifty, and with his background. But he had an ideal of living. He knew what he wanted, or imagined he wanted. And now that he had sold his business in New York, he was in a position to attain what he wanted, under certain conditions.

He was describing his status when he heard Mrs. Deming's daughter, the girl who had been on his ship and who was now married to Jack Bannister, correct her mother in a high, aristocratic voice.

'Mr. Romaine isn't on the boats now, Mother. He's retired. Mr. Spenlove told you over the phone.'

'I'm always terribly stupid over the phone,' Mrs. Deming said, but without any real remorse.

'In one ear and out the other,' her daughter added calmly.

'Not that it matters,' Mrs. Deming said brightly. 'I envy you just the same. More, in fact.' She smiled in a way Mr. Romaine remembered.

'Don't *you* like the Old Country?' he said. He was honestly taken aback. She was a very nice woman, a very nice woman indeed. She was a lady. She didn't look a day older, he reflected, than when she sat in his cabin and showed him snapshots of the kid, who now sat opposite, regarding her mother with a blend of criticism and concern, as though she were her mother's guardian.

Mrs. Bannister, of course, looked much more than a day older than she did when she was a passenger. She was a handsome girl, Mr. Romaine thought, very aristocratic in a manner quite different from her mother, who was aristocratic in a way Mr. Romaine liked much better. The daughter's low-cut dinner dress and her manner showed she was a lady all right, and knew her way around. She was only a kid still, however, he reflected, say twenty-one or two. Her manner made her seem more mature than otherwise, but he knew, from the way she looked a few years ago, she was only a kid.

As he asked Mrs. Deming about her feeling for the Old Country he looked around the table. There was a space between the clergyman and Mrs. Price. A chair had been removed and the others had not quite filled up the gap. Mr. Romaine's side of the table had four chairs. Where was Bannister?

He realized that Jack Bannister had not turned up and he saw Mrs. Bannister's glance following his. He bent his ear to Mrs. Deming.

'I can stand it,' that lady was saying, 'but I often wish I was back in the States. I suppose you know my husband died some years ago?'

Mr. Romaine was buttering a roll. He said, 'Mr. Bannister not at home?'

Mrs. Deming smiled and shook her head. 'He had to go to London. You knew him? Weren't you on the same boat?'

'Not well,' Mr. Romaine said slowly, as though trying to remember just how well he knew Jack Bannister. 'Heard a lot about him, from time to time.' Mr. Romaine did not want to talk about himself. An idea had come into his head which made him just a shade excited. A real idea! 'Matter of fact, I lost touch with a lot of the fellows when I came ashore.'

'When you retired, you mean? Mr. Spenlove said something.'

'No, I didn't retire. Just the reverse, Mrs. Deming.' He smiled as though Mrs. Deming had made a joke. 'I went into business. I'm a businessman. I have just sold my business.'

He had gathered from something he had read in the past, that ladies looked down on business. He had a suspicion that Mrs. Deming was different. 'Well, now you've retired. Is that it?'

'No, ma'am. Just taking a breather, you might say. Mr. Spenlove, we had some business together once; he wrote me I better see the Old Country, now I was free for a while, so I took a vacation. Plenty of changes from the old days.'

'Some for the worse, I think,' Mrs. Deming said crisply. 'I can't think why anybody would want to stay if they can get away.'

Mrs. Bannister's gaze was fixed on her parent. She made a gesture of hopelessness and said to Perdita, 'Mother wants to go back to live in America. Can you imagine why? She says it's so slow here. A ghastly idea.'

She addressed the table and then said, 'Don't you agree?'

Mrs. Deming had heard this before and laughed brightly. Mr. Romaine looked shrewdly from one to the other. He was thinking. He relaxed. He dismissed for good the notion that women like Mrs. Deming merely tolerated him. He said that he thought Mrs. Deming had something there. He himself was going back, all right, and pretty soon too. He thought of his visit to Glasgow.

'Good for you, Romaine,' Mr. Spenlove called out from the other end of the table. 'Pity more of us don't take that line. The pioneer spirit is dying out! Here we stick, sunk in ineptitude!'

Father Soames said he wouldn't call it ineptitude. Mrs. Price exclaimed that she would say not! Miss Soames said she thought it essential to support home industries, and, of course, the Empire.

'Mother's terribly patriotic,' Perdita said to Mr. Romaine and Mrs. Deming. 'She thinks everybody ought to stay at home, and buy nothing but British goods. So does Miss Soames.'

'Absolutely!' Mrs. Price was very much the duchess. Her rings, which were large, flashed fire in the candlelight.

'You're right, of course,' Mr. Spenlove said. 'Those days, the pioneer days, are over. They won't come back in our time. Instead of visions of empire we have visas and quotas. Mrs. Price thinks the Chinese had the right idea, a great wall to keep the Chinese at home. The young squirts in consular offices, who put a rubber stamp on your passport and collect two pounds, are in the saddle. They and their creators at home. It's easier to do that than fight, or learn a trade, or sell our stuff against competition abroad. The British Empire is now entering a period like the Roman Empire at the end of the fourth century. Huns and Goths, you know. The Germans were as troublesome then as they are now.'

'Now, he's off,' Perdita said, smiling at her guests. 'It's his pet subject.'

'There's no possible comparison,' Mrs. Price announced with great energy. She and Mr. Spenlove often wrangled amicably about politics. Her large, benevolent features glowed with righteous and patriotic sentiment. 'You and your old Roman Empire!'

Mr. Spenlove beamed. 'Mrs. Price prefers the new one, the gimcrack, jerry-built affair ruled by a sawdust Caesar. There's a huge mosaic map in Rome, showing the British Isles as part of the Roman Empire. The trains will run on time from the Bosporus to Broxburne. Sir Oswald will be our pro-consul. I expect the concession for the sale of black shirts and castor oil will be valuable.'

Mrs. Price appealed to the table. 'What can you do with a man like that?' she inquired. She turned to Mr. Spenlove. 'You can't possibly deny that they've made simply marvelous progress! I didn't see a single beggar all the time I was there last year. If you ask me, it wouldn't be a bad idea to try it here at home. It's absolutely the coming thing!'

Mr. Spenlove continued to beam. 'All right, so long as

we get a big mosaic map in London showing Italy as part of *our* empire. The Germans, of course, are preparing a map of the world as *their* empire. So are the Japanese, I believe. Then the Spaniards have a dream of restoring *their* Hispanidad empire in America. And as Philip the Second married Mary Tudor, they expect us to hand over England!' He turned to the others, 'You mustn't take us too seriously,' he said. 'Mrs. Price doesn't really mean it. She just means she likes to see foreigners, especially poor foreigners, toe the line. It gives her a thrill. And of course, from our point of view, working-class people are a sort of foreigner, so they ought to be made to toe the line pretty smartly. You remember Disraeli's remark about the Two Nations in England, the rich and the poor. We don't notice it in the country, but they are at war. And the rich, including people like us, who are near to the rich, don't like it at all. They think Sir Oswald has the answer to their prayers. I used to hear the same sort of thing in America. My old friend, Mrs. Colwell, one of the kindest persons I have ever known, extremely charitable and more than usually intelligent, came back from Germany simply blazing with enthusiasm. Because they had abolished trade unions! And started the Strength-Through-Joy business. The workers had been put in their place and were being taken care of properly. Like cattle! Strikes were unheard of.'

'I'm with her there!' Mrs. Price cried. 'The General Strike . . .'

'Of course you're with her there!' Mr. Spenlove agreed. 'The sentiment crosses all international boundaries. It's the new internationalism. We've always had it, *sotto voce*, of course; but now it's like a new religion, a new salvation army, organizing a crusade to capture the New Jerusalem in England's green and pleasant land from the paynim rabble. It's a pity uniforms are no longer legal. When I was here in

141

1928, it gave one a thrill to watch those young Blackshirts on their black motorcycles, or marching in black jerseys and black leggings, and getting some black looks from the British working man, as they went strutting along. They even had a black soap-box for their orator when he made a speech. It resembled the block in the Tower, a truncated pyramid. All gone now. Not allowed. A Fascist in civilian clothes is no more impressive than a plumber, and not nearly so useful.'

Mrs. Price said, 'They looked awfully smart in Italy. And so wonderfully polite, if you know what I mean.'

'We do, we do,' Mr. Spenlove said. 'In America the gangsters, I have been told, are most gentlemanly. They are extremely courteous to strangers who wander into their haunts. They provide bodyguards to escort you back to your hotel.'

'Have it your own way,' Mrs. Price said calmly. To Miss Soames she added that Mr. Spenlove's radical talk was all moonshine. 'He's absolutely capitalistic, really. A conservative.'

Mr. Romaine said that was so.

'Romaine is the real capitalist,' Mr. Spenlove said. 'He really believes in it.'

'Capital's only stored labor,' Mr. Romaine said, sententiously.

'He doesn't tell us whose labor.' Mr. Spenlove regarded his old shipmate with benevolence. He only smiled when Mr. Romaine said that Spenlove's bark was worse than his bite.

'He was very socialistic on the boat,' Mrs. Deming said.

'When was this?' he inquired, smiling. He had been wondering how much truth there might be in Mrs. Bannister's statement, that her husband was in London on business. Girls nowadays, he reflected, were sphinxes. They never fainted or shrieked. They gave no signs of joy or grief. They kept their emotions completely under control. You never knew what they were thinking.

'On the boat,' Mrs. Deming said. 'I forget the exact words, of course. I was reading *The Tatler*, or *Bystander*, one of those papers, and looking at the pictures of county people. He said they were all no good. *Not worth the price of a second-hand guillotine.*'

Mrs. Price shook her finger in Mr. Spenlove's face. 'Our very best people!' she exclaimed.

'I was just being conversational,' Mr. Spenlove remarked, going on with his dinner. 'What can you say about people in *The Tatler* or *The Bystander*? You tattle, of course.'

'Why shouldn't they be in the paper?' Mrs. Price inquired, in great dudgeon.

'We were in *The Tatler*,' Mrs. Deming said. 'As it happens. No, it was *The Lady*, I think. When we came to Moat Farm.'

'I'd like to see that picture,' he said. 'I expect Mrs. Bannister has it at home.'

Mrs. Bannister looked at Perdita and shrugged her shoulders. She glanced back at Mr. Spenlove, her face pink and her eyebrows raised in that characteristic way of hers. 'What makes you so sure?' she inquired.

He was not sure about anything concerning that competent and handsome young woman. His imagination had been captured by the accidental discovery of Jack Bannister's most recent romantic achievement. The affair seemed to him almost fantastically perfect. It was the finishing touch to a career remarkable for a seaman. Jack had been what Mr. Spenlove called a hardworking, professional lover, and he had had no luck until he rescued Candace Deming from her family. Now he had arrived. Onward and upward he was

143

on his way, to sink at last magnificently into the richly up-
holstered existence of an English county. And Candace,
with that aristocratic, slightly supercilious tone, not cold
but competently authoritative, was exactly what Mr. Spenlove imagined would be the perfect complement, the lovely
guerdon, for Jack's incessant knight-errantry. He had done
so much for girls who really did not deserve it! Candace
would train and domesticate him, and drive him in silken
harness. They would found a new county family. Descend-
ants in the year A.D. 2,700, would gaze respectfully at the
worn, partially defaced brasses in the church at Tollemache
St. Marys, of John Bannister Esq., with Candace his wife
. . . Mr. Spenlove allowed his fancy to rove. It was not
really so fantastic. Most of the knights, baronets and barons,
sprang from the loins of sharp peasants, if you delved deep
enough into the past. Even those who came over with the
Conqueror.

Mrs. Bannister's question, 'What makes you so sure?'
required no reply save a smile. She was a fine girl. He remembered her as a somewhat waspish chit when she was a
school-girl traveling with him across the Atlantic. She was
much more attractive now. She had character. He wished
Jack Bannister had not been such a fool as to find a business
engagement in London on an occasion like this.

They had given no explanation of the business which
made Jack's presence in London so urgent. Thinking the matter over, Mr. Spenlove discovered that the transformation of
his shipmate Jack Bannister, into John Bannister Esq. of Moat
Farm, Tollemache St. Marys, was not easy to imagine.
Jack was an unknown quantity. Of course, he might have no
desire to meet an old shipmate under such circumstances. He
had some queer crankinesses in him. He was, in a way, like
those old pirates who came home to England and settled

down as country gentlemen. Tradition said they were never eager to meet their old friends of the Spanish Main. Jack might, on the other hand, simply be scared of the social complexities of such meetings. How would he behave, Mr. Spenlove wondered, in what is called good society? Would Jack be able to form an opinion as to the propriety, or the reverse, of his wife's visit to Perdita? In a way it was a pity, Mr. Spenlove reflected, that he, himself had not been at home. Ah! he thought, there was I, too, in London, on business. And glancing along at Mrs. Bannister's face, it seemed to him she was looking at him, in that attractively super-cilious way of hers, and reading his thought. How about you? she was saying. You were in London on business, weren't you? Well, then!

Mr. Spenlove had been much preoccupied, during his years at sea, with the relations between his shipmates and passengers, particularly women passengers. Suddenly there flashed into his mind that affair of the stewardess on the Gloriosa. How had he ever forgotten it? The reason probably was that he himself on that occasion had been a passenger, returning from a special job in Havana. One of the ships had been in trouble there; Mr. Spenlove being ordered by cable from the office to turn his job over to his second-in-command, remain in Havana and take charge of the disabled vessel. This he had done, and after the ship had been re-paired and gone south, he had taken passage on the Gloriosa, where Jack was chief, for New York.

Mr. Spenlove recalled that episode of the stewardess on the Gloriosa; the elderly businessman clutching and grinning, as the girl tried, gently and tactfully, to disengage herself.

Jack might not want his wife to keep in touch with a former shipmate. Marrying a passenger involved a man in an almost metaphysical maze of social problems. Mr. Spenlove,

145

as he pondered, saw many difficulties in the new environment at Tollemache St. Marys. Jack might not be entirely
at ease in Zion. It was a nice question. Mr. Spenlove wanted
very much to have it answered.

He sat at the head of his table, watching the faces and
enjoying his thoughts. Old Romaine seemed to be getting
along very well indeed with Mrs. Deming. Well, in a way,
they were old friends. Perdita was smiling at them, and then
caught her husband's eye as she glanced along the table,
ready to ring her bell. Mrs. Bannister was talking to Sonia
diagonally across the table. She had what Mr. Spenlove believed to be the traditional aristocratic voice of the English
high-born dame from Rowena to Jane Austen's young ladies.
A soft, clear voice, the antithesis of the hard, flat tones of the
women of New York, where the climate seemed to dry out
their vocal chords.

Now she was a confident young matron talking of life at
Montreux when she was there. Sonia, leaning her cheek on
her hand, was listening raptly, her lower lip caught in her
small teeth. She was a jolly person now, very poised and
good-tempered, but she had lost the air of having just arrived
from fairyland, which had enveloped her in America.

Mrs. Price was talking to Father Soames and his sister.
They were very fond of her. She put them at their ease.
Miss Soames read Mrs. Price's serials with pleasure. The
plots were so simple and the characters just like the people
one met in real life, or as Miss Soames imagined real people
to be. She had no illusions about village morality. She had
the attitude of a nurse who preserves an intense personal
respectability while carrying out her duties at a foundling
hospital.

Mr. Spenlove regarded them over his glass of Beaune
with affection. He had done nothing, absolutely nothing, to

146

deserve his good fortune, he reflected. It had been entirely accidental, a casual concatenation of events. First there had been old Mr. Merry, a stray passenger who had taken to Mr. Spenlove, with whom he dined. They had seen something of each other from time to time in New York, and when Mr. Spenlove had asked advice about an investment, Mr. Merry had suddenly suggested a first mortgage as a nice safe way of getting five per cent without risk. Then, when he retired, Mr. Spenlove had bought the place and had lived in it. Sonia's dog had chased the old cat, and Sonia had brought her mother to pay a call. From then on they had all three been borne irresistibly on a powerful current.

Of course that wasn't quite the whole story, he thought as he drank his wine and reached for the decanter. What about his own stored wisdom? That was probably lucky accident, too. It was the heritage of hundreds of years of yeoman forebears. Forty-shilling freeholders, Holinshed called them. Their gray, mossy headstones had sunk almost out of sight in the Hampshire churchyards. Some, of every generation he had knowledge of, had gone overseas. They were in New Zealand, Australia, Canada, and even China. As a boy he had heard tales of 'the China Trade,' a fabulous family business where fortunes had been made, and then, unfortunately, lost at home. The point was, no matter where they were, they did not maintain any solidarity. They wrote rarely or not at all, and their children not at all. There were never any 'reunions,' no 'old home weeks,' as the Americans said. They went their ways, standing on their own feet, and achieving what he liked to call 'a distinguished anonymity.' Who knew, he would ask rhetorically, whether mute inglorious Miltons did not have a long-term value?

Going back twenty years, when Jack was his chief on the *Sandringham*, he realized that unless Jack had undergone a complete metamorphosis, going to London was exactly what he might do on such an occasion. He might be inspired by a blend of panic and bluff, or perhaps merely shyness, bad manners and obstinacy. He was one of those men who suffer from a fatal lack of faith in their authentic ability, who suddenly throw their weight around to assert themselves, only to appal their shipmates, who are willing to concede the ability if they themselves are only left in peace.

If he took that caper ashore with him, and had it in working order over at Tollemache St. Marys—there might be family trouble, possibly.

Candace would be worth cultivating if he could get her alone. She had been full of character on the ship. She had been realistic enough about her father and mother. What would be her traditional attitude toward the man who, as a knight-errant, had carried her over the abyss between her father's disintegration and the falling-in of the family bequests? If Mrs. Deming had not exaggerated, it was quite an abyss. Was he still a knight-errant? The trouble with that occupation was that it was usually a form of casual employment. Nobody ever secured a permanent billet as a knight-errant.

Mrs. Price chuckled comfortably and put her heavily ringed hand on his arm.

'Is that an absolute fact?'

'I didn't catch . . .' he said courteously.

'Miss Soames says you told Father Soames American girls go on cruises to get husbands. Is that a fact? Or is it just one of your sailor's yarns?'

'Why shouldn't they?' he inquired mildly. 'What other inducement could there be to make them spend so much time and money?' Mrs. Price waved this away.

'Travel,' she said. 'Picture galleries, and all that. You see them in Paris. Swarms!'

'That's Europe. You mentioned cruises. Do you know, we had a special development called "Cruises to Nowhere?" I once clipped some of the advertisements. "Be an Explorer! Fare out to Fairyland!" That sort of thing.'

Miss Soames gave him a faint smile of complete non-comprehension. Mrs. Price made a gesture to indicate that her opinion of Mr. Spenlove as a modern Munchausen was confirmed. Father Soames smiled in a sporting spirit. He knew Mr. Spenlove generally had some foundation in fact for his extraordinary yarns about America.

'I don't blame you for being skeptical,' he said, 'but it's the truth. We would sail out Friday nights, moonlight if possible, with four or five hundred passengers, a couple of orchestras, one of them Hawaiian, of course, a cruise director who acted as master of ceremonies, and we would cruise around in the Atlantic for a few hundred miles at three-quarters speed, turn around and sail back to port, arriving early Monday morning. That was a Cruise to Nowhere. Only metaphorically, of course. Some of them reached heaven, some purgatory and a few an alcoholic hell. I never saw any statistics, but I believe there were quite a few husbands caught that way.'

'Is that so difficult, then? Marriage in the States? Can't they . . . ?' Father Soames was unable to find the phrase to express his confused reactions. Miss Soames, looking down at the gold cross on her bosom, remarked in a severe voice. 'Of course, for them it isn't a sacrament.'

'Now we're generalizing,' Mr. Spenlove warned. 'We all do. It's an international vice, I'm afraid. I don't know about the sacrament. They are largely a secular race. At any rate, it's a secular country. Of course, I know only a micro-scopic fragment of it. We used to have English passengers who had been in the country, mostly in New York, a couple of weeks, and knew all about it! My own experience was less exhaustive. We would have two or three hundred Americans for several weeks. They would land, and we would never see them again. We'd take on another crowd. A cross-section of the prosperous middle-class. The rich don't go on those cruises, as a rule.'

'What about that rich friend of yours, the one you're always quoting?'

'Mrs. Colwell? She's the exception which proves the rule. It's a long story, how she came to be with us. She had a niece who had been the victim of an unfortunate love affair. She was in such a state over the break-up of her engagement that the doctors recommended a cruise to take her mind off her troubles.'

'And to find a husband?' exclaimed Mrs. Price. 'The doctors actually prescribe?'

Mr. Spenlove, very much amused, shook his head. 'Oh, no! Doctors don't prescribe a cruise for a broken heart or for matrimony specifically.' He thought of young Jacques, who had tried so frantically to insinuate himself into the Colwell family. Agnes Colwell had done better for herself than that. Jaques, in his suburban villa at Cedarhurst, Long Island, was very much married to a girl who had been in the auditing department. Jaques was a born husband. Mr. Spenlove smiled to himself as he thought of Jaques being audited so efficiently by his wife. 'No, the rule still holds, in spite of exceptions like Mrs. Colwell. And doctors don't prescribe a cruise as heart balm, as Americans call it. You know,' he said to Mrs. Price, 'instead of asking me, why not go over and see for yourself? They'd welcome you with open arms.'

'I'd much rather they welcomed me with open check-books,' Mrs. Price said. She had a friend who got the most marvelous prices from American magazines. And her work, in Mrs. Price's view, was not so wonderful either. Inferior to her own, in fact.

'I have no doubt they will eventually,' Mr. Spenlove said, sincerely. 'You can't keep a good woman down. I was thinking of the cruise passengers. They are your public, of course. They read the women's magazines. If you can call it reading. The point I was making was that cruises give one a very limited view of America. You don't learn much about Americans on a cruise. They adopt a special kind of behavior at sea.'

'Want to create a good impression, I suppose,' Father Soames suggested, in a deep voice. Keeping up in foreign affairs, Father Soames wished to think well of America. He was startled by Mr. Spenlove's laugh. Everybody looked at their host. Perdita, smiling, rang for the maid.

'I wouldn't call it that!' He laughed again. 'Oh, no!' He shook his head, as if in despair at ever making these quiet English people understand what he was talking about. 'They aren't out to create a good impression. Nor do those who go to Europe, which in their case means Paris. They think one of the advantages of travel is that you can leave your inhibitions at home. They are fond of that word, inhibition. There was a girl at my table one voyage. She was from the West. Psychologically, she was a combination of a prairie fire and a Mississippi steamboat with the calliope going. She told me that when she was abroad or on a boat, she had no inhibitions. It was the first time I had heard the word in conversation. I told her I'd watch her career from a safe distance!'

Mrs. Price said, 'Oh, I know I'd hate that country!

It would be too disconcerting. Don't you agree?' she asked Miss Soames, who nodded silently.

'They find *us* so,' Mr. Spenlove pointed out gently, 'for precisely the opposite reason. They resent the fact that we remain ourselves and have no particular desire to visit their country as they do ours. They think it argues a lack of vitality. They accuse us of being preoccupied with the past. We accuse them of thinking of dollars and cents. They say *we* have that trouble in an acute form. They have a lot of convincing figures about it, I'm afraid.'

'Six of one and half a dozen of the other,' Father Soames surmised.

'They're a jolly sight more successful in getting the dollars than we are, you must admit,' Mrs. Price said. She smiled as the apple-cheeked maid set down the desert in front of her. 'No,' she added to Mr. Spenlove, who held the decanter invitingly. She placed her finger over her glass. 'Madeira's bad for me, really, thanks.'

'There you go again,' he said, setting the decanter down. 'You're like a lot of people in this country. You think there are no poor Americans, no unsuccessful businessmen. In a hundred and thirty million people you find all sorts. We think of Americans as the Italian and French and Swiss hotel-keepers used to think of the English milords on the Grand Tour. They never saw any other kind of Englishmen, except domestics. They thought we at home were all rich. Think of Beckford in the eighteenth century, taking his servants, his coaches and horses, and even his furniture, with him to the Continent. I read somewhere that men like him even remained shut up in their coaches during the trip across the Channel. Americans take a suite with a trunk-room, bath-room and sitting room, with maids' quarters adjoining, when they cruise. They take their cars.'

'Is that a fact?' Mrs. Price said, in a low voice. It was an exciting thought. If she could only achieve one of those amazing American successes, of which she had heard, like *The Constant Nymph*, for instance, or *The Sheik*, she would take a cruise like that. She would take a maid and a Rolls Royce, as well as a secretary. She had never heard of this Beckford lad, but he had the right idea. After all, she noted, the Americans had got the idea from the British!

'You ought to talk to Mr. Romaine,' Mr. Spenlove said. 'He could tell you more stories than you can shake a stick at. Scandal, of course, I mean.'

'If he knows more scandal than you do, he must be marvelous,' Mrs. Price said. Miss Soames smiled tolerantly. Miss Soames was not always completely sure about Mr. Spenlove. She had never met anyone quite like him before. Socially, he refused to be classified in her narrow world. A naval officer, or even the retired captain of a merchant ship, could find a niche in her mind, but Mr. Spenlove was neither. He had told her, in a tone of feigned shock, when she asked him if he had been a captain, that he had never fallen so low as that! Then again, he was not churchy. His wife went to church occasionally, but not he. He told her he was already so holy he did not need ghostly consolation. Her brother advised her not to worry too much about Spenlove. He was, Father Soames said, 'all right.' Well, in Miss Soames's view he might be all right, but he was sometimes extremely confusing.

'We used to have scores of good-looking widows and spinsters,' he told Mrs. Price. 'And there were big business men, too, widowers or divorced.'

Mrs. Price knew he was being facetious. She knew he knew she had no intention of marrying again. This was not due to devotion to the memory of the defunct producer of innumerable serials in magazines and weekly newspapers. Marriage had been only one of her interests. As Perdita had said, now she was free from her responsibilities and her children were on their own, she was really enjoying her life. So she said, 'Really!' and regarded Mr. Spenlove with indulgent affection. She had told Perdita, 'It must be fun to be married to a man like him. You don't have to pretend you're anything but yourself. He *knows* what you are, ducky.' Perdita, smiling, had asked 'What?' and Mrs. Price had said, 'As if you didn't know! He adores you.'

Perdita rose now and said they would have coffee in the drawing room. Mr. Spenlove's suggestion, to Father Soames, that they leave the ladies to sit over their wine, was received by Mrs. Price as 'a darned good idea.' She said men had had the best of it long enough. They had had their feet on women's necks for centuries.

Mr. Spenlove, as he left the room to seek a cigar, said the necks were as beautiful as ever. He went down into the billiard room. He heard someone follow him and looked in the mirror over his head. Mrs. Bannister was examining the Hogarth prints on the walls.

WOULD you like a Creme de Cassis?' he said, looking around.

She nodded and he brought out the bottle, remarking that it was a bit sweet for him. He preferred whiskey, or rum, or cognac. Or ale in a tankard. He smiled to make it clear he was talking merely to make conversation while she made up her mind what she wanted to say to him. He knew she had come in for that purpose. He told her of Hilaire Belloc's aphorism, never to drink anything made since the Reformation. He thought Mr. B. allowed his prejudices to run away with his judgment. He wanted the oldest in liquors but the newest in political systems. Before they had had time to mature, he added. Fascism, for instance, was still fermenting.

He lit his cigar.

'Sorry my husband wasn't able to come,' she said, a little breathlessly. 'I wanted to explain. . . .'

He poured the liqueur and handed it to her. Then he went on quietly arranging the other bottles on a tray.

'You don't have to apologize for him,' he said in a low tone. 'I knew Jack long before you did. You don't have to explain unless you want to. It's warm tonight. Let's take a stroll outside. I'll just carry these things in.' He put a box of cigars with the liqueur bottles and glasses and went into the drawing room.

When he returned she was standing in front of a Hogarth drawing. 'What are they supposed to be?' she said.

He drew on his cigar. '*Marriage a la Mode*,' he said, mildly. 'In Hogarth's time, of course. We have made some improvements I suppose. Well . . .'

He led the way to the garden.

The elms rose tall beyond the apples trees which surrounded a tennis court. There was a faint radiance from a light outside the kitchen door, beyond a high brick wall with a doorway. The cocker spaniel sat in the doorway watching them as they walked toward the gazebo. Mr. Spenlove called him and he joined them silently.

'What did you mean just now, when you said you'd known my husband longer than I had? What made you say that, just at this time?'

'I merely meant that I wouldn't be surprised at what I might hear about him. Anything wrong?'

She seemed to be considering. She began to walk more slowly. 'If I'm not intruding,' he added, taking her arm. He felt her press his hand to her side.

'I'm in a funk.'

Mr. Spenlove stopped and looked closely at her. 'What about?' he inquired.

'He isn't coming back.'

'What makes you think so?'

'It's happened before, you know. Only not so long.'

'What? London on business?'

'He's seeing someone.

'Is that a fact? Or just a suspicion?'

'It's a fact, Mr. Spenlove.'

'How long since he was away before—on business?'

'Oh, he has a business, all right. Don't misunderstand us. He has a business. Yes.' She gave a short laugh.

'What's the idea? Is he in business?'

'That's what I said.'

'He's seeing someone. So he isn't coming back. But he came back before.'

'These things don't stand still, do they?'

'But how long is the—ah, period? Does he go regularly?'

'Last May. He has a car. It's not a London business exactly, you know.'

'I don't know,' he reminded her. 'I know nothing about it. I *am* surprised at Jack going into business, if that's any use to you. I wouldn't have thought it of him. What is it?'

'Insurance.'

'Come, come! You mean, he goes around, door-to-door business?'

'Not exactly. It's commercial insurance. He's an inspector of machinery for the insurance company at Norwich.'

'Oh! Industrial! I see. Lots of our fellows went into that. Hm!' Mr. Spenlove smoked silently for a moment. This was a new line on Jack. 'What you haven't explained,' he said suddenly, 'is what made him take up this business. You aren't living on what he makes, are you?'

Mrs. Bannister leaned over the dog sitting at her feet and appeared to be studying him as though he held the answer to the riddle of her life. Rover contemplated the darkness of the orchard.

'That wasn't the reason he took it up,' she said. 'He had a reason, of course.'

The bulb Mr. Spenlove had switched on in the gazebo was dim and cobwebbed, but he could see that she hesitated to explain the reason.

'I think I understand,' he said. 'What it amounts to is, he found country life rather different from what he expected? Yes?'

'When we were married he thought I hadn't any money. I hadn't, in fact, then. He never really believed me when I told him of my family.'

'Then why did you leave America? Why did he want to come back to England if he thought he had to work?'

'It was his idea. My mother wanted to stay in America, but the family wanted her to come back. And he hated America.'

'Oh, did he? I never knew that. He certainly never had any enthusiasm for America. But hate . . . ?'

'He had the idea he was saving me from America,' Mrs. Bannister said gently. 'I know it sounds batty, but . . . My father, I think, gave him some wrong ideas about America. So, when we had the legacy from Uncle Fabian, and my great-aunt was ill and wanted Mother to come and take care of her, we came too.'

'This was after your father died, I suppose.'

'Not quite, but we weren't seeing anything of him. As a matter of fact, we were living in Florida when Uncle Fabian died.'

'I don't see you in Florida,' Mr. Spenlove said, frowning.

'Just as well,' she said, smiling at her own thoughts.

'Were you married then?'

'Yes, married and, except for what Jack had, broke. He didn't have very much.' Her voice trailed off as though she were thinking of that time. Mr. Spenlove was incredulous.

158

'Jack ought to have had as good a bank as the next,' he protested. 'He lived on the ship, didn't drink, didn't gamble, didn't—you know . . . No vices at all, and over three fifty a month. I ought to know. I had a little more, on account of the seniority he lost while he was on the coast. Did you know he was a beachcomber once? In Costaragua. I don't mean he was a bum. He had a good job on the beach, or in the bush near the beach. Yes, he should have had something. Something substantial.'

'He had some losses in the market,' she said. 'In 1929, about that time, you remember?'

'Did he? I thought he would have had more sense than to buy stocks. Hm. Well, it does let new light on Jack, to know he was married and living in Florida. In one of those plushy places, was it?'

'I said it was just as well you couldn't see us in Florida,' she said, looking out into the darkness. She had put the glass of liqueur on the small rustic table and now she looked at it as if she did not recognize it. 'We were pretty broke at first.'

'Where? I was in Fort Lauderdale once. And Miami for the day.'

'Nothing like that. We went there because we had so little money, and Mother wanted to live in the country. Jack said we could keep chickens. He said there was a fortune in chickens.'

'Was there?'

'I'm afraid there wasn't for us.'

Mr. Spenlove nodded and patted her arm. 'I'm afraid not,' he said. 'It seems an extraordinary idea to keep chickens! What could he know about it?'

'It was an idea he had,' she said lightly. 'He said all sailors, when they retired, kept chickens.'

'We do say things like that,' Mr. Spenlove admitted, 'but it never occurred to me anybody ever took the phrase literally. Dear me! And what happened to the chickens?'

'We lost them eventually. But that wasn't Jack's fault. He really worked awfully hard down at Heavenly Haven.'

'Heavenly Haven? A name like that would scare off anybody with any sense,' Mr. Spenlove suggested sharply.

'It didn't scare off the mosquitoes and snakes,' Mrs. Bannister told him simply, smiling. 'The real trouble was Grandfather, my mother's pater. He came to see us.'

'He did? The county-cricket player? You know, your mother told me quite a lot about herself. But she didn't mention Heavenly Haven.'

'Grandfather was very well off. He treated Mother badly when she got married. . . .'

'I heard about that. About the elopement.'

'Did you ever hear how she climbed out of the window and hung in the ivy for ten minutes before they could pull her out of it? Father was waiting at the wrong window, of course! Grandfather sent her to Coventry, as he called it. Then he cut her off with a shilling. Father used to keep a shilling on his watch fob. While we were in Florida, Mother wrote home for money. For her own money, you know. Mother's rather sporting that way. When it was a case of getting money for us she would, as she said, eat humble pie. There was no answer to her letter, so she sent a cable. No answer to that, either. And then suddenly Grandfather came himself. His second wife, my mother's stepmother, had taken her side often. He had gone off on a world cruise, and when the cable came from Mother it was sent off after him. He got it in San Francisco on his way home. Instead of going straight to New York, he came to Florida to visit us.'

'That must have been a situation. What did he think of

it?' Mrs. Bannister reached out and took the glass and drank what was in it. She laughed and wiped her lips.

'He took it rather well. He expected what you did, that we were living in some place like the Breakers, or the Royal Palm in Palm Beach. He found us in a shack on the shore in a rather poverty-stricken village near Boca Raton. It was May and rather warm. We all wore shorts, of course, and I hadn't worn shoes for a month. Just sandals. The kid was as red as a lobster. He's named Vivian, after Grandfather.'

Mr. Spenlove rose and patted her shoulder again. 'We have to go back to the house,' he said. 'See how they're getting on. What you're telling me simply takes my breath away,' he added. 'I must have the whole story, of course. How did he take it? Your grandfather?'

'He nearly had a fit!' she said. 'He came down in a very large Lincoln he had hired in Palm Beach, with a chauffeur in uniform. What with the palms, and the chickens, and the boat we had, and the kid being practically a nudist, you know, he told us afterward that we were more like a Robinson Crusoe family on a desert island. When he heard we really were broke and not doing it for a lark, he sent the Lincoln away and stayed with us for the night. We found him a room in Boca Raton and he bought a second-hand Buick for us. He said the trouble with our chicken business was, it wasn't big enough. We knew that, but we were broke. He ordered a thousand more by telegraph and got a contractor to start a new run at once, with electric lights and an incubator. He sent for a whole library of books on poultry raising and told Jack he ought to study every night.'

Mr. Spenlove led the way across the lawn. 'He did? And Jack, did he study?'

'I'm afraid Jack went fishing,' Mrs. Bannister said. 'They both went fishing, as a matter of fact. It was Mother who had to wrestle with the chickens, and the books too. When the new lot came, our troubles began all right. I had the kid.'

'What about your father? Was he . . . ?'

'He was in New York. Didn't Mother tell you what happened?'

'Yes, but not the exact date. I suppose all this you're telling me was during the depression.'

'Of course! That's why we were there. You could buy a big estate in Florida for a thousand dollars. But that's not much good if you haven't a thousand cents.'

They entered the house and Mr. Spenlove was amused to see that Mr. Romaine was getting along very well indeed with Mrs. Deming. It showed, Mr. Spenlove thought, how impossible it was to foretell what will happen when you bring people together to dine. He had had the notion that the Deming party would take to Father Soames and his sister, while he himself and Jack Bannister and Romaine would have a yarn about old days. This was more interesting.

'What are you two talking about?' Perdita said. 'Don't you want any coffee? It's still hot.'

'Black, no sugar, please,' Mrs. Bannister said, setting down her liqueur glass. 'Life in America was the subject of our discourse,' she added.

'The same for me,' Mr. Spenlove said. He relit his cigar, but he did not sit down. He rarely sat down in his wife's drawing room. 'She was telling me about the chicken farming,' he said to Mrs. Deming, who laughed, throwing back her head and closing her eyes, as though the memory of the chickens was irresistibly funny.

'You know about poultry?' Mr. Romaine inquired. Mrs. Deming said she ought to, after what she'd gone through. Mr. Romaine became even more preoccupied with their conversation.

Mr. Spenlove saw the party was going along nicely enough. The Soames contingent would be moving out soon. Miss Soames was an early riser. He took his coffee with him into the billiard room and Mrs. Bannister followed him. The drawing room was not large enough to allow more than two simultaneous conversations to function comfortably.

She walked around and studied the Hogarths more attentively.

'So you were stuck with a thousand more chickens.'

'Yes, and the catch was, they had roup. And they gave the others roup. We nearly got roup too!'

'What is it?' he asked. She told him what roup was. 'It's a sort of sinus trouble. We had to dip all their heads in permanganate of potash, and as they were white birds they looked strange. In the dusk they seemed to be walking around with no heads! Those who hadn't roup got cholera, or coccidiosis, or bronchitis. By the time we found out how to cure them they were all dead. A dead loss too. Healthy birds are bad enough. Those were a horror.'

'You've had a lot of adventures in your short life,' Mr. Spenlove said, musing. 'What did your grandfather think of the head of the family leaving everything to you and your mother?'

'Oh, he'd gone. He had to catch the *Rex*. He had a cable that his brother, mother's uncle Fabian, was seriously ill in Bellagio.'

'Your mother told me what seemed hard to believe. She said that uncle of hers was a Fascist.'

'Of course! He had bought this villa and put a lot of his money into Italian things, and when the Fascists came in, well, he had to use a certain amount of common sense, or they'd have taken everything. From what Mother said, too, he really believed they were going to save the country.'

'Made the trains run on time, eh?'

'Don't you agree?' Mrs. Bannister raised her fine eyebrows. Mr. Spenlove smiled. 'Napoleon made the coaches run on time, I expect,' he said gently. 'He had many admirers in England. I couldn't argue about it. It's like Transubstantiation. If you believe, the miracle happens. If not, not. Credere, Ubedire, Combattere, is a fine gospel, for those in the saddle. My wife's brother is one of them. A disciple, not an apostle.'

'Well, we seem to be in the same boat. Uncle Fabian was the head of the family, you see, so Grandfather had to go at once, on the *Rex*, to Bellagio. And we were left to struggle with those darned chickens.'

'They won, I gathered.'

'They did. When we got a cable about Uncle Fabian leaving us Moat Farm, we went to New York. I hated the place after what we had gone through. I wouldn't have minded if we had made a fortune, but to have all that dirty work and then lose, it was too much.'

'What happened then? Did you come back to England? You said you were left this place. . . .'

'Mother wanted to sell it and stay in America, but I wasn't having any. You heard her at dinner.'

'I was surprised.'

'Mother's rather a colonial type,' Mrs. Bannister said thoughtfully. 'She seems to enjoy roughing it.'

'You're not? What are your plans? You can confide in my wife. Jack seeing someone in London?'

'I was telling you, but you asked me about Florida. It's not easy to explain. Jack isn't the flirty type, you know. It isn't that sort of thing. I have had the idea he ought to have someone to advise him.'

'A nice job! Don't count on me! Haven't you any address or telephone number to call him when he's in London?'

'Of course. He isn't concealing anything. He just doesn't

come home. He goes on tours of inspection, Norwich, Harwich, Felixstowe, Colchester, all 'round. When he does come home, he keeps to himself. As if he was in some sort of hole and can't make up his mind what to do about it.'

'Yet you say he isn't concealing anything!'

'In that sense, I suppose. I meant in the usual sense. He is what they call faithful. He wouldn't be unfaithful.'

'Then why the funk? You said you were in a funk.'

'I am, too! It's like what Grandfather called being sent to Coventry.' Mr. Spenlove nodded. He had only sour memories of his own schooldays, and disliked the expression and what it implied. He frowned as he reflected that perhaps Jack had that sort of mood in him. It would be all the worse if he continued to be what she called 'faithful,' and sent her to Coventry.

'Well,' Mr. Spenlove said, crisply, 'who? Who is the cause of the funk?'

'Where he stays in London.'

'Not at a hotel? He stays with someone?'

'I suppose you could call it a private hotel,' Mrs. Bannister said, looking down at her cigarette. 'Yes, a private hotel.'

'What's the matter with that? You say he isn't the unfaithful type.'

Mrs. Bannister, who suddenly looked very young and forlorn, glanced around at Hogarth's *Marriage a la Mode*, as though she might discover assistance for her own predicament.

Mr. Spenlove watched her for a moment and drew on his cigar. He was at a loss what to say to clear the roadblock in her mind. They were not thinking of the same things, he suspected. He waited. He heard her say, in a small, tight voice, that there were possibly worse things in married life than unfaithfulness. He nodded.

'Quite! Such as . . . ? You aren't referring to what is known as incompatibility, are you?'

'In a way. Not incompatibility between us, you know. We got on very well, in America.'

'Oh! In America, eh? But not here. You mean you two and England are incompatible?'

'No.' She gave a little laugh and pinched out her cigarette. 'Couldn't you come and see us, soon? It would be easier to explain then. Couldn't you? We'd love to have you. My great-aunt . . .'

'Your mother's aunt? You have a lot of uncles and aunts.'

'Yes. This is my mother's aunt on her mother's side. They are Enderbys. Our family is Enderby-Breton.' Mr. Spenlove nodded. 'That's how we have Moat Farm. It's the old Enderby place.'

'She must be very old.'

'Very old. And she can't stand Jack. He can't stand her. It's a difficult situation.'

'Hm. Incompatibility. Jack often meets with incompatibility. I knew him before you were born. It's possible Jack was passing through Paris when you were born.'

She stood up, staring at him. 'He never told me that.'

'It wouldn't occur to him. He might not remember it. He was on a ship in Alexandria, in Egypt, and he went home overland. I got his job when he left us.'

'What did he go home for?'

'He said it was family trouble. His wife had run away. Didn't he ever tell you he was married before?'

'A stewardess, wasn't it?'

'Oh, no! That was *much* later. In America. That only lasted a short time. She was a Dane or something. We called her the Blonde Venus. No, I'm speaking of his first marriage, in England. To a Belgian girl. He never told you?'

166

'He never spoke much of his early life,' she said. 'He did tell me about being on a ship with you in the war. How many times has he been married?'

'Several times. I am embarrassed. I naturally thought you'd have known. . . .'

'Yes,' she said, looking down at her hands.

'Well, I know what I think you ought to do.'

'Have it out with him?'

He nodded.

'That's what I was suggesting. He might not remember it all. You could say it was never an actual experience for him, that journey. He was very much upset at the time, and he was probably in a sort of trance all the way from Alexandria to Liverpool.'

'Did he find her?'

'In a way, but he may have forgotten that now, chasing other dreams. I used to live at the same lodgings in Liverpool, with some old friends of mine, so I heard he had come home, and after he failed to discover who the fellow was she had gone with, except he was a Belgian, like her, he went to London to get his discharge papers so he could sail again. According to the story, he met his wife there. She was living with another man. Or so I understood. Then later he turned up in America when I was over there in the Line. He was in Costaragua for a while too. Or didn't he mention that either?'

'He said he used to go there in the ships.'

'We all did that. What I meant was, didn't he tell you he lived ashore down there? On the beach, as we say?'

She shook her head slowly. 'No,' she said, and added, sharply, 'I don't expect him to tell me every blessed thing he ever did!'

'That's right,' Mr. Spenlove said. 'We've all been

around a bit in our time,' he said vaguely. 'I was only trying to find out what you did know and what you didn't. Well, Jack was in the hospital. I was in the hospital once myself. Only Jack, instead of rejoining the ships, got himself a job on a construction contract. Well, he's changed, I suppose.'

'What did you mean by saying he was chasing another dream?'

'That was how he used to strike me, in the old days. He may have changed. He was always rescuing girls! He got a medal when he rescued his first wife. She was a passenger.'

'Like me,' Mrs. Bannister said lightly. 'I was a passenger. Then there was that stewardess. I suppose she could be called a passenger too. In a sense.'

'He mentioned her, eh? Well, I suppose he would. There was nothing to be ashamed of. For that matter, he has always had the noblest motives, with regard to women. The very noblest!'

'Thank you. In my case, at any rate. And yet it doesn't always work out, noble motives, I mean.'

'Do you suppose he has another noble motive now?'

'If I knew that . . . !' Mrs. Bannister shrugged her beautiful shoulders slightly and looked at Mr. Spenlove with the clear honest eyes of a girl whose experiences had never touched her integrity. 'Of course, if it's medals he's after . . . He didn't get a medal when he rescued me, you know.'

'He should have, I suppose,' Mr. Spenlove said slowly, studying her. She smiled.

'Of course,' she said lightly, 'one doesn't quite expect to hear such a long list of distressed maidens, I must admit. All beautiful, no doubt.'

'You don't need to worry about that,' he said briskly. 'It just happens that it's true; they were all beautiful. I have never thought about that angle, and I am not clear about it. I mean, I don't see what there is about Jack to have attracted them. As you say, he isn't a philanderer. In fact, he used to strike me as a bit the other way; puritanical, in fact. I don't know the answer, unless it's just that he's rather romantic.'

Mr. Spenlove's voice trailed off. He was thinking, as he sometimes expressed it, of the days that are no more. He found it easier than to face the problem of the young lady, who was looking at him steadily, digesting the obviously fresh information that her husband was a chronic romantic. It was supposed to be an occupational disease of sailors; but although he had been to sea for the great part of his adult life, it was absurd to think of Jack as a seaman. That was the trouble with the sea nowadays. You were constantly thinking of it in the terms of a bygone age. Take the phrase, 'The lass that loves a sailor.' It was as empty as the emptiest journalistic cliché. Had it ever been anything else, he wondered sourly? Had it ever been anything more than the landsman's feeble imagination working on a theme of which he had no knowledge, like the stage Irishman and the stage American in English comedies? Passengers inquiring archly if it were true that sailors had a wife in every port! Was it possible to change these misconceptions? He himself wanted to, but at times he had a feeling that it was impossible. The trouble was, it required the genius of an artist, and when a man had that he would inevitably transmute the reality into a new legend about seamen.

He heard Mrs. Bannister speaking. He looked at her in astonishment. She was actually remarking that possibly philanderers were easier to handle than romantics.

'You know where you are with them, anyhow,' she said.
'And you don't with romantics? That's true, I suppose.

What do you mean by handle? Keep them on a collar and chain? Drive them with a curb and snaffle?'

She flushed delicately and assumed that characteristic air. Her chin lifted and she looked at him with candid eyes.

'No,' she said, and looked down at her hands. 'Nothing of that. Only I am not always able to understand what you call noblest motives. She heard a movement in the other room and rose. 'Oh!' she said in a low, thrilling tone. 'Sorry I've talked so much about myself. You have been awfully decent. Do come to see me.'

'Of course. And take it easy, as they say over the water. I don't see you wilting like a lily. You know, I once saw your grandfather, close . . .'

'You? Where?'

'At Lord's Cricket Ground. He was playing for England against Australia. I was one of the crowd watching him going into the pavilion. He had made a century. I saw him plain, like the man who saw Shelley. I remember him too! A great experience!'

'For what? His appearance? Tall, of course!'

'For the character in his face. I thought of him as a sort of pro-consul! I don't know much about pro-consuls even now, but that gives you the impression he made on a young man. Well, you're his grand-daughter.'

'It doesn't follow, but I appreciate it. Perhaps you will tell me more. You seem to know so much.'

They moved toward the hall where the others were saying good-bye. Mr. Romaine was bidding Mrs. Deming farewell with much ceremony, and she was laughing very much indeed. Mr. Spenlove heard her high, bright voice saying how sweet it was of Perdita to ask them, and do come soon, soon . . . Father Soames and his sister, smiling

suavely, sidled out to their small car and crackled away
down the drive.

Upstairs, a half hour later, Perdita said, 'Come in.'

'I thought Sonia was in here,' Mr. Spenlove said, standing at the door.

'She's playing tennis tomorrow at Brandiston, so she
went to bed. What were you talking about to Mrs. Bannister? I mean, really.'

He told her. Perdita made a face.

'Then I suppose we'll be in at the death of another
romance. I'm sorry. I like her.'

'Don't be too hasty about the funeral,' he said, walking
across to his favorite chair. He did not, however, sit down.
He stood for a moment in thought, and then smiled. 'I promised we'd pay them a visit. Romaine might enjoy seeing the
country. He says he would much rather see Mrs. Deming.
He says they had a good talk. Do you know what he said
just now?' He lowered his voice. 'What he said about her?
He thinks she's refined.'

Perdita laughed. 'Well, isn't she? Of course I know how
a remark like that tickles you, you old ruffian. I hope he's
comfortable.'

'I looked in and he is. It is remarkable how the human
animal adjusts himself to any sort of environment. He's there
under the tester in that four-poster, looking like an eighteenth-century nobleman after a hard day at Newmarket.
And I was afraid he would feel a bit out of it all!'

'He made a remark about your life in that place, Costaragua, was it? You must explain it to me. Not now. I'm
sleepy.'

'I can explain anything,' he said smiling. 'I'm sleepy
too. We'll call it a day.'

WHAT did he say?' Mr. Spenlove inquired, at breakfast.

'It was while we were discussing how people change when they go to live in the tropics. Warm countries anyway. I said I used to wish it would snow or something, in Hollywood. Hot sun every day. That sort of thing. And those people you'd meet who'd hole up in Mexico for various reasons. Mr. Romaine said it was much worse in places where you had to find your own amusement. He knew people who made pets of snakes and ocelots. In Costaragua, I suppose. He said there was a place where they kept snakes to collect the venom. He said you thought it would have been a good idea in the Garden of Eden.'

Mr. Spenlove smiled and pulled his nose.

'That was where Jack Bannister holed up, as you express it. And the serpents weren't all in the serpentarium, I can assure you. Otherwise Jack mightn't be here at all. Yes, everything would have been different. He might still be in his Garden of Eden. As it was, I think it was all for the best.'

'I thought he was on those ships.'

'He was, but before he came to us he had been in the West African trade. As far as I could make out, from the few hints he let drop and the rumors my old friend Annie in Liverpool had picked up, when he got home from Alxandria that time and found his home in ruins, he went into a decline. Annie said he went back to London to get clearance papers from the Ministry of Shipping. When he got back to Liverpool he had what Annie called a breakdown. I think it was something like the one he had when I found him in his cabin, only worse. And he accused Annie of driving Roxane away and ruining his life.

'He had met Roxane in London. First he went to the Belgian family in Hatton Garden. They said she was living with a relation in Bloomsbury. He could see what kind of place it was as soon as he saw it. They may have been related, Roxane and the woman she lived with, but it was obvious to Jack and Roxane had been unfaithful to him. They had a furious quarrel. He wanted Roxane to return with him to Liverpool and she refused. Whether the man she ran away with had deserted her or was at sea, was never cleared up. What really mattered in Annie's view was Jack came back and had a breakdown.

'She said he lay on his bed for hours, his chest heaving, his body shaken by sobs. And he said she was responsible. He said she never understood Roxane. If it hadn't been for the lack of sympathy, she would never have gone away.'

'I can see that,' said Perdita slowly. 'It might have made all the difference.'

'It might, but Annie did the best she could. Finally Jack went to sea again, to West Africa. He got a job on the Niger River steamers. That was where he got his first dose of malaria, which came out again in Costaragua. There was some rumor about him and a nurse out there, but I never heard him say much. I do remember him saying the English girls in West Coast had no morality. As he put it, "Some of them were very immoral." Then he came home, and the ship was torpedoed, but he was saved with the other passengers. Then he signed on one of our new ships building in Glasgow.'

'Tell me about the native girl business,' Perdita said, 'the one you said he had a grand passion for.'

'That was in Puerto Balboa, in Costaragua. I mentioned the malaria. While he was chief of one of our ships he took sick and had to be taken ashore. They left him there. That was how he came to be around Puerto Balboa, a convalescent.'

'I never knew the girl's real name. We called her Chiquita. When Jack met her she was a nurse-girl, but she had lived most of her life in the Casa Raquel, a cantina house run by her aunt, or great-aunt, old Raquel. Everybody knew Chiquita, but everybody knew she was not one of the girls at Raquel's. Then she got a job taking care of Captain Berg's baby. Captain Berg was the Swedish harbormaster. Mrs. Berg was German. Chiquita was about sixteen, a pale gold color, and abnormally shy, considering where she had lived most of her life. Her hair was black, but if you saw it with the sun shining on it, there was a faint hint of rust in it. She was a sturdily built girl for her age and the single garment she wore, a cotton dress, rather short and without sleeves, showed what she was to anyone who wanted to look. And when she walked on the dock in the evening with other girls, there was a lot of looking.

'It was understood by everybody that old Raquel's niece was out of bounds. I heard discussions among our fellows, about what good it did the girl. According to our experts, she would be on the town eventually, so why not now? She had never looked at a man, until Jack came along, a convalescent. She would see him reading a paper in the little Plaza de Armas or along the sea-wall.

'The contrast between her and the regular professionals old Raquel got from the Canal Zone was shocking to the young fellows. One of ours remarked that it was like seeing a lovely lily, pure and spotless, growing in a garbage dump. If anyone had attempted anything the other girls would have ganged up on him and torn him to ribbons. So Chiquita, when she got this nursemaiding job, was unusually circumspect. Her routine was to take the baby in its perambulator, with the double mosquito screen tucked in all around it, to the park, and wheel it around for an hour or so. That was how she and Jack got acquainted. She would sit on a seat and read. And during the forenoon, they would have the place to themselves.'

Mr. Spenlove drank coffee and looked out of the breakfast room window, smiling.

'It might have been a private garden in a chateau on the Mediterranean. Or a villa in Ventimiglia,' he said. 'There was this low wall, and outside a lot of vast concrete blocks strewn around on which the long rollers smashed into irridescent spray against the sunlight. Far out there was a hard blue horizon. Behind the point, covered with palms, the harbor. All quiet and secret save for the endless crash of the seas, and the occasional scream of a cockatoo. It would have been strange if those two hadn't found each other under such favorable circumstances. The first time I saw them they were sitting on the same seat and the baby was asleep in the perambulator between them, invisible under the mosquito netting.

'I had been to the office and was taking in the park as a

refresher from the dust and heat of the port. I didn't recognize Jack at first. He was wearing a big native straw hat. If he hadn't looked up with that well-known who-the-hell-are-you expression, I wouldn't have paid any attention. A bummer working on a native girl, was what I thought, and let it go at that. I knew he had been in the hospital; but here he was, on the beach. We shook hands. The girl sat with her hands on her lap, one foot moving the baby's pram to and fro and looking at me with curiosity but quite without any self-consciousness. I suppose she had been so familiar with men coming and going all her life in the Casa Raquel, we seemed quite different from what we would have been to an English girl of that age.

'I made the usual remarks—what are you doing here? How long have you been out? When are you going back to New York? That sort of thing. He was very easy after he found I paid no attention to the girl. He introduced her. "This is Chiquita. She works for Mrs. Berg. That's Mrs. Berg's baby." I asked if Chiquita spoke English. She smiled and nodded. "Some," she said. Jack said, in his dictatorial way, "She speaks as much English as anybody else. Knows how to keep quiet too. More than some of ours do."

'This was praise from Sir Hubert and I said so. Jack gave me a sidewise look and stroked his mustache, as though he was wondering how far he could trust me. Then he said he might not return to the ships. I was thunderstruck. What did he plan to do? Go on the beach? Become one of these . . . ? He waved that away. "I think I've got a job here," he said. "In fact I know I have, as soon as the doc says I'm okay. I'm not okay yet." I said he looked pretty good. What was this job? Ah, that would be telling. He said I'd know soon enough.

'It was like Jack to take the line that I might sneak

176

up and snatch the job from him, if I knew of it. He even gave the girl a knowing look as if to say, see, I know how to handle these johnnies. She was so terribly young. You should have seen the way she looked at him. That told me all the story. I asked him if he made a habit of hanging around the park. He said he went there every day and what about it? Oh, I said, looking at the girl, don't let me keep you. I got up and offered him my hand. The best of luck, I said. He took my hand and after a moment, nodded. He didn't wish me the best of luck, you notice. I doubt if he ever got out of his own skin long enough to realize there were other people in the world beyond his own particular sacred circle. I wonder if he isn't the same now, after what his wife told me last night. I very much wonder what he's up to!'

'Doesn't she know, really?'

'Apparently not. As she says, he isn't a flirtatious chap. He doesn't pick up women. Don't laugh. I know he picked his first wife up out of the sea, and he must have, in a way, picked up this Chiquita in the park, and he picked that stewardess out of her tangle with the fat, rich and amorous passenger. He must have thought of this new wife of his as a brand plucked from the burning when he saw her at that Christmas party, when the genius was on the rampage. But I know what Candace meant when she said she believed he is faithful. He is probably faithful to this lofty conception of himself as a knight-errant. The point is, with whom is he being errant now?'

'Well . . .' Perdita said, holding out her hand for his cup.

'Well, as you say, I left him there and went on my way. I had my own problems and they excluded Jack and his new life. When we returned to Puerto Balboa we heard the news. Jack had this job on the construction gang of the new drainage canal they were digging into the bush. That sort of thing gets around like wild fire. The passion men have to be the first to tell a yarn about someone everybody knows! Talk about women being gossips! I sometimes think they are tongue-tied by comparison with the men I used to work with! My first assistant came rushing into my room as though the sheriffs were after him, to tell me about Bannister being on the beach. "Fancy, Chief! He's quit; he's got a job on the beach!" I said perhaps he liked the climate. I said it made a chance for everybody else to get his job on the *Sansovino*.

'More news came. Old Raquel was dead. She had had a stroke. The Casa Raquel was closed. There was a lot of glory-hole and messroom talk about what would happen to that kid she had in the house. The girls were all gone to the other houses, I was told by my assistant. No, he hadn't been there, but he had heard. The main fact was, the kid was gone. And Mrs. Berg had taken to walking in the Parque Colon with her baby herself.

'After this glut of small talk, we had a rest. Gossip on a ship is like will o'-the-wisp flares on a marsh. It gives no real illumination and it means nothing. I might have forgotten all about it if I hadn't met an old friend who worked in the hospital. She had come down with me and I had her at my table on her trip home for a vacation. A Miss Calhoun. She was in the commissary store and she wanted to know at once if I had brought her any perfume from Havana. I hadn't, but I promised to bring it next time. We went into a café for a gin rickey. Miss Calhoun was from Edinburgh. No, not a nurse. I would say she corresponded to a chief steward on a ship. She was in the procurement department. Very executive. Anyhow, she had a great tale to tell. Had I heard about Mister Bannister, the chief engineer of the *Sansovino*?

I said I had heard this and that, but what was it? She told me.

'She said I could have knocked her over with a feather when she heard about it. First there was the case of that old thing, Senora Raquel they called her, who was brought to the hospital unconscious. Stroke. She never rallied. To their consternation, Jack Bannister, who was about to be discharged, attended the funeral. There he was, among the girls from the house and some of the other citizens, and the young girl who was supposed to be a by-blow of the old woman's daughter, long dead. What did I think of such a thing?

'I had no idea at all. She said Jack suddenly appeared in a new role, construction engineer. Hospital people hear everything in a small place. The engineer who had been in charge of the big dredge had gone home after an accident, or at any rate he had been sick and then, as Miss Calhoun put it, he got sick of the job, or the country, or was homesick for the States.

'So there was our Jack in charge of the gang driving a big drainage ditch into the bush. First the track was laid and then Jack and his entourage followed and dug the ditch parallel to it. He was about three miles in the jungle at the moment. And what did I think about his morals? He had that young girl with him.

'I asked if they were married. She shook her head smartly. There was nothing grundyish about Miss Calhoun. She was reporting what happened. The priest had refused. Jack was a Protestant and the girl herself was a vague proposition to the Church. Miss Calhoun believed that Jack had not made any strong attempt to do much about it. I was sure of that, and said so. I said Jack was a very romantic man and the situation was tailored for his temperament. Having been at sea with him years ago, I knew him pretty well. Miss Calhoun said, "Weel, why don't ye go oop the line and pay him a veesit? They're leevin' in sin, and from what I've heard they're verra happy. She's cookin' for the gang, ye see, and . . ." '

'And of course you went,' Perdita said, smiling. 'It was right up your street, darling.'

'It was. As soon as I had a chance I got a ride with the inspector going up in his rail-car. I saw Jack in his new role of pioneer in the wilderness.'

'It's an extraordinary story,' Perdita said. 'I don't suppose his wife knows anything about it.'

'Well, he wouldn't speak of it to her, naturally. But don't forget, Jack is the sort of chap who fails to speak of things, not because he wants to hide them, but because it doesn't occur to him. He did tell her about the stewardess he married later, but not about Chiquita. It may be he felt it was too sacred to discuss. It had a tragic ending. But while it lasted Jack was the happiest man in the world.

'He had not hesitated for a moment when the old woman, old Raquel, died. He knew from Chiquita just what lay in store for her. She would have to take up the life of the rest of the girls, the life old Raquel and her own dead mother had lived. The family profession. Going to the company school and learning to read and speak English had changed her. And she and Jack were so in love she would have followed him on foot across the ranges. The construction company manager knew all the facts, and when he found that Chiquita was a good cook, she got the job. What went on out of office hours didn't concern him. He was in a hole and Jack, by taking the job, had got him out of it. In fact, he told Jack it seemed an ideal combination. Jack had his girl, he had an engineer and the fellows had a cook.

'Jack was earning twice what we were paid on the ships, and his girl was well paid too, for it was a desperate business to get any of that sort of worker to stay on the job more than one month, or one pay-day. Our fellows were always chattering about the big wages in the bush. The catch was, you had to sign a year's contract and there was a stiff forfeiture clause. You had to sign it in New York and get a medical certificate and so on, and then travel south in an inside cabin on Deck C.

'So I dropped off one morning and stood looking at Jack's little outfit. The dotted-swiss curtains caught my eye and I heard a girl singing to a radio. There was a wire strung from two rods on the roof of the car. Fifty yards away the shovel was making a growling, gurgling and smacking racket as it scrabbled another two tons of dripping muck and began to chuckle and groan as the wire ropes took the strain. The girl saw me through the door screen and came out. I asked her if she remembered me and she nodded, holding the door with one hand. Then she skipped down the steps and ran to the machine. She made a vigorous signal and Jack looked out to see what was up. Chiquita came back and made a sign that he would be coming. The crane swung round and dumped its load on the far side of the ditch. It swung back and the scoop plunged into the muck again and stopped. Jack, wearing huge leather gauntlets and sun-glasses, stepped down and came forward.

'He was tremendous! No other word for it, after seeing him for so long, at long intervals, in uniform, generally white. Now he was in soiled khaki, with a khaki helmet smeared with dried mud and grease. He wore high leather boots, and a wide belt on which he carried a large automatic in a leather holster. There was a change in his style too. He had taken on the pose of a frontiersman. He reminded me of one of Kipling's verses—"He shall desire loneliness, and his desire shall bring, hard on his heels a thousand wheels, a people and a king. He shall come back o'er his own track, and by his scarce-cooled camp, there he shall meet the roaring street, the derrick and the stamp." That was the impression he gave me. An empire builder! The derrick and the stamp were there all right and some of the thousand wheels. The people and the king would follow. Meanwhile Jack, with his big revolver and his stern jaw, was pinch-hitting for the king. I don't suppose he ever used that gun, but he had it and the others hadn't. When he had shaken hands with me, he put his arm around Chiquita's shoulders and we walked toward his caboose. I had the ridiculous notion that I was an explorer who had stumbled onto an unknown white kingdom in the bush!'

Perdita reached for a cigarette and struck a match. She looked at her husband over the flame, and he gained again the impression that she had the most marvelous eyes in the world, of the rarest color and intelligence.

'It sounds wonderful, the way you tell it,' she said. 'Romantic is the word, as usual.' She smiled. 'I understand now what you were getting at when you told Mr. Romaine about the Garden of Eden. Fig leaves and all!'

'I'm telling you exactly the way it was,' he insisted. 'We went into the caboose. It was a regular little cottage in the country. I mentioned the dotted-swiss curtains. There were pictures on the walls, cut from magazines. There was a sacred picture over the bed in the corner and a snowy mosquito bar hung on a steel frame all round the bed, so that it looked like a larger edition of the perambulator she used to

182

push around the park in Puerto Balboa. I mentioned this and Chiquita looked bashful. She even glanced at Jack for approval before she smiled. Jack didn't smile but he did not disapprove. We sat down and she got out a bottle and glasses.

'Jack said it would be six months work to finish the main ditch. They would then be thirty or more kilometers in the bush. He wasn't sure whether he would renew. The climate wasn't too good in the rainy season. They wouldn't be able to get ice regularly. And there were a lot of snakes around. This happened to be a ripe area for them. I asked, what kind of snakes? He looked at me for a moment before answering. The girl was coming with the bottle and glasses. He said in a low, warning tone, "Cascavels. I tell her . . ." he nodded to Chiquita, who was rinsing the glasses at a little sink. "I tell her never to leave the camp without those," He glanced up at a small pair of high boots hanging upside down on a thin wire from the ceiling. "Especially in the *potreros*," he went on. He reached out and took hold of her as she came forward and held her a moment, "Get that?" he said quietly. "Watch out for the cascavels, Chick." That was his diminutive for Chiquita.

'I said I thought those things belonged up country. Jack gave me a gloomy look and a nod. "Supposed to," he said. "A fellow was killed in a cane field near here not long ago. Died in three minutes."

'I steered the conversation away from *Crotalus Terrificus*, but not before Jack had shown me his portable medicine-chest with syringes, antiseptics, anti-venins, anti-toxins and so on, all ready to rush to the spot. He never traveled away from the rail without it, that and—he tapped his holster—his gun. I asked him if he was going to settle there. Had he given up the idea of returning to the Line? We had a drink while I was making these inquiries. He swallowed his and set the glass on the table. He said, if he could work it he would stay in Costaragua. It was a good life if you took care of yourself and let the booze alone. He said this was an occasion or he wouldn't have had a drink until evening, when he had a tot before bed. He patted Chiquita on the thigh— he had this! He gave me exactly the same look of superior condescension I had noticed that time in London, when he introduced me to Roxane. Chiquita looked down at her hands. She was sitting with her feet crossed, and her yellow house dress, her artificial silk stockings and her red shoes formed a composition. I mean an aesthetic composition. The passion those two had for each other was something you could feel in the atmosphere! But then'—Mr. Spenlove finished his coffee and took out a cigar—'with Jack it was always that way. That's why I am so curious as to what he's doing now. He's getting on, you know. He was over thirty then. Of course there was Casanova. . . .'

Perdita shook her head and began to rise. 'I have to go into Colchester,' she said. 'Want to come?'

'Gladly. We won't disturb Romaine. He didn't use to eat breakfast when he was at sea. Cup of coffee without milk or sugar. He'll be all right.'

Mr. Spenlove stood in the porch entrance and watched old Mr. Bobey puttering around under an immense straw hat. Perdita thought Mr. Bobey an excellent gardener. She said he had green thumbs. A crackle of tires on gravel accompanied the Virago as Perdita eased it around the corner between the high hedges. It never failed to impress Mr. Spenlove with its size and what he called capitalistic arrogance of demeanor. A haughty vehicle! He thought at times it was too large and expensive to keep up. The tax alone was nearly thirty pounds a year. However, it meant something to Perdita, and she handled it superbly. She said it gave her a feeling of superiority. What she really liked was that it was the very best of its kind. She said it out-lasted at least half a dozen cheap cars, and you had a first-class thing all the time. It was hers and she liked it. Mr. Spenlove got in beside her. One of these days, he said, he would buy a Baby Austin or Renault. Perdita thought such a vehicle would not be suitable. It would be undignified. The fact was, driving was not a hobby of his. He preferred to walk, and the trains from Marks Tey to London were convenient enough. He had found that he could not think while driving. He doubted if anyone could. It was destructive of cogitation, which might be the reason for its extreme popularity in America, he suggested. Perdita retorted that at any rate in America they knew how to drive, which was more than she could say for most Englishmen and all Englishwomen.

He liked to watch her and Sonia drive. They were both good. He got into the Virago.

'What sort of things are cascavels?' she asked when they reached the high road. 'Poisonous?'

'Extremely!' he said. 'Three minutes is all you have left if they get you. They're rattlesnakes which do very little rattling. In fact they give no warning at all, as a rule. Anti-Crotalic Serum very soon after the bite is the only chance, and you have a tough time even then for a while. I wonder if there were any in the Garden of Eden.'

'Oh, don't! she said, accelerating and passing a car in a flashing curve. 'I can't understand how you can call that place the Garden of Eden. That ditch-digging in a jungle.'

'It was, to him,' Mr. Spenlove said. 'He had a high-paid job; he was the boss of all he surveyed, he had a child-wife who was extraordinarily attractive, apart from her youth, who adored him, and who was, in addition, a good cook. Can you give me a better definition of Paradise?'

Perdita gave him her special smile, which wrinkled her nose. 'Go on,' she said, 'what happened?'

'Nothing for a while. Each day found them a few hundred yards farther from Puerto Balboa. That doesn't sound much, but it is not the same as living in one spot. I forget how long it was after my visit that I saw Jack again. He had come in on business, pay-roll probably. I went into the hotel bar and he was there, a foot on the rail, khaki shirt and riding breeches, big revolver in the holster and a large Western hat on the back of his head. When he saw me he gave me his usual look of which I've spoken. I dare say I don't describe it very well. It was as if he were saying to himself: "This chap! I've been stuck with him half my life and he keeps turning up, and I can't avoid him. No sense in being rude, but there's something queer about him for all that. How he keeps his job is just one of those mysteries. . . . Must have pull with the shore people."

'He was friendly enough. Shook hands and asked the usual questions. How are the pumps? Any smashes? etc. I suppose he felt superior. He had been my chief long ago and now he was making twice my wages. Would I have a drink? The way he said it was like a friendly slap on the jaw. I was interested in his new adventure. I said I would have a drink. He introduced me to the other man, a Mr. So-and-so, of the construction corporation. After Mr. So-and-so had gone away I asked Jack how Chiquita was making out. He said Chick was okay. Did he leave her alone in the camp? Oh, no, he said, she was in town now.

'That was his way. He would never come straight out with a statement about his own affairs. She was okay, but I

186

had to put another question to bring out the fact that he had brought her to town with him to see the doctor. What was the matter with her? He said she was all right, at present. Well, I supposed it was a general check-up, preventive measures, something like that, eh? He stood erect, pushing out his upper lip and looking down at the small mustache he had been cultivating. Now and again he would rock back on his heels. I went on looking at him. He was evidently coming down with another case of adolescent pride in his virility and power over women. Finally he told me that she was expecting. I asked him why he hadn't said so at first. I congratulated him. She would have to go to the hospital for that, of course. He said he was making all arrangements. We had another drink to celebrate his future paternity and I went off on my business. He made no offer to take me along or upstairs in the hotel, to see his girl, and I let it go at that.'

Perdita drove on without speaking for a moment. Then she said their little friend's husband was probably fretting because of the quiet life one always led in the country in England. What had we, to compare with what he had in Costaragua? The best way would be, in Perdita's opinion, to persuade him to go to sea again.

Mr. Spenlove nodded. 'You've said it!' he remarked. 'That may be the solution. Yes!'

'It's your idea,' she said, slowing down for the traffic in the High Street. 'You've often said that marriages of sailors were preserved in brine.'

'I've known them preserved in alcohol too,' he said. 'Where 're you going to put up?'

'The Cups, as usual. If I leave this thing at the curb the kids climb all over it and the policeman makes remarks about parking. It's only a bob at the Cups.'

'It's too early for a bottle of stout,' he remarked. 'Or

I'd wait for you there. I think I'll drop around to Ancient House. He may have picked something up for me. In Foyles.'

'You'll have that study of yours so full of books you won't have room to sit in it,' she pointed out. 'I won't be more than a quarter of an hour. A little more, possibly.'

Mr. Spenlove, walking along to a shop right out of the Middle Ages, its upper story hanging over the sidewalk and bulging with elaborately carved bow-windows, pondered the ease with which Perdita achieved common sense without ever seeming to be aware of it. It was a thoroughly sound suggestion she had made. He was concerned about that girl, Candace. She had quality. She had character. That might be the trouble. Jack was a knight-errant out of a job there!

And yet she insisted that he was "faithful." It appeared, from her attitude, that she could handle a case of infidelity; almost that she would have preferred it to the present situation. What was the bloody fool up to? Mr. Spenlove wanted to know, exasperated. He liked to see through people, and Jack had had a trick, all his life, of being partially opaque, of keeping the omniscient Spenlove guessing at what was going on inside.

The senior salesman, a gray, precise person, with that peculiarly detached manner old booksellers preserve toward their merchandise, and even on occasion toward their patrons, watched Mr. Spenlove scanning rapidly the mounds of bright, shiny new fiction as he walked through the shop. The Ancient House did not, of course, deal in pornography, but there were small houses in New York and Chicago publishing special illustrated editions of special authors, from Juvenal to Joyce. Very often the illustrations were by absolutely first-rate artists, and the pictures were the feature of the edition. They fetched a nice price in sterling. The old gentleman knew Mr. Spenlove was in the market mainly for

188

memoirs of old seamen, and anything about London, from Stowe to Besant, but he held up a large volume to show it. 'Ever read this?' he whispered.

'Curiosa?' Mr. Spenlove inquired, smiling. 'Suetonius, eh?' 'Yes, I have read him.' He turned the pages and looked at a drawing of an emperor torturing birds and mice by putting them in a cage with a snake, while a grim matron held a nude frightened virgin by the wrist in the background. 'Not for me,' he said, still turning the pages. 'He was just an old gossip and scandalmonger. I wouldn't hang a cat on his evidence. First-rate pictures, I grant you. Remember that story of Tiberius, was it? Swimming with small boys? Oh, no! Got anything in my line?'

The old gentleman offered a bright, shiny-blue pamphlet. It was "The Channel Lights, in Hexameters, With Some Sonnets on the Most Famous Lighthouses." Mr. Spenlove took it, and noted the price, three bob.

'Fancy grinding out all this! Passed the time on watch, I suppose.' He looked into it. 'Thames lights too. Right, I'll take it. What's this? More curiosa?'

'Autobiography of an English sailor. Seventeenth century. Claims he had a wife in every port.'

'How many ports?'

'Quite a few. A Suffolk man.' The gray, precise person showed the title page. Mr. Spenlove, his attention captured, and some private thought making his eyes sparkle for a moment, took the small volume to the light. The print was small and the paper stained. He read:

The Perilous Adventures, By Sea and Land, of John Lushington, of Aldeburgh, in the County of Suffolk, Of The Several Adventures By Sea, With the Dangers, Difficulties and Cruel Hardships, and the Many Deliverances Enjoyed in Numerous Havens, Where were Safe Anchorages and Careenings For Which

*I Have Cause to Give Thanks unto God. Also an Account of
the Time I was taken Prisoner by a Female Potentate in Algiers,
Who made me Her Vizier, to my Great Glory.*

'Careenings, eh! I suppose that's a euphemism.'

The bookseller would not offer an opinion about that,
but he saw the point and his features might be said to relax
a little. Mr. Spenlove said he would take it.

'Every port, you said?' he remarked, and the other man
said, 'Practically. Not legally, though. Lady-friends.'

Mr. Spenlove went off up the street to The Cups. He
felt he could do with a Guinness now, while he examined his
purchase. It was easier for those people to get things for
him than to spend days, himself, covered with dust, in
Foyles.

Here, in the great yard of The Cups, approached through
an immense archway suitable for mail coaches, he thought
was something not only genuinely English and Dickensian,
but belonging to Europe. A groom was whistling through his
teeth as he worked on a carriage horse. Another minion was
polishing a tremendous Daimler. The Virago stood between a
couple of baby Austins. There was also an ancient Rolls,
with elaborate carriage lamps, a gleaming brass radiator and
with gilt flower-vases inside, shining as if it had just come
from a showroom. It was marvelous how the English maintained their traditions of back-breaking menial labor.

He went into the private bar and ordered stout. The
extraordinary thing, he reflected, was that it seemed impossible to create this atmosphere in America. He had
noticed it over and over again while he lived there. They
called their places taverns, inns and 'lounges,' but they could
never introduce the peculiar quality of the bar-parlor or a
good private bar. The privacy of the public-house was beyond their powers. He liked it. It symbolized for him the

great permanence of the national character, as the outdoor café did for France.

Perdita's brash young brother, Tad, who was doing so well in London as an advertising consultant, wanted to sweep all this away. He thought Sir Oswald Mosley had brought a new Ten Commandments back from Rome. He thought Mr. Spenlove was a hidebound old reactionary, a Bourbon and a Tory, because he believed England would outlast a few pip-squeak neo-Fascists in Fleet Street. Mr. Spenlove had once quoted Emerson's great words on England, and the young man had pretended to faint from nausea. They now avoided each other. It was understood that Mr. Spenlove and those who had his antique notions would be the first to be liquidated when Sir Oswald and his cohorts took over.

He began to read the book he had bought. The allusion to wives in every port had given him the idea that this autobiography of a Suffolk seaman might be about a predecessor of Jack Bannister. It took a strong hold on his sardonic imagination. Seamen, he believed, were all the same, no matter where or when you found them.

John Lushington, of Aldeburgh, in the county of Suffolk, wrote in a style usual with illiterate men in the seventeenth century. There was nothing of Swift, Pepys, Dryden or Sir Thomas Browne about it. Mr. Spenlove thought he had probably never heard of those gentlemen, though Browne had not been far away. The structure of his sentences showed he really did suffer the agonies of composition, and conveyed those agonies to the reader. Strange how men, whose life demanded that they react instantly to circumstance, squirm and wriggle when they take pen in hand. Lushington had gone to sea in a hoy at the age of twelve.

Perdita came in briskly and sat down beside her husband

in the bar-parlor. 'How is it, ducky? Find anything good?' Like many impractical women, she could shop with speed and efficiency and get it over while real housewives were gaping in store windows.

He showed her the book and told her his theory, that it had been written by Jack Bannister in a former existence. Perdita waited while the bar-maid brought her a claret and soda.

'Sounds interesting,' she said, sipping. She knew he would have some reason for making such a remark. She glanced at the open page. 'Taken prisoner by a female potentate, hm. Is that what you mean?'

'You get the point,' he said, nodding. 'Making allowance for the two periods in history, and so on. Jack probably thinks of himself now as a prisoner.'

'Oh, how can you!' Perdita laughed a little. 'She's a lovely person. And I like her mother. Do you know Mrs. Deming's simply crazy to go and live in America again? Wouldn't you think she'd know when she was well off?'

'Perhaps she does. Old Romaine is really keen to get back to New York. He's only stopping now until he can get his passage changed to the *Berengaria*. He has just heard that an old friend of his is her chief steward. Saturday week.'

'He's having a good time, don't you think? Sonia says he plays croquet like a champion, now he's learned the rules. He's getting younger every day.'

'I hope we see Jack, you know, before Romaine goes. I'd like to have his reaction. Romaine's, I mean.'

'From what Mrs. Bannister said we can't count on it. Mr. Romaine wants to go, but not to see Mr. Bannister. He thinks Mrs. Deming a charming person. So do I. That's why it seems so strange to me she would even think of going back to live in America.'

'I'm not too sure about that. From what her daughter told me about their life there, Mrs. Deming isn't the true-blue British matron you imagine. It's her own affair, however. It's old Jack I'm intrigued with. I try to figure him out, what he's like now and what he's up to, and I get nowhere.'

'You may get a hint from that book,' Perdita said, good-humoredly, nodding at it as it lay open on Mr. Spenlove's knee.

'I'm not so sure,' he admitted, taking out a cigar. He finished his stout and lit the cigar slowly and with care. 'We can tell better when we've been over to see his wife.'

Perdita rose. He followed her out to the yard. It was all very well for him to say that his curiosity was aroused by the Bannisters, but there would be no fun if he could not share it with this woman of his. She was a marvelous person, he thought. The old-fashioned phrase, that she had made him the happiest of men, seemed to express the actual truth. But of course, he had always been happy in the deeper sense. Looking back now, he saw that with clarity. Perhaps it was only in such rare cases that a woman was successful! No woman, he thought, had ever made Jack happy in his spirit. If Candace couldn't, it was impossible. It gave him a pang to face this fact. He admired that young lady so much.

He said so as Perdita drove slowly out of Colchester. 'You couldn't imagine a finer person,' he mused. 'I had a long talk with her and she confirmed my early opinion. Fine character.'

'Yes,' Perdita said, nodding. 'It begins to look as if we are taking her side.'

'We don't know his side,' he pointed out. 'We haven't the Recording Angel's advantages.'

'You call them advantages?' she said lightly. 'I'd hate to have *his* job.'

'Because you have an angelic nature,' he informed her. 'The angels keep away from him, I am certain.'

'They don't take sides either, ducky,' Perdita said with emotion. Now and again she had a sudden sharp memory of what she went through in Hollywood. *Safe; I'm safe!* she cried silently, and thankfully dismissed the past for the present.

It was there as she swung the car into the narrow road leading to Layer-de-la-Pole. Sonia was riding on her bicycle and looking over her shoulder at Mr. Romaine, also on a bi-cycle, who was proceeding slowly, with an occasional wobble. At the tap of the horn he dismounted and stood to let the car pass. Mr. Spenlove was amazed.

'I didn't know you could ride a bike, Romaine,' he said.

'Not so sure I can either, after all these years,' that gentleman said. He wiped his brow. 'Too much top-hamper now.'

'All right,' Perdita said. 'Come along. We're late for lunch, already.' She drove slowly past the two cyclists.

'How do you account for those two getting on so well?' Mr. Spenlove said. 'Attraction of opposites? You can't imagine any two human beings with backgrounds more different.'

'Well, Sonia's very intelligent, as you may have noticed. Then, she is naturally agreeable to older people. And do you know what she says? She says she's really an extrovert, but she gets very fed up with it at school. She means com-munity team-work and being one of the crowd. So, for a change, she likes it here.'

'Esprit de corps? She'll do old Romaine good.'

He went to his study and laid his purchases on the table. The narrative of Master John Lushington opened at a page which caught Mr. Spenlove's eye. He sat down and read it.

The sentence continued over to the next page, which was uncut. He cut it.

> Our lodging was a dark dungeon in a castle hard by the palace of the sultana, whereby we had sight of her when she went abroad with her women and eunuchs. Here, as we lay in shackles made fast to a great chain, one of our number made a great cry, so that she, hearing it, turned aside and came to the great door of the prison. Whereupon the gaoler, making obeisance, told her that we were no more than wild beasts; but she, being a woman, was not to be denied and demanded that he bring forth one of the beasts for her satisfaction. By chance when the fellow came among us took hold of my person and ordered the blakamoor to unshackle me and bring me forth. Thus it was I came into the presence of the sultana, a most comely and well-favored female. . . .

He skipped a few paragraphs to where the prisoner was taken from the chain-gang and made a gardener in the sultana's private seraglio. No longer terrified by the enormous chinches and other vermin of the dungeon, rid of his lice by the slaves, and given fresh clothing, the young man from Aldeburgh, thin as a rake from his diet of bread and water with some horse beans and olives, took on a new lease of life, waxing fat on the fresh fruits and rich meats, dates and goat flesh he had from the sultana's kitchen. He became, he said, extremely goodly in appearance and the sultana commanded him, when she walked in the gardens, to give her lessons in English. Which he was very glad to do, whereupon he was given quarters in the steward's house, and being quick at accounts, soon had a place made for him in the treasurer's offices.

Mr. Spenlove glanced ahead again and then smiled, closing the book. Master Lushington was a smug narrator of his own success with the sultana. So, far from fleeing and leaving his garment behind, he regarded himself as a benefactor, teaching the poor heathen lady the elements of English grammar and lovemaking.

Mr. Spenlove laid the book aside for the time being. He thought it might be of use to him in the work he was doing, or getting ready to do, but it was stretching things a little to see Jack Bannister as a modern John Lushington. There was nothing of the knight-errant in the earlier John. He voyaged about the seas of the world seeking what he called divers entertainments. There was no thought in his head of rescuing anybody save himself.

CHAPTER

9

MRS. PRICE came down to lunch and said she had nearly finished her number for the week. It was her custom to seclude herself wherever she might be, until her "number" was ready for the post, to be sent to her special typist in London. She would then relax, and when at Layer-de-la-Pole, beam on the others. As Mr. Spenlove put it to Perdita, one would think she was purring like a cat who had safely disposed of a canary.

Perdita now inquired how many more numbers she had to do to complete her current serial. Mrs. Price said it all depended on the editor and how the story was coming out with the news agents. He might want it cut and another started, or he might want her to add a number. It didn't matter. She had plenty of ideas.

'You're fortunate,' Mr. Spenlove said. 'I'm just the opposite. I often sit for hours and have no ideas at all. Only other people's ideas. I have plenty of *them*.'

'You're fortunate too,' Mrs. Price said, much amused and not a bit offended by the suggestion that her ideas were pilfered from other writers. 'Very fortunate. You don't have to get a number out every week, old boy.'

'I doubt if that is the whole story,' Mr. Spenlove said, shaking his head. 'You wouldn't do it if you didn't enjoy it. I have been exceptional, I suppose, but in my experience, people never act as they do in fiction. Your fiction, anyway. I read that last serial, you know, just to get some hints.'

'You're wrong. They do. Nowadays they do.' Mrs. Price gave a hearty laugh. 'They've read so many stories they unconsciously imitate the stories in their lives. Read the papers, my boy, and see if I'm not right.'

'Oscar Wilde had that theory,' Mr. Spenlove admitted. 'Very neat. The London fogs imitated Whistler's etchings and nocturnes. I used to wonder, myself, sometimes, whether Brooklyn weather near the docks hadn't been imported from Hollywood, where it always rains in tragic scenes. I doubt if you could make it stick on my level of thinking.'

Mrs. Price inquired what that might be. He told her what they had been saying about the Bannisters. Perdita took up the tale. Mrs. Price was at once alert to the possibilities of the situations.

'I suppose she'll find him in another woman's arms,' she said. Sonia laughed and Mr. Spenlove guffawed. It was Mrs. Price's solution for all secondary crises in a serial. Sonia laughed again and went back to the *Morning Post*, which was propped against the cruet. She was lunching on dry toast and milk, because of the tennis.

Perdita said that was just what she wouldn't do if they understood her correctly. Mrs. Bannister insisted that while she thought he was seeing someone in London, he was not unfaithful.

Mrs. Price looked as if the foundations of her profession

198

were giving way under her feet. She shook her handsome head slowly and continued with her lunch.

'Come, come!' Mr. Spenlove said. 'You surely don't imagine you can explain everything that happens to humanity by sexual irregularities, do you?' Mr. Romaine kept his eyes on his plate. He knew old Spenlove when he was in this mood. He could floor a Congressman. In fact Mr. Romaine had heard Mr. Spenlove tell a Congressman off on one occasion and shut him up too. That had been in the good old days of Prohibition. The Congressman and his fellow junketeers had been set on shore during a special call, ostensibly for fuel, at Norfolk, Virginia, with their wardrobe trunks filled with case-goods from Cuba. No change to be had out of old Spenlove.

'Tell us the tale, old boy,' Mrs. Price said, comfortably. 'I know you're dying to.'

'That's not the point,' he observed. 'You're dying to hear it. Right? You see? Well, here we have this neighbor of ours, a charming young lady, whose husband, we are led to believe, is estranged.'

'Isn't he?' Mrs. Price demanded.

'How do we know? Estrangement isn't as simple as you make it in your stories. I suppose you have to simplify in the interests of art, but . . .'

'It's in the interests of the public,' Mrs. Price said. 'They aren't quite bright, very often; they wouldn't catch on to *your* ideas, my boy. Black has to be black and white as dazzling as you can make it. There isn't anything vague about estrangement in *their* lives! Art be blowed, if you'll excuse the unparliamentary language.'

'Well, she has the idea that he is tired of the whole business, doesn't like the quiet of country life after his exciting existence at sea and in the tropics. There is a bit of tropical love in the story too, you understand, and while she, Mrs. Bannister, doesn't know much about that part of it, she has a general suspicion that Jack Bannister doesn't fit into country gentry life. That's the set-up, as the Americans say. There's nothing, so far as we know, to go on. No home-wrecker to be identified. How would you work that out?'

'Why, it's as plain as the nose on your face. Reconciliation.'

'Yes, but how? When you don't know what he's up to?'

'Mother would bring in a Handsome Detective,' Perdita said. 'Mrs. Bannister sees an advertisement for private inquiry agents. She writes, or telephones, and the H.D. arrives and gets the particulars of the case. How would that do, Mother?'

'It wouldn't do at all, ducky,' said Mrs. Price. 'How would you bring about a reconciliation if you have a handsome detective? She's supposed to be reconciled with her husband. No, we would have a very plain detective, a rough diamond who has lived in the tropics, catching emerald thieves in the mines, you know, and he has met her husband, and knows of a heroic action, where he rescued the detective's sweetheart from bandits. Oh, yes, it works out beautifully. I may use it, yes . . .'

Mr. Spenlove roared with laughter. Sonia, looking from one to the other, smiled.

'You have a fertile imagination. What's the use of my telling you the story? You know a better one.' Mr. Spenlove shook his head, as though he was licked.

'Don't be silly,' Mrs. Price said. 'I really want your version.'

'It isn't my version. It's what happened to Jack when I knew him, a long time ago.' He gave Mrs. Price some of the early facts of the Mediterranean period, when Jack made off to look for his wife.

'That was his first,' he explained. 'He's had several, you must remember. One lasted a short time only. A stewardess we had. We used to call her the Blonde Venus.'

'You're making it terribly complicated,' Mrs. Price said. She handed her coffee cup to Perdita. 'Is he one of these promiscuous lads? Glad eye for every pretty face?'

'You aren't even warm,' Mr. Spenlove said. 'He is rather an ascetic type, really. I know it sounds odd, but I sailed with him and knew him well enough, and there's nothing promiscuous about Jack. Quite the opposite, in fact. He has a knight-errant streak in him.'

'Come off it! I never heard of a knight-errant with a wife and children.' Mrs. Price chuckled and looked at Sonia with affection and amusement. She was enjoying herself.

'That's because you've always lived such a sheltered life,' Mr. Spenlove said. 'The knight-errant business in England is reserved for bachelors. That's the tradition. Jack is romantic. A knight-errant has to be. I happen to be familiar with three episodes in his life and in each case he has gone all out to rescue the girl from a desperate situation.'

'And you think that's what he's doing now?'

'I'm not sure. I didn't offer to tell the future. It is the past I know about.'

'People change when they get older,' Mrs. Price said sagely. 'And circumstances alter cases. Don't you agree? I mean, if this friend of yours has been living in the country, he must have a bit. That changes people, having a bit.' She looked at Mr. Spenlove with more attention. 'It isn't his wife's money, is it?'

'I suppose that gives you another idea,' he said. 'I really don't know. I could make estimates, of course. I know how long Jack has been with us in the Line and what he made. He had a good screw for years and had nothing to spend it on and so he may have had what you call a bit. His wife told me he had losses when stocks tumbled. Yes, she told me that. I remember being surprised because I hadn't associated Jack with investments. Jack was the sort of Britisher who would send his money home to a bank in England, and let it lie, at one per cent, for years. Seems he didn't. What do you think, Romaine? Ever hear anything about Jack's bank?'

Mr. Romaine, without looking up from his plate, shook his head.

'He never had any money to speak of,' he said in a low tone. He cleared his throat and seemed to concentrate. He shook his head again in finality. 'Fellows used to talk a lot about stocks then. Not Jack. Never joined in when the fellows talked about buyin'. He had some insurance one of the office men sold him.'

'I remember that chap,' Mr. Spenlove said. 'He sold me a policy too. You may be right about Jack. Yet I don't see him saying he had losses if he didn't. But that's the trouble with all of us. We magnify losses. We even invent them if it gives us any feeling of importance. Of course,' he said to Mrs. Price, 'I'm speaking of seamen. Shore people never exaggerate.'

'All men are liars,' Mrs. Price said calmly. 'All landsmen, at any rate.'

'There you are. I was speaking of exaggeration, though. And Jack wasn't an exaggerator in that sense. What he exaggerated was his own significance in the world outside himself. That's a rather pompous way of putting it. We can say his life was a romance in which he was the hero. But when he came back to England and tried to live the life of a country gentleman, he probably found it wasn't in his way, after all. Especially when it was largely, you may say, a matriarchy he had to live in.'

'Henpecked?' Mrs. Price said.

'Not for me to say,' Mr. Spenlove said in a hollow tone. 'I was referring to the fact that there is, in addition to his wife and his mother-in-law, Mrs. Deming's aunt, who makes her home with them at Moat Farm. Three women, relatives. A matriarchy. In fact, I think it's the aunt's home. She's an Enderby. It's theirs when she goes.'

'That would be pretty rugged for him,' Mrs. Price admitted. 'It makes a difference. He may have simply run away!'

Mr. Spenlove was amused, but he nodded his head in agreement.

'Still,' he reminded the world at large, 'we're guessing. I was going to tell you how this all came up. It happens I knew Jack when some of those present were not yet born. That was in 1915. Twenty years ago.'

'Perdita was telling me about that,' Mrs. Price said.

'Well, Jack turned up in America. At that time seafaring men, officers, were at a premium. Anyone with credentials who applied for work in New York was taken on at once. But Jack arrived on a new ship. He burst into my cabin down in Puerto Balboa to borrow some calcium chloride. Jack had never been in the American-style ships before and he found himself caught with a leaky brine-tank just as he was sailing from New York. Lost a lot of brine and used all his reserves. I gave him a couple of drums of the stuff and he told me a long tale of woe about his juniors, who were no good. He had seven of them, and according to him there wasn't one he could trust. He was excited and on the jump, full of suspicion because he was new to the peculiar atmosphere of

America. He called Americans Yanks. He said he hadn't been out of his overalls the entire trip south. I told him he would find things easier if he didn't interfere too much. I even asked him how he thought the other chiefs managed. They had the same sort of men. I expect he had got his crowd into a thoroughly ugly state of mind. And why spill it to me? I couldn't do anything for him. I got on all right. He could tell it to the boss in New York.'

'When was this?' Mrs. Price said.

'Why, it must have been some time in the twenties. Jack was a new broom. He had a new set of juniors every trip. The superintendent finally suggested he go a bit easy. They didn't care about such a high labor turnover. Jack seemed to demand lofty standards of perfection. One of his rejects came to me as first assistant and I found him all right. It wasn't safe to get him onto the subject of his late chief, however. He told me the engine-room was like a madhouse. I knew what he meant. I had been through the same thing but I didn't mention it.

'Jack got into the way of it after a while. When he came to see me that first time he had on a rather soiled suit of whites and his hands were stained with oil and dirt, and he even had a streak on his face. He still had at that time the British mechanic's conviction, that unless you were smothered in grease you weren't really working. He disdained gloves, another British prejudice. Imperceptibly he got out of these insular customs and began to see some good in other men. Not much, but a little. Then he discovered that he could get himself dressed and go top-side, and even have his dinner in the saloon with passengers to talk to. That made another great difference in his life. It was a step forward when he could sit through a meal without suddenly jumping up and rushing down into the engine room to find fault because of a flicker in the lights. He was on his way to becoming quite a regular, civilized person when he got a touch of his African malaria again and went into the hospital down in Puerto Balboa, Costaragua.'

'Was he in Africa?' Mrs. Price said. 'I have a brother there.' Mr. Spenlove smiled at the phrase. It was as though, to Mrs. Price, Africa was about the size of the Isle of Wight. 'He has a cocoa plantation. I can't bear cocoa, but that's what they do out there.'

'I don't think Jack was in cocoa,' Mr. Spenlove said. 'River steamer, I fancy. It doesn't matter. All he brought back was a touch of this malaria.'

'You know, ducky,' Mrs. Price said, 'your friend sounds to me like one of those johnnies who have adventures every-where. I bet you tuppence he had an affair with a nurse out in Africa.'

'It's possible,' Mr. Spenlove said. 'He never said much about it. But don't imagine Jack is the Lothario type. He's rather austere in his standards. It is his high standard of chivalry which gets him into these things. Remember the Blonde Venus, Romaine? The stewardess who was having trouble with a passenger. The old boy was trying to pull her onto his knee. Right in front of a lot of us in the palm court. Remember?'

'He didn't have to marry her,' Mr. Romaine said.

'You or I wouldn't, but Jack has unusual standards.'

'You think he is being chivalrous and all that over some woman in London?' Mrs. Price inquired. Mr. Spenlove nodded.

'We'll cross that bridge when we get to it,' he said. 'He rescued his first wife, Roxane; he rescued the stewardess, the Blonde Venus, and married her, and he rescued Candace Deming and married her.'

'What did he rescue *her* from, I'd like to know?' Mrs. Price folded her napkin and lit a cigarette. 'A fate that was worse than death?'

'It's a bit more complicated than that. You have to know what sort of man he was when he was ashore in Costaragua. Remember he rescued another girl there. He didn't marry her, but he lived with her. It's my belief he'd be living with her still if he hadn't had bad luck.'

Mrs. Price blew out some smoke and sat back looking hard at her son-in-law. 'I thought you said he was austere,' she said.

'He was, and probably still is.'

'That makes four, and you seem to think he may have had another adventure in Africa. What austerity!'

'It was your idea in the first place. If you can go back in thought to those days, you'll remember it was the era of economic and social independence of the women. They began to smoke in public, to make up, not in public as they do now, but to use cosmetics and lipstick. I have often remarked that after the war young virgins first began to make up their faces and expose their limbs as courtesans would do when working at their profession. Not in private. The courtesan was demure, discreet, and intensely respectable when off duty. The virgin was a raging exhibitionist in public. Jack was a very austere and prudish chap in some ways. I told you he was always getting into his emotional crises because he was rescuing girls from their misfortunes. The girls whom he saw behaving in what he called an immoral manner didn't want to be rescued. The Lost Generation were enjoying their new liberty very much and didn't care what he thought of them.'

'It sounds simple, the way you explain it, old chap, but

what about the rescue in that place you mentioned, Costa-ragua?'

'Let us go on the terrace,' Mr. Spenlove said. Perdita was already there, arranging the chairs and tables. Mrs. Price said to Mr. Romaine that the Lost Generation was a lot of hokey-pokey, in her opinion. What did he think?

'Never was any good at riddles,' he said.

'You put the problem the wrong way around for Romaine,' Mr. Spenlove said, when he had lit a cigar. 'He's seen plenty of them in his time on the cruises. Eh, Romaine? Remember that trip when some practical joker found where the main switches were for the promenade and boat deck? At two in the morning the entire ship, on a dark moonless night, was suddenly flooded with light. Quite a show, I heard. Those people, caught flagrante delicto, were members of the Lost Generation. They weren't all young, either.

'It was a period of change. A period of adjustment. And Jack didn't keep in step. He never really liked the modern girl. I have a suspicion that when he got a touch of fever again and had to go into the hospital in Puerto Balboa, he didn't mind at all. My friend, Miss Calhoun, in the administration office of the hospital, had the right idea about Jack. She said he was a true Britisher. "He was always ready to take up the White Man's burr-den, if the burr-den was a female." '

'He didn't dress for dinner in the bush, did he?' Mrs. Price wanted to know. 'They tell me that's the sign of British character.'

'White drill. That's the tropical formal attire. I had dinner with him. I wouldn't stress that point! Jack wasn't a pukka sahib in that sense. He came from another class, or I wouldn't be so interested in him.

'Jack came aboard, the trip after I met him in the bar. Not to see me, but the ship's surgeon. He wanted something the local hospital didn't have. I was surprised he took the trouble to come down to my cabin. We had a drink and a chat. As he was leaving, he said suddenly, "Why don't you come out and have supper? The car will bring you back if you have to be aboard tonight." I said I must certainly be aboard, but I'd be glad to come. I took the liberty of saying he must be hard up for company if he had to come to me. He said he was never hard up for company. He said it was Chicky who had the idea. He said she had an idea I was a doctor, on account of my beard, but he got that out of her head. She talked about me and asked when I was coming again. So there it was. Women were queer creatures, he thought. They got strange ideas into their heads. I told him not to apologize. The truth was, you know, I had noticed her in the past.'

'Where?' Mrs. Price said. 'I thought you said . . .'

'In the Casa Raquel,' Mr. Spenlove told her mildly. 'I remember the first time. I had three women from a town named Crackersburg or some such place at my table. They belonged to what I called the groundgripper class. One was a widow. She was in partnership with the other two, spinsters, in a successful florist business they had just sold to a chain operating in the Middle West. They were traveling at leisure. I suppose they were between forty and fifty, good fellows socially, perfectly independent of men in every way. If they took liquor, I never knew it. They didn't smoke either. They wore sensible clothes, and merely spoke guardedly among themselves when the young girls took to the sun-deck almost nude. They played deck games very well. They read sound books. They had a lot of stuff about the places we were going to visit, Havana, Kingston, Canal

208

Zone, and all the rest of it, and they were going to "do" every country except Spain, for which they couldn't get a visa. They were going to "do" Puerto Balboa too. No place too small for them to take a tourist interest in. They had bags of golf-clubs with them and they had the fresh, wholesome, weathered complexions of naval officers.

'I warned them Puerto Balboa didn't have many facilities for tourists and it would be better to get the purser to advise them. They had done that and he had said the place was "Impossible—nothing to see, nowhere to go. Better stay on board until you get to the Canal Zone." I agreed with the purser, and said so, but these ladies insisted that as they could see the sailors going on shore and evidently going somewhere they wanted to go and see for themselves. Would I go with them?

'They had an immense curiosity about what went on in such a place. They had read a lot of novels and they had decided to find out if the novels were true to life. Take that book Somerset Maugham had written, or was it a story? They had seen a movie of it called "Rain." They had seen a play on it. Was that sort of thing to be seen in a tropical port? Then that book, The Moon and Sixpence. And White Shadows on the South Seas. They didn't want to go to see standardized tourist attractions. They wanted to look on at the real life of beachcombers and sailors. They had their cameras and were all set.

'The only thing I could think of was to take them along to the Commissary bar in the hope that some whiskered beachcomber might be on view. It was after dinner before they were really ready to go ashore. The heat in the afternoon had done for them. We left the cameras behind and took a walk. First there is the jetty, where the local residents walk for the breeze in the evening. I mean the respectable

Costaraguan residents. Particularly when a ship is in. They would come on board if their men were connected with the port. They would sit in the smoke-room and drink soft drinks. It was their one contact with northern life.'

'There is a long dusty stretch outside the dock gates lined with small grog-shops and warehouses. There's a small plaza with the inevitable equestrian statue of Bolivar. Then you come to the main street. The hotel is there, and the commissary. Away to the right is the park I spoke of, where Jack met his girl, behind a row of houses standing in their own gardens, hidden by tropical foliage, facing the ocean.

'They accepted my escort into the bar and we sat down. They were disappointed. Not a single disreputable human being in sight. There were a few men, who worked in the plantations, down to the port for a night. They were very bronzed and dressed in khaki so washed and ironed it shone in the electric light. They wore big hats and high boots. Some had changed into white drill and wore panamas. They sat at tables drinking and smoking as quietly as if they had been in Crackersburg. I couldn't take these ladies into the club; I wasn't a member; but that would have been no more exciting. They left their ginger ale and rose. Puerto Balboa was not rising to the occasion.

'After a day's work, Puerto Balboa was subdued. They said, "No night life at all?" They expected night-clubs! They wanted to see how the people lived. We walked along in the dust, going nowhere in particular, the air very hot and still. What puzzled them was the secrecy of the houses we passed. They had been accustomed all their lives to people sitting on the stoops and the porches or verandahs in full view of everybody else, with the shades up when they turned their lights on, and neighbors walking in and out at pleasure. I said these people didn't do that. We didn't do it in Eng-

210

land. And then we came to the turning where the real concrete pavement ended. They saw a lot of lights far down this
street and there was music. They said "Let's go down there."

'I was in a fix. I said, "Don't you know what that part of
town is? It's what you call the red-light district, in America.
You don't want to go down there." They murmured something to one another and then the widow said, "We can
walk past, maybe. We've heard so much about that sort of
thing." And they started to go on down.

'I think the Crackersburg ladies were a little daunted
when they came to the first cantina, and heard the noise of a
big gramophone in the bar. Some sailors were dancing with
the girls. One mariner was lying under the awning outside.
What daunted our passengers was the sort of girls who were
dancing. Costaraguan girls have a fierce, fixed glare when
they don't know who you are and cannot place you in their
world. These Crackersburg ladies were conspicuous in the
bright light of the inevitable naked bulb in the ceiling. We
passed on slowly until we came to the end of the street. The
Casa Raquel was on the other side.

'The widow said, "Let's go over there. It's a café, isn't
it?" I could see some of the local big shots sitting at tables.
I said it was, but perhaps we had better go back to the ship.
I couldn't explain to those ladies that the gentlemen she
saw all had respectable wives and families at home in another part of the town. They did not wish to be disturbed
by ladies from Norte America spying on them. It wouldn't
do me any good either; they would think I had put the
women up to it. Even more shocking, they might think I
had brought those women down here for my own purposes.
The Latin American mind would have found it impossible to
understand the ladies' motives. Pure motives!

'One of them exclaimed, "That child!" A girl of thirteen

211

or so, sitting on a folding chair by the door of this house of sin, was sewing intently, her head bent over the work. That was my first view of Chiquita. As we came up she rose and went in to serve the customers.

'Old Raquel's music was not so loud as the other places and the lights were not so pitiless. There were alcoves along the rear wall on either side of the door leading into the house. Unfortunately, as we reached the sidewalk, a girl entered the café with a young man. They passed Chiquita as she went to get the drinks. They began to dance to the music. My lady-friends recognized the purser at once. He didn't see us, and I managed to get my charges out into the shadow. "Don't you think we'd better go now?" I said. They didn't answer. We were moving away all the time. When we got back to the hotel bar they ordered ice-cream sodas, and while we were waiting one of them said, "Is he in love with that girl?" meaning our purser.

'I wanted to suggest she ask him herself. I just shrugged and said, what a man did when he was off duty was his own business. It would be the part of discretion to let the matter drop. The widow inquired if he was married. I really didn't know. I had nothing to do with him most of the time. I said a little irritably that I never interfered with other officers' private lives. He was an American, and had been only a couple of trips on the ship. When the sodas came and I drank a whiskey there was a silence. One of them said, "I keep thinking of that lovely child. Something ought to be done. The authorities. . . ."

'I said she was probably the daughter of the old woman who owned the place. I went on to warn them not to jump to conclusions. There was a code. It was difficult to explain, but she was probably as safe as if she lived in the United States—even safer. The widow said, "Code? You mean she isn't one of those creatures?" I said, "She's out of bounds."

'It was only a guess at the time, but I was right. I would see her at the door if I was down that way. One of my skippers used to like to walk into the Casa Raquel and have a drink with old Raquel herself. I think it had been his house of call when he was younger and unmarried. He it was who told me that Chiquita was Raquel's grand-daughter. He claimed to have known her father, the Swedish mate of a fruit steamer. He had been on the beach and Raquel had taken him in as a boarder because her daughter fell in love with him. He was a "big, yellow-bearded blowhard," my skipper said. He had shipped in a windbag to get home and had died at sea. Old Raquel had adopted the kid. She had grown up in the Casa.

'That was the background. I knew that much about Chiquita when Jack asked me to pay them a visit. I found him at the hotel bar and we started off in a station-wagon that ran on the rails. It is not a comfortable form of traveling, but Jack reveled in it. He had that expression of proud complacency which you see on the faces of men achieving paternity. He let her rip when we got over the freight-siding points and were banging along between two walls of tropical jungle.

'We reached the clearing in the jungle overshadowed by the big excavator. Smoke was drifting peacefully from the chimney of the cookhouse. One of the men had shot a huge eagle and they were nailing it on a tree, upside down. A gramophone was scratching away in the bunkhouse. Jack was very pleased with himself. I could see he was proud of the whole outfit. And when his girl stood at the door of his own private car, as you may call it, looking down at us, he was even prouder. Yes, as far as it is possible in the world, I suppose it really was the Garden of Eden for him. Paradise.

Looking back at it, I can even begin to understand how living over at Moat Farm, Tollemache St. Marys, might be boring for Jack, after what he has had. I don't know, mind you. I'm merely speculating. What do you think, Romaine?'

Mr. Romaine changed his position and knocked the ash from his cigar. The idea of discussing Jack Bannister and his native girl was not to his taste. His calm large face took on a faint flush.

'I couldn't say,' he said in a low tone. 'He wasn't a friend of mine, remember. Not like he was with you.'

'No,' Mr. Spenlove admitted. 'He was never one of the boys. Don't imagine he made a friend of me either. He used me to show off his success. He had always been a seaman. He had had no shore life since he had finished his apprenticeship. I think he had built up a dream world of domesticity. I dare say we all do at times. His first wife, Roxane, had awakened him from the dream by running away. Then this girl in the tropics had built it up again. He saw himself in that shack in the jungle, with his gang of workers and his Chiquita, achieving a success he understood. She was going to have a child too. I could see him, if all went well, settling for life, becoming a power in Costaraguan politics, a rich *administrador*. If all had gone well.'

'What happened?' Mrs. Price asked. Her own favorite literary credo was "cut the cackle and come to the 'osses," but she knew Mr. Spenlove had his own way of telling a story. He came to the 'osses in his own good time.

'Nothing that day,' he said. 'The girl was pretty near her time, but she had the supper ready and she gave me a steady grave look when she shook hands. Jack said, "Here he is, Chick. You said you wanted him to come again." He put his arm around her and took her chin in his hand, looking at me with pride. Then he said, patting her gently and looking at

214

her with passion, "Proper little woman! Goin' into dry dock, she is!"

'The only word for the look she gave him was adoration. She had changed from a child into a madonna. She had a severely angelic expression. We sat down to supper, brought by a boy from the cookhouse.

'I asked Jack what he would do when he was a family man. He said he would take a house he knew of in Puerto Balboa. Was he going to stay there? He wasn't sure about that. The contractors had plenty of other work coming. No hurry.

'When I asked him if he had no idea of going back to England, he became very agitated. What would take him to England? he asked. What put that into my head? He said there had been a time when he might have wanted to go back, but he was trying to get all that out of his system.

'He was very agitated. I had merely wondered if he would like to see Annie Collins and her Harry again. He said he did not want to see Annie again as long as he lived. He had had a shocking experience at home and it had been Annie's fault. He would never forget what had happened.

'When the girl was outside for a moment, I said I thought he did Annie an injustice. He got up and took a couple of steps. He shook his head. He said there were things a man could never forget. He was trying to forget. He had burned his bridges. He would have to stay there, now she was going to have a kid. He even had the idea of going into contracting himself. He could get a contract if he settled down in the country.

'I asked whether he would stay in Puerto Balboa. Wouldn't Chiquita want to go north? He said no. All she wanted was to be with him. They might move up country. Whatever he wanted was all right with her. He reached

215

over and took her face in his hand and said gravely, "It's all settled, isn't it, kid? All settled. You and me, eh?"

'I began to wonder why he wanted to bring me into this, and after dinner he told me. He wanted me to get him an insurance policy. He had one, but it was for only a thousand dollars. He wanted one for five thousand to cover everything, accidents and so on. I said I'd do it next time we got to New York. He was going to make the girl the beneficiary, of course. He went into a long speech about the hazards of living in such a place of Costaragua, as though nobody's life was worth much. It was plain enough, he said, that everything was a risk when you got fifteen per cent for your money.

'Well, he drove me back that night and I was glad to get on board. I felt he was making a mistake. He was tying a millstone about his neck. I thought no Englishman had any right to cut himself off from his own traditions and people by becoming infatuated with a girl with such a background. I couldn't put any faith in the success of such an experiment. It was too romantic. But it wasn't my business and I let it go at that.

'I told you about Miss Calhoun, the Scotch lady who worked in the hospital administration department. She used to come down to the ship and have a drink or two in the smoke-room with us. She came down the next evening. We were sailing very early in the morning. There was a nurse with her. I remember she was talking about a landing-field they were to build about a mile out on the route Jack was using to dig his canal. They thought it would be grand to take a plane and get up to the capital in half an hour instead of that horrible eight-hour trip on the train, full of squealing babies, smelly mestizos and cigar-smoking women. Miss Calhoun said what she couldn't stand was the awful creatures, the beggars, who stood silently beside the train at the stations, with enormous goiters or shocking abnormalities of face or body, with outstretched claws, picking their sores to make them bloody, and showing their gashed abdomens.

'The capital, Lord knows, isn't much, but it was a change for those ladies. The most you can do in San Benito is walk around the plaza, listen to the band or see a movie you saw in New York a year before. You can go to the Club Commercial if you know somebody who will give you a card, or the Jockey Club if you know the Minister's secretary. After that you go to bed. Everybody goes to bed at nine sharp.'

'You'll have to tell me about that,' Mrs. Price said. 'But what about the girl? Didn't you say . . . ?'

'I'm coming to it,' he said. 'Miss Calhoun and her friend had several drinks that night. When it came time to go ashore, they felt it would be better if they had an escort. It was past ten and the port would be in darkness. It was beginning to rain. It wasn't the rainy season, but we had showers.

'We started. I had a raincoat and an umbrella. It's some distance to the hospital, nearly all uphill, and Puerto Balboa has no taxis, no carriages, no buses. There was no rail-car available or we might have had a ride part of the distance. So we footed it along the rails. The ladies took the umbrella and I led the way with a flashlight. They were both from north of the Tweed and a drop of rain meant nothing. I expect they felt a little jingled, and were a shade uncertain of themselves. I didn't mind. I was glad to have a brisk walk before turning in.

'We trudged along in the dark until we came to the bend in the line where we would have to follow the spur up to the hospital. There was an arc-light sputtering in the rain. Miss Calhoun stopped and said, "What's that?" She pointed.

'Coming round the curve a hundred yards up the line was a single headlight. It was low down and shone on the rails, so that they seemed to be made of silver wire in the rain. I said it was a rail-car, and guided the women to one side. It was slowing for the points. Those machines jump the rails if you take a switch too fast. We could hear the brakes squeal. Almost before it stopped Jack Bannister leaped off the car, ran to the switch and threw it, so the car would go up to the hospital. He ran back without even looking at us, and started with a jerk. We stood watching him rattle past us. I saw a woman's form in the back of the car very faintly, her head lolling as though asleep. I thought to myself, "He's bringing her in!" Miss Calhoun was offended. She said, "It's Misterr Bannister! Well, he might have stopped . . ."

'I said, "It's his girl. I saw her in the car. She's going to have a baby. He told me he was bringing her down soon. He's probably excited."

'Excited or not, he was way out of sight by that time. It's about a quarter of a mile up the road to the hospital. Miss Calhoun said to me, "Now you needn't come any farther, Chief. We're a' richt noo." I told them about my visit to his camp, and all the rest of it. Jack was probably unable even to see us when he met us on the track. Too excited. So we went on up through the dripping trees and shrubs of the hospital grounds. There was Jack's rail-car at the door.

'I waited in the big patio, covered in with glass and fine screen-wire, with a fountain playing among the palms. Miss Calhoun said she'd come back and tell me the news. I had the place to myself. I could see a few night workers in the offices under the arcade that ran around three sides of the patio. Miss Calhoun came in from the main door. She beckoned to me and we walked along a passage and through a door into an office, switching on the lights and starting the fans. She said, "Misterr Spenlove, it's a turrible business, this. She's been struck by a snake, a cascavel. And she's having her pains now."

'I had a sudden picture in my mind, not of what had happened there and then, but of Jack going to pieces in his cabin years before, because his wife had run away. Because she had encountered his conceit and complacency and given way to panic. He had gone to pieces in front of me and his captain.

'I saw him that way while Miss Calhoun was telling me what was going on upstairs. She had a strong Scotch face, full of fine lines, with a big sensitive mouth which smiled but never grinned with a great show of teeth. It was grave as she spoke of the girl's condition. Struck in the knee as she was getting into the rail-car on the siding. Getting in on the dark side, next the trees. She had given a scream and flung herself into the seat while Jack had flailed away at the snake with a machete he carried among his tools. Whole camp in an uproar as he yelled, "Cascavel! Cascavel!" He had twisted a tourniquet on her leg and started off at once without giving her an injection. I expect he wasn't too sure he could do any good that way. He got frightened. Who wouldn't? It was probably a wise decision. Half an hour and she'd be in hospital. Her condition, Miss Calhoun said, was "Not good."

'I said she'd better see Jack was taken care of. He wouldn't go back to camp. She told me he was "distracted." As I had seen him distracted, I didn't wait. Miss Calhoun told me about it next voyage, when it was all over.'

'She died?' Mrs. Price said.

'A couple of hours later. I dare say she died of shock as well as venom. Jack said, one day, after he came back to the ships, those creatures aren't like anything else in the world. Most wild creatures are only dangerous if you disturb them or attack them. But the cascavels, *Crotalus Terrificus*, may be looking for you. He comes for you, and if you retreat he puts on speed and strikes as he rushes straight at you. No coiled stance for him! He is in the bush, alongside the trail, or under a car, watching and hating. Jack said the bastards would bide their time and strike when they had you careless. He said they were the originals of the one in the Garden of Eden. Which'—Mr. Spenlove turned to Mr. Romaine— 'gave me the idea in the first place.

'Miss Calhoun went to the funeral. You will understand that such things as I am telling you now aren't part of our regular life at sea. We sail when the schedule says so. We sail! Life and death, love and hate, all the things people on shore are so preoccupied with, have to be left behind. We have to keep time; eternity can wait. This business of Jack's happened on a rainy night, a few hours before we sailed. I was the only person on the ship who knew about it. Don't imagine for a moment that I was in an agony about it either. That's a convention of modern story-telling. Most of us don't give a damn about the other fellow's woman troubles. If I had a feeling at all it was regret that I knew so little about Jack's girl. I remember her because of Jack. I dare say Jack's own memory of her is pretty vague now. He found in her something of his dream woman, a mysterious maiden chained to a rock, or sinking in the waves, or overborne by furies. He was the Perseus who slew the monster and set her free. Perseus married Andromeda. Jack would have married his Chiquita, I am perfectly certain, if she had lived and had had a child. But my conviction gives me only very vague clues to her hold on Jack, except her youth, and the appealing circumstance of her childhood in a brothel. That would be irresistible to Jack.'

'I don't follow,' Mrs. Price protested. 'I don't know what you mean by that.'

'Jack was fundamentally a very strict moralist,' Mr. Spenlove said. 'I know it sounds strange, but he was. For all we know he may be still.'

Mrs. Price was ironical. She counted off on her fingers. 'His first wife, this native girl, a stewardess, possibly a nurse in Africa, didn't you say? Now he's married again, but he's off with a fresh Andromeda. You find wonderful names for them, old chap! And he is a strict moralist. I'd like to meet one of your loose moralists. I'd give him in charge!'

'You don't get his character at all,' Mr. Spenlove said. 'Even his present wife insisted that he is faithful. She seems to know him well enough to be certain he doesn't run around with women in the way you suggest.'

'Well, let's have it,' Mrs. Price said. She looked around. 'He could convince you black's white any day in the week.' Mr. Romaine nodded to confirm this. 'You think he's shot himself in remorse, or something like that?'

'You're trying to make a dramatic ending to one of your serials,' Mr. Spenlove said. 'A knight-errant rarely commits suicide. Most of them live to a ripe old age. I am only telling you what happened. I didn't see Jack for a long while after that. If it hadn't been for Miss Calhoun coming on board the following trip I might not have heard the story.'

CHAPTER

10

I WOULD have expected Jack to have got another job.
He might have gone into the wilds and cherished his grief,
perhaps. He didn't. He has, or had, a certain realism about
life and death. You find it most unexpectedly in the English,
who are otherwise sentimental. He walked behind the coffin
to the cemetery. It must have been a motley group, with a
small band playing a mournful tune. He never flinched from
paying the last rites. But when Chiquita was buried and the
grave filled in, he never mentioned her again. He settled his
business, quit his job and came north. He rejoined the company and was soon chief of a ship. The Costaragua business
was over and done with. He was our Jack once more, but
with a difference. He was easier to get on with, I heard, and
he kept his staff, voyage after voyage.

'Then I got sick and went to the hospital. I had a rather
bad mastoid and our ship's surgeon ordered me to go. I
came back north in Jack's ship as a passenger. Which was
how I was in on the episode of the stewardess. I suppose it
was about time for Jack to go into the rescuing business again.

A knight-errant, when his time comes, has to start, you know. I must say, she was an impressive eyeful.'

'That's a very vague description,' Mrs. Price complained. 'Can't you make it a bit more definite, old chap? An eyeful! What a way to talk! I suppose you mean she was beautiful. I want to see her, if you know what I mean.'

'Someone called her the Blonde Venus. That was after she was seen in a swim suit. I didn't see her that way, but I saw a snapshot of her about to dive. Miss Nelson was the name. I expect it was Neilson in Sweden, or Denmark. Elsa Nelson was a Nordic edition of Lady Hamilton. She could never have been painted as a Bacchante, however. She was a very quiet girl, about twenty-five. Something like that, Romaine? You engaged her, didn't you?'

'Bornholdt, the second steward,' Mr. Romaine said. 'He was a Swede, remember? She was livin' with Mrs. Bornholdt in Brooklyn. Around twenty-five or -six. Good-lookin' gel.'

'That's right. The word for her—I was a passenger that trip, going home after being in the hospital—was "retiring." She was a very quiet girl. Never in the way and never out of the way. On duty, but in the background. I have seen her walking along an alleyway with a tray for a sick passenger, almost like an automaton, the tray in front of her like something mechanical, it was so still, her eyes never wandering from straight ahead, no expression at all. She'd knock, and wait. Then she'd open the door and go in like a beautiful priestess entering a shrine. You couldn't imagine anyone with more propriety, more reserve. Her white uniform was invariably immaculate. Her face was never made up like the young Latin-American girls', all paint and chalky powder. She didn't need it. Her heavy, corn-colored hair was coiled closely around her head and she wore an apron with the Company's houseflag symbol on the bosom. She also wore a neat cap. I think the most magnificent thing about her was her walk. Like a Viking queen. You couldn't help thinking of Vikings when you saw her. But in real life she was a competent working girl earning her living in an exemplary manner, taking care of young children when their mothers were sick, carrying trays to women who couldn't get up, associating pleasantly with the other stewardesses and respected by all hands. Then she ran into trouble with an elderly passenger, whose bad-tempered wife was an invalid.'

Mr. Spenlove nodded toward Perdita and made a gesture with his cigar. 'She will tell you I do not like being a passenger,' he said. 'I was a passenger that trip. I had nothing to read except what was in the ship's library. The *Sansovino* was the latest thing when she was launched, but she had a lot of leather-bound books, things like *The Valiants of Virginia* and Marie Corelli's *God's Just Man*. I spent a lot of time watching the other passengers, who were average human beings. Passengers have a tradition going back to the Ark. Every ship which carries them is a little like an Ark. All kinds of animals. One sardonic cruise director we had used to call our ships cattle-boats.

'Our passenger who caused the trouble with Miss Nelson was a type. He was president of some extremely prosperous organization in the Middle West which nobody had ever heard of. I think he made parts for washing machines, or perhaps it was farm implements. His suits seemed to be cut out of sheet metal. He wore a short, clipped, white mustache cut straight across over a hard mouth that was always smiling. The impression he made on me was, I would not care to work for him.

'We were sitting around the palm court at the after end

of the promenade deck, and Miss Nelson was serving iced tea and coffee. Another stewardess followed with hot tea and sandwiches. It was a new experiment the line was making. It evolved eventually into a tremendous splurge called Ye Olde Cocktail Hour, with an orchestra accompaniment, ham-and-chicken for snacks and unlimited side dishes.

'In those early days it was merely tea and pastry at five o'clock. The bar opened at four, so the patrons who drifted into the palm court were likely to be already primed. Our friend, the manufacturer of whatever it was in the Middle West, a prohibition state, was an ardent patron of the bar. He said, in my hearing, that he himself voted for prohibition. He believed in it because it kept his employees sober. He himself had laid in a large cellar of good bonded stuff.

'He was well oiled on this occasion. He came in, teetering on his toes, looking around the palm court for some of his cronies. It had soon got around that he was the richest man on board. I heard a rumbling rumor from a man I talked to in the smoke-room that he was worth "a million dollars." He had a court around him. His word was accepted among them as the ultimate opinion. On this occasion there were no courtiers in sight. He sat down and relit his cigar. Miss Nelson came along from the pantry with a tray of tea-glasses.

'She was not a frigid, standoffish girl, mind you. She was affable in a polite way. She would always reply to a compliment. I told her one day she was smart to remember I took no sugar. She said, "Thank you, sir. I try, sir." If a young man was persistent, she would ease him off with a nice smile and an "Excuse me, sir."

'The old fellow was different. I don't know if he had noticed her before. Perhaps she suddenly filled a place in his dreams. She was extremely attractive, bending over carefully to serve the people. She had a good figure and that rich creamy skin you often see in Scandinavian girls. As she offered this old tycoon the tray, he put it down on a table beside him and drew her onto his knees. He put his arm around her and laid down his cigar. I could feel the sensation among the others, a rising tenseness. An old hag with heavy diamond jewelry, across the court, gave a spasmodic jerk of her body, and bridled. I expected her to neigh!

'The girl exerted her strength, which was considerable, and stood away from the old man. Jack Bannister, who was chief engineer, remember, at that moment came along on his way to the bridge, and saw the whole thing. He saw the passenger reach out and catch again at the girl's arm. She slapped his hand away and shook her finger at him, her expression becoming grave for the first time. She said, "Excuse me, sir."

'She wasn't really angry. She didn't lose her head. She didn't want to lose her job and she didn't want to have the reputation of being shrewish or bad-tempered. When he grabbed her she had to be definite. The old fellow sat there smiling, alcoholically unaware of the spectacle he was providing. Unaware too that the bridling hag was already resolved to tell his wife about it.

'Otherwise that might have been the end of the business. We knew he had had a few too many, and the girl herself knew it. She had more sense than to complain. She was probably used to fending off satyrs. But the lady, who had a husband of the same kind as our friend, lost no time in informing the recumbent wife. And the recumbent wife became active. She complained to our friend Romaine here that one of the stewardesses was carrying on with her husband, and insisted on the captain being informed so that the hussy should be sacked the minute the ship docked. Pretty embarrassing for Romaine.'

Mr. Romaine nodded and shrugged his shoulders.

'She went to the skipper,' he pointed out. 'He sent for me, to get the rights of it.'

'Correct. He did. And then, when you simply had her word, the girl's word, against a passenger's, and the old fellow went to the skipper and said he would make trouble with the management if the matter wasn't dropped, Miss Nelson was called on the carpet again.'

'Formal reprimand,' Mr. Romaine said shortly. 'For the record.'

'And then Jack Bannister butted into the business. He heard about it in the purser's office, like everybody else on the ship. He went to the skipper and said he had seen the whole thing and the skipper sent for Miss Nelson again and the skipper believed her. However, a complaint had been lodged and the matter would go to the office. The Line had a rule in those days, that if a passenger lodged a complaint, you had to quit. For the good of the service. There was no argument, no appeal. The passenger was always right.

'It was the hag who reported the matter to the office. She too had a friend in the management. You were not actually fired, of course. Oh, no! You stayed ashore for a week or so, and then you were put on another ship, or sent to another division. So Miss Nelson was paid off when we got to New York.

'The injustice of the business was plain enough, but most of us were resigned to seeing a nice girl fired. We knew that nice girls generally got along somehow. Jack took another view. The scene he had witnessed in the palm court had fired his imagination. It had made his blood boil. He had been a recluse since his Puerto Balboa experiences. Now he was a knight-errant again. The ship went over to Brooklyn that voyage to have her regular survey and Jack took a room at Mrs. Bornholdt's. Before anyone had an inkling of what he was up to he had married Miss Nelson over in New Jersey. She didn't take any more jobs as stewardess. Nobody of our crowd ever saw her again.'

'I bet you found out all about it, though,' Mrs. Price spoke with conviction.

'Romaine told me.' Mr. Romaine, looking thoughtful, nodded assent. Mr. Spenlove smiled at Mrs. Price. 'Remember,' he said, 'that all this time we were sailing out and coming in, trip after trip, preoccupied with our own anxieties, each of us in his own department, meeting a fresh batch of passengers every trip. A trivial thing like that faded in a few days. I have known a skipper, whom we had known for years, who jumped over the side on his last voyage. He was due to retire on a pension. He was forgotten in a few weeks! I dare say his widow remembered him, but all I ever knew about her was what another skipper, who did know her, said about her. He said he would jump over the side himself rather than live with her. The dramatic act of that man, with a fine service record, with money in the bank, and a pension, without any financial worry, walking out of his cabin off Barnegat on a misty night and going over the side without anyone knowing about it until eight bells, left no record on our minds at all. I remember he used to talk about some day keeping chickens!

'Bornholdt spread the story that Jack Bannister had married Miss Nelson, and we took it in our stride. Bornholdt himself was promoted and sent to manage the commissary in Puerto Balboa and we soon forgot him except when we met him in the commissary. Mr. Romaine found it a convenience to get stores from him on occasion, for instance, and I had a bottle of good Scotch out of bond from him. Very obliging chap, and his wife was well liked too. She'd come aboard with Miss Calhoun.

'That was how Romaine learned what had happened to our Miss Nelson, who was now Mrs. Bannister. When the Bornholdts gave up their apartment in Brooklyn, Jack was at sea on the Atlantic run. That meant six weeks away.

'Mrs. Bornholdt, coming on board in Puerto Balboa with Miss Calhoun to have "a wee drappie," as Miss Calhoun called it, said Mrs. Bannister wanted to come down with them; make Puerto Balboa her home port, so to say. Jack wouldn't hear of such a thing. He didn't tell her what Puerto Balboa meant in his life, but he made it clear that it was out so far as he was concerned.

'Jack was in Southampton when the Bornholdts left for the south, having stored their furniture. The new Mrs. Bannister shared a room with another Swedish or Danish girl just come from the old country. This new girl, hunting employment, soon heard about stewardess's positions in the Line. She turned up at the office, where the personnel director was a Dane with a Swedish wife, so she was taken on. She wasn't in Puerto Balboa long before she heard all about Jack's experiences on shore. When she got back to New York, it was a matter of hours and Mrs. Bannister heard about it too, in Swedish. I wonder what it sounded like as those two calm, blonde young women exchanged their information. Mrs. Bannister decided this was why her husband did not want her to live in Puerto Balboa.

'After her room-mate sailed, Mrs. Bannister had three weeks solitude before Jack arrived from Bremen. I suppose she had developed a state of mind about seafaring men. From her point of view she had merely exchanged liberty for a rather dull captivity by marrying a sailor. The Line had a strict rule about marital relations. Not even a skipper could take his wife on a cruise in his own ship. He could get her a pass on another vessel. As for a chief engineer and a stewardess, it was unheard of. Mrs. Bannister did not like it at all.

229

'I am not sure just what she had expected. She might have had some hint from Jack that he would get a job on shore and live with her. She was an extremely conventional Lutheran girl; but Lutheran girls, when they get married, have husbands to live with them. You can see she was in a predicament. Jack wasn't even an American citizen, so she wasn't getting anywhere in life, as an immigrant sees it. The weeks of solitude passed; the simple, short, secular ceremony at City Hall became less and less important. After she heard of Jack's life in Puerto Balboa, Costaragua, a tropical place as she remembered it, living in the jungle with a native girl; you can bet the tale lost nothing in the telling; she must have begun to wonder whether she was married at all in the Lutheran sense. A passenger once told me that it is an old American custom to make a ceremony impressive in inverse ratio to its importance, so they get married with less formality than is needed for a license to drive a Ford or use a gun. He probably exaggerated; another old American custom.'

'Mark Twain,' Mrs. Price suggested. Mr. Spenlove said Mark Twain was in the tradition, but a timid practitioner.

'Jack came home and found she'd moved. She'd left a message with her landlady that she had got a job in Manhattan. She gave her address, somewhere in the West Seventies. He went after her as soon as he could leave his ship.

'What she had done was something, I suppose, Jack hardly expected. He had, of course, left her some money. She had enrolled in a school that taught the art of the beautician. She was determined to rise in the world, and she had been told that American women spent seven million dollars a day making themselves beautiful. She thought it would be sensible to get some of that money for herself.

'Jack objected to a wife working, especially at a job he thought hardly respectable. He had almost no knowledge of life ashore in America. He thought beauty-shop girls and manicurists on a par with fallen women. Elsa was not only very good-looking, but she was Swedish, or Danish, and she was unusually blonde even for a Scandinavian. Jack had heard strange things about how some of the Swedish massage parlors were run.

'But nothing Jack could say to her had any effect. She had found she had a talent for the work and she was resolved to earn her own living. She was very sensible about it. I happened to meet Jack in Havana one trip. He was going south and my ship was sailing for New York. He told me something of his new family trouble. Elsa was resolved to live her own life. She told Jack that, since he was away so much, it was only the sensible thing to do.'

Mr. Spenlove moved in his chair, as though he had experienced some sudden physical discomfort.

'There never was such a sensible creature!' he said, irritably rubbing his nose. 'Everything she did was sensible, but to a husband it didn't make sense. She was beautiful, she was calm and she was virtuous. She was like a Viking ship which had been accidentally launched on the waters of American life and at once sailed away, without a jar, without a ripple, in perfect trim fore and aft, with ballast and a fair wind. And she sailed right out of Jack's life, hull down, and out of sight!

'I had this from Jack as we sat at a bar off the Malecon, in Havana. He leaned back in his chair, looking around contemptuously at the Cubans near us, his hands in his trousers pockets, telling me about his ex-spouse as though it was a relief to confide to a fellow countryman how he had been treated by a woman whom he had rescued from what he called "a damned compromising situation." The fellow, he said, was "absolutely immoral." There was nothing so loathsome, in his opinion, as a rich man taking advantage of a virtuous girl earning her living.

'I tried to get him away from that. My own experience doesn't lead me to believe that girls who earn their living, if they are as good-looking as Miss Nelson, have such a hard time. I asked him why he married her in the first place. I hadn't asked for his confidences, at least not more than an ordinary human interest in one's companion might be called asking.

'He launched into the story as though it had been bottled up inside him, under pressure. He assumed I had a right to know how he got himself into this mess.

' "It was a mistake," he said. He looked glumly at me, as though I had been responsible. Maybe I was. I was present when the immoral rich old man had started to make his passes at the inviolable Miss Nelson. It was hard to say what I could have done. "The whole thing was a mistake. I was taken in. I didn't realize . . ."

'I said "It was a failure, then?" And Jack had an illumination. I can't call it anything else. It was almost as if he were a medium in a trance. He finished his drink and looked away to where the sea was exploding in towers of spray behind the Malecon breakwater. He said, in a hoarse mumble, "Every marriage is a failure, for one of the parties."

'It seemed to me that Jack had reached a certain stage in his adolescence, had in fact grown up a bit. I said, why didn't he go after her and make her see reason? Why did he let her take that line? He had enough to support a woman as well as she had been supported in wherever it was she came from. Why didn't he?

'He said he couldn't. He had to get back to the ship.

He said, as if it explained everything, "I had to go back to the ship." And it did explain a great deal. It is the crux for a seaman. He has to go back to the ship. His wife may be having a baby or she may be running off with a piano-tuner. If the ship needs him he has to go back. If he doesn't, he isn't a seaman. He has broken that inexorable law of duty. He is merely an unreliable casual laborer who happens to go to sea.'

Mr. Spenlove paused and smiled at his audience. 'I am a bit old-fashioned, I'm afraid. Romaine thinks that sort of thing is over and done with.'

'It don't matter what we think,' Mr. Romaine said. 'The unions won't let ye.'

'Well, that was how we used to look at it. Of course, before that they had slaves, and in the distant past they chained us to the oar. Never mind! Jack had to go back to the ship. He *had* to. It is a problem every man of principle has to face, the conflict of two cardinal loyalties, his ship and his woman. Jack was a seaman.'

'Perhaps that's why he isn't happy now,' Mrs. Price said.

'We don't know that unless we see him. That's what has been in my mind ever since I heard he was here, living the life of a country gentleman. Do you know what he said to me, that time on the Malecon? He had just remarked that every marriage was a failure for one of the parties, and I had asked him how he was so sure. I said it could only be proved by experience, and if you go to sea you couldn't get that ex-perience. I was going on to point out that he was trying to square the circle matrimonially, when he said, "Fred, why don't you get married?"

'I said, "With your example?" He said I wouldn't make the mistakes he had. I was too damn satisfied with myself.

233

"Then," I said, "you mean it would be failure for the other party. Is that it?" '

'I still don't understand what you mean by that. You keep saying, "He was a seaman." Just what do you mean?'

Mr. Spenlove gave Mrs. Price a glance and then looked out into the orchard.

'It's a fair question,' he said. 'And I'll answer it. You'll bear in mind, of course, that I am describing'—he smiled—'an extinct, or almost extinct species. The war blurred the minds of shore people to the realities of seafaring. They discovered that, by Jove, they depended on poor Jack to bring in the food they ate. They began to realize his existence and they glamorized him. He was a hero. He fought back. He went down with his ship—if he couldn't get away, of course. He was found exercising his heroism in small boats under the blazing tropical sun and in frozen seas. Nothing was too good for him. A couple of skippers were knighted. A few owners were made lords. What intrigued the landsmen was that they themselves, some of them, who had gone to sea to do their bit, as they called it, were as good at being heroes as any old salt. They got medals and bonuses, and high pay. To hear them tell it they won the war.

'They weren't seamen. They went ashore long ago. The men I am speaking of had a desperate time after the war. Many of them died and left families in straitened circumstances. Many took low-pay jobs. We had a deck-steward who had been master in the old Baronial Line. They had nothing for him, so he took what he could and got going with us as third mate. He made good. Retired now. Meanwhile the times were changing. Ships were different. Crews were very different. Owners were even more different. The wireless tied us to the shore. Instruments took the places of men. I can see the time coming when a ship will be navigated from the office ashore, all automatic. Crewless liners with automats for dining and musical boxes bringing in wireless music for dancing. . . . Nothing preposterous about that, is there? Progress!

'The men I speak of had a different sort of sea to sail on. They—we, I was one of them—were on our own almost as much as explorers in Africa were on their own after they left the coast. We were a team under a commander. We developed a special mentality, and the basis of our religion was something we called principle. Integrity, if you like, or loyalty. Not to the owners, or to a union leader making a fine fat salary in an office, but to the ship herself, to our shipmates, to our cloth. We would say, "So-and-so had principle." We meant that in the secret casket of his soul there was a jewel beyond price. We could depend on him, come hell or high water. He was one of us. He had been through the same mill and refining fire in youth. He might be a steward, like Romaine here, or a mate, or a fireman. I have known a cook who had our regard after a bad voyage. We thought of him as we thought of the commander. Good men, by God!'

He paused to let his emotion subside. This was no place to get rhetorical; but he wanted Mrs. Price to understand what he meant about Jack Bannister, who was otherwise not a comprehensible Englishman to her. She would not see why it was impossible for Jack to run around after a wife who was intent on her own career, far uptown, in New York.

'Jack said to me he could see she had no intention of living with him. When he told her that it was her duty to live with him, in a place near the ships, she said, calmly, "This is America. Women can do things here." Jack said the atmosphere of America was very bad for women. They got ideas in their heads! They read about divorces, and thought

235

of marriage as a temporary business. He even went so far as to say the whole system was immoral.

'It wouldn't be easy to state in so many words just what a man like Jack really thought of America. By the time he married his present wife he had a strong dislike of the country. He disliked it simply because he didn't understand it. And he wanted to go back where he came from.'

Mr. Spenlove paused. He did not dislike America himself, but he was suffering from a sense of confusion. He had thought much on this theme, the mentality of seamen exiled for years from home ports, from their wives, families and friends at home. Even more confusing was the fate of the young single men, whose opportunities of discovering America was so meager, and whose contacts were so fragile.

Reflecting on this, he had understood that Jack's visit to the Demings that winter night, when Deming acted like a madman and Candace ran screaming up the stairs like a woman in a Greek tragedy, must have given him a highly charged picture of life in America.

'Think of it!' he said suddenly. 'Mrs. Deming and her daughter were, in Jack's view, English ladies, the peak of our social achievement. They represented the upper classes, or perhaps I had better say the upper middle-classes, who for us are the finest manifestation of the national genius. Jack would never aspire to that class himself. But to him they were ladies of quality, beings of another world, but an English world, a world he deeply venerated. He had never met an artist. He had never met a man like Deming. To him the terrifying drunk, who turned a quiet Christmas party, in his own house, in the quiet country, into a pandemonium, represented an alien civilization, something he did not understand. I have an idea he never recovered from the impressions of that evening.'

236

CHAPTER

11

YES, he had been taken in; he had made a mistake. The calm, chaste Miss Nelson had taken to American life like a duck to water and had gone swimming beautifully away from him. To her, who wanted at once to become an American citizen, he was nothing at all, an alien who was so stupid he did not realize the necessity of becoming a citizen without loss of time. He did not realize, either, that to her, being on a ship carried with it a stigma. It was a mark of lowly origin, whereas if he had come ashore and taken to selling, he would have raised his status. So I gathered from his account of his attempt to get her to return to his way of life. He had to get back to the ship. That again to her was a sign of being no-account.

'He always seemed to have some sort of family trouble. Romaine here was with him for a while, and he says Jack got into the way of not going ashore at all, having his meals in his room, and getting his ship along fast.'

'He got her along, all right,' Mr. Romaine said. 'Never any trouble, either. Always on good terms with my crowd.'

'You see? He was growing up. I ought to explain what Romaine is talking about. There was often a lot of inter-departmental squabbles on those ships. With two or three hundred passengers and a hundred and fifty crew, there was a lot of refrigeration. Sometimes the butchers would leave the doors open, and the refrigerating staff wanted to fight the butchers. Those fellows thought it was too much trouble to close the doors every time they went in for something. You can imagine what that meant for Jack's department in the tropics. Jack managed without any fights, as some of the rest of us did. But so far as his own life went, he became very dull.

'Used to tell him to come along up for the captain's dinner,' Mr. Romaine said heavily. 'I'd say, there was a couple o' good-lookers at his table. He wouldn't bother. Used to say, to hell with the captain and his dinner. The skipper didn't care. Jack was getting the ship along. That's all the old man cared about; all any of us cared about. But the Line wanted this captain's dinner, with paper hats and crackers and balloons all over the place. Fine mess to sweep up, after. They'd all get drunk that night.'

'Americans insisted on that sort of thing,' Mr. Spenlove went on. 'It was the current conception of life on the ocean wave. That was what they made the trip for.'

'Well, that was how it stood when I met Jack in Southampton. He had just come in from Hamburg and I was heading there. He came over to borrow some special requisition sheets. We had a drink in my cabin and chinned a bit about things in general. I remember Romaine came in and said how-do. He had come over too, to make a quick touch from his opposite number on my ship.'

Mr. Romaine made an unintelligible sound and nodded.

'We used to do one another little favors. It was one of

238

the things Jack had not caught on to at first. When our business was settled, I asked Jack how it was with him and the beautiful Miss Nelson.

'She had got a Mexican divorce. In those days Mexican papers were sent by mail-order through an agent in New York. It was the most remarkable racket I ever heard of. We had a passenger from Havana on one occasion, an elegant, diplomatic type of Mexican, who had an elegant office on Park Avenue, and he gave us some of his publicity. For a few hundred dollars he would send you a beautifully engraved divorce certificate. The wife, or the husband, did not even have to know about it. He was doing an immense business in New York, and Jack's wife had got one. I am not at all sure that it wasn't illegal. It became so later. While they lasted they were extremely popular.'

Mrs. Price said she had never met an American woman who had not been divorced at least once. It seemed to be essential.

'Mother's very Victorian,' Perdita said, quietly. Her mother patted her knee.

'It's a wrong impression,' Mr. Spenlove said. 'Most Americans live with the same wife all their lives. But that isn't news, and as we see only those who have lots of money we get the feeling they are moving in and out of marriage like a revolving door.'

'Was Mr. Bannister divorced when he married her?' Mrs. Price said suddenly. Mr. Spenlove nodded.

'A Paris divorce. I was telling Perdita. They got Jack's address from the Line's London office and he received a certificate that his wife, Roxane Heller Bannister, née Vermandois, had been granted a divorce. I saw it. He showed it to me in Costaragua. He made to me an astonishing remark at the time. I'll tell you, if you're interested some time.

'It was Mrs. Deming we met first. Mrs. Deming was at Jack's table when she returned to America after visiting her daughter, then a child, in Switzerland, and her brother, who was a retired civil servant living with an uncle in Italy. They were all obviously people of wealth and position. She'd been in England too, visiting her aunt at Moat Farm. When Jack told me about them I could see he was impressed, not by their fortunes but by their quality. At first I thought it had been Mrs. Deming he was interested in, but it wasn't so. He was flattered when she told him her child would be coming over alone at the end of the school term, and she wanted her to be looked after.

'Mrs. Deming unconsciously touched some long latent chord in Jack's character. She was gentry, and most Englishmen are sensitive to the appeal of quality. No matter how long a pedigree an American may have, we don't feel the same. I know something about that. My people were yeomen, and we never lose a special feeling for gentry. I used to think Lord Balfour was right when he suggested that the very qualities that make a man an agnostic, or a socialist, have been derived from the ancient faiths and traditions he is attacking.'

Mrs. Price said she thought that was nonsense.

'Well, we can say that Mrs. Deming is a lady. She isn't a grand lady, or even what is called ladylike. She has had a number of harrowing experiences, but nothing ever altered her fundamental goodness and gentleness. And when she asked Jack if he would take care of her child when the young person came over, it aroused the old knight-errant instinct in him. It stimulated his imagination. He happened to be unmarried at the time, which was fortunate.'

'I should think so!' Mrs. Price said.

'That's how he and I happened to assist at that Christmas party when the genius, the formerly successful illustrator Deming, the creator of Deming's Damsels and other famous features in the magazines, gave one of his remarkable performances.

'I don't blame Jack for being outraged. We were both accustomed to have sailors, firemen, stewards, and even officers go ashore and get extremely drunk and get into jail for breaking up a bar. But for a man who made a lot of money, living in a fine country house, with a wife of high breeding, and a lovely, aristocratic daughter, to do such a thing, was an outrage. It was unforgivable. Apart from that Jack was always extremely abstemious. He took a drink as if he didn't really care about it.

'The voyage he had the girl at his table and "took care" of her, exalted him. He saw himself as a knight-errant in a new role. Perhaps he saw this girl as the embodiment of his Chiquita without any of Chiquita's disadvantages. She was Chiquita and Roxane and Elsa Nelson, all blended into a glorious young creature with a background of wealth and aristocracy; and she was in distress, for the wealth was non-existent during the depression. When Deming, after abandoning his wife and child, took his life, Jack saw his duty. The schoolgirl he had taken care of with the most chivalrous solicitude, who had given him her grateful affection, needed him. He had made a mess of things with Roxane when he married and left her. He would not make that mistake again. He was faced with the alternative of leaving the girl to her fate or leaving the ship. The ship was laid up on account of the depression, and Jack went ashore to assume the guardianship of his new family.

'The depression had not done anything to him at the time. He had several thousand dollars in the bank, and the bank was one of those which remained open until a year or two later, when they were all closed for a while. Jack lost some of his savings when stocks tumbled, I believe, but he wasn't badly off.

'You had only faint impressions in England of that period in America. There was a lot of unemployment. On the other hand, if you had money it bought much more than it does now. And it was Jack Bannister's first experience of American life! It was an adventure. They bought a jalopy and went to Florida. To a certain extent it was a repetition of his adventure in Costaragua. He began to learn about America.

'They call it a melting pot, which always seems to me a simplification. To me it is a fermenting vat. Some parts of it are blending casks, where different distillations are changed into something we call American.'

'Intoxicating, I suppose?' Mrs. Price sniffed.

'Even inebriating! They go to your head sometimes!' Mr. Spenlove said, seriously. 'There is a quality you can call tang. I don't say it's good for us in large doses. Some Americans seem to be permanently drunk on their native spirit! Never mind! It's there; it's new; it hasn't been aged; and we have to wait a while. We wouldn't have cared for a daily diet of the Elizabethan Englishman, I fancy—or the Renaissance Florentine! Let us say that some of us find America exhausting, and prefer to remember it in tranquillity. That ought to please everybody. There is also the pathos of distance.'

Mrs. Price, laughing in her throat, said she wouldn't expect an American to accept a piece of cheek like that in tranquillity! However, she added, let's get on with Mr. Bannister. She remarked to the others that they were 'getting warm.' She could see 'the germ' of a story in what he was telling them. It was one of her favorite phrases, 'a germ.'

'Only a germ?' Mr. Spenlove was shocked.

'So far, old chap,' she assured him, affectionately.

'Well, there's no need to invent anything about Jack's early career, so far as I know it,' he said. 'I am a bit involved now, you see, because Mrs. Deming and her child, the present Mrs. Bannister, traveled with me as well as Jack on one or two occasions. I needn't go over that. As Romaine says, Jack swallowed the anchor. And there was no subscription list in the mess-room for a wedding present this time. There was no announcement in the papers about a maritime hero marrying a beautiful creature from over the sea!

'He had again saved a girl from drowning, not in the sea, but in family trouble; from being overwhelmed by the hazards of matrimony on an international scale. It would be easy to say that Deming would have been as great a failure if he had married an American. An American girl of Mrs. Deming's class would have simply left him. Mrs. D. has old-fashioned prejudices. There is, as she put it to me, smiling, "no mud on their petticoats." Mrs. Bannister finds the present situation more complicated than her parents' troubles ever were.'

'Does she still love him?' Mrs. Price inquired.

'I think so, but you can't be sure. The impression I had was that she has a feeling of mortification, a feeling that she has failed as a star attraction. That's my impression. There is wounded pride because he has taken a job, although she is *very* well off, and will be very much better off later on. And then there is the kid.'

'I remember, when I first met her, as a schoolgirl on the ship, and she told me how dissatisfied she was with her parents, she used the word "imbecile" to describe their behavior. She said, too, that to her it was "ghastly." She said her father lived "like a lunatic."

'Very strong expressions; but young girls, when their emotions are aroused, always use strong expressions. I asked her what she meant by them. She said, "Don't you know? Didn't you read about my father?"

'We read a lot of things in the papers which don't stick in our memories unless we have some special reason for it. I had forgotten the case in which her father had figured. It was one of those cases which intrigue the tabloid public because of its intricacy.'

Mrs. Price sat waiting for the story. She was as interested as anyone else in such cases. The reason people wanted to read about them was their *humanity*, she said.

'Well, it involved a woman who did the same kind of work as Deming, one of these highly paid and successful illustrators in magazines. She and Deming had been intimate during his periodical flights from domesticity. At the time of this scandal in the newspapers, however, she was having an affair with another married man, and Deming came into it merely because he had loaned her his cottage in the country. Her friend was described in the papers as a Wall Street man. He had a big house on Long Island, a wife, and children at fashionable schools. He would drive down from New York to his love-nest in Connecticut.

'His wife had suspicions, and she used them to bring action for divorce, naming this woman artist. When private inquiry agents followed the Wall Street man's car and broke in on them, the Jap houseman said the woman was Mrs. Deming. So the fat was in the fire. Neither Mr. nor Mrs. Deming were within fifty miles of the place at the time, but the reporters did not know that. Deming was on Cape Cod with another artist. Our Mrs. Deming was on the Atlantic somewhere.

244

'There were a lot of complications in the affair which made it absorbing to the picture-papers, but they had nothing to do with Deming. He had merely done a friendly act for an old friend. The Wall Street man's wife wanted a divorce for her own reasons. The long-estranged husband of the woman artist decided *he* wanted a divorce. Mrs. Deming, however, the real Mrs. Deming, had no such intention. Her theory was that she was Deming's wife until death did them part.'

Mrs. Price shook with laughter.

'Fred, you have to admit it's an extraordinary country. Mail-order divorces, private detectives breaking in, reporters dashing about getting names and addresses, and pictures of the love-nest in the papers! Never a dull moment over there!'

'You can read about that kind of thing if you want to,' Mr. Spenlove said, smiling. 'I mentioned this case because Deming's daughter heard of it and while she felt that he was a lunatic to get mixed up in such a smelly business, what she felt aggrieved about was that with such a parent, she could not live a normal, sensible life. She had a dark feeling that possibly it was her mother's job to make Deming over into a rational human being. She gave me a hint, that if her mother had more imagination she might keep Deming from wandering, as he was always doing, to seek solace with another woman. Mrs. D. never had any such ideas. Her mind stopped at the normal limits of conventional living. If Deming wandered, all she could do was wait until he came back, which was when he was broke, as a rule. He seemed to have the most extraordinary ups and downs of financial prosperity. If he had it he blew it. As Mrs. Deming once told me, when she was narrating her adventures, if he got a check for a thousand dollars he thought he got it every week, and spent it in a week. So, when he was broke and he had ended one of his emotional benders, he went back to his wife and she would get some money from her people.

'What gave the matter its unusual interest for me,' Mr. Spenlove went on, 'was that Candace, even as a schoolgirl, did not seem to feel her father, who was a genius, was doing anything out of the way in having these periodical pilgrimages into Bohemia. It was his stupidity in getting into the papers, as though he had been running a disorderly house, that she disliked.'

'What else was it?' Mrs. Price inquired, and laughed again with some violence.

'Not from his point of view,' Mr. Spenlove said. 'He had done what he considered a decent thing. An old flame of his was in love, and wanted a place where she could enjoy an affair in comfort. Deming was always a stickler for doing the decent thing, except for his wife and daughter. I believe he would have thrown *them* out of the house to make room for a "friend" who was having a love affair with another man. She would have done the same for him, if occasion arose, of course. Those people have their own code. Wives and daughters don't enter into the matter.

'It would have suited Candace much better if her mother had got a divorce. Mrs. Deming could not do that. She told her daughter that it would be immoral. She once referred to a divorced woman, another passenger, as a trollop, but that was because the woman was behaving like a trollop in the bar. She invariably forgave Deming when he returned, which infuriated her daughter. She would say that now everything would be all right and they would live happily ever after!

'It never worked. Deming would be off again, or he would put on a show like the one Jack Bannister and I saw that night at Christmas. It was Deming himself who finally decided it was no use, he could not carry on, and left for good. When Jack took the matter up, so to speak, mother and daughter were in very straitened circumstances. Deming's vogue was waning, and he vanished into limbo until one day, during the great depression, he got into the papers again by going out of a hotel-room window.

'Looking back to that time, I have no clear memory of Jack leaving the sea. He had left it once before. Men were always coming and going. I heard in the office he had left to get married and had gone back to England. No details. So when I heard a Mrs. Bannister had called I wasn't sure who she was. Then she,' he nodded at Perdita, 'said she was very young, and it flashed on me that Jack really had meant it when he said he was going to get her out of that. He must have married her almost out of the schoolroom, as Deming married her mother.'

'And now this,' Mrs. Price said. 'I still think you'll find it's another woman. It always is.'

'His wife insists he is faithful. She means he would not do anything clandestine. I have the same conviction, though I admit I haven't any solution of the mystery.'

'She's probably imagining things,' Mrs. Price said, making a move.

'That's to be seen,' Mr. Spenlove said. 'It's only twelve miles. We are going over. It is now time for my walk.' He took a heavy ash stick from a corner and made for the door of the garden. Mrs. Price rose too, looking at her watch.

'I have time to finish my number by tea time, if you'll excuse me, ducky.'

CHAPTER

12

THE Virago stopped under a row of fine plane trees bordering a short private drive ending in a high box hedge. On their right was a calm expanse of water with reeds and water-lilies, over which a white-painted wooden bridge led to an iron-studded gate, in an ivy-covered red-brick wall. Beyond they could see the clustered chimneys of a house, of the same rose-colored brick. On a black panel, stuck in the bordering turf, were the words, in gold leaf, Moat Farm.

Perdita, leaning on the steering wheel, sounded a musical note on her triple horn. The gates opened at once and Mrs. Bannister, waving cordially, came toward them, followed by a stream of dogs and a small boy in bathing trunks.

Mr. Spenlove was fascinated by the idea of his old friend and shipmate Jack Bannister turning up as the master of this ancient mansion. Even more absorbing was the realization that Jack had apparently run away from it.

Mrs. Bannister explained they had to keep the gate closed because of the dogs, who would get into the moat and then make a mess in the house. She introduced the little boy.

248

'This is my son, Vivian. Will you drive in now?'

The bright little boy opened the door of the car and climbed in. He glanced around agreeably and then concentrated on Perdita's movements as she backed the car and drove slowly over the bridge into the yard.

It was a very old place, part of an ancient abbey. An enormous red-brick chimney was out of proportion to the main structure, which had probably been the refectory. Tall box hedges, very old and so close in texture as to suggest walls of black-green material, stood around two sides of the court. The front of the house was densely covered with ivy, and the mullioned windows, with leaded panes and overhung with steep red-tiled roofs, maintained the medieval atmosphere. Mr. Spenlove found it more difficult than ever to imagine Jack Bannister settling down in such a setting.

They followed Mrs. Bannister into a large garden. A maid was laying a tea table under a tree, and a very old lady in a wheel chair was staring straight at them as they walked toward her. Mrs. Deming suddenly appeared at the French doors opening on the garden. Bustling and smiling she gave her hand to each and welcomed them with a short sharp shake.

'Lovely of you to come,' she said. 'This is my aunt, Miss Enderby-Breton.' She introduced them in turn to the very old lady, who continued to look at them but made no move of any kind. As Mr. Spenlove said to himself, she seemed to be wondering who they were and how they got past the men-at-arms at the drawbridge of the castle.

Mrs. Deming leaned over the ancient dame, still looking at her guests and smiling at them while she explained.

'In America, Aunt,' she said distinctly. 'We met Mr. Spenlove and Mr. Romaine in America. On a ship, you know.'

Miss Enderby-Breton had a tall ebony stick with a gold knob beside her. She held it in her pale mottled hands, on which could be seen large freckles. Her face, long and imperious, was lined and gray in its pallor.

'America?' she said in a faint, thin voice. It sounded as though she were a long way off. 'Are you Americans? I don't like Americans. They didn't tell me Americans were coming.'

'We left the Americans in America,' Mr. Spenlove said, sitting down beside her.

'What were you doing there?' the old lady said, turning her gaze on him sharply.

'Just having a look around,' he said, and he began to tell her, slowly and politely, who they were, how they had met her niece Mrs. Deming and her grand-niece, Mrs. Bannister, and what they were doing in England after living in America. He knew, from his childhood experience, that the old aristocracy and gentry were that way, abrupt and oblivious. They were not intentionally rude, but their life behind the high walls of privilege and caste was isolated and narrowing. He knew they cherished an intense residual dislike of the America of the Reconstruction Era. It was impossible to erase the impression of that kind of American. They believed the South ought to have won the Civil War. And they were unaware that there had been any change in America or in England, since the seventies, except for the worse.

When Mr. Spenlove said he had been 'giving the natives a treat' in America, she looked sharply at him and then took a cup of tea from the maid. 'Natives?' she said.

'She thinks they're all black over there,' Mrs. Deming said cheerfully. She was not a controversialist. If her aunt wanted to think Americans were colored, she was welcome.

Miss Enderby-Breton stared at Mr. Spenlove as though he were from another world. 'Natives?' she said again.

Mrs. Bannister waved her small son away from the tea-table after giving him a macaroon and came forward.

'Aunt is taking you seriously,' she said to Mr. Spenlove. 'Wouldn't you let me show you the gardens?'

'Very much,' he said at once. He drank his tea and rose. He asked Miss Enderby-Breton to excuse him. She gave a faint gesture of assent, watching him as he walked beside Candace across the lawn to a gap in the box hedge. She turned to Mrs. Deming. 'Who is that man?' she said.

Mrs. Deming looked at Mr. Romaine and smiled. She was known to Miss Enderby-Breton's private thoughts as a fast modern girl. She had made a runaway match with an American. She had lived in Paris with him. A bomb had destroyed the marriage records in the war. A likely story! Mrs. Deming, however, never made any effort to rehabilitate herself in the old lady's mind.

Now she explained that Mr. Spenlove was an old friend whom they had met on the boat coming over from America.

'Old friend of Jack's,' she added. Miss Breton said 'Humph!'

Mr. Spenlove walked beside Mrs. Bannister until they were out of sight. They were proceeding down a narrow passage between high hedges of box leading to the rose garden. When they reached a recessed iron seat, he motioned her to it and sat down.

She stood looking down at him, without resentment, without any discernible emotion save that she seemed to re-gard him as having a perfect right and competence to assume his present role.

'I'm not intruding, am I?' he inquired. 'If you won't regard it as an intrusion, has anything transpired? No news of Jack?'

She sat down and composed her hands and feet.

'I think I told you he wasn't coming back.'

'I understood you to say you thought so. You said he'd been away before. Have you had any news of him? Any clearing of the mystery?'

'I have an idea . . .' she began, and her voice faded. 'It's only a theory, so perhaps I'd better not discuss it.'

'You stick to your opinion that Jack is what you call faithful? I understand how you feel. You're probably right. But that doesn't explain what he's up to, does it?'

'My theory does,' she said, looking down at her hands.

'When I came in here,' Mr. Spenlove said, feeling for a cigar. 'That moat, you know, I had a theory too. I have an idea he wouldn't be able to stick this sort of life.' He studied the fine, gravelly floor of the alley and sniffed the roses. He shook his head. 'Rather a change, don't you think, from his former life? Or the chicken farm in Florida?'

'Well, what am I supposed to do? Go and live in a slum? Or in one of our cottages? I don't see *you* going off and leaving *your* wife!'

'The cases are not the same. I'm not Jack. Mrs. Price isn't your great-aunt. I'm not defending Jack. I resent very much this happening. I was looking forward to seeing Jack's expression when he found me and old Romaine waiting to have a yarn with him about old days! I didn't expect this.'

'He isn't particularly in love with the old days,' she said. 'He once made a very peculiar remark about that. He told me, when I suggested, if he was so damned unhappy living in the country, why didn't he go back to sea? He said, if he hadn't been a fool he would have given up the sea years

252

ago. He said, that was the great mistake of his life. He had just come back from London when he said that.'

'He did?' Mr. Spenlove sat back and stared gravely at the girl beside him. 'Well, you've told me something I didn't know about Jack. I wonder what gave him that idea.' He plunged back into the past for a moment. 'No,' he said. 'No, even when he went on the beach in Costaragua he didn't make any such remark about going to sea. Why, he'd always been at sea, ever since he finished his apprenticeship. He's never been anything else but a seagoing man! And a good one too. He always got the ship along. I wonder what made him say that.'

'He said it,' Mrs. Bannister said. ' "The greatest mistake of his life!" He said his life would have been altogether different if he had made a decision when his chance came.'

'Let me think,' Mr. Spenlove said, holding up his hand.

He was reluctant to admit he was wrong. Having discovered, he liked to think, the knight-errant motif in Jack's career, it would be humiliating to find it no longer offered a key to the future. It had worked all right so far.

Mrs. Bannister looked at him quietly, her chin slightly raised, with an air of haughty yet friendly attention, as though she thought he might be able to solve this problem, having had so much larger experience of what a roving life did to a man.

But that was just what he seemed unable to tell her.

'I've heard of cases,' he said thoughtfully, pulling his beard. 'Cases of men who simply quit. I mean, they quitted matrimony. They didn't run off with anybody else. If they had been religious, they might have entered a monastery. As it was, they merely resumed their single existence. They could not stick double harness. They wanted to live their lives *alone*. But I don't see Jack doing it unless he's changed

253

since I knew him. He had such lofty ideals about the way women should be treated. And wasn't he in love with you? Weren't you . . . ?'

'Very much so,' she said in a low tone. 'It's only since we've been here. He began to change when we came to live here.'

'I see. Well, I see something. Tell you what. Suppose I go in to London and look him up? My girl wants to go to Harrod's and that sort of thing.'

'If you would! Of course . . .' she became much more animated for a moment. 'I don't care! If he wants to go, I'm sure I wouldn't want to keep him! Only it's rather a rotten situation. And it can't go on indefinitely. I'd like him to know that.'

'You don't suggest he wants to go on indefinitely like this?'

She shrugged slightly. 'Looks like it,' she said. 'He's like a very considerate stranger in the house when he comes home. Oh, I haven't any complaint about that. You know we, well, we made an arrangement—on my account . . . I hope you don't think I'm suggesting he is being cruel, or anything like that. But I wouldn't want him to stay if he wants to go. If you know what I mean.'

'Yes, I understand. But we can cross that bridge when we reach it. Where does he live in town?'

'I'll write it down. It's a boarding house. It's near Gray's Inn Road. He doesn't board there, I think. He's a member of a club. . . . He writes from the club.'

'Not the Neptune?'

'That's it. You know it?'

'Very well, though I've never belonged to it. It's popular with the senior skippers of the big lines, P and O, British India, Blue Star, Royal Mail, and so on. I've been there as a guest. You'll find more dignity there than in White's and the Bath Club combined. I was introduced to a man who worked in the Nautical Almanac Office. Mathematical men. They work out the tides years ahead. Jack is in respectable company. They are very particular, I know that. Jack must have changed. How old is he?'

'Forty-five.'

'Hm. It's a problem.'

'Because he's forty-five?'

'He's a very young man for his age. Young in his mind, I mean. That's not the problem I was thinking of. It's this. No matter what he may say to me if I meet him, he won't come back here if he doesn't want to. This job he has, I know what it is. It gives him an unusual amount of freedom of movement. He has his district to cover. I suppose part of the eastern counties. He goes from town to town, from plant to plant, making inspections, putting up at hotels, and living what some people would call an ideal life. He's a sort of semi-commercial traveler. His salary is secure. He doesn't sell anything. So far from selling anything, in fact, he's like a bank-inspector. He is a highly respected and sometimes feared man, for he can order a lot of expensive repairs if he isn't satisfied. The more I think of it the more complicated the problem seems. Far more so than when he went to sea. I'll go and see. You understand, with a job like that, he's *somebody!*'

'And here he's nobody? Is that what you think's the trouble?'

'You know better than I whether you're talking nonsense. I'll see if I can get hold of him. Think of it! I knew Jack before you were born. We ought to get on with the roses. One thing I'd like to be sure of. It's all his fault, of course? He hasn't any grievance?'

255

'I'm not aware of any. Of course I think of Vivian. And the family. Vivian is to have everything.'

'I had that idea,' Mr. Spenlove shook his head. 'I am beginning to see a little of Jack's side of it.'

They walked through long lines of roses now in their full glory. They went on to beds of flowers Mr. Spenlove recognized, though he had forgotten their names. This, too, was a part of the girl's life which Jack would not be able to share. She spoke of Anchusa, of Periwinkle and London Pride. There was a yew hedge and a sunken garden with Saxifrage and Canterbury Bells. There was a tub with a mass of small things with tiny labels on them, and Mr. Spenlove noted, by bending over it for a moment, that the names were in Latin and very long. Jack wouldn't be interested in Genista Dalmatica or Myonotis Explanata. Mrs. Bannister said she had an uncle who was a great traveler, and collected rare plants and sent them home. She pointed to a long greenhouse with a brick chimney at one end.

How can she expect him to settle down here? he asked himself. He saw Jack's side of it more clearly than ever. He became aware of a strong and secular curiosity to find out what Jack was up to. He formulated a quick scheme in his mind to go to the address, close to the Euston Road, and spy around when he took Romaine to town to go to Southampton. He knew this was not a wise thing to do. Always leave people alone, he had learned, was the best way in the long run. But he was fascinated by the problem. This Candace was a special article. If she had been a rich manufacturer's daughter, it might have worked. But this closely entailed, centuries-old patrimony, all concentrating on the girl's son as heir, this ancient place and immemorial quietness, was a bit too fantastic for a man like Jack Bannister.

As they walked back to the people on the lawn, he saw no reason why Jack should imprison himself in such a place. That was strange, surely! he thought. What about Layer-de-la-Pole? Wasn't that the same kind of prison? It was not. He wasn't the same kind of man as Jack. Perdita wasn't the same kind of woman as Candace. Nor was that old crone on the lawn anything like Mrs. Price, who was being tremendously impressed by the whole place, he could see. It was right up her alley as an Englishwoman and a writer; but it wasn't her sort of life at all, any more than it was Jack's.

He heard Candace say something about 'duty.'

'Duty?' he said. 'You mean his duty to you?'

'Shouldn't he come back here?' she inquired. 'Isn't it his duty to come back? What do sailors do? Even if he used to have a wife in every port, as they say . . .'

'He was never that sort,' Mr. Spenlove said firmly. 'He used to be a rather puritanical blighter! He disapproved of what he used to call the "absolutely immoral habits" of sailors. He did! As for duty, duty is a strange word. Renan said no philosophical theory could account for the idea of duty. Jack's duty is what he thinks at the moment is his duty. You too, eh?'

'The boy,' she said, in a faint tone. 'You can't argue about duty when you have a son. I know all about that. Sometimes I wonder if it wouldn't have been better if we had stayed in America. Things were all right between us there, before . . .'

Mr. Spenlove knew that she meant, before they came into the money. He did not say this. He had seen it happen before. He had known other men who had had difficulties when they had married a woman with money. It was particularly hard on men who went to sea.

'You are not to blame,' he said, patting her arm. They came to a gate in the garden wall leading into a small secluded churchyard. He saw a small and ancient church shaded by enormous trees. Mrs. Bannister looked at him with an expression of inquiry, her delicate brows raised ever so slightly. She opened the gate and led the way through long grass to the dark porch.

Mr. Spenlove found himself standing with the girl in front of a tomb on which lay the marble recumbent figure of a Crusader in chain armor and with a round hole in one of his thighs, to indicate how he had been wounded. His hands were folded in prayer. Sir Giles Enderby had been killed at the siege of Acre in 1191. His heart had been brought home.

'Your ancestor?' Mr. Spenlove said in a low tone.

'One of them,' she said, waving her hand to the tablets on the walls, and then pointing to the worn brasses under their feet. 'Place is full of them. Do you suppose Jack gets fed up with this sort of thing too?'

'You're not to blame for them,' Mr. Spenlove said, severely. 'Don't be foolish! I can't speak for him, but he ought to be proud of his man-child, with this behind him.'

'It doesn't seem so!' she said, and led the way out into the sunshine again.

Mrs. Price was standing, ready to depart, when they returned to the party on the lawn. Mr. Spenlove went over to Miss Enderby-Breton to say good-bye. Give her a suit of chain-mail, a hauberk like the one the ancestor was wearing on his tomb, and a casque, she would look a lot like him.

She put up her hand for him to bend down.

'You a friend of Jack's,' she said, in a hoarse whisper.

He nodded. 'Since nineteen-fourteen. One of my old shipmates.'

258

'Tell me, is he any good?' Mr. Spenlove hesitated. 'Is he?' she insisted. 'Oh, one of the best,' he said at a venture. He was not sure what she was driving at.

'What's he up to, then?' she said. Her pale, freckled old hand held his sleeve. 'Got mixed up in some business. Doesn't come home to his family.'

'He'll be back,' he said firmly. 'I'm sure he'll be back. I'm going to see him, you know, in London.'

'That's what you think. I know better. He isn't coming back. Know why? I can't stand him, and he knows it. And I know he can't stand me. That's why.'

Mr. Spenlove hesitated again. He stood up, but Miss Enderby-Breton beckoned him to bend over again. 'I like your wife. Thoroughbred! Nice of you to bring her. I haven't been up to the mark today. Know why? Thought you'd be like Jack. You're all right. Come over and see me again. Tell me everything.'

As the Virago swung into the high road, Mrs. Price said she thought the old lady was quite a character. 'You got very matey with her,' she told Mr. Spenlove. Then she frowned and bit her full lips. She was beginning to see where she could work in a description of Moat Farm in her current serial.

'What it all adds up to,' she said to Mr. Spenlove, 'is that he's terrifically romantic. From what you told us about his past. Terrifically romantic. And while the fit lasts he believes he's doing something frightfully noble. The question is, who's the subject of his nobility now?'

'That's for me to find out,' Mr. Spenlove said over his shoulder. 'So you can go on with the story.'

'That's for you to find out. I know some wives who would jolly soon find out, and without help too. You believe she really wants him back? She's a cool young woman.'

'I can't tell you. I'm not sure. In some ways Candace is rather old-fashioned in her ideas. She thinks it is his duty to stay with her and the boy, and . . .'

'What's so old-fashioned about that? Oh, of course it's her money.'

'It's not the money,' Mr. Spenlove said. 'Jack is not mercenary. And the property is entailed. It's the whole way of life that goes with the property. She showed me the tomb of an ancestor, a Crusader. She told me the little boy was entered at Harrow when he was born. The idea is to get the family running on the old rails. No more Americans! That's the least the old, barren branches of the great tree can do now. In the old days the heir of such a family would marry a French or Italian singer, or a chorus girl, who would bring new blood to old stock. Now it is American blood that revives. Some of these old creatures imagine they will get a touch of the tar-brush, or Red Indian blood. When they look at that little boy they are reassured. They'd never understand that Deming's family were good people in colonial times. From their point of view Jack's duty has been done. He's produced an heir. I'd like to find out whether Jack thinks so.'

Mrs. Price wasn't sure she could use a theme like that. In her stories a guilty man was always discovered in another woman's arms. 'Cherchez la femme?' she said.

'His wife thinks otherwise,' Mr. Spenlove said mildly.

'But no woman would care . . .' she began and then was silent. Spenlove might be right. He often was.

The car sang softly on the smooth road. In the early evening light Mr. Spenlove meditated on the strange destiny of Jack Bannister, the knight-errant of so many diverse distressed damsels. The point was, did the damsels regard him as a knight, or a dragon?

260

He felt very strongly that if he could settle this problem he would have what the statisticians called a yardstick for human behavior. It was no use expecting any help from women themselves. Those who were articulate on the subject were rarely the objects of knight-errantry. Distressed damsels were even less satisfactory. Candace, for instance, would never know that it was that terrible cry of hers, as a young girl, rushing up the stairs away from the maddened, intoxicated Deming on that Christmas night, which settled her fate with the romantic Jack Bannister and set him after her until he rescued her from what Mr. Spenlove cynically called a fate worse than death. Nor would that dumb Brunhilda, Elsa Nelson, whom he had married in New York, feel that she owed her later success to his recklessly quixotic contribution to her fate.

In the billard room that evening, with a cigar and the old Jamaica rum decanter at his elbow, he mused on the various destinies of three men: himself, old Romaine, now playing cribbage with Mrs. Price, and Jack Bannister. Three rolling stones! Jack, the fortunate young prodigy, the hero of the first great war in the history of his generation, who had plunged into matrimony as he had plunged into the cold North Sea, to rescue the beautiful widow of an enemy agent! By the rules, Jack should have achieved the heights.

Mr. Spenlove, wondering in passing whether Candace had ever heard of that early heroism of Jack's, found himself with another conundrum on his hands. What was the essence of paternity? For himself, he had developed a sentiment, as they used to call it, for Sonia, as a child, and now as a charming young lady, a replica of her mother, which transcended anything he had ever experienced in his life. She was his child in every way except that she had not sprung from his loins, and he had been thinking for some years now that that was the least important part of paternity.

He was forced to put Jack Bannister among those men, a fairly large class nowadays, who had no particular feeling for their children. He had seen them on the ship. He had sailed with them. They were at times unpleasantly articulate about it. They left their wives, and they seemed to have no feeling for the offspring at all. It was unconventional to call attention to their existence, yet they were very common indeed in America. It occurred to him that possibly it was the other way round in America. The children disowned the fathers.

It was confusing, however, in Jack's case. What about that girl in Costaragua? If ever a man was complacent because his woman had conceived, and nearly lost his reason when he lost both mother and child, it was Jack Bannister that night in Puerto Balboa. Then look what he had done! Wiped the whole thing out of his life. Gone back to sea and closed the books on the life he had lived ashore. Resumed his former career. And suddenly donned his armor, and with trusty lance in rest, had galloped to the rescue of the peerless Viking maiden, Miss Nelson. Miss Elsa Nelson.

Mr. Spenlove had another idea. What if this business were none of Jack's doing at all? What if he had had no particular desire to sire a son? It was possible. There were some who insisted that a woman often had a lot to do with unpremeditated procreation, especially a son.

Was she that sort? He didn't know. He was too far away from her, in age and background, ever to know. But he could guess! That old great-aunt would have made no bones about going to stud for the family when she was a young woman. She'd make conditions, of course. He would have had to be a thoroughbred, as she called Perdita; bred in the same paddock, with his name in the stud-book, and a long pedigree. Under the surface culture of the upper classes one could always detect their preoccupation with breeding. Mr. Spenlove was ready to admit that, granted their philosophy of hereditary property, they were right, they were realistic and they were logical. But their philosophy wouldn't mean a thing to poor Jack.

He glanced around the room. He liked to read here, and when the mood came, he had a large writing pad and pencil at hand. On a side table, folded neatly, he saw the *Morning Post*, the *Athenaeum*, last Sunday's *Observer*, and an astonishing affair still called *The Saturday Review*. Anyone coming into this place, he reflected, would decide that the master of the house was Colonel Blimp in person, a pulpy-headed old duffer who thought *Punch* was a humorous paper.

It pleased him to avoid any harsh dissonances in his life these days. He didn't like the way things were going. He had watched for half an hour one day in London an almost interminable procession of "workers" through the West End, holding aloft their clenched fists in the Communist salute. And he had also watched the Mosley hoodlums strut and thrust out their jaws like Mussolini. Perdita's young brother, Tad, was one of them. His dear friend Mrs. Price thought they were fine fellows. The people who lived in houses like Layer-de-la-Pole all thought they were fine fellows, who would take care of the radicals and protect Old England.

For once in his life Mr. Spenlove was not at all sure what he himself thought about the state of the world. He knew that there had been changes, but he remembered that when he was a young man starting out, the struggle to get a job, to keep a job and to earn a living had been appalling. You had had to hold onto any kind of position with both hands, your feet and your teeth. The permanent reservoir of unemployed had consisted of millions. It had been dog-eat-dog. There were then no Labor Exchanges, as they were called, where you could register and wait to be assigned. There had been no security at all, except the workhouse if you became destitute.

On the other hand in those days one lived in spiritual security. Even the socialists had been Englishmen and human beings. You could travel in any country except Russia without passports or visas. Those who wanted to escape from the despotism of their own lands could come to England and be safe. London was full of them. The craziest anarchist in the world could preach in Hyde Park on Sunday and the police would protect him. The Kaiser might act like a lunatic, but he was the Queen's nephew and he knew his place, by Jove!

Now there was peace in his time; but Mr. Spenlove was occasionally uneasy. In the deep privacy of his life in the English countryside the sounds of strife were muffled, but he was aware of them. He was occasionally irritated by the lack of imagination of the people with whom he lived. Not Perdita. She was perfect. But when Mrs. Price and Miss Soames, and Father Soames too, talked as if all they had to do was to turn the Mosley fellows loose with machine guns on the radicals, and England would once more become a green and pleasant land, he felt that it would be a fine experience to savor the brash, boisterous intellectual atmosphere of America again. It would be like getting out of a stuffy, Victorian parlor and taking a walk on an open road in the wind.

It was not so easy, nowadays, he found, to be a philosopher. He wanted to remain where he was, meditating on this theme which had captured his fancy, the influence of sea life on history, a sort of metaphysical interpretation of a calling which had always been the helpless victim of romantic writers, or reformers whose hearts bled for poor Jack aloft, afloat or ashore. His aim was to expound his private theory that the best civilizations evolved from sea-faring communities, rather than from great nations with sea-faring fringes. This was what he wanted to do, but the restlessness and the rumbles of the outside world reached even to his quiet haven, and he had to ask himself, what was the future for that son of Jack's, already put down for Har-row; and for Sonia, who would soon be leaving the school in Switzerland, and who was already announcing that she wanted to qualify for "a job." For some obscure reason it was impossible to feel safe about that future.

He went upstairs and found Perdita reading. She had developed a liking for Trollope and was taking in the entire series. 'He's so *sensible!*' she had said, and Mr. Spenlove had agreed with enthusiasm. She had added, 'Half the time I never know what these modern writers are talking about. They aren't interesting. I suppose it's an unfortunate heredity, ducky, but I want a story. I want to know how it comes out.'

She put down *The Duke's Children* and looked at her husband. 'How d'you like it?' he said. She patted it af-fectionately.

'I'm sorry for the girl,' she said.

'What girl?'

'Lady Mabel Grex. She's worth a dozen of Silver-bridge.'

'You know what I think? Trollope missed a chance there.'

'For what?'

'To jump a whole generation ahead of his time. He ought to have made the Duke of Omnium marry her! Think how that would have finished the book! A sensation.'

'Finish with a bang, my father used to say. Yes, it would be grand, that. You ought to write novels, ducky!'

'You think I could finish with a bang? More likely be arrested for indecent exposure of my private life.'

'You and your private life!' She watched him take his accustomed seat in the armchair under the high-pitched ceiling. 'I suppose you expect me to believe you've had a career with women like this Mr. Bannister.'

'My girl, he has led a most exemplary life! He never had an improper thought. No breath of immorality ever tarnished the shining mirror of his soul. I thought you understood that.'

'It's one of your paradoxes. You think he's taken a vow of poverty and is living in a top-back room in a slum in London?'

'If he had the excitation, he would! If something, or somebody, stirred his romantic imagination he would. Make no mistake, it isn't something he is ashamed of, I'll be bound. And it isn't anything immoral that makes him run away from Moat Farm. Oh, no!'

She watched him stare frowningly at the carpet.

'Oh, it's impossible!' he said, as if he had had a sudden revelation. She looked at him in silence.

'Jack,' he explained. 'He could never be a gentleman. Never!'

'And you think that is the trouble.'

'Ah! What he used to call family trouble. It's probably the fundamental reason for all that's happened to him. A knight-errant who isn't a gentleman!'

Perdita gave a little laugh and then she laughed again as she took the idea in. She reached for a cigarette. 'Well,' she said, 'nowadays . . .'

'There's no nowadays inside that moat,' Mr. Spenlove said gravely. 'He has none of their instincts. Your father and mother, for instance, professional people, may be modern in many ways, but they would share the Enderby-Breton instincts. Candace took me through their garden to a tiny

266

churchyard full of old gray stones buried in long grass. We went into the church and I saw an ancestor's tomb, a Crusader. The walls were covered with tablets to Enderby-Bretons and Enderbys. Jack has no idea at all of how they think of things, and being a first-class man in his own right, he doesn't want to learn. He doesn't give a damn. He has probably fled to keep possession of his own soul.'

Perdita looked at him through the cigarette smoke. She was reminded of her own past, when she fled the rich Byzantine splendor of Elliot Ducroy's mansion on Long Island Sound, to keep possession of her own soul.

'Just like me,' she said.

A S THEY drove back from Marks Tey station, they discussed Mr. Romaine's sudden decision to return to town on the same train as Mrs. Price. Mrs. Price had explained that she wanted to stay, but had engagements. Mr. Romaine suddenly chimed in with engagements of his own which he had to attend to before he sailed.

'I thought he was getting so interested in Mrs. Deming we were going to have him here another week at least,' Mr. Spenlove said.

'Well, he knows his own business,' Perdita said. 'It'll be nice to be quiet for a while. You know we are having Tad tomorrow week. Miss Soames wants us then for supper Saturday night. Do you think Mrs. Deming would take a step like that?'

'She might. They've had a lot to say to each other. Romaine told me about this place he has an option on in New Jersey. He said his plans called for a woman on the job there. When he heard Mrs. Deming had had experience keeping

268

poultry, he became more interested in her than ever. His idea is, if you are going to serve chicken dinners it pays to keep chickens.'

'Two hearts that beat as one,' Perdita said. 'He's a decent old chap. Mrs. Deming is old enough to know her own mind.'

She concentrated on the approach to Layer-de-la-Pole.

'He was telling me,' Mr. Spenlove said, 'he'd be scared to live in England any more. He said what he'd seen since he has been here scares him. I asked why? And what? He's been visiting a sister in Glasgow. Married to a foreman in shipyard work who's been out of work for years. I believe Romaine has given them some help. He says he advised them to get out and go to America if they could. His idea of helping the old country is to advise everybody to get out of it.'

'He has his limitations. I noticed it.'

'So has Mrs. Deming,' Mr. Spenlove said. 'As you put it, two hearts that beat as one. Would *you* like to go back? How about that cottage of mine for a month or two?'

'I shouldn't mind that. But not for keeps, darling. I'd rather stick around, even if we do pay ten bob income tax. I know you say there's no truth in that old gag about rats leaving a sinking ship, but it expresses an idea, don't you think?'

She turned into their drive and both uttered an exclamation. Standing in front of the house was a car.

It was a touring car with the top down, a large, dusty and not very new model. There was a man at the wheel with his arm along the seat-back and they could see a woman in the rear seat sitting sideways, her hat and a veil visible over the folded top.

As they arrived, the man got out of the car and stood with his hand on the door. He was a heavily built, youngish man, high-shouldered, and there was a vague familiarity about his pose. Mr. Spenlove, coming forward, thought of Cecil Rhodes. The man was wearing a suit of Donegal tweeds, and his hat, which he wore at a rakish angle, had a small feather. He was wearing brogues, dark and well polished. For a second Mr. Spenlove thought the visitor was from Scotland Yard. Then he recognized him.

'Well, I'm damned!' he said.

'Remember me?' The man withdrew his hand nervously and then, as Mr. Spenlove extended his own, they shook firmly.

'You've changed!' Mr. Spenlove said. He turned to Perdita and introduced the stranger. 'This is my old friend, Jack Bannister.' He glanced involuntarily at the woman in the car, who was regarding them through her motoring veil. 'Jack,' he went on, 'I thought at first you were from Scotland Yard. That shooting suit isn't how I imagined you.'

'Yes, I've changed,' Jack Bannister said quickly, 'but not you.' He looked at Perdita. 'He's just the same. Always imagining funny business.'

'You'll stay to lunch,' Perdita said. He glanced at his wrist-watch and frowned.

'I'm on my way to Norwich,' he said. 'Our head office is at Norwich.'

'Who's your friend?' Mr. Spenlove asked.

'Very old friend of mine,' Jack said, leading the way. 'This is my car, but the company takes care of maintenance, gas, oil, tires, and service jobs. This is Roxane. Remember, Spenlove? My friend, Roxane. She's taken her maiden name again. Miss Vermandois. Darling, remember?'

The woman stretched her hand toward Mr. Spenlove and he caught the old brilliant smile. 'Oh, yes!' she said softly. There was still a faint foreignness in her speech. 'You do not remember? You sink I 'ave *change*, no?' Her smile dazzled.

'Of course I remember Roxane,' he said. 'We were talking about you not long ago. Come in, come in.' He opened the door of the car. Jack Bannister intervened.

'Fact is,' he said hurriedly, 'she can't walk now. Just a minute. If you'll hold the door I'll lift . . .' He scrambled into the car and picked the girl up, rug and all. He backed out carefully, turned around and they formed a procession into the house. Jack lowered his burden on a chaise-longue in the drawing room.

Mr. Spenlove noted a subtle change in Jack Bannister's personality. He had been rather spare and wiry at sea. Now he was built up. He had retained his vigor, but it was encased in a massive body. He had presence and solidity. He was in command of the situation. He showed no embarrassment over suddenly turning up with a woman whom Mr. Spenlove had imagined he had cast off forever years ago because she had left him.

Perdita said she would go and see about having lunch early. She would not think of allowing one of Mr. Spenlove's oldest friends to leave without lunch. She went out, followed by the brilliant gaze of Roxane and Jack Bannister's frank, almost incredulous curiosity.

'What sort of accident?' Mr. Spenlove said, to give Jack a chance to recover from his tense mood. For he was tense, Mr. Spenlove could see now.

'A long story,' Jack said, walking about the room, his hands in his pockets.

'You've been a long time coming to see us,' Mr. Spenlove took a new line. 'Sit down, Jack. We're glad to see you. We expected you when your family came to dinner. Want a glass of sherry?'

'Not me. She,' he pointed, 'she'll have one. I'm teetotal. Got to be, in business.'

'I hear you're a surveyor. Is that right? A surveyor?'

'You can call it that,' Jack said, sitting down and crossing his legs. Mr. Spenlove went out to get the sherry. When he came back Jack was standing behind the chaise-longue bending over Roxane, her hand in his.

'You have a lot to explain,' Mr. Spenlove said, pouring the wine. 'Begin at the beginning.' He handed a glass to the woman, who gave him her great eyes, like stars, and said, 'Ah-h! We arrive! At last we arrive. He . . .' she indicated Jack. 'He tell me of his frien'.'

'Did he?' Mr. Spenlove said. 'What have you been doing with yourself all this time?' He made a gesture toward the rug that covered her. 'When was this?'

'You been to Moat Farm?' Mr. Spenlove nodded. Jack shrugged and sat down again. 'I think that's a closed chapter in my life,' he said. 'That's really why I came to see you, knowing you'd been over there. I don't want you to have any wrong ideas. I thought she might have given you wrong ideas.'

Mr. Spenlove glanced at Roxane. She said, looking at each of them in turn, 'That is all right. I know all about this Moat Farm. Jack tell me everyt'ing.'

'How do you know we have any wrong ideas?' Mr. Spenlove said in a flat tone. 'Let's have your story. How long has this been going on.'

'In a way,' Jack said, 'ever since we were married.'

Mr. Spenlove looked incredulous. 'All these years!' he said. 'I thought you were divorced. Weren't you?'

'I said, in a way,' Jack said. 'Of course not all these years. We have been parted, as you know. There was a misunderstanding. Now we have found each other again. In London, about a year ago.' He and Roxane exchanged glances and she nodded. 'By an accident. That's a joke. It was an accident, all right! Now we're together.'

'What happened?'

'I told you. Accident. She had a business. After her husband died she started a business. Artificial flowers. Did it all herself. Employed several girls at it.'

Mr. Spenlove, meeting Roxane's brilliant eyes, and noting the blending of her own rich brunette beauty with the rust-colored veil that lay beside her and the snowy chamois gloves, that she looked a little like an artificial flower herself. He said, 'Yes; and the accident? Serious?'

'Explosion,' Jack said. 'Printer's shop next door. Gas-engine in a shed in the yard. It exploded, or the gas-tank did. Wrecked the entire building. Brought down the girders. She was pinned down . . .' Jack Bannister thrust out his own legs in front of him and drew his right hand slowly across his thighs, just above the knees. He covered his eyes with his left hand for a moment. 'Amputation,' he said, in a stifled tone.

'Hm! And that was where you met. Or had you . . . ?'

'That's how we met again. By an accident, as I told you. I had to report on the explosion for the underwriters. It was a sort of miracle, to find her there. She was buried . . .'

'It's quite a story.' Mr. Spenlove reflected that Jack had a genius for being in such stories. 'What became of the artificial flower business?'

'Wrecked, of course. She got compensation. The landlord had a big suit on his hands. He'd been warned about that gas-engine being too close to the gas and electric mains. She was living with a relation in Bloomsbury, a private hotel in Bloomsbury. I live there when I'm in town. The Continental. It's convenient for me in several ways. She can't get about much, so I take her with me when I'm on a trip. That's one reason I don't go to Moat Farm even if I wanted to. I thought it would be an idea, why not drop by and see old Spenlove? I've had it in mind ever since I heard you'd been living here.' He nodded at Roxane. 'She was always asking about you. She remembered you, all right. When I spoke about you, one of the first things she asked when she was in the hospital, and getting better, was where was that man with the beard she met before we were married? That was nineteen-fifteen wasn't it? Ah, twenty years ago. Time flies. And she remembered you! Used to ask about you. I didn't know much. Of course, then I had no idea you'd come back to the old country.'

The door opened and the apple-cheeked maid looked in. Mr. Spenlove rose and said, 'Lunch. How about . . . ? Can she sit at table?'

Jack Bannister had risen too and shook his head. 'She has a tray,' he said. He went over to her and bent to speak to her. She put up her arms to hold his shoulders. Mr. Spenlove went into the dining room to see about the tray. Perdita said that was quite all right. She would send a tray.

'So she used to ask about me,' he said when they sat down. Jack had got up and set the door slightly open, so that he could see the chaise-longue. Sonia, coming in to lunch, was introduced, but Jack hardly looked at her. He was still a little tense from the strain of his great experiment. He was not entirely sure of himself.

'Often,' he said. 'I'd have brought her down before, after I heard you were here, but I wasn't sure whether you hadn't got some wrong ideas from over there. I was always in the wrong pew with them, you know. Yes, the wrong pew.' He laughed shortly. 'You knowing her when we were in London, you had a claim, you might say. But I didn't know.'

'Must have been a great shock,' Mr. Spenlove said. He explained to Perdita about the explosion.

'Terrible!' Jack said. 'Touch and go, whether she'd win or lose. It was due to that I lost touch, you might say, with Moat Farm. Difficult thing to explain. They wouldn't have understood about her.' He nodded toward the chaise-longue. 'Never!'

'No doubt,' Mr. Spenlove said drily, and he laughed. 'You haven't changed inside, Jack,' he went on. 'You've put on weight, and I hardly recognized you at first, but you're the same Jack. Always after a new thrill.'

'I haven't changed about Roxane,' Jack said. 'You have to get that straight. I've never really lived before. She's the same. She often says it was a mistake, her leaving Liverpool.'

'Annie Collins said the same,' Mr. Spenlove said. Jack shook his head.

'It was Annie drove her away!' he said. 'She didn't understand Roxane at all. But it was my fault, in the first place. I didn't fully realize what I'd got. I ought to have stayed to look after her.' He bent his head over his plate. 'I shouldn't have signed on for that voyage. I was carried away.'

'You came home quick enough.'

'That's not the point. I should never have left her. She's one of those who need a man, their own man, close beside them all the time.'

'And you mean you're anchored, tied up for life? You have finally found what you want? Swallowed the anchor?'

'I'm pretty busy now,' Jack said. 'I have eastern counties and London north of the Thames. It's a big assignment, and a big thing for me eventually. There's a lot of new factories going up. I live in London mostly, on account of Roxane, but the head office is Norwich. That's where I'm headed now.'

'I hear you go to the Neptune Club,' Mr. Spenlove said.

'That's right. Meet a lot of the other fellows in the business there. British Association men. She tell you? Candace?'

'That's so. She told me a lot of things.'

'Well, I wanted to be sure you hadn't got the whole thing wrong. Are you taking her side?' He got up to go into the other room as the maid carried in a tray. He stood looking around the table. 'I was thinking that—well, never mind.' He went after the maid.

Mr. Spenlove said to Sonia in a low tone to make no mention of this to Candace. Perdita kept her eyes on her food. Sonia shrugged slightly. 'Of course,' she said.

He looked at her and said nothing. Of course she would say nothing. Sonia had been through a number of family crises in childhood. Hollywood must have been a queer experience for a small girl before Elliot Ducroy had come on the scene and married Perdita. Then there was Elliot's death. He knew Sonia had some knowledge of the other crises that preceded his death, but that was a period which he and Sonia never mentioned.

Jack came back to the table, looking at his wrist-watch.

'Have to be pushing off,' he said. He accepted a piece of cheese. He glanced around the room, as though he had not seen it before. 'You're very comfortable here, Spenlove. You own it?' Mr. Spenlove said no, a lease. 'Snug as a bug in a rug, as we used to say.' Jack continued, 'I was surprised when I heard you had come back to the old country. Lot of water under the bridge since we were on the ships together. We've got on, both of us. When I get my affairs straightened out, I may have a place in the country, too. Take a little time, though.'

'You aren't coming down this way, I suppose?'

'Not on your life!' Jack Bannister gave a faint laugh. 'Not my line, not our line at all, this part of the country.' He looked down his nose, that nose which had a distinct resemblance to the nose of Cecil Rhodes. 'Somewhere near Bourne End's more what I had in mind. Near the river. A lot of our fellows have places there. Oh, no! I wouldn't think of the eastern counties, or anywhere near Tollemache St. Marys.'

'I admit I'm surprised, Jack,' Mr. Spenlove said. 'I didn't give you credit for swallowing the anchor. At least not here, in England.'

'It's what I should have done years ago,' Jack said. He stirred his coffee and frowned. 'The sea's an absolutely wasted life. I was never able to settle . . . I feel I'm really living now.' He inflated his chest. 'I was dying of dry rot. That was a mistake from the start. Coming back to England, I mean, and doing the country gentleman business.'

'I gathered that. But it's a very serious thing and I can't discuss it just now.'

'Wouldn't do any good to discuss it if you take her side.' He looked at Perdita and smiled. 'He always wants to discuss things. Talk the hind leg off a donkey in the old days. I told Roxane I bet Spenlove'll have a fine tale to tell if we go and see him. So she said, then let's go and see him.'

'We are very fond of your wife,' Perdita said, quietly.

'Sure. She's fine. Don't get me wrong, Mrs. Spenlove. It's my fault. Always is. Always was. I'm the fly in the ointment. I've been told so often enough.'

He looked around the room again and out into the garden

277

past the open French windows. He shook his head. 'I know now,' he said. 'I guess I'm one of the working classes.' He glanced again at his watch. 'I really do have to push off.' He started for the other room.

They followed him out as he strode to the car and laid the woman carefully on the rear seat, tucking the rug around her. She held out her hand to them with a sudden gesture of dazzling friendliness. Mr. Spenlove noted that her hand was very white and waxen in texture. Seen close, there were tiny lines at the corners of her eyes, but she was extremely brilliant. She said, 'Zank you so mooch! Nex' time I tell you everyt'ing.'

They watched Jack start the engine. Mr. Spenlove explained that if he continued right around the buildings he would find another way out.

'Tradesmen's entrance,' Jack said, and gave Mr. Spenlove a sardonic grin. 'Okay. See you again soon.' He drove forward slowly. They saw Roxane's white-gloved hand wave over the back of the car and heard a short toot of Jack's horn. They were alone.

Mr. Spenlove went into the billiard room to get a cigar. Jack was running true to form. Here was one of those timeless passions which modern men regard with skepticism and uncertainty. Jack had retained his first love with all the vehemence of his youth and strength. The other adventures had been merely inadequate substitutes for that matchless first experience he had missed when he left Roxane and gone to sea at the call of patriotic duty. Now that she was back in his life not even the shocking misfortune she had met altered his feeling for her. In fact Mr. Spenlove had a suspicion that this set a seal on her for Jack. His devotion was now a selfless and sexless exaltation.

Mr. Spenlove had a sudden illumination. He began to

recall what their first meeting would do to a man of Jack's starved imagination, the clutching of the girl's inanimate body in the cold North Sea, when Jack's first ship, the Lavenham, had been almost blown out of the water, the refugees struggling to reach life-belts and the boats from the destroyer. He remembered the furore, as one of the juniors called it in derision, when it became known that Jack had been a hero. What had become of the citation, and the medal? No kind of achievement was so transitory, as a rule, as heroism. He remembered the Crimean war medals and ribbons in the pawnbrokers' shops when he was a boy.

But the value of that episode, in forming Jack's character and shaping his career as a romantic, was enormous. It had been the great event of his life. It had become a symbol. It was the nucleus around which all his subsequent actions had functioned. He had formed a conviction that his fate and Roxane's were intertwined, even after she had run away with another man, and after she had divorced him and married a man who was able to give her much more than a wandering seaman. He had wandered, certainly, and he had sought solace all over the world, as a substitute for his loss. Nothing had come of it except, possibly, the little boy at Moat Farm. With some men that would have been very important indeed, but with Jack Mr. Spenlove believed it had no validity.

Then again, Roxane was far more glamorous to a man like Jack than Candace. She was forty, nearly twice the age of Candace, but she had a quality Candace never would have. She was no longer young, and it was obvious that she had been in London, for all Jack's idealistic account of it, what would have been called in the old days demi-monde. Damaged goods was another euphemism. To Jack that mattered not a snap of his fingers. She had something which had

279

struck fire in his soul at the first glance. He had of course been terrifically inexperienced then. He had made every possible error in dealing with the situation. He had lost her, but he had retained the dream. He had followed the dream all over the world. He had become a knight-errant, and he had squandered his emotions on all kinds of women, but he had kept the dream, and the hope.

And so, wasn't he, in his own way, in the great tradition?

He had turned what most men would have called a fluke, an impossible barrier to happiness, into something exclusively fine and heroic. He was giving all he had to a woman who had deserted him and who had now nothing to give in return save gratitude. Mr. Spenlove, however, was not too sure about that. He recalled that dramatic gesture, when Jack covered his eyes with his hand and spoke of the accident and its tragic denouement.

Walking out into the garden to watch Sonia and her friends playing tennis, he wondered what was going to happen over at Moat Farm, Tollemache St. Marys. He felt a pang. It might indicate a definite difference between himself and his old shipmate, but he felt a pang. He admired that young lady very much indeed. Next to Perdita and Sonia, she was more to him than anyone he knew. It was obvious to him that they would stand by her now.

CHAPTER

14

PERDITA said at breakfast that she and Sonia were going to Felixstowe. They were taking Miss Soames. He ought to come too, she said, but her tone was without emphasis. One of the secrets of their private happiness was their reluctance to take charge of each other.

'Swimming?' he said. Sonia nodded. She inherited her mother's delight in the sport.

'I would,' he said, 'but I have an appointment. The telephone rang when I came downstairs this morning.' He was an early riser and took his morning tea on the porch at six.

'You want to go somewhere?' Perdita said.

'No, it's Jack Bannister, he said he would call and see me. He's alone, and he wants to see me. He called me from Cambridge. He's on his way to Ipswich and said he'd drop in.'

'I suppose he realizes we are on his wife's side,' Perdita said. 'I am, anyway.'

'We all are. He realizes it, but he wants something. It isn't support so much as confirmation of what he is doing.

And I want to see him when she isn't around. He thinks he's one of the luckiest fellows alive and he wants me to think so. He was always convinced he was luckier than anyone else. When he had that affair in Costaragua there was nobody like him while it lasted. Now he has reached the heights.'

'If he thinks so,' Perdita said, calmly. 'Don't you think Candace came to see us because she knew we'd be on her side?'

'Very likely. She needed somebody who understood what she had been through. Her mother, Mrs. Deming, said she had been mother as well as grandmother to the little boy, Vivian. I said I expected she loved it. She said, "That's what *you* think!" She said now she had to be father too. She was laughing as she said it, but she's not an old woman.'

'She's very efficient,' Perdita said. 'They have five maids at Moat Farm, and a house-boy. Old Miss Enderby-Breton has a chauffeur for a Lanchester as big as a church. I don't know how many gardeners they have. But Mrs. Deming's very domestic, and does a lot of work herself.'

'She had a tough apprenticeship with Deming. I expect she had to be father as well as mother to her own child when Candace was small. Deming had a way of making any woman efficient and self-reliant.'

A couple of hours later, as he sat in the garden, he heard a car and got up to receive Jack Bannister. Jack came striding across the lawn, high-shouldered and vigorous, a touch of the sporting man about his attire. There was the tiny feather in his hat-band and now he had a dog's head on a stickpin. It was obvious that this was what he had really wanted all his life, a middle-class, provincial businessman's career. This was what he had subconsciously worked toward for years.

'They've gone to Felixstowe to swim,' Mr. Spenlove said. 'Are you alone?'

'She didn't want to come this time,' Jack said hurriedly. 'She's got the idea we don't fit in here just now. She's got it into her head you're on my wife's side.'

'We are,' Mr. Spenlove said frankly. 'But I understand your side of it, Jack. Tell her I understand. You see, we like Candace. We think she has a right to know what you're going to do. She's been expecting to hear, so she can make her own plans.'

'She give you that idea? She knows well enough it would do no good for me to go back there and start it all over again. She knows I'm in the wrong pew. All that moated grange business.'

'Crusaders,' Mr. Spenlove said, smiling.

'Ah, and Battle of Bosworth, Battle of Hastings for all I know. Crusaders?' he said loudly. 'Well, Spenlove, I can beat that. Roxane can, I mean. By a hundred years!' He drew out a pack of cigarettes, tapped one and lit it with a sweep of the match on his thigh and threw the match on the grass. He drew deeply on the cigarette, exhaling it in jets from his nostrils.

'I'm to blame for everything,' he went on, as Mr. Spenlove looked at him in wonder. 'I should never have left Roxane. I should have stayed. She was in a terribly difficult position.'

'Annie Collins told me.'

'Annie Collins told you? I bet Annie Collins gave you a fine yarn! She made Roxane's life a hell! I don't wonder she ran away. That again was my fault. I must have been mad. Cut off my nose to spite my face. It would have served me right if—well, it's all over now.'

'All that doesn't help your wife,' Mr. Spenlove said

in a dry, distant tone. 'She's your wife. Mother of your son.'

'Mother of my son? You see *me* with a son named Vivian? He's *her* son. Nobody there ever thought of me as having anything to do with him. Her uncle Vivian entered him at Harrow as soon as he was born. Harrow! He'll have an Old School Tie! Uncle Vivian went there and Uncle Vivian's uncle. I don't fit in! I felt like a whore at a christening. You see those people in the *Sketch* and the *Tatler,* and they're the only people who read about themselves. They don't know it, but they're a thing o' the past. They're as dead as the dodo. And nobody's going to keep *me!* I can stand on my own two feet. That's what I'm doing right now, standing on my own two feet. It's better than being a rich lady's pet dog.'

'Don't get excited,' Mr. Spenlove said. 'I told you I understand your point of view.' Jack Bannister was drawing so hard on his cigarette it was blazing and dropping. He gave a final pull and threw it away, where it sent up a thin blue reek. He stared down the vista to the vegetable garden beyond the apple trees, frowning and gnawing the short ends of his clipped moustache. Mr. Spenlove thought to himself: he's an able man; a much abler man than I've been in the habit of thinking. There may be something in the theory that he ought never have gone to sea in the first place.

'I tell you,' Jack went on, more quietly. 'It's put new life into me. I was dying on my feet. I was tired, tired, tired!' He looked scornfully at Mr. Spenlove for a moment. 'You know how it is usually, when there's family trouble; a girl goes home to her mother. Candace has never left her mother!'

He got up and took a step or two. He looked suddenly down at the book Mr. Spenlove had been reading, as though trying to focus its significance. 'You read that sort of stuff?'

The title of the book was *What Marx Really Meant*. Mr. Spenlove said he did. He was surprised to hear Jack mutter that it was time those damned Communists were sent back to Russia.

'Well, don't look at me,' Mr. Spenlove said. 'I'm just as vague about what Marx really meant now as Marx was. It passes the time to keep in touch with modern thought.'

'Passes the time? I don't know how you stand it, Spenlove. It seems to suit you, but I would have thought you would go crazy among these *Sketch* and *Tatler* people. Still, I suppose it's not the same thing.'

'It certainly is not the same thing,' Mr. Spenlove said. 'This isn't a moated grange, Jack.' He saw old Rover coming across the lawn to them. 'No rich lady's pet dogs. Only old Rover. And my stepdaughter.'

'You always had a way with passengers,' Jack said. 'Where's old Romaine?'

'London. Sailing Saturday for New York. He is buying a new business. He was having a vacation.'

'I wonder you haven't got a business,' Jack said. 'What d'you do with yourself? You can't read all day.'

'I manage all right. I happen to be in love with my wife, and we have a daughter, as I mentioned. It's a matter of temperament, I suppose. I'm glad you've found what you wanted. I wonder you live in London?'

'If it wasn't so far for me, we'd live at Brighton. We go there week-ends. Or Bournemouth. If I get shifted to the southeastern district we'd have a place at Torquay.'

'You've found what you wanted,' Mr. Spenlove said again. 'That's the great thing. You'll get settled now. No more rushing around . . .'

Jack Bannister sat down and looked at his feet. He made

no immediate reply to this. Then he said, 'What's Candace going to do? Any idea?'

'You'd better ask her yourself. There's the telephone. Give her a ring.'

'I wouldn't do that. I'm not sure that would be a good idea at all. We've never been able to look at each other since we came to that place.'

'She said she thought perhaps you'd have been happier if you'd gone back to sea.'

'That's the sort of thing she would think. Shows how little she knows about me. Roxane would never say that. She wants me near her. I often dash back to London from Norwich, just for the night. And there's not a thought of anything sensual in the business. You understand that, Spenlove? I've dedicated my life to that girl. She's everything in the world to me. *She was at first.* Like a fool I let my happiness slip . . .'

He looked at his wrist-watch and got up. 'I must be in Lowestoft after lunch,' he said. 'I'm glad we've had this talk. I don't want this to make any difference to us. Roxane wants you to come and see us in London. Will you be here all summer?'

'Not all summer.' He thought suddenly it would be a good idea for Perdita and himself to have a few weeks roaming. 'We may go to New York and to my place in Connecticut.'

'Lucky you,' Jack said. He came out of himself and looked around at the garden. For a moment he was at a loss. There was slight fissure in his self-confidence. 'It takes all sorts to make a world,' he went on. 'It'd kill me, not to have a job of work.' Only for a moment. Then he was himself again.

They walked around the house to the car. He shook hands vigorously. He seemed so much larger than when he was at sea that Mr. Spenlove said his new job must agree with him.

'Don't forget Roxane,' Jack said. 'She's made a new man of me. Good-bye. Don't forget, either, she wants you to come and see us.'

'Perhaps I will.'

Mr. Spenlove watched him turn and drive past, raising his hand in salute. Then Jack was gone again.

Mr. Spenlove went back to find out further what Marx really meant. But he found his attention wandering. It was not Marx he was thinking of, but Jack's wife. He had enjoyed telling Perdita the story of Jack's odyssey, but he was not sure that he wanted to keep in close touch with it. Jack couldn't be said to have returned to Penelope. It was rather as if he had deserted Penelope and gone to live with Circe, with a view to spending his life with her. And Mr. Spenlove reflected that there are many more Circes about nowadays.

It might be a sign of advancing age, but he took Penelope's side. At the same time he admitted that Jack would never settle down as the lord of the manor at Moat Farm. He would not be able to comprehend the struggle in his wife's bosom to return to the family traditions. Her mother's departure from the strait and narrow path—so it would appear to the Enderby-Bretons! What a tragedy, to have contracted that alliance with an American! Candace herself was the living embodiment of that first error. When Deming threw himself out of the hotel window, a penniless suicide, what must have been the sensation of this ancient clan, in Davos Platz, in Bellagio, in Torquay and in Tollemache St. Marys! When the uncle Vivian died and Candace returned with a son and an heir and with Jack Bannister, would not their sensations be even more difficult to analyze?

The more he thought of it, with the remembrance of old Miss Enderby-Breton in mind, the more rational Jack's actions appeared. He had said, 'She had never left her mother!' Was that it? Was that a clue?

Whatever it was that had made their marriage possible had disintegrated when they left America, he thought. That was an awesome illumination into human relations. The little boy hadn't disintegrated, however. Mr. Spenlove was somewhat dismayed at the line his thoughts were taking, but he was enjoying them all the same. He had no compunction about following them to their logical conclusion, which was that you never know what will emerge when you meddle with traditions.

After lunch he took his stick and Rover and set out for the rectory in the next village. Four miles along a pleasant country road. Father Soames had a mellow brick house facing the green, with a gate leading to the churchyard from his garden.

Seeing the little two-seater car in the old coachhouse, Mr. Spenlove knew the owner was somewhere near, so he walked into the garden and sat down. The rector came through from the church almost at once. He found his guest reading a pamphlet that lay on the table. Mr. Spenlove put it down hastily and shook hands.

'I'm glad you came in,' the rector said. 'I was thinking of coming to see you. I've had a visit from a friend of yours.' Mr. Spenlove waited. 'Mrs. Bannister.'

'It's a lawyer she needs, not a parson,' he said.

'Possibly, but she came to see me. She wanted you to know. She thought she might come here to see you. She's in a rather nervous state.'

'It's not surprising. Did you advise her? About her husband?'

'It was about her mother she came. Mrs. Deming is leaving Moat Farm.'

'Leaving . . . ?'

'To go to America. Mrs. Bannister thinks it unwise.' He hesitated. 'As a matter of fact, she's already gone to London. She's going to be married.'

Mr. Spenlove looked at Father Soames without saying anything.

'To Mr. Romaine,' the rector added. 'Mrs. Bannister had a telegram yesterday from her mother. They are to be married tomorrow morning.'

'In a registry office?'

'No, in church. St. Gabriel's.'

'I don't see what you could do about it, Father. Mrs. Deming's a mature widow. If you ask me, I think it's all right. I suppose her daughter thinks she ought to stay at Moat Farm and spend her life taking care of the son and heir.'

'Thinks it's her duty,' Father Soames said. He stood by the green-painted table folding the pamphlet, which was on the subject of the laying-on of hands. The title, *Are Bishops Priests?* had startled Mr. Spenlove. It had made him put the thing down. He respected the Church of England because he had been born and bred in it, but he avoided theological controversy. He knew Father Soames did too, being a practical Christian and often giving consolation and hope to his parishioners without making a single remark about religion. It was probably this shining goodness which had inspired the visit of Candace, poor girl.

'I dare say she does,' Mr. Spenlove said. 'And the old aunt, who has all the money, or a great deal of it, thinks so too, I expect. Mrs. Deming inherited her own money from her grandfather, or somebody. I didn't pay much at-

289

tention when she told me. It was in a trust and she couldn't touch the principal for I don't know how long. During the war she couldn't get the interest either. She's the sort of woman who gets into all kinds of trouble but who bobs to the surface every time.

'Mrs. Bannister told me her mother had a small independent income,' the rector said. 'She thinks her mother should have stood by her in this trouble about her husband.'

'How do you look at it? I suppose you couldn't advise her to have a divorce.'

'They could live apart. The Church . . .'

'But my old friend Jack Bannister has burned his boats. He thinks he's doing a virtuous thing. He is devoting his life to a former wife who is now a hopeless casualty. He told me he had never really loved any other woman. It sounds fantastic, but he's a fantastic fellow. He's as fantastic as Chinese Gordon, or Lawrence of Arabia, or Jonathan Swift, or Lord Nelson.'

The rector's good-humored features expressed a tolerant amusement. He knew Mr. Spenlove's weakness for casuistry.

'You ought to have been a Jesuit,' he said, smiling. 'She isn't one of my communicants, and even so I couldn't do more than suggest patience. It isn't spiritual assistance she wants so much as friendship. You can do more for her than I, in fact. She likes you and your wife so much. What she is afraid of is this business is going to throw up a barrier. She thinks you will take her husband's side, or withdraw to a certain extent. Since she came back to England she hasn't made many friends. This trouble, and her great-aunt, and having the child, of course . . . You see what I mean?'

'Well, invite us over and see she comes too. We are very much on her side, but of course I couldn't actually tell a man I've known for twenty-five years or so not to come.

He came without being asked, anyway. He was over again this morning. He wanted me to have his side of it.'

'And you have it? His side of it? I don't see . . .'

'Yes, I have his side of it. In a way,' Mr. Spenlove relit his cigar, a sign to the rector that he was about to make a pronouncement. 'In a way Jack almost makes me believe in what we used to call metempsychosis. Nobody believes in it now—only in psychoses. But it's a special kind of reincarnation. He seems to me to have got his lives telescoped. He's living them all at once, if you know what I mean.'

'You're an arch-heretic as well as a potential Jesuit,' the parson said. 'I don't have any jurisdiction over either of you. Fortunately. All right. He's burned his boats, you say. She can stay where she is and take care of her son.'

'But she's only twenty-one or so. She'll want to marry again.'

'She says she has no intention. She told me she wishes to have no further troubles with men. She told me a little of her childhood, about her father.'

'I dare say she says that now, but you can take it from me she would never make it stick. She's a handsome and intelligent girl. Nonsense!'

'We can cross that bridge when we come to it,' Father Soames said.

'And meanwhile her mother's left home,' Mr. Spenlove said. 'She'll be Mrs. Romaine tomorrow. The more I think of it the more I admire that lady. She isn't intelligent in the way her daughter is. There's a lot of the father, the artist, in the daughter. And Romaine has got hold of the very woman to make his life a success. He always did like her when she was a passenger. He used to say she was very refined, and that's the last word with Romaine. They'll raise thousands of chickens and they won't all die, as they did when Jack was running things. They both have a solid hold on life. They think we should let the dead past bury its dead. They have both buried actual wife and husband and their idea is, I fancy, to let Candace dig herself out. Is that unchristian, Father?'

'I'm not going to be pinned down,' the rector said. 'It's what many people do. Candace is here and we are here. We can wish your friends all happiness. I wonder why Mrs. Deming went off like that.'

Mr. Spenlove laughed.

'I can hazard a guess. For a good many years she was married to a man, a genius, her daughter called him, who went off whenever he darned well pleased, with other women. For years more she has been on hand, always on hand, as a sort of assistant mother, unpaid. She's been busy in that big old family mansion since she came back to her native land. She's been regarded as a permanent blot on the family scutcheon because she eloped with an American. So she has slipped her collar and decided to live on her own. She's a very fine woman. To an infinitesimal degree she has added to the gaiety of the nations.'

'I'm glad to know it,' Father Soames said, smiling. He gained a certain amount of amusement from Mr. Spenlove's extravagant interpretations. That gentleman rose to walk home. Rover roused himself from his meditations.

'My sister will give your wife a ring. Saturday, I think.'

'Her brother is favoring us with a visit on Saturday. For the week-end.'

'Bring him too,' said the rector. 'I've met him.'

'You'll have a party of heretics. Young Tad, a corruption not of tadpole but of Theodore, may grow more mellow with time, but I doubt it. He thinks I am a museum piece.'

'British or South Kensington?'

Mr. Spenlove went away swinging his ash-plant and shaking his head.

Perdita was grave when she heard. They were both silent for a moment. Suddenly Mr. Spenlove struck one hand on the other.

'Now I know what he was talking about,' he said. He made a gesture of impatience with his own intelligence.

'Who?' Perdita said.

'Jack. We were talking about his wife's ancestors. Crusaders. He said Roxane could beat that by a hundred years. And I never even tumbled.'

'I don't tumble now,' Perdita said patiently.

'I don't blame you. It was thinking of her name that gave me the key. Sir Somebody Enderby was killed at the Third Crusade. I suppose Jack has found out that it was a Vermandois who led the First Crusade. Roxane's ancestors, possibly.'

Perdita smiled. Then she laughed. Mr. Spenlove laughed too.

'You have to hand it to him,' she said. 'He has a lot of imagination.'

CHAPTER

15

THEY were at lunch the following Saturday when loud honking of an automobile horn in front of the house announced that the week-end was begun.

'I bet that's Tad,' Perdita said. 'He always makes such a noise.' She got up to go to the door. Mr. Spenlove continued to investigate a veal-and-ham pie.

He rose to shake hands with an extremely handsome and alert young man of thirty. He had been wearing a leather aviator's helmet with goggles and he still wore a leather jacket and held huge gauntlets. Tad Price drove a long, low, open two-seater Napier. One of his aphorisms was, a man could support a wife or a Napier, but not both. His ambition was to turn it in for a long, low, open Bentley, a six-liter one for choice, custom-body with aluminum panels, and supercharging. . . .

'Did you get arrested?' Mr. Spenlove inquired. Tad was well-known to the police, he admitted, as a speed demon. He had made an elaborate chart of all the police traps in the southeast of England, sending it out as complimentary publicity to his firm's clients, most of whom drove long, low, open two-seaters, parked Saturday nights near the Hind's Head at Bray, or the Metropole at Brighton. There was no doubt as to Tad's enjoyment of what he called a change, but it would have been the greatest change of all if he had spent a Sunday at home.

'Lunch?' Mr. Spenlove said. He never quite knew what to say to Tad. He was pretty sure Tad made fun of him in the City. He certainly did down at Layer-de-la-Pole. 'You must have knocked off early to day.'

Young Mr. Price walked around the table and kissed Sonia with relish and she hugged him with enthusiasm. Sonia liked her uncle Tad, and Mr. Spenlove was honest enough to admit to himself that it was a perfectly proper relationship.

'Listen to the voice of experience!' Tad said. He threw down his helmet and gloves, drew out a chair and sat down, pulling the claret bottle toward him. Sonia got up and gave him a glass from the side board. 'Five-day week, old chap. Another vicious radical innovation!' He poured carefully, set the bottle down and, because he knew Mr. Spenlove hated smoking during a meal, lit an Egyptian cigarette. 'However, it saves electricity and so on. And what have the idle rich been doing with themselves? I wanted to come last week. Perdita said you had a guest.'

Perdita told him it was an old friend of her husband. Then she gave him a sketch of what they were doing later in the day. 'Father Soames said we were to bring you. Want to come?'

'I'll drive Sonia over in my car. Or Sonia can drive me. I know she likes the machine.' This was true. There was a great thrill in the sense of terrific power under that long, slender hood, with its wide leather strap, 'To keep it from flying off and hitting you in the face,' as Tad said blandly.

Perdita said some people from Tollemache St. Marys would be there. This brought up the connection between the recent guest and the people at Tollemache St. Marys.

'They are sailing today,' Perdita said, 'for New York.'

'Lucky bloke,' Tad said. 'It's what I ought to have done years ago! New York! No real scope for a man of my transcendent abilities in London. Advertising is in its paleolithic stage here. The stone age of advertising! We want a boat, and we burn out a hollow log! Instead of building a speed-boat with a hundred-horse-power petrol engine.'

'I thought you were doing remarkably well,' Mr. Spenlove said. 'You haven't taken a vow of poverty, I observe.'

'You have no conception of the opportunities we have to pass up,' Tad said, staring at the plate of veal-and-ham pie the maid set down in front of him. He drank some claret.

'Perhaps the trouble is, so many of the public haven't any money to buy anything.' Mr. Spenlove said a few words about Mr. Romaine's trip to Glasgow, and the dole.

'What else can you expect with a socialist government?' Tad inquired. 'Bread and circuses! I did a thing the other day. It was called "A New Use for Lampposts." '

'I can imagine it,' Mr. Spenlove said. 'But hanging cabinet ministers to lampposts, *pour encourager les autres*, won't make work except in the hemp trade. There's something fundamentally wrong when good mechanics don't work and other good mechanics want to eat.'

'Remember Phil May's cartoon about the fisherman and the lunatic looking over the asylum wall?' Tad said, smiling impudently at Mr. Spenlove. ' "Caught anything? No? Come inside!" The people you despise so much have been harping on that for several years now. We'll have you with us yet, old man.'

'He's going to make the trains run on time,' Mr. Spenlove said to Perdita.

'We'll make the radicals run on time, and do time,' Tad said. He was very good-natured about it. 'We'd keep a few lampposts for journalists. Editors.'

'What about advertising? If there were fewer papers . . .'

'Oh, we'd leave the advertising managers at liberty,' Tad said. 'In fact we would subsidize them,' he laughed. 'No need to talk shop on a week-end. Tell me some more about the people we're meeting this afternoon. I always like to have some sort of dossier. It saves such a lot of beating about the bush.'

Perdita told him. She made no mention of Jack Bannister's abdication from the throne. She said Mr. Spenlove had known Mrs. Bannister long ago as a child in America. Then she mentioned the name Enderby-Breton.

'I've heard of him,' Tad said. 'We did some advertisements for the Southern Fidelity Company. He's a director, or was a director.'

'That's Mrs. Deming's uncle,' Mr. Spenlove said. 'The old man died and the grandson succeeded him. Fire insurance.'

'That's right. All kinds of coin!' Tad said, eating with animation. Talk of money always animated him.

'Most of that coin comes eventually to the son of the lady we are talking about,' Mr. Spenlove said.

'Is she a widow?' Tad inquired. 'I suppose you know I'm in the market for a widow. Independently wealthy. Is she a widow?' He gave his brother-in-law an impudent look.

'I wouldn't call her a widow,' Mr. Spenlove said. 'I think we might change the subject.'

They changed the subject, but Tad's spirits were high

and derived much enjoyment from challenging Mr. Spenlove's views, whether he was fortified with information or not. He had had a very successful week professionally, but he did not mention this. He was merely extremely gay.

'I ought to come down oftener,' he told them. 'You need a breath of the bracing city air. You get into a rut. It's a question of personality.'

'We're grateful,' Perdita said. 'Want any more salad?'

Tad pushed his plate away and turned his chair. 'No, thanks. No more of anything. I'm on a diet.' He took out a fresh cigarette, crossed his legs and struck a match. 'It's a popular fallacy,' he said, and dropped the match in the wineglass, 'that country air is bracing. It's largely birella and blethers. I'm much more alive in the City! Or in Fleet Street, anyway. Monday morning I'm fresh as a daisy. Here one wilts and languishes. I was looking it up the other day. Most men who have ever done anything got out of the country as quick as they could. They used to say God made the country, Man made the town. Which is much like saying, go to the country when you're dead, but stay in town to keep alive.'

'It's an interesting theory,' Mr. Spenlove admitted. 'It makes your visit all the more valuable. You're sacrificing yourself in our interest.'

'Precisely what I was leading up to,' Tad looked at Sonia and winked. 'And the best you can do for me is to invite me to visit a parson!'

'He won't do you any harm,' Mr. Spenlove said, getting up to get a cigar. 'He's a good man. I mean genuinely good. It does me good just to be in his company.'

'What about me?' Tad inquired, raising his voice to reach Mr. Spenlove. 'Doesn't it do you good to be in my company?'

Sonia got up to get ready for tennis. Tad wanted to play. Mr. Spenlove was heard to say that it all depended what Tad called good. Good Discipline possibly. Tad got up too and lounged out into the garden. He removed his coat and dropped it on a chair in the porch. The fact was, he was having a very good time. It pleased him to have his sister living so handily for town. He did a lot of sponging on his mother in London. Perdita said to her husband one time, 'Tad has money in the bank, but he buys a suit and sends the bill to Mother! She has a room for him, or a friend.'

A week-end at the Hind's Head was all of a five-pound note, if you included room, dinners, drinks and tips. Layer-de-la-Pole wasn't quite so gay, perhaps, but it cost nothing apart from the petrol, a box of chocolates for Sonia and a tip for Polly. Say ten bob. Tad Price always exaggerated to himself the boredom of country life. He was not in a dissipated set. Perdita confided to Mr. Spenlove. 'You have to give Tad credit, ducky. No women. He isn't a celibate, but he's a jolly clean young gentleman.' Mr. Spenlove had replied, 'I'm glad to know it. In fact, I did know it. Sonia wouldn't be fond of him if . . .'

It was even possible, Mr. Spenlove thought, as he went out to watch the tennis later, that the disruption was a good thing for an older man. Tad was a very vital person. As he said, it was a matter of personality. If only he weren't so damned sure of himself! At his age, thirty, Mr. Spenlove knew well enough that he hadn't been sure of himself at all. He had been groping in the dark about a lot of things. He had also, not long afterwards, been in love. Tad seemed immune. He wanted a rich widow!

Very vital indeed. He had changed to shorts and an old yellow sweater and he was bounding about the court like a young stag, sending down what he called "whizbangs" to

Sonia. Sonia was in shorts too, and seemed competent to send a few whizbangs of her own.

No women, Perdita had said. The pursuit of radicals might be Tad's substitute for Paphian rites. Just as young men became Jesuits in the old days, Tad was a kind of secular Savonarola, an advertising anchorite! That was far-fetched.

It was pleasant, sitting in the shade, in that secluded place, watching two beautiful young people at play. The thought crossed his mind that it was as good a way as any of forgetting about rationalization, and the dismaying clots of idle men and boys around the labor exchanges. Men and boys who had had no work for months and even years. Apprentices who had not worked at their skill since they finished their time. That was going on all over Britain. Tad insisted there would be no change until the socialists were hanged to lampposts. Romaine had suggested, with a surprising insight, that Mr. Spenlove would want to get away from it and return to America.

Mr. Spenlove had inquired once, if the country were in such a state of indigence, who were the people riding in all the dozens of Rolls Royces and Daimlers in London. Tad had told him at once that they were all Brazilians and Argentines. They did not resemble any South Americans Mr. Spenlove had ever seen, but he let it pass. It all added up to a profound change in things, and the best way for a retired philosopher to forget it was to live in a place like Layer-de-la-Pole. Try as he would, he was unable to bring the responsibility home to himself for the condition of England. He thought it might be a good idea to ask Father Soames.

He had seen the socialism of his own youth disintegrate into quarreling sects. He had watched the Fabians become a coterie of doctrinaires who had married rich wives. Now the so-called socialists had been thrown out of the saddle, but nothing was altered in the depressed areas. But he was distrustful of Tad's black-shirted friends. Those young hooligans were sinister. He thought there was more hope in a red flag than a black one.

It was more agreeable to think about old Romaine. Mr. Spenlove was sorry the old chap had gone. His visit had been a wholesome experience for them all. And to think that he and the woman who had been born Delia Augusta Enderby-Breton had taken to each other at once when they met on a social level! It would have been unthinkable to either of them to have had such a rapprochement while on the ship. Mr. Spenlove was not sure what it signified, but there it was.

What was going to happen to Candace? Father Soames would not counsel divorce. As far as Mr. Spenlove could make out, the Church forbade it and the rector disliked it in any case. He had remained celibate because the woman he loved had married another. She had died, but he was still a celibate because it was a Sacred Memory. Mr. Spenlove could not follow that line of emotionalism. It seemed to him that the world would come to a standstill if everybody did that. Love, he felt, was not immortal. Everything grew old and died, even thought. Perhaps it was just as well.

THE combined attractions of a Virago and a Napier two-seater in front of the rectory drew the boys of the village from the cricket match on the green. The rectory garden had a table on which there was a bowl of claret cup. Miss Soames did not serve spirits, but Father Soames had a bottle of sherry in reserve.

'I thought you said some people were coming from Tollemache St. Marys,' Tad said to his sister. He took the claret cup and smiled charmingly at Miss Soames.

'Well, a girl. Candace,' Perdita said. 'Mrs. Bannister was coming, at any rate. She's not here yet. It's twenty miles.'

'The widow?' Tad said.

'Don't be troublesome, ducky,' Perdita suggested. 'She's not a widow. I told you.'

Father Soames was in a gray alpaca coat with a clerical collar, his concession to worldly informality. Seated in a large wicker chair was a gentleman known to Mr. Spenlove as Dr. Sellers. He was one of the rector's old friends, a one-time sporting man who had traveled to various countries to judge sporting dogs. He had lost an eye in a shooting accident. Mr. Spenlove, who had never become intimate with the doctor, insisted that there was more intelligence in the glass eye than in the real one. The two organs were not completely focussed and the doctor's stare expressed to many people his suspicion of modern ideas. It took Tad's light touch to thaw Dr. Sellers. Tad did not know that the old gentleman was the deputy-lieutenant of the county, and was accustomed to deference.

Tad's social talent was one of his important assets in business. He called it personality and assumed that it could be acquired. The fact was, he really liked people and was able to make them feel good. Once on the theme of sporting dogs, and finding that Tad knew what he was talking about when it came to terriers, the old fellow thawed. The party began to move.

After his third claret cup, Tad said to Perdita, 'What about your friend? The one who isn't a widow?' She was about to say something when Father Soames came out of the rectory.

'Mrs. Bannister's on the telephone,' he said. 'She's had a breakdown. Her car. She's at Sudbury.' Tad sprung up.

'I'll go and bring her,' he said. 'It's only a few miles. You keep dinner a few minutes. We'll be back in two twos.'

He hurried out to his car. Father Soames followed him to say Mrs. Bannister was at the Crown Inn. Tad waved his hand as he got into the Napier and started the engine. The crowd of small boys moved away from the wheels. The car went off with a swish of tires on gravel and a spurt of blue vapor. They could see Tad in a practically recumbent position at the wheel. The rector went back to his party, shaking his head gently.

'He seems to be full of energy,' he said to Mr. Spenlove. 'I was going to suggest . . .'

'Tad will know what to do,' Perdita said. 'There's a garage at Sudbury. They'll be here in a few minutes. I hope he doesn't try to do eighty on these roads.'

'I doubt if there's anything he would like better than to do eighty,' Mr. Spenlove said. 'We can only hope. It may be a very good thing,' he added, musingly. Perdita looked at him. 'It will take Candace out of herself,' he explained.

'Oh, I see. You think Tad's rushing to help a fair lady. I thought he wanted a rest from . . . Miss Soames, dear, let me help you with that tray.' Perdita left her husband to talk to Sonia.

Sonia said it was an absolutely marvelous car.

'And he's an absolutely marvelous uncle,' Mr. Spenlove suggested, but without conviction. Sonia said, yes, he was, really.

'He works awfully hard,' she said. She had the same rhythm as Tad, Mr. Spenlove perceived. They were of the same generation. They were on the other side of a gateless barrier of the soul. 'He's been telling me. He has just landed a wonderful contract. That's what's made him so frivolous all day.'

Beyond that barrier everything was marvelous, wonderful, topping and priceless. The words expressed moods rather than definitions. He looked at Sonia with love. He saw her as one sees a person broadcasting on the wireless, through a wide window. One hears the voice, but it comes from a distance and there is a great pathos in the distance.

He wondered sometimes whether Sonia remembered the days in Connecticut. Still more he wondered whether she appreciated the fact that he deliberately avoided being reminiscent with her. He had learned, somewhere along the long road of his life, that young people remember, but do not want to talk about it, or be reminded of times past, not even the times they have loved and still cherish.

'I wasn't aware that a contract made a man frivolous,' he said. 'Tad's a special case. He'd tell *you* about it, but he wouldn't believe I give him credit. He thinks I don't take him seriously.'

'Oh, I'm sure he doesn't. It's just that he's rather sensitive.'

'That's a new one,' Mr. Spenlove said. 'He didn't impress me as sensitive. Not on one's ears,' he added. There was a loud snarl from Tad's horn outside, a raucous squawking. Sonia hurried out to meet the marvelous uncle in his marvelous car.

Tad was helping Candace out of the Napier. Her usually calm features were flushed and she was full of a novel brilliance. She hurried in to express her regrets.

'Something went wrong with the carburetion,' she said, shaking hands and bowing to Dr. Sellers. 'Sherry, please.' Tad came in beaming, having achieved, not eighty but something well over sixty, on the return journey.

'I call that an understatement,' he said. 'Mrs. Bannister's car ought to be in the South Kensington Museum. In fact I'm not sure it shouldn't be in the British Museum. You know, among the Assyrian chariots and Egyptian things.'

Mr. Spenlove saw the girl look at him and hold back a smile. He was impressed at Tad's ability to make her see that he was giving her time to adjust herself to the company.

'I'll probably live longer in my car than in yours,' she said, and sat down beside Sonia. 'Does he always drive like that?'

Tad rubbed his hands vigorously and made for the claret cup. He thought it a very insipid drink, but he wished to make Miss Soames feel good. It was a trivial sacrifice for him. He was feeling good himself. He had had an adventure.

'Invariably,' Tad said over his shoulder. 'Faster, if any-thing. We've moved out of the ox-cart age, you know.'

'Dr. Sellers is a Justice of the Peace,' Mr. Spenlove said. 'He'll want to hear your views.' Tad cocked a bright brown eye over his sherry glass at the old gentleman.

'I believe it's fourteen days without the option of a fine.'

They went into the somewhat bare rectory dining room to dinner.

It would have been a quiet, rather humdrum evening but for Tad, who was in electrically high spirits. He avoided Candace, yet it was obvious that he was performing, as a male, for her. Later, in the rococo and over-furnished draw-ing room, full of Victorian knick-knacks, he opened the piano and accompanied himself, playing by ear. He gave an imitation of a popular floor-show performer in London, an American whose success was achieved on two levels, among those who took his jokes seriously and those who enjoyed the unconscious humor of his sketches. It was Sonia's con-viction that Tad was marvelous as a take-off.

Mr. Spenlove found himself reflecting on the amazing diversity of temperament in so small a circle. He was even more amazed as he thought of the differences between Tad and himself; between the rector and his sister, living serene lives of goodness, sacrifice and celibacy, having no commerce with either the flesh or the devil, and Jack Bannister and Deming, romantics and everlasting exiles from home. It was obvious that the former were happy in a sinful world, but it was not their virtue so much as good fortune. Jack and Deming were sinners, of course, but they were the salt that gave savor to life.

When the time came to break up, the question arose, expressed by Miss Soames, how was Candace to get home? Tad at once stepped forward, tapped himself solemnly on the breast, and indicated that he and he alone would see the lady home. Miss Soames looked at Perdita, who looked at her brother and then shrugged.

'I was going to suggest she come with us,' she said, as they drove back to Layer-de-la-Pole. 'But she seemed to have no objection to Tad. He won't drive fast at this time of night.'

They were in the billiard room, and Mr. Spenlove was having a nightcap of Scotch and soda, to take the taste of the claret cup and Miss Soames' orange wine out of his mouth, when they heard the two-seater return. Sonia had gone to bed.

Tad came in, walking lightly on his toes, whistling a bar or two from the 'Tannhäuser Overture,' beating time with both hands and extending himself along the club-fender in front of the fireplace.

'Did you go in?' Perdita said. He shook his head.

'Oh, no! Plenty of time for that. It's an extraordinary place, eh? In fact I've had an extraordinary evening. I owe it entirely to my own enterprise, too.'

'How do you make that out? Didn't we invite you?' Perdita inquired.

'You didn't give me the, ah, the *élan* to volunteer to get Candace,' he pointed out.

'Candace already? You've got very matey with Mrs. Bannister.'

Tad put up his hand.

'Don't mention that name to me,' he said gravely.

'What do you know about it?' Mr. Spenlove interjected. Tad took a tumbler and poured himself a double Scotch. As he pressed the siphon lever he raised his eyebrows and smiled.

'I know all about it,' he announced calmly. 'She told me on the way home. Everything! She's a marvelous person.' He lifted his glass and looked at his sister and her husband. 'I knew something would happen,' he went on. He drank quickly and set the glass down. He pointed his finger at them, jabbing it as though accusing them of contradicting him. 'Fate!'

'I can remember you telling me that men made their own destinies,' Mr. Spenlove said. 'Fate, according to you, was an exploded superstition. You compared it with examining the entrails of birds, as the Romans used to do. You were most elegant on the subject.'

'I've changed my mind,' Tad said, and he took another quick drink. 'I mean I've changed my mind about my own fate. But this was what I was going to tell you. Coming out on the Finchley Road this morning, I saw three rooks flying in triangular formation. I felt it was an omen! They were flying toward Colney Hatch. That's a lunatic asylum.' He gave Mr. Spenlove a brilliant smile. 'I knew that meant something would happen to me. Good fortune. So it has.'

'You've had too many drinks,' Perdita said.

'This is the first drink of spirits I've had today,' Tad said seriously. He drank again. 'A marvelous girl. Leave it to me. Not a widow, you said. It's a pity murder is frowned on in our circles. Of course I don't mean that. But you'll see what goes, in two twos. A chap doesn't get a chance like this twice in his life. Did I tell you she is a marvelous person? We have the same ideas on so many things. Music . . .' He began to do the 'Tannhäuser Overture' again, but broke off and finished his drink. 'Everything.'

'Politics?' Mr. Spenlove inquired.

'Absolutely. Particularly politics. This effete, archaic,

obsolete government must go! She took the words out of my mouth. And what a marvelous son she has! She had a snap of him in her bag. I saw it.' Tad walked up and down on his toes for a moment.

'What's all this leading up to, Tad?' Perdita said. 'You haven't been making a fool of yourself, I hope. You haven't been rushing that girl, have you?'

'It will lead up to something wonderful. No details at present. As soon as I get back to town, wheels will turn. Take it from me.' Tad raised himself again on his toes and put his hands in his trousers pockets. He began to walk to and fro briskly in front of Mr. Spenlove. He was evidently in an exalted mood.

'Tad!' said Perdita. He turned on his heel to face her.

'Sis,' he said, 'she's the girl for me. As the Yanks say, she has everything. She's been wasting her time up to the present moment. Well, I'll say no more tonight.'

'Are we to understand that you've made up your mind to marry her?'

'If I'm not mistaken I've made up her mind too,' Tad said, as he made for the door. 'You've never seen me really on the ball,' he added. 'A bit of luck, having me over there.' He opened the door. 'I'll have to go over to Sudbury to-morrow to see about that car of hers. She ought to have a silver-plated Rolls with Chinese silk upholstery and solid gold ash trays. We'll have to see about it. Good night, sweet friends. Thanks for a divine evening.'

They heard him whistling, as he went up stairs, the 'Tannhäuser Overture.'

'Tad's a bit elevated tonight,' Perdita said, as she got up. Mr. Spenlove shook his head.

'It may be real,' he said. 'He's fallen hard for our friend Candace. And he unconsciously uses the language of his profession. Oh, yes, it may be real. It may be the solution of the problem. There's nothing improbable in a modern advertising man talking like an Elizabethan hero. She's captured his imagination. She's a princess in an ogre's dungeon. He'll get her out. But he'll get no help from me. I wash my hands of them. I shall devote myself to you, my girl.'

As they went out into the hall and he turned to lock the front door, Tad, removing his tie, could be seen at the top of the stair.

'Did you say you were thinking of going to the States for a visit in the autumn?' he said softly.

'We did,' Perdita said. 'Why bring it up now?'

'This would make a perfect house for a honeymoon,' he said and vanished, still whistling.

Mr. Spenlove stood still for a moment before returning to the billiard room. He put the bottle on the sideboard and was about to switch off the lights. But he walked around the room first, examining, with earnest attention, the series which William Hogarth called "Marriage à la Mode."